Carrie Duffy grew up in North Yorkshire before moving to Paris at the age of eighteen. After studying PPE at ...ity College, Oxford, she trained as an actress. ...e has worked professionally as both an actor and ...ncer, and she currently lives in west London. Her ...st novel, *Idol*, was published in 2011.

www.carrieduffy.com

Also by Carrie Duffy

Idol

CARRIE DUFFY

Diva

HARPER

Harper
An imprint of HarperCollins*Publishers*
77–85 Fulham Palace Road,
Hammersmith, London W6 8JB

www.harpercollins.co.uk

A Paperback Original 2012
1

A catalogue record for this book is
available from the British Library

ISBN: 978 0 00 742153 4

Set in Melior by Palimpsest Book Production Limited,
Falkirk, Stirlingshire

Printed and bound in Great Britain by
Clays Ltd, St Ives plc

To Amy and Cleo
My Selby divas!

PART ONE

1

Dionne Summers sashayed down Rosa Parks Boulevard in cheap white heels and a butt-skimming mini that revealed acres of firm, chocolate-brown thigh.

'Hey, Dionne. Lookin' good!'

'Drop dead, Mikey,' snapped Dionne to the twelve-year-old kid who was checking her out. She wasn't wearing any underwear and she wondered how much he could see.

'Headin' someplace special?' Mikey persisted, cycling alongside her on a beaten-up BMX. Cocky, overweight, and dripping in fake gold jewellery, he hung around in the same gang as Dionne's younger brother, Shawn, and like every poor kid on the block he was desperate to get out of Detroit.

'I said leave me the fuck alone,' Dionne growled, bending down towards him and unintentionally flashing eye-popping amounts of cleavage.

Mikey shrugged. 'Hey, doll, if you want a good time, you know where I live,' he quipped, before flipping her the bird and pedalling off.

3

Dionne laughed in disbelief. The kid was *twelve*, for chrissakes!

But today she had more important things to consider than the growing pains of pre-teen wannabes. She had a meeting about a modelling job – no, a casting, that was the right word. After all, if she was going to walk the walk she ought to learn how to talk the talk, Dionne grinned to herself.

Dash Ramón had set it up for her. The burly Colombian was a powerhouse in Dionne's neighbourhood, a guy who made a formidable ally and a deadly enemy, and now he had a soft spot for Dionne, thanks to all the effort she'd put in over the last few weeks. She'd spent evenings at his favourite club, bringing him his favourite drink, looking fabulous and saying little before he finally agreed to do her this favour and organize a meeting with Luis Fernandez.

Luis Fernandez.

Just saying his name sent a thrill right through Dionne. She'd never heard of him, but Dash assured her he was the best and Dionne wanted to believe it. He could get her a spot in *W* or *Harper's* – maybe even European *Vogue*, Dash had told her. He'd slipped her Fernandez's card, told her to be there Monday afternoon.

'I've got school,' she blurted out stupidly. She was still only sixteen.

Dash raised an eyebrow as the intimidating crowd of black-clad heavies who were never far from his side laughed patronizingly. 'Skip it,' he told her, menacingly.

Dionne bit her lip nervously, but didn't argue. If there was one thing you didn't do, it was piss off Dash Ramón.

So that morning she'd remained huddled under her sheets while her younger sisters got ready around her.

'Are you sick, honey?' asked her mother, running a cursory hand over Dionne's forehead.

'I don't feel too good, Momma,' Dionne swallowed weakly. She knew her mom would be in too much of a rush to argue – her shift at the local deli started at seven a.m., and she couldn't afford to be late.

'I really can't stay home . . .' Natalie Summers looked torn.

'I'll be fine. I just need to rest. You get off to work, Mom.'

Dionne lay immobile, waiting until the sounds in the house had died down and the front door had banged half a dozen times, signalling that everyone had left. Well, almost everyone. Her daddy would still be in bed but Dionne wasn't worried about him. He'd be out cold until he dragged himself up around midday, slumping in front of the TV and working his way through a bottle of Jack until her mother came home from her gruelling twelve-hour shift to fix him some dinner. Earl Summers hadn't had a job since he'd been let go from General Motors more than five years ago, and since then it had been down to Dionne, as the eldest of the six kids, to help her momma keep everything together.

As soon as she'd turned sixteen, she'd found herself a Saturday job, working as a salesgirl in Macy's over at Oakland Mall. It was a prestigious job, one which wouldn't normally have been given to a young, black kid from the wrong side of the tracks, but Dionne was possessed of a natural charm and a disarming beauty, and she'd persuaded the manager to give her a chance. He hadn't regretted it: Dionne was a born saleswoman and had no trouble persuading the rich suburban housewives to part with their husbands' hard-earned cash. She gave her basic salary straight to her momma for housekeeping, but the commission she made was all hers. She'd opened up a savings account, and already there was almost a thousand dollars in there.

But if Luis Fernandez liked her, she'd be made for life, Dionne thought, offering up a quick, silent prayer that Ramón's contact would give her the break she needed.

She knew she looked a million dollars. She'd spent yesterday in the African Princess salon, having her luxurious afro relaxed so that it hung straight and sleek down her back. She'd had her legs and bush waxed, her nail acrylics reapplied and decorated with small crystals.

And now she was tottering along Twelfth in tight, plastic heels that were already hurting her feet, her tiny skirt leaving little to the imagination. She'd made herself up carefully, applying fake eyelashes and clear lip gloss that made her bee-stung lips even more enormous. Dash had once told her that the first thing a man thought of when he saw her was what it would be like to be sucked off by those lips. Dionne had simply smiled and blown him a kiss. She hadn't been blessed with much in life; she figured she might as well make the most of what she did have.

Dionne stopped, searching through her purse and checking the address she'd been given. She studied the badly printed card on its cheap paper, then glanced up at the house in front of her. It didn't look anything special. In fact, it was a typical example of the houses in downtown Detroit – sprawling, ramshackle and falling to pieces, so the rent was dirt-cheap. The place looked as if it hadn't been painted since the '67 riots, and the garden was a jungle.

Taking a deep breath, Dionne pressed the buzzer firmly. Then she thought better of it and knocked;

the buzzer looked like it had long since been disconnected.

'Yeah?' A small, wiry Hispanic guy opened the door just a crack and peered suspiciously at Dionne.

'Mr Fernandez?' she asked, trying to sound confident.

'Depends who's askin'.'

'I'm Dionne Summers. Dash Ramón sent me. For the casting?'

'Diane, hi!' His lips crawled back over his teeth as he smiled charmlessly, his gaze flickering over her appraisingly. Dionne could tell he liked what he saw.

She smiled politely as she followed him into the house. It was a pigsty. Discarded takeaway cartons with their half-eaten contents rotting inside littered the floor, barely covered by the old newspaper cuttings and torn magazine articles that were strewn carelessly around the lounge. A couple of twists of foil lay on the stained coffee table, surrounded by crumpled beer cans. Fernandez didn't even seem to notice the mess.

As he pushed open the door to one of the back rooms, Dionne began to feel a little calmer. It was set up with professional-looking equipment; a couple of large studio lights on adjustable stands, a silver reflector lying in a corner and a neutral-coloured backdrop hanging from a rail.

There was a camera mounted on a tripod that looked like an antique. Fernandez didn't touch it. He simply picked up a cheap, digital camera and told her, 'I'm gonna take a few test shots first.'

Dionne stepped tentatively into the centre of the room, trying to look as if she knew what she was doing. 'What do you want me to wear?' she asked, hoping that Fernandez might suddenly produce a selection of beautiful designer gowns.

He didn't even look up. 'What you're wearing's fine. Don't worry about it.'

Dionne nodded, pouting self-consciously and jutting out her hips in what she hoped was a provocative pose.

Fernandez fired off a few shots and checked his camera. 'Hey, babe, lose the jacket. It's not the fuckin' Arctic in here,' he yelled.

Silently, Dionne did as she was told. She didn't want to piss him off and have him tell Ramón she was no good.

She shrugged off her fake-fur bomber jacket to reveal a white tank with a deep V-neck that couldn't fail to draw attention to her full breasts and silky, dark-brown skin.

Fernandez let out a low whistle and Dionne felt a pang of triumph. He liked her! This was going to be a success!

'Okay, honey, I want to see innocent,' Fernandez commanded as Dionne tried her best to oblige, changing her body and her expressions the way Luis instructed.

Fernandez was pleased with what he saw. Yeah, she was getting more natural, more confident at playing with the camera. The girl – what was her name again? – definitely had something. And she was starting to trust him.

Luis smiled lasciviously, walking across his make-shift studio towards Dionne. He stood close to her, but she didn't flinch. Guys invading her personal space was nothing new. Slowly, Fernandez looked her over, then his eyes caught on the gold necklace that sat just above her cleavage. He twisted it between his thumb and forefinger, his fingertips brushing her skin.

'Nice,' he commented.

Dionne's gaze didn't falter. 'It was a present.'

8

'From your boyfriend?'

'From my parents.'

Fernandez flashed that sleazy smile again, seeming pleased with the answer. 'Okay, take off your top.'

'What? I—'

'Just take it off,' he drawled, suddenly sounding impatient.

The request was unexpected, but Dionne wasn't ashamed of her body. Hesitating for only a second, she pulled her vest over her head. Hell, it was only like a bikini shoot, right?

Fernandez stared at her cheap white bra and raised an eyebrow.

'As well?' Dionne asked. 'Do I really need to?' Alarm bells were beginning to ring.

'Come on, honey, I ain't got time for this. If you want out, get out.'

He gestured towards the door, but Dionne remained motionless.

'I'm serious. I ain't gonna kidnap you or nuthin'. If you don't wanna do this, then get out and stop wasting my time. But if you do wanna make it big, you gotta be prepared to start gettin' 'em out. Look at Kate Moss – she's always naked in the Europeans. French, Italian *Vogue* – do you read 'em? You should do if you're serious about this industry. And you can't move for the titties on their pages.'

Dionne hesitated. She remembered the precious stolen moments she'd spent poring over an ancient copy of British *Vogue*. The cover had shown a model giggling as she slipped a hand inside another girl's dress, pretending to touch her breasts. Maybe it was the norm over there.

Reaching round to her back, Dionne unhooked her bra and let it fall away. Her breasts were heavy, the large, dark nipples swaying deliciously on her superb body.

Behind the camera, Luis Fernandez broke into a sweat. He checked three times that he had enough battery – he wasn't going to miss getting those babies on camera – and fired off a dozen shots without a pause, as Dionne raised her arms above her head like he told her to. 'It makes them look higher, more pert,' Luis explained.

More pert? thought Dionne indignantly. She was sixteen years old. How much more pert did he want?

'Right, I wanna try something different,' he barked, as he crossed the studio and dragged an ageing chaise longue into the middle of the floor. It was covered in fading red velvet, heavily worn and edged in dark wood. Dionne could tell it had been nice . . . once. Now it was covered in unsavoury-looking stains and leaking yellow stuffing. Dionne sat down tentatively on the edge.

'How about we try a few nude shots?' suggested Fernandez, hastily wiping his perspiring forehead. Jesus, was it hot in here, or was it just the girl? He rearranged his trousers uncomfortably. Maybe she'd let him bang her after the shoot. 'Upmarket stuff, of course,' he continued. 'Nothin' funny. That's why I brought the couch.'

He gestured to the dilapidated chaise longue, and Dionne looked at him doubtfully.

'Look, sweetheart,' he began, trying to sound kind. He placed a hand on her naked shoulder and Dionne flinched. 'I know you're only a kid, but you've got a great future ahead of you. I'm gonna put the word out about these shots, and I guarantee you'll have jobs lined up like that,' he insisted, clicking his fingers. 'But I gotta have something to show my contacts, and the wider your portfolio, the better. They wanna see all the different things you can do – you gotta be able to project different images y'see, kid – that's what makes you sellable.'

Dionne nodded.

'Now I'm doing you a favour here, because you're a friend of Ramón's and he's an amigo of mine. I ain't charging you nuthin' for these pictures, but they're gonna be your passport to the big time.'

'So what's in it for you?' Dionne challenged him. She was poor, from a neighbourhood full of Hispanics, African Americans and a handful of Eastern European migrants, but the one language everyone talked was money.

'Me? I get to help make a big star. I have faith in you, Diane, and if you get to the top, I want you to repay the favour to Luis Fernandez. I make my money from shooting the big jobs – *Vogue*, *Women's Wear Daily*, ad campaigns, see? It means I can afford to do a favour for a friend and help out a kid with huge . . .' his eyes lingered on her breasts . . . 'potential.'

Dionne took a deep breath. 'Okay,' she agreed, standing up and slipping out of her skirt to reveal a perfectly waxed pussy.

Fernandez nearly fell over. Christ, the kid was bald! Was she really that young?

'Just lie back on the couch,' he told her, trying to keep his cool. He didn't want to alarm the girl – he had her exactly where he wanted her. 'Put your arms above your head, and relax . . . that's it . . . Make like some British rich bitch. You're born to this kind of life. Elegance, luxury, that's what we want . . .'

Dionne suppressed a giggle. It was hard to portray elegance and luxury when she was stark naked. If she'd been dripping in diamonds, it might have been different. She arched her back slightly, trying to get comfortable, and Fernandez caught his breath.

'Legs a little wider, honey . . . that's it . . .'

Unconsciously, Dionne did what he told her, following his instructions and letting her mind wander over the scenario he had set up for her. She was the lady of the manor – rich, beautiful, glamorous . . . she had servants to look after her mansion, and a devastatingly handsome, successful husband who bought her everything she wanted – fast cars, trinkets from Tiffany . . .

Fernandez moved slowly across the room towards her, his feet silent on the grotty carpet. 'I'm just gonna do some close-ups,' he said softly.

Dionne barely heard him. There would be no more clothes from the Goodwill, no more sharing a room with three of her sisters in a grotty, roach-infested house that smelt of damp and stale bourbon. Instead she would be treated like a princess and hold grand balls in her country house, where exquisitely dressed, beautiful men and women would flock to her parties. She wanted it so badly it was almost tangible. She would be admired and in demand, she would be loved, respected, and—

'What the fuck do you think you're doing?'

Dionne jumped up from the couch and grabbed a nearby dustsheet to cover her body. Fernandez had been kneeling at the foot of the chaise longue, pointing the camera between her legs.

He grinned lecherously. 'You know, you're even more beautiful when you're mad. And you're the best bit of cunt Ramón's ever sent me.'

Dionne felt sick.

'Give me that camera,' she yelled, lunging at him.

But Fernandez was too quick for her.

''Fraid not, cutie pie,' he sneered. 'I ain't letting these go. You're a natural, you know that? You should be a model.'

'I *am* going to be a model,' Dionne insisted, blinking back tears.

Fernandez laughed loudly and Dionne pulled the sheet more tightly around her. 'You ain't never gonna be no supermodel, honey. The public – they don't like black trash, see? And that ass ain't never gonna fit into any sample sizes.'

'Give me those pictures!' Dionne screamed again, snatching furiously at the camera. But Fernandez held on to it tightly.

'Get the fuck out of my house,' he snarled, pushing his face up close towards her. Dionne could smell the stench of his breath, see his yellowed teeth.

With a sob, she grabbed her clothes and ran down the corridor, leaving the door open behind her as she ran outside. Tears were streaming down her face as she sprinted barefoot into the street, her thick, black hair streaming out behind her. Passing cars honked their horns, amused by the spectacle of this beautiful girl running down the road with only a sheet wrapped around her, but Dionne was too upset to care.

How could she have been so fucking stupid? She'd thought this was going to be her big break, but he was just some fucking pervert. Jesus, he had those pictures of her – God only knew what he'd taken when she wasn't paying attention. He'd been pointing the camera right between her legs, right up . . .

Dionne stopped running and collapsed into sobs. The photos would go all round Dash Ramón's crew, she knew that. She wanted to kill him for humiliating her like this. She thought he'd been doing her a favour, but Dash Ramón was only looking out for himself, as usual. Shit, what if her daddy saw those photos?

'Hey, Dionne! You okay?'

It was Trey Williams, one of the guys from her neighbourhood. They hung out with the same crowd and she'd slept with him a couple of times.

'Baby, what happened?' he asked, looking genuinely concerned as he pulled his car over to where Dionne was standing, shivering, on the sidewalk. 'Come on, get in,' Trey told her, opening the passenger side door.

Miserably, Dionne did as she was told.

'What happened?' Trey repeated, as she slid into the seat beside him.

'I don't want to talk about it,' Dionne insisted, wiping her eyes furiously on a corner of the filthy sheet.

'You wanna go back to mine – get yourself fixed up?'

Dionne nodded. He was a nice guy, and she didn't want to go home yet.

'Oh, Dionne, baby, you're so good . . .'

Dionne lay back lifelessly as Trey writhed and moaned on top of her.

'I told you Trey would cheer you up, didn't I, baby?' he whispered, pushing deeper into her.

Dionne lay silent, closing her mind as he used her body.

She didn't mind, not really. It was all the same to her. Men always wanted sex, and she wanted to feel loved. It was a fair trade.

Dionne lay back passively, running over her options as Trey thrust inside her, grunting and squirming. She had to get out of here. She'd known it for years, but this afternoon had made her see there was no future for her in Detroit.

Ever since she was a kid, people had told her she

ought to model. She was beautiful, with soft, flawless skin, high cheekbones, huge, liquid-brown eyes and legs that went on forever. But as she'd grown up, her body had refused to cooperate with her dream. Dionne had wanted to be tall and skinny with a flat chest and no hips, but nature wouldn't play ball, obstinately blessing her with large breasts and a full-on booty that never seemed to get any smaller no matter how much she exercised. Whenever Dionne tried the big agencies, she always got the same answer: 'Try glamour work. You haven't got the right look for runway modelling.'

But Dionne refused to let them crush her dream and turned her attentions to Europe; after all, didn't they like different-looking girls over there? Dionne was no Cindy Crawford, no all-American, California-tanned cheerleader type. But in Europe, the fashion world adored the tiny, bohemian Kate Moss, the doll-like Lily Cole and the Amazonian Naomi Campbell.

Trey began to thrust faster, and Dionne could tell he was close to climax. Obligingly, she moaned and arched her back, clenching herself around him. With a final groan, Trey came and collapsed onto her. He was heavy and sweating, and Dionne hoped he'd get off her soon.

'Dionne, you're the best, you know that?' he told her, pulling out and rolling away from her. 'I told you I'd cheer you up,' he winked, clearly pleased with himself as he lit a spliff and lay back contentedly.

Dionne smiled weakly. 'Thanks, Trey,' she said, getting up and dressing hastily. 'I'd better head off.'

'Sure,' he told her, unconcernedly. 'I'll see you around.'

Dionne paused. 'Yeah, see you around.' She let herself out, closing the door behind her, and stepped into the grimy streets, breathing in the polluted air.

Suddenly she knew with absolute certainty that she had to get out of here, whatever it took. If she didn't, the city would grind her down, her life becoming a carbon copy of her mother's – marriage to a deadbeat drunk, a cluster of kids, a minimum wage job that exhausted her and made her look old before her time. There was no way she could let that happen. Dionne Summers wanted something more from life.

She thought of the money in her savings account. A thousand dollars. Enough to buy a plane ticket, a motel for a few nights. The possibilities swirled tantalizingly in her mind. She could go to Europe, find work, be a model. It all seemed so easy, so obvious.

Dionne looked around her, taking in the familiar streets for one last time. She felt something harden inside her, like steel, and she knew what she had to do.

2

Manchester, UK
Eighteen months later

Alyson Wakefield scurried out of school into the freezing February air. Her head was bowed, her shoulders rounded in her habitual pose, in a desperate effort not to be noticed. Standing just shy of five feet eleven in flats, with a rail-thin body and endless, coltish legs, being unobtrusive was not something that came naturally to seventeen-year-old Alyson Wakefield.

Her fine blonde hair had been hastily tied back with a simple band, revealing razor-sharp cheekbones and enormous blue eyes. With her clear porcelain skin and enviable poise that naturally lent itself to elegance, Alyson was on the verge of blossoming into a true beauty. But all she saw when she looked in the mirror were startled eyes and a skinny body that never filled out, no matter how much she ate. With her lean, gangly frame she felt clumsy and masculine, gauche and out of proportion compared to the other girls in her class. The boys teased her about her flat chest and towering height, the daily taunts ringing in her ears so that it was impossible for her to be anything other than self-conscious about the way she looked.

'You workin' tonight, Alyson?' asked Kayleigh, a small, freckled girl with a shock of red hair and a prominent overbite.

Alyson nodded as she hurried to catch up with her friends. They were known as 'The Misfits', a group of five girls each as physically awkward and insecure as Alyson herself. Staying together meant safety in numbers.

'Yeah, it's going to be another late – ouch!'

She broke off as she was shoved in the shoulder by the group of boys walking towards her. Instinctively, Alyson spun round and saw Callum Bateman grinning at her. Dark-haired and good-looking, he was also cocky and arrogant, and did his best to humiliate Alyson whenever he saw her.

'Fancy a fuck?' he yelled. 'I could do you up the arse, you'd love it.'

The ever-present group of admirers hanging off his every word burst out laughing as Alyson flushed bright red, her whole face lighting up like a beacon that was probably visible from the other side of the Pennines. But she kept her mouth shut and didn't reply. She wasn't about to get into a war of words with Callum Bateman. There would only be one winner, and it wouldn't be Alyson.

Instead, her friend Leanne took up the challenge. Short and round, almost as wide as she was high, with a perma-orange fake tan and a face obscured by a mass of jet-black hair extensions, she relished a good argument.

'Shut your face, you bell-end,' she screeched, her voice carrying halfway across the car park.

'Piss off, Leanne,' sneered Callum. 'I'd rather chop my dick off than put it in your rancid midget fanny.'

'Go fuck yourself, gaylord,' Leanne shot back venomously.

'I've got to go,' Alyson said under her breath, as she saw her bus pull up to the stop. Already the other kids were piling on, and she couldn't afford to miss it. If she did, she'd be late for work. 'I'll see you guys tomorrow.' She sprinted off, her long legs quickly covering the ground, leaping onto the bus as the doors closed behind her.

There were no seats left and she stood awkwardly at the front, speaking to no one. Instead, she kept her head down, pulling her tatty old duffel coat tightly around her like a security blanket and glancing out of the filthy windows from time to time as the bus made the short journey from Oldham to Manchester.

Three nights a week she travelled into the city centre to waitress at Il Mulino, an upmarket restaurant catering to the city's most affluent residents. Her shift finished around midnight, when it would be a dash to make the last bus home and grab a few hours' sleep before college in the morning.

It was a punishing lifestyle, but Alyson knew she was lucky to have been taken on by such a reputable restaurant as Il Mulino. It paid minimum wage but the tips were excellent, the clientele being predominantly the flashy, new-money set: media workers, property developers, footballers with their wives or girlfriends or mistresses. The footballers were the worst, their eyes roaming over her as she walked back and forth to their table. Men often looked at her like that, with a predatory, covetous gaze, and Alyson found it unsettling. She didn't realize it was because she was beautiful – stunningly so, ethereal almost – and ripe for the picking.

The bus pulled into Piccadilly and Alyson jumped

off, walking briskly towards Exchange Square. The pavements were already glowing with a thin sheen of frost, the bus covering her with slush as it drove away. But Alyson simply sunk her chin deeper into her knitted scarf and moved on.

She reached the restaurant in a few minutes, hurrying into the back and quickly saying hi to the other girls who were crowded round the tiny mirror applying mascara and lip gloss, spraying their slicked-back hair firmly in place. Alyson didn't even glance at herself as she slipped out of her school uniform and into her well-worn white shirt and black skirt, pulling on thick black opaques and her smartest shoes. Stashing her bag in her locker, she dashed back through the double doors into the mania of the kitchen and grabbed the dishes that were waiting on the hot plate.

'Table twenty-four,' yelled the sous-chef, and Alyson was on her way.

It was an exhausting, spirit-crushing way to live, but it had become so routine that Alyson rarely stopped to think how tired she was. It was a necessity, a way of life, and it had been like this ever since her father walked out on them.

Alyson slammed down a plate with more severity than she had meant to, apologizing profusely to the indignant-looking woman at the table. The woman arched an over-plucked eyebrow, then smiled graciously – well, as far as she could manage with a face full of Botox. Alyson smiled politely, hoping she hadn't just blown her chances of a good tip, and scurried away.

Even after all this time, memories of her father were still painful. Alyson had been just nine years old when Terry Wakefield had walked out on them, taking her younger brother, Scott, who was only six at the time. She remembered all too clearly the feeling of abandonment, the painful realization that her father had opted to leave her behind, that she somehow wasn't good enough for him.

The reasons behind his departure were complex. For as long as Alyson could remember, her mother, Lynn, had had issues. Her erratic behaviour had characterized Alyson's childhood – there were periods when she wouldn't leave the house for weeks, convinced that the neighbours were plotting against her, or that Mrs Davidson next door was trying to communicate evil thoughts through the wall. Alyson wasn't frightened, simply confused.

From time to time, her mother found work – low-skilled, low-paid appointments, like factory work or cleaning – but she struggled to keep a position as she swiftly gave her employers reason to get rid of her. Sometimes she stayed in bed for days on end, simply not turning up for work, until her employers got sick of trying to contact her and her P45 arrived in the post. Other times they would be disturbed by the bizarre things Lynn did – refusing to drink the mugs of tea she was offered for fear they were 'contaminated', or completely forgetting how to do a task she'd been shown a few hours earlier. It was only when she went to clean for an affluent and compassionate doctor that someone finally recognized what was wrong. When Alyson Wakefield was eight years old, her mother was diagnosed with schizophrenia.

For a while, life got better. With an accurate diagnosis, Lynn's condition could be treated, but the run of good behaviour didn't last long. Some of the side effects were unpleasant and she became increasingly reluctant to take the medication prescribed, treating her pills like headache tablets – taking one if she felt unwell, not bothering if she was having a good day.

And as someone who enjoyed a drink, she didn't see why being on heavy medication should stop her.

For Terry Wakefield, the final straw came one night when he awoke to find his wife standing in the freezing cold kitchen, wearing only her underwear and holding a heavy metal pan high above her head. She claimed Mrs Davidson was trying to tunnel through from the house next door, and she wanted to be prepared for when she surfaced through the dirty lino floor.

The following day, Alyson came home from school to find the house unusually quiet. Her mother was slumped in an armchair, her eyes staring blankly into the middle distance and a near-empty bottle of vodka beside her chair.

'Where's Dad?' asked Alyson, an ominous feeling creeping over her.

Lynn glanced up at Alyson. She looked exhausted, huge purple bags under her bloodshot eyes. 'He's gone.'

Alyson swallowed. Her father had left before – so many times that she'd lost count. Often he'd disappear for days at a time and there would be furious rows when he got back, her mother crying and screaming and drinking, while Alyson and her brother huddled together at the top of the stairs, longing for them to stop. But this time there was something different in Lynn Wakefield's tone, an air of finality.

'He's taken Scott with him,' she confirmed resignedly, picking up the vodka bottle and swallowing the final dregs.

From then on, it was just the two of them. Alyson never heard anything more from her father and grew to deeply resent him, furious at the way he'd abandoned them to struggle, choosing her brother over her and splitting up their family.

Alyson had had to grow up very quickly, learning

to care for herself and her mother, ensuring she was always presentable for school lest the teachers became suspicious. One of the kids in her class had been taken away by social services, and for nine-year-old Alyson that seemed every bit as terrifying as being snatched by the Child Catcher. She was determined to avoid the same fate; after all, her mother was all she had left now.

Lynn Wakefield gave up looking for work when her husband left, the pair of them getting by on benefits and disability payments. There was barely enough to cover bills and food, let alone any money for extras like school trips or new clothes. Alyson dressed as cheaply as she could, buying clothes from charity shops and wearing them until they were threadbare. She wasn't like the other kids, with fashionable outfits and designer trainers. She was different, obviously so, and was ostracized accordingly.

She began working as soon as she was old enough – a paper round, babysitting for the neighbours' kids, then glass collecting at the local pub when she hit sixteen. Every penny she earned she took home to her mum, to help pay the heating or the water or whichever bill was coming through the letterbox stamped 'Final Demand' that week.

Sometimes, in her rare, quiet moments, she secretly dreamed of getting out; of escaping and going far, far away, like an adventurer in a fairytale. But in reality, she couldn't see an end to this life. There was no time to think about her own dreams and ambitions, to consider what she wanted from the future. She was too busy fighting tooth and nail to keep everything together – school, work, home. She couldn't stop for a second. If she did, she might break.

'Alyson?'

Alyson jumped as her shift manager's voice cut into her thoughts.

'Yeah?'

'I really hate to ask, but Carmen's just rung in sick and I wondered if there was any chance of you covering for her tomorrow night?' Helen bit her lip and looked pleadingly at Alyson.

Briefly Alyson thought about the English essay that was due in two days' time, and the French verbs she was supposed to learn by tomorrow. She was a good student, bright and hard-working, but her troubled home life meant she couldn't always finish her work on time or study as hard as she wanted for that exam. Her teachers got frustrated that she wasn't reaching her full potential, but Alyson simply bowed her head and took their criticism, unwilling to go into details about her problems.

'Sure,' she told Helen, with a little shrug of her shoulders. Schoolwork could wait – they badly needed the extra money.

'Great!' Helen smiled gratefully at her, before disappearing back through the double doors into the restaurant.

It was raining lightly when Alyson climbed wearily off the night bus and set off through the darkness towards her house. It was almost one a.m., and the dank drizzle for which Manchester was renowned only added to her bleak mood. She was exhausted, longing to collapse into bed, but she dragged her aching body one step at a time through the deserted streets.

She lived in a small two-up two-down, just one of many on an estate with identical rows of red-brick terraces, built at the turn of the century for Oldham's millworkers. Each opened directly onto the street in front, with a small yard out back and a narrow lane running behind. Beyond lay the rugged moorland, stretching for miles, but currently invisible in the blackness of the night.

Alyson slipped the key into the lock and opened the front door, surprised to find that the house was dark. Her mother was usually waiting up for her, watching TV or dozing in an armchair. With a strange sense of foreboding, Alyson flicked on the light and hurried through to the kitchen.

The first thing she saw was her mother's red and white pills, scattered across the old, cracked lino. Her eyes followed the trail, refusing to take in what she was seeing. Lynn Wakefield lay slumped on the floor, her eyes closed and the pill bottle clutched in her hand.

The neon striplights at the hospital were harsh and draining, making it impossible to know whether it was night or day. Her mother was comfortable, they told her. Critical but stable. As yet, Alyson hadn't been allowed to see her.

She'd been asked question after question, filled out form after form.

'Who's her next of kin?' asked the young, male nurse, who'd introduced himself as Martin.

'I am,' Alyson answered clearly.

'Is she married? We notice she's wearing a wedding ring . . .'

'He's gone,' Alyson said, and her voice was hard. 'I don't know where he is.'

The nurse looked at her sceptically. 'Well, if you manage to think of anything, let us know. A contact number for your father would be very helpful.'

Alyson remained mute. Her father had been out of

25

their lives for so long and she wasn't about to invite him back again. *I'm the one who looks after her*, Alyson thought fiercely. *I'm the one who's cared for her every day for the past eight years. He doesn't deserve any part of this.*

Martin left, and for the next few hours she remained ignored, seated on a hard plastic chair in an endless white corridor, her head in her hands. She had no idea how long she kept up the vigil. She was on the verge of dozing off, her exhausted body finally running out of energy, when she heard a voice that made her think she was hallucinating.

'Ally?'

Her head shot up. There was only one person who'd ever called her that.

Terry Wakefield stood in front of her, and he had the good grace to look embarrassed. Alyson stared at him in disbelief. He looked older than she remembered; his hair had grown thinner, the lines on his face etched deeper. Beside him was a tall, lanky guy that Alyson barely recognized – her brother, Scott. She hadn't seen him since he was six years old, and he'd altered almost beyond recognition, becoming a sulky, sullen teenager with pale-blond hair and a bored expression. He looked as though he'd rather be anywhere but there – in the hospital, visiting the sick mother who was a stranger to him.

'How . . . What the hell are you doing here?' Alyson burst out. Her voice was anguished, a strangled cry.

Her father's forehead creased anxiously. 'They contacted me . . . The doctors. How is she?'

'Like you even care,' Alyson spat. 'How did they get your number? I never gave them it.'

'They found it . . .' Terry began awkwardly. 'In your mother's things.'

Alyson felt a slow, heavy, sinking feeling in her stomach, as though she'd just eaten a pile of lead.

'We kept in touch, now and again,' her father continued. 'Sometimes I sent her some money . . . when she was struggling.'

Alyson felt sick. Her mother and father were still in contact, yet her father had never once asked to see her, her mother keeping silent about the clandestine meetings. And all the time she'd been slaving away, working until she dropped, her mother had failed to mention the extra money Terry Wakefield had given her. She'd probably spent it on alcohol, or something ridiculous from QVC, Alyson thought furiously.

'Why didn't you help me?' Alyson demanded. Her voice was growing louder, more hysterical. 'Why didn't you want to see me?' The room was spinning.

'Ally . . .'

Her father stepped towards her, but at that moment a white-coated figure appeared from her mother's room.

'I'm Dr Chaudhry,' he introduced himself, shaking hands with the three of them. 'Would you like to come in now?'

They followed him through; Alyson went first, shocked to see her mother looking so small and fragile in the hospital bed. She was hooked up to all manner of machines, an IV tube attached to the back of her hand. She was sleeping right now, the machines around her beeping at regular intervals.

'Please, take a seat, all of you,' suggested Dr Chaudhry. They sat down, her brother rolling his eyes and sighing like this was all a big inconvenience.

'I understand you're her primary carer,' he said, turning to Alyson. He looked tired but patient, and his dark-brown eyes were kind.

'Yes, that's correct,' she said determinedly.

27

'It's a lot of responsibility for someone so young.'

'I didn't have a choice,' she retorted, with a pointed glance at her father.

The doctor nodded, understanding. 'Well, now you do.'

Alyson stared at him, her brow furrowing in incomprehension.

'We think it might be better if your mother went somewhere she could get the help that she needs. Her condition is obviously serious, and Lynn might be better served in a place where they have the specialization to really look after her. Now, there are a number of care homes in the area—'

'*I* look after her,' Alyson burst out. 'We've managed fine all these years.'

'Ally, you're clearly not coping,' her father cut in.

'We'll be *fine*,' Alyson insisted, her voice small and tight. She stared hard at the motionless figure in the bed, fighting back tears. 'We don't need you.'

'Perhaps I'll give you some time to talk this through,' Dr Chaudhry suggested tactfully, sensing the atmosphere. 'They have all the details you need at reception, and I'll be back after my rounds if you have any questions.'

'Listen, Ally,' her father began after the doctor had left. '*Think* about it. And I mean seriously. You can't spend the rest of your life looking after your mother – it's just not fair on you. Now the doctor thinks this is the best option, and maybe he's right. You've got to think about her too, not just what you want.'

'Why not? That's what you did, isn't it?' Alyson retorted. She was lashing out, all the anger that she'd bottled up over the past decade finally finding an outlet.

'You need some time for yourself, sweetheart,' Terry

28

said adamantly. 'And maybe it's best for both of you. It could be that Lynn's become too reliant on you . . .'

Alyson felt a swathe of guilt and hated her father for making her feel like that. Was he right? Was this somehow her fault, for encouraging her mother to become too dependent on her?

'Look, love, I can give you a few hundred pounds, maybe more. You can do what you want, go where you want.'

'I don't need your money,' Alyson spat, her eyes flashing dangerously. She couldn't believe that her father thought he could just walk back into her life and pay her off.

Terry Wakefield leaned forward and caught her hand. His hold was strong, a little painful even. He stared straight into her eyes, the pressure on her palm getting stronger. When he spoke again, his voice was cold, threatening almost. 'Think about it, Ally.'

3

Paris, France
Three months later

Cécile Bouvier was late. She hurried down the *rue de Rivoli*, dodging tourists and taking furious drags on the Philip Morris cigarette dangling from her pillar-box-red lips. *Everybody* stared. A few tourists took pictures. No one could take their eyes off her.

Despite the heat of the day, she wore black drainpipe trousers with black brogues, and a Frankie Says Relax T-shirt that she'd slashed to her midriff so only the top half of the message was visible. At five foot four her frame was gamine, petite in that particularly French way, with her flat, porcelain-white stomach extending beneath the T-shirt, her small breasts jutting through the thin cotton fabric. She wore armfuls of bangles and Wayfarer sunglasses, while enormous earphones were clamped over her head, attached to a tiny iPod.

But the most striking thing about CeCe was her hair. On one side of her head it fell in a thick, dark curtain, straggly and gloriously unkempt. The other half was shaved in a severe buzzcut. The whole look was eccentric, edgy and individual. She'd been compared to early Madonna, Agyness Deyn and Alice Dellal, but as far as CeCe was concerned, the look was all her own. One hundred per cent original and impossible to replicate.

CeCe was twenty-one years old, and lived and breathed fashion. She was obsessed with clothes – and not in a superficial, Beverly-Hills-socialite way. CeCe saw clothes as an art form, a true expression of the individual. She was fascinated with the way they were conceived and created, the way they could alter moods, launch a star or destroy a career.

CeCe's dream was to make it as a designer. She wanted her own fashion house, to be known the world over for her bold, glamorous designs. She'd sacrificed a lot to make it happen, but there was still a long way to go.

She came to a halt outside a large store at the less salubrious end of the *rue de Rivoli*, in the midst of shops selling tourist tat and cheap clothes. The sign above read 'Rivoli Couture', and the window display showed rail-thin, black plastic mannequins modelling ostentatious designer clothing. It was where CeCe worked as a sales assistant. The job was soul-destroying, but she had rent to pay.

She threw down her cigarette and burst through the door, pulling off her earphones and stuffing them into her bag. It was vintage Chanel tweed, and she'd customized it herself with ribbon and lace.

'*Bonjour, tout le monde,*' CeCe greeted everyone.

'Morning CeCe.'

'*Buongiorno!*'

'*Cześć*, CeCe, how are you?'

A chorus of languages greeted her as she pulled off her sunglasses to reveal dark black circles under her eyes.

'Christ, CeCe, you look like shit!' exclaimed Maarit, a waif-like Finnish blonde, whose foul mouth belied her demure appearance.

'I stayed awake until five a.m., designing,' CeCe explained in her thick French accent. 'I had an incredible idea that wouldn't leave me, and I could not sleep until it was finished. Is Dionne here yet?'

'Yeah, she's out the back.'

'*Merci*,' CeCe smiled, as she made her way across the shop, past groaning shelves overflowing with garish clothing. Rivoli Couture bought up the dross from France's top designers, last season's pieces that those with taste and money found too hideous to actually buy. Yet the tourists seemed to lap it up, leaving with bagfuls of designer labels at heavily discounted prices.

'CeCe!' Dionne exclaimed, kissing her on both cheeks. 'Girl, I am loving your outfit! But hell, look at your eyes – you're exhausted, honey.'

'I was up the whole night working on something new: a beautiful full-length dress made of crêpe de chine, with shoulder draping and an asymmetrical hemline.' Her hazel eyes sparkled as she described it. 'I have made the toile and I need you to try it, Dionne, I just know it will look amazing on you. But where were you last night? You did not come home, no?'

'No,' Dionne giggled. She was wearing an obscenely short, cherry-red bandage dress that clung to her incredible curves. CeCe realized she'd come straight to work from wherever she'd spent the night.

'Are you still drunk?'

'Maybe just a little,' Dionne admitted, as she broke down in another fit of giggles. 'Shit, that reminds me, help me get these back before Khalid notices them,' she hissed, pulling a pair of neon-yellow peep-toe stilettos out of her bag.

'You wore those?' CeCe asked disapprovingly. 'They're vile.'

'I thought they were kind of fun,' Dionne disagreed, as she turned them over to inspect them. The soles were badly scuffed, and a cigarette butt clung to the bottom of the right one. Dionne quickly shoved them back on the shelf with a shrug. 'If anyone complains, just say they're shop-soiled and give them ten per cent off.'

The way Dionne saw it, there was no point working in a clothes shop if you couldn't borrow the occasional item. It was one of the few perks to this job, and meant she was rarely seen in the same outfit twice.

'So where did you go?'

'David took me for dinner, then we went on to Bijou,' Dionne gushed, naming the hot new nightclub that had just opened in the Marais. 'I had so much fun – you should have come. The champagne was flowing, I was dancing on the tables all night long, shaking my booty . . . And the best part . . .' Dionne paused for effect, ensuring she had CeCe's full attention. '. . . *The owner.* Philippe Rochefort. Man, that guy is hot! Loaded too – like, serious money. David introduced me to him and I couldn't take my eyes off him. *Very* good-looking. Very French, you know what I'm saying?'

'Poor David.' CeCe smiled sympathetically. 'He adores you.'

'David's a sweetie,' Dionne conceded. 'He's a great guy but—'

'But what?'

'I don't know.' Dionne sighed despairingly. 'There's just not that spark. I want totally intense chemistry where you can't keep your hands off each other, where there's an orchestra playing every time you're together and you think you might die when you're apart.'

33

'Life is not like in the movies, Dionne.'

'My life's going to be,' Dionne replied indignantly. 'There's gonna be drama and passion and—'

'Ah, ladies, much as I hate to interrupt you, I had hoped you might get round to doing a little work today.'

It was Khalid Hossein, owner of Rivoli Couture, a short, pot-bellied man in an ill-fitting beige suit. Egyptian by birth, he was a now a French national, for reasons neither Dionne nor CeCe could understand. Khalid never had a good word to say about the French, complaining about the Parisian weather, the taxation levels, and especially the liberal employment laws which, in his view, gave workers every excuse to slack off whilst making it virtually impossible to sack them.

'I was just . . .' CeCe began, then trailed off.

'Putting these away for me,' Dionne interjected, dumping a pile of lavishly decorated Christian Audigier jeans in her arms. 'And I was about to—'

'Do the coffee run,' cut in CeCe, in a flash of inspiration.

'Absolutely,' Dionne purred, batting her eyelids at Khalid. 'Can I get you anything?'

'Well . . . an espresso,' he agreed grudgingly. Dionne might have been lazy and unreliable, but she could charm the pants off anyone, employing the same skills she'd honed at Macy's back home in Detroit to sweet-talk the Parisian tourists into leaving Rivoli Couture with bags full of overpriced, end-of-line designer gear. For Khalid Hossein, the bottom line was money. He would overlook a lot as long as the cash tills kept ringing.

Dionne slipped out to the café next door – the young guy there had a hopeless crush on her and gave her such a generous discount the order was practically free – as CeCe began straightening hangers. Khalid was OCD about having them all face the same way round.

There were times when CeCe hated this job with a passion. She put zero enthusiasm into it, saving her energy for her designing and her partying – the two great loves of her life. She and Dionne moved in moneyed, hip circles, and she loved the lifestyle, but she had to find some way of supporting herself. Her socializing was always paid for – her friends were rich and generous – but rent, food, the basics, all needed to be covered, and since falling out with her parents, CeCe had been on a steep learning curve, quickly discovering the harsh realities of working for a living.

CeCe had grown up in Clochiers, a small town in Auvergne in central France. It was stunningly beautiful, but boring as hell, and from a young age CeCe had been desperate to move to the city.

Her family were wealthy – CeCe had fallen in love with Paris when she'd accompanied her mother, Inès, on her regular shopping trips to the capital – but CeCe had little interest in money. Like Marilyn Monroe, she just wanted to be wonderful.

As a child she'd been given dolls to play with and she used them as her first models, cutting up old dresses then stitching them together in provocative, sensual designs that outraged her conservative mother. Whilst Inès's wardrobe comprised chic, classic pieces by traditional French fashion houses, like Yves St Laurent and Givenchy, CeCe's passions lay elsewhere. She loved the overt sexuality of Jean-Paul Gaultier, the high drama of Alexander McQueen and the punk-inspired eccentricity of Vivienne Westwood. Soon she was experimenting with her own style, mixing her father's battered old walking boots with her mother's vintage Dior, or using an Hermès scarf as a sash for her school uniform. She dressed to get attention – everyone in the small village knew her name, and that was just the way CeCe liked it.

When she hit her teenage years, CeCe cranked the rebellion up to max. She experimented with drink, drugs and sex, sleeping with both boys and girls – anything to push the boundaries. But there were dark times too. After the highs she would crash with depression, hiding beneath her sheets and refusing to get out of bed until her mother despaired and her father became white-lipped with fury. She remembered with horror the demons that had chased her down, pulling her deeper into a web of darkness that seemed impossible to escape from. It had taken a long time to fight her way out. There had been visits to a clinic – private and discreet, naturally – a startling array of pills and a course of counselling.

And then suddenly CeCe was back, as out of control and outrageous as ever, her behaviour even wilder than before. The summer after she turned eighteen, the issues came to a head and CeCe knew she needed to make a decision about her future. Her parents threatened to cut her off unless she curbed her ways and went to university to study for a proper degree. They wanted her to go into one of the professions, to become a doctor or a lawyer. Better still, to *marry* a doctor or a lawyer, and stay at home being a good housewife. CeCe couldn't think of anything worse.

After a particularly heated argument, CeCe packed up her little Citroën and drove non-stop to Paris. She went first to her mother's regular hairdresser in *rue Cambon*. Sitting in the stylist's chair, CeCe stared hard at her reflection and took a deep breath. 'I want you to shave off all my hair,' she declared.

It was an exclusive salon, catering for well-heeled Parisians and known for its elegant styling.

'Absolutely not,' the woman replied in horror.

CeCe walked out, heading towards Les Halles, where she found a far less discerning establishment. She intended the haircut to be a gesture of liberation – her mother had always told her that her long, brunette hair was her best feature, and the childish locks reminded CeCe of the old life she was leaving behind. But halfway through, she told the hairdresser to stop. She liked it like that. She was half rebel, half princess. It suited her perfectly.

'One double espresso for Madame le Designer.' Dionne came back in, the pungent scent of freshly ground coffee filling the air.

'Thanks, Dionne.' CeCe took it gratefully, knocking it back in one. She felt the caffeine kick start her body, the jolt of energy hitting her instantly. She needed it after her late night.

'Hey, I totally forgot to tell you,' Dionne said, as she began refolding a pile of sweaters. 'Elise is moving out.'

Elise was their flatmate.

'Shit, really?'

'Uh huh.' Dionne pulled a face. 'She told me last night. She's moving in with her boyfriend.'

'Fuck. I hope we find someone.' CeCe sounded worried.

'I'll ask around, see if anyone we know wants to take the room,' Dionne suggested. 'And I can put a couple of ads up. We'll get someone. After all, who wouldn't want to live with the two most gorgeous, most popular girls in Paris?' she exclaimed dramatically, as CeCe raised a sceptical eyebrow.

'I hope you're right. I can't afford to make the rent between just the two of us.'

A flicker of an idea crossed Dionne's eyes, and she

smiled wickedly. 'Well, if you need the extra money, you can always cover my shift this afternoon . . .'

CeCe groaned. 'Dionne, I'm totally exhausted,' she protested. 'I barely slept last night.'

'Please,' Dionne begged, pouting like a child.

'What is it for?' CeCe asked resignedly. It was all a charade; they both knew that CeCe would agree.

'Just a few go-sees, doing the rounds, but I'm booked all afternoon.'

'Well, I suppose I—'

'Thank you, honey, you're a star!' Dionne exclaimed, throwing her arms around CeCe. Then she caught sight of her reflection and was instantly distracted. 'Do you think I've put on weight?' Dionne frowned, turning from side to side as she scrutinized her incredible body. She was twenty pounds lighter than she had been in Detroit, and staying that way was a constant battle. 'My agent told me I need to lose a little, and the last casting I went on I could barely fit into the samples.'

'Dionne, you are gorgeous – *vraiment parfaite*,' CeCe assured her. And she meant it.

When CeCe first met Dionne, she had hated her on sight. It had been in VIP Room, a cool nightspot catering to *les branchés*, the hip, well-connected crowd. Dionne had been loud and brash, impossible to ignore.

Typical American, CeCe thought, wrinkling her nose in distaste. Dionne was desperate to be the centre of attention, that curvaceous body poured into some little black dress that was so tight CeCe wondered how she could even breathe. Her hair ran wild in a tightly curled afro, and she held an ever-present glass of champagne in one hand while gesticulating wildly with the other. She didn't stop talking, dancing, flirting the whole night.

By the time they left the club at six a.m., CeCe was converted, totally under Dionne's spell. Within a month, the two girls had moved in together and were inseparable. They rented a beautiful apartment in the upmarket, 8th arrondissement, with high ceilings, polished wooden floors and even a baby grand piano in the living room.

'It's a lifestyle choice,' Dionne had explained, and CeCe agreed.

The rent was killing them, so they let out the third room. CeCe had planned to use it as a small studio, but there was no way she could afford to. Her designs quickly took over the rest of the flat and there were always offcuts of calico draped over the sofa, the sewing machine permanently left out on the dining table, even rolls of fabric stashed upright in the bathroom.

The pair of them would get gloriously drunk on champagne as CeCe draped and tacked, while Dionne tottered up and down the makeshift runway between the living room and the kitchen, resplendent in a pair of fuck-me stilettos and whatever creation CeCe had pinned to her body.

Dionne was the perfect choice for CeCe's flamboyant designs. Unlike many of the gay, male designers, CeCe appreciated a woman's body and designed accordingly. She cited beautiful, strong, independent women as her inspiration and declared that Dionne was her muse – a title that fuelled Dionne's already unfettered ego.

CeCe favoured bright, bold colours in shimmering, body-hugging fabrics. An aquamarine sheath, slit dazzlingly high at the thigh and decorated with over-size silver and gauze butterflies. An outrageous scarlet ballgown, with petalled layers of chiffon skirt and a beautifully boned corset that gave the wearer a figure to die for. The audacious colours looked stunning against Dionne's dark skin, and she certainly had the confidence to carry off even the most outrageous designs.

One drunken night, CeCe and Dionne had made a pact. They vowed that whoever hit the big time first would do everything they could to help the other. So Dionne swore that when she became a top model, she would wear CeCe's creations to every event she could to help raise her profile. And CeCe assured Dionne that even when the most beautiful women in the world were clamouring to wear her designs, it would be Dionne debuting them on the runway and heading up the ad campaigns.

'Man, I can't wait to get the hell out of here,' Dionne sighed, glancing round the shop to where an obese woman was wrestling with a skintight lime-coloured T-shirt. 'All I need is a chance. I mean, you know I'm a good model, right? I've got energy, personality . . .' She struck a bold pose against a set of shelves, her hip jutting out, her neck elongated to emphasize her superb bone structure.

CeCe couldn't help but smile. 'You and I are destined for the top, *chérie. This,*' CeCe waved her hand disparagingly to indicate their uninspiring surroundings, 'is only temporary. One day you will be the famous supermodel, and I will be the most celebrated designer, and the whole world will know our names. We are a partnership, no?'

'Right,' Dionne agreed, finally cracking a smile. 'You and me, boo.'

'You and me,' CeCe repeated.

4

Alyson Wakefield stood in the sleek glass offices of Masson International, France's leading shipping company and a regular on the Forbes Global 2000 list. Located in the west of Paris, in the famous business district of La Défense, the Masson building was spectacular – thirty-six floors constructed in steel and glass, it even boasted a three-storey-high granite fountain in the lobby. Alyson would have given anything to work there.

But right now that didn't look likely. The uptight receptionist stared distastefully at Alyson, making no effort to hide her hostility. The girl in front of her was undoubtedly beautiful – her fine, blonde hair was scraped back in a functional ponytail, and even the fact she wore no make-up and a shapeless grey suit couldn't conceal the tall, slender figure and the stunning features. But she was clearly playing at being a grown-up – she could barely have been more than eighteen years old, and she looked utterly terrified.

The receptionist smiled tightly at her. 'Monsieur de Villiers is in a meeting and cannot be disturbed. And no, I don't know what time he will be finished.'

Alyson felt the heat rising in her face and willed herself not to be intimidated. 'Can I at least leave my résumé?' she asked, fighting to keep the note of desperation out of her voice.

Raising a pencil-thin eyebrow, the receptionist took it from her. Alyson knew it would be going straight in the bin the second she left, but she smiled brightly.

'*Merci. Bonne journée,*' she called, holding her head high as she turned and walked smartly across the polished marble floor. The exit doors hissed open to let her through as she emerged into the warm, still air outside, and headed straight across the square towards the métro.

She didn't notice the way the men turned to stare as she strode past, their attention captured by this willowy young girl with the strikingly long legs.

She reached the station, quickening her step to catch the train that was pulling up to the platform. It was only when the doors slid closed behind her that Alyson let her composure drop, slumping down in her seat with an exhausted sigh.

What on earth was she doing with her life?

As soon as her mother had been settled in a home, she'd accepted her father's offer to get away for a while. Perhaps he was right – perhaps she *did* need to do something for herself. The chance of escape was tantalizing, and she fled before it was retracted, bolting across the Channel to Paris. It was all so easy – a train to London, a short hop on the Eurostar and there it was: a whole other city, a whole other world. It was a place of dreams, so familiar to her from countless television programmes and movies and black-and-white posters.

In spite of the dirt and the pollution, Alyson felt as though she could breathe for the first time. It was all too easy to forget about home; she just wanted to keep on running and never look back.

She had no idea what she wanted to do with the rest of her life, but she got organized fast. Her money would last barely a month, so she needed to find work quickly, and she set her sights on an office job. At school she'd been interested in business studies, and she was intelligent, presentable and hard-working. How difficult could it be?

Impossible, turned out to be the answer.

Within days of arriving in the capital, Alyson sent a copy of her CV to every single one of the top one hundred French companies, along with a personalized letter of introduction specifically targeted at each firm. She knew she'd have to start at the bottom, but she didn't care. She would make the coffee, photocopy, do whatever it took – she was buzzing with ideas and all she wanted was a chance to prove herself.

She heard nothing. Not one single reply.

So Alyson decided to take a more direct approach. Catching the métro out to La Défense, she hawked her résumé round every office that was willing to take it. And she hated every minute of it.

'I'm sorry, we have nothing available at the moment,' Alyson was told over and over again, in haughty Parisian tones. The supercilious secretaries, with their dark-framed glasses and chic suits, looked disparagingly at this terrified young girl who clearly wasn't good enough to work for *their* firm. Her French might have been faultless, but she didn't even have a degree, and her contact address was some two-star hotel in the 5th arrondissement. She was lucky they didn't laugh her out of the building.

But there was no way she could go home. The idea was terrifying, and was what drove her on every single day. Now she'd got out she couldn't bear to go back. She'd finally been given the opportunity to really make something of herself – although, as yet, she had no idea what that might be.

And Alyson adored Paris. The longer she stayed, the more she fell in love with it – the people, the energy, the cosmopolitan vibe and the stylish way of living. She didn't know a soul and the freedom was exhilarating.

The first day Alyson arrived, she had walked and walked, with no real aim in mind, eventually finding herself at the Eiffel Tower with a crush of other tourists. Alyson made her way to the top, just another anonymous face in the crowd. She looked out over the city and the sight took her breath away – the wide river snaking far below, the distinctive cream buildings with their sprawling rooftops and the magnificent white dome of Sacré Cœur high on the hill to the north. She didn't think she'd ever seen anything so beautiful.

Overwhelmed by a fierce determination, Alyson vowed that, one day, one way or another, she would conquer this city. There would be no snobby secretaries looking down their nose at her, no 'sorry, he's not available' or 'sorry, she's not interested'. Alyson Wakefield would be someone they wanted to see, someone they respected. One day.

But it was easy to make vows, Alyson reflected, as the train pulled into Saint-Michel. The hard part was fulfilling them.

She exited the station, walking back through the vibrant neighbourhood that was already so familiar to her. The smell of fresh crêpes drifted deliciously on the air, and Alyson's stomach rumbled hungrily. She'd eaten nothing all day except the apple she'd grabbed for breakfast.

Alyson checked her purse as she walked towards the stall, then stopped in shock. Was she really that low on cash? Shit, things were getting dire. She'd been walking everywhere she could to try and save money, living on little more than bread and fruit from the market, but Paris was an expensive city and the money she'd arrived with was being eaten away at an alarming rate. If she didn't find work soon . . . Alyson swallowed. There was no way she was giving up on her dream.

As she stood fumbling with her purse she noticed the café on the corner, the waiters bustling in and out in their smart uniforms. Alyson thought for a moment, gathering her nerve. She could do that easily.

It felt horribly like a step back – she didn't want to return to waitressing – but surely it would only be temporary, until she got a real job somewhere. Right now, earning money was her priority.

Before she could change her mind, Alyson crossed the road.

'*Pardon*,' she began, in hesitant French. 'Do you have any jobs available?'

It had been an impulsive gesture, completely out of character. She hoped the gamble would pay off.

The waiter she'd approached shook his head. '*Non*,' he offered curtly, before heading back inside. Alyson stood on the pavement, feeling stupid. Then she mustered her dignity and moved on. She'd taken enough blows today – a little more humiliation was hardly going to make a difference.

The Latin Quarter was a mecca for cheap tourist restaurants, but everywhere she tried she got the same response. It was like a replay of her morning spent at La Défense. *So much for being proactive*, Alyson thought in frustration. She couldn't even get a job as a waitress.

But she persevered, making her way from one low-rent eaterie to another. Some kind of dogged determination kept her going, a perverse instinct to keep putting herself through the wringer. *One more place*, she told herself. Just one more, and then she would go back to the scuzzy little hotel room she was staying in. It was hardly a cheering thought.

The final bar on the street was illuminated by a gaudy green and white flashing sign. It was an Irish theme pub, all shamrocks, leprechaun hats and pints of Guinness. Even the name was a horrible cliché – Chez Paddy. Alyson walked in without hesitating.

Inside it was dimly lit, decorated in dark wood panelling to give it a rustic feel. About half a dozen of the tables were occupied, and Alyson walked straight up to the bar. At first she thought no one was serving, but then a guy appeared out of the back room.

He was tall and slim, with dark hair, and he smiled when he saw her.

'What can I do for you?' he asked, in a rich Irish accent.

'Do you have any jobs?' Alyson blurted out, not even trying to hide her desperation.

The guy smiled, his blue eyes crinkling at the corners. 'When can you start?'

'Straight away?' she suggested, wondering if he was joking.

'Well, get behind the bar then,' he laughed, throwing her a black T-shirt with Chez Paddy stitched in green just above the left breast. 'I'm Aidan, by the way.'

'Alyson,' she told him, shaking the hand he was holding out. His grip was firm, his skin warm.

'Welcome to the team,' he grinned.

*   *   *

For the next month, Alyson worked solidly, six-day weeks and taking on any extra shifts she could. Life was reduced to little more than travel, work and sleep – *métro, boulot, dodo*, as the French said – but hard work didn't faze her: it was all she knew. She was so busy that she forgot no one had rung her back with a more serious job offer.

To her surprise, Alyson found she was enjoying life at Chez Paddy. Aidan was a lifesaver – funny, warm and patient as he showed her round the bar, teaching her how to pull a pint of Guinness and make a shamrock design on the head, or how to mix cocktails over the back of a spoon so they sat in perfect layers.

She found that she was far more relaxed than she'd been at home. Back in Manchester, Alyson had always been something of an outsider. Her natural shyness was often misinterpreted as hostility, the other, more popular, girls labelling her snooty or stuck-up.

Here she was less defensive, confident enough to let her guard down and make small talk with the endless stream of tourists that were passing through, or the Irish expat regulars who came in to get drunk on Jameson's whiskey.

She didn't realize that, night after night, Aidan watched her and marvelled at the difference in her already – from the nervous young girl she had been when she'd first come in to beg for a job, to the incredibly beautiful, confident woman she was fast becoming. He knew she had a history. That much was obvious. She didn't like to talk about herself, and she was clearly running away from something. But he didn't ask her, and he didn't rush her. Almost instantly, Aidan felt incredibly protective of her and wanted to help her in any way he could. He daren't ask himself what his motives were.

'Any luck finding a place yet?' Aidan asked one afternoon as they cleared away the tables after the lunchtime rush.

Alyson shook her head. 'I haven't had time to look. I've been so busy here.'

'You're not still living in that crummy hotel?' Aidan asked in disbelief. 'Go on. Take the afternoon off.'

Alyson stared at him in confusion.

'I mean it. Seriously, I can manage here. Have you been to the American Church?'

Alyson shook her head.

'It's on the Quai d'Orsay, along the river. They have ads for flat shares, au pairs, hostess work, that kind of thing. But don't go getting another job! There's no way I can do without you here.'

'Thanks, Aidan,' Alyson grinned shyly, as she grabbed her bag and slipped out of the door, stepping into the bustle of the busy street.

It was a beautiful day and she decided to walk, eager to see as much of the city as she could. She took a left and followed the curve of the river. Heavy sycamore trees swayed gently in the light breeze as the traffic rumbled incessantly on the other side of the Seine.

A group of young Parisians, not much older than herself, whizzed by on rollerblades, their bronzed limbs sleek and toned as they yelled to each other. Their French was rapid and full of slang, but Alyson was learning fast, the colloquial phrases quickly becoming familiar to her. Yeah, she was really making progress, she thought happily, as she strolled along enjoying the warm spring sunshine.

'*Mademoiselle?*'

Alyson felt a hand on her arm and turned sharply. A man stood in front of her, nervously clearing his throat. He was in his forties, a touch overweight and beginning to go bald. There were sweat patches under the armpits of his shirt, and the top of his head barely came up to her chin. '*Vous avez l'heure?*' he asked.

Alyson checked her watch. '*Oui. Quinze heures trente.*' She went to move on, but the man stopped her.

'*Vous êtes très belle, mademoiselle. Vous voulez prendre un café avec moi?*'

Alyson reddened, looking away sharply. '*Non, merci.*' She began to walk off. The guy watched her go for a moment, as though considering whether or not to pursue her. He decided not to. He didn't stand a chance, and he knew it.

The incident had unsettled Alyson. She hated the way men came on to her like that. It had happened ever since she'd arrived in Paris. They would follow her down the street, hit on her when she was sitting in the park reading a book – even chat her up when she was in the launderette, trying to wash her clothes She knew that the French reputation was legendary when it came to romance, but so far all she'd encountered were a bunch of sleazeballs with appalling chat-up lines. Besides, she'd lost her trust in men when her father had walked out on them . . .

Angrily, Alyson stomped up the stone steps of the American Church, trying to banish the unhappy memories. Away from the road it was quiet, and the cloisters were cool after the heat of the street. Shading her eyes from the sun reflecting off the windows, Alyson skimmed the 'To Let' adverts. There was very little that was suitable – too small, too expensive, too far out of the city. But then her eye landed on one that sounded exactly what she was looking for. She took her new mobile out of her bag and dialled the number.

*   *   *

'Oh yeah, baby, that's right . . .'

'Fuck,' swore Dionne, as her cell phone began to ring, completely distracting her from the job in hand.

'*Laisse tomber!*' David shouted to her. 'Leave it, Dionne.'

'It could be important,' she protested, climbing off him. 'A job or something.'

David Mouret, dark and gorgeous with a body to die for, lay back heavily on the black satin sheets, his unsated cock rock-hard and throbbing in frustration.

'Come on, Dionne,' he pleaded, in heavily accented English. 'What am I supposed to do?'

'Just shut up for a moment,' she snapped, rummaging through her purse. 'Shit,' she swore again as the phone stopped ringing.

'Thank Christ for that. Perhaps now we go back to fucking, yes?'

'Wait! Maybe they'll leave a message.'

David sighed as Dionne tapped her nails impatiently. Her phone beeped and she pounced on it.

'Hello? Hi, this is . . . well, my name's Alyson,' stammered the girl at the other end. 'I'm phoning about the flat-share you're advertising.'

Dionne groaned, feeling something inside her sink. She had hoped it would be from her modelling agent, but it was just some girl with a weird voice calling about the apartment.

'If the room's still available, I'd be interested in viewing it. You can call me on my mobile . . .' – *A mobile?* She must be British. And check that accent! – '. . . and just leave a message if I'm at work. My name's Alyson Wakefield and I look forward to speaking with you soon. Thank you.'

Dionne hung up. She could phone the girl later; right now, she had David to attend to. CeCe had been right when she said that he adored her, but Dionne knew she had to keep him sweet. She was counting on him to take her out for dinner later, then onto the hot new club, Bijou, so she could get another look at the luscious guy who owned the place.

Moving across the bed, Dionne placed one manicured fingernail firmly on the dark, wiry hairs on David's chest and gently pushed him backwards. He let out a groan as Dionne began to kiss his stomach, teasing the soft hair on his belly, until her lips gradually worked lower, and David Mouret remembered exactly why he bought her all those expensive presents . . .

5

'Is that it?' Dionne asked incredulously, as Alyson came into the apartment carrying a single suitcase.

'Yeah,' Alyson nodded self-consciously, wondering what all the fuss was about.

'Honey, I take more than that for a weekend in Cannes.'

'I don't have . . . I don't *need* a lot of stuff,' Alyson explained. It was true – she carried the bare minimum of clothes, only the essential cosmetics. She had a couple of books, including the French dictionary she'd used at school, three pairs of shoes and one handbag. No photos, no keepsakes. She'd taken very little when she left home.

'Maybe I could take over some of your closet space . . .,' Dionne wondered, but broke off as a bedroom door opened and another girl staggered out. She was wrapped in a dressing gown and her eyes were barely open, narrowed into tiny slits. One side of her head was shaved, but the hair on the other side was sticking out at crazy angles. It looked as though she'd just woken up.

'Hey, I'm CeCe,' she said warmly, kissing Alyson on both cheeks. 'Nice to meet you.'

'You'll have to excuse her,' Dionne apologized. 'We had a big night last night, and poor CeCe's still feelin' it.'

'It was wild,' CeCe added, by way of explanation.

'Sounds like fun . . .'

'Oh, it was,' Dionne assured her. 'Nobody parties harder than me and CeCe. We're *legends* in this city. Anyway,' she chattered on. 'Your room's through here – but you already know that . . .'

Alyson followed them along the corridor, looking around her as she took in her new home. She'd seen the apartment before, when she came to view it, but that had been brief and Dionne hadn't stopped talking. Although the whole place was beautifully decorated, it was also incredibly cluttered – half-finished garments, rolls of material and fashion magazines dominated the communal areas. Alyson began to think it was a good thing she hadn't brought much with her: space was clearly at a premium.

She dumped her suitcase on the single bed, padding across to the window to look out at the view. It was far from spectacular. Instead of a skyline vista over the rooftops of Paris, Alyson's room looked out on a small courtyard where the refuse bins were stored, a couple of long-forgotten pot plants wilting in the corner. It was hardly the Parisian dream.

She turned round to find Dionne and CeCe standing in the doorway, looking at her expectantly.

'Shall we help you unpack?' Dionne asked brightly. 'Not that it'll take long . . .'

Alyson thought about it, a sudden embarrassing vision of them going through her secondhand clothes and greying underwear. 'It's fine,' she said hastily. 'I'll do it later.'

'Sure. Come through, sit down, let's get to know each other,' grinned Dionne, grabbing her hand and pulling her back through to the lounge. 'Can I get you a drink?'

'Yeah, that'd be great.'

'Oh my God, I *love* your accent,' Dionne squealed. '*Yeah, that'd be great,*' she repeated, trying, and failing, to imitate Alyson's flat Lancashire vowels. 'It's just too cute! So what would you like? We have champagne, wine, gin, vodka, brandy . . . There's probably some other stuff lying around, but I wouldn't recommend the absinthe.' She pulled a face.

Alyson smiled, assuming she was joking. But Dionne was staring at her, waiting for a response.

Alyson checked the clock on the wall – just gone eleven a.m. 'Um . . . do you have anything nonalcoholic?' she ventured, wondering if she was making some kind of terrible faux pas.

'Oh, sure. Will coffee do ya? CeCe looks like she could do with some.'

CeCe, curled up in a chair with her eyes closed, merely grunted.

'Coffee would be lovely, thanks,' Alyson said politely.

'You got it.'

As Dionne left the room, Alyson turned to CeCe, who was dragging herself upright, wincing at the light as she tried to open her eyes. She reached out to the coffee table, fumbling for a pair of Ray-Bans.

'Sorry for being shit,' she apologized as she pulled on the sunglasses, the phrase sounding odd in her strong French accent. 'We go out a lot. Last night was a killer.'

'That's okay,' Alyson said easily. 'Hopefully the coffee will help.'

'I think I need a triple shot,' she groaned. 'I've developed an immunity.'

Alyson smiled, unsure of what to say next. 'Dionne said you're a fashion designer,' she commented, trying to start a conversation.

'Yes. Undiscovered, but hopeful,' CeCe grinned. She seemed to sit up straighter, her face becoming animated as she talked about her work. 'I love it so much – the creative process, making something beautiful, something totally original and unique. It's my life,' she finished, lighting a cigarette and offering one to Alyson. Alyson shook her head. 'And you? Are you interested in fashion?'

'Um . . . not really,' she admitted.

'Ah, that will change,' CeCe asserted confidently. 'When you live here, in this apartment, you cannot help but be consumed by it. You will become a true, chic, Parisian woman.' She smiled at the look of doubt on Alyson's face. 'So, Alyson, tell me about you. You do not love fashion, so what do you do?'

'Well, at the moment I work in a bar,' she explained, her tone apologetic.

'No problem,' CeCe shook her head. 'Do not ever apologize for yourself. After all, that is not where you are going to finish, yes? All of us, we are starting at the bottom, but we have our dreams, *n'est-ce pas?*'

'Right,' Alyson agreed, feeling a huge surge of relief and unexpected kinship towards this girl. Finally, someone who understood that she wanted something more out of life!

'So what is your plan?' asked CeCe, exhaling the smoke from her cigarette in a long stream. 'What is the grand ambition of Alyson?'

'I'm interested in business, actually – the corporate world,' Alyson confessed. 'I think it seems really fast-moving and exciting.'

'Perhaps not the words I would use to describe it, but . . . as you wish,' CeCe remarked, a smile playing on her lips. 'So you are intelligent, yes? It will be good to have someone in the apartment who has a brain.'

'What's that?' Dionne walked back through, balancing three cups of coffee. She'd changed while she was out of the room, into the tightest pair of jeans Alyson had ever seen, and a very thin, form-fitting sweater.

'I was saying to Alyson, it will be nice to have someone of intelligence living here.'

'Speak for yourself honey,' Dionne told her, as she handed round the drinks. 'I'm borderline genius.'

CeCe looked amused. 'What is it they say? A fine line between genius and bullshit, I think.'

'Fuck off, darling,' Dionne shot back good-naturedly, as she plucked the dying cigarette from CeCe's fingers, took a drag and stubbed it out in the ashtray.

Alyson watched the banter between the two women with interest. They were obviously close, and had a great relationship.

'I think this calls for a toast,' Dionne announced, rising to her feet and raising her coffee cup. 'To our new recruit – officially the third most fabulous girl in Paris. CeCe, you're second,' she grinned, as the three of them clinked mugs.

'But of course,' CeCe shrugged, resignedly.

'We'll celebrate with champagne later, I promise,' Dionne insisted, turning to Alyson. 'Hey, we should all go out tonight! I'll call David – he can take us to dinner, then on to a club . . .'

'I have to work tonight, I'm afraid,' Alyson cut in, before Dionne got too carried away.

56

'Man, that's lame. Another night then?'

'Sure,' Alyson replied uncertainly.

'Oh, we are gonna have so much fun!' Dionne squealed, clapping her hands together in excitement. 'Seriously, doll, CeCe and I know everybody. And I mean, like, *everybody* in Paris. We know all the club owners, all the door staff, so we never have to pay for anything. We can introduce you to so many people – all the guys are gonna *love* you. You're gorgeous, isn't she CeCe?'

'Beautiful,' CeCe nodded seriously.

'And I've got the most amazing wardrobe, so if you ever need to borrow anything, feel free. Although ask me first, in case it's something I'm planning on wearing . . .'

Dionne chattered on and Alyson began to feel over-whelmed; it was like being slapped round the face repeatedly. Dionne was sweet, but she was also incredibly full on.

'Shit, is that the time?' Dionne swore, gulping down the last of her coffee. 'I've got a casting to get to. Wish me luck.'

'Good luck!' Alyson exclaimed; it seemed churlish not to.

'We *have* to go out one night this week – let us know when you have an evening off and we'll arrange something,' Dionne insisted, picking up her mobile and throwing it into her bag. She wedged a pair of sunglasses on top of her head and threw Alyson a dazzling smile. 'I've gotta head. *Ciao*, ladies.'

The door slammed shut behind her and she was gone. Alyson felt as if she'd just survived being caught in a tornado. 'She has a lot of energy,' she managed to say.

'Yeah, she's incredible,' CeCe agreed, staring wistfully

at the door where Dionne had just left. 'So beautiful, with such passion for living, such *joie de vivre* . . .'

Alyson nodded, looking thoughtfully at CeCe. Whatever her reservations about living here, one thing was for certain: with those two around, life would never be dull.

Dionne turned her hand over to examine her nail extensions – they were long and square-tipped, painted a deep purple and decorated with a small piercing at the end of each thumb – then stared listlessly round the room, all thoughts of her new flatmate long gone.

She was at a casting for Pierre Gavroche, some new designer fresh out of Esmod, and around her sat a dozen other models clutching their black leather portfolios, each wearing the identical model 'uniform' of skinny jeans and a cotton tank. They all carried an oversized bag, which only served to make them look even thinner and more fragile by comparison, and in which they carted their whole lives around – mobile, diary, modelling cards, high heels, nude underwear and a bikini. You never knew what the client would request and the girls had it drilled into them that – like a good boy scout – they should always be prepared.

Models really were a different race, Dionne reflected, as she stared round at the others. They were almost alien-like with their long, racehorse limbs, angular features and striking faces scrubbed bare of make-up. One or two were clearly anorexic – their hair lank, skin flaky, bones protruding just that little too much. There was a girl sitting across from her who Dionne was certain couldn't have had her period for months.

Looking round, she was the only black girl at the casting. The others were a mixture – mostly white, mostly French, with a scattering of mixed-race women in a nod to the country's colonial heritage – fourth generation Moroccan or Algerian. In spite of what anyone said, the fashion industry was still overwhelmingly racist. Of course, there was the occasional girl that broke through – Naomi, Tyra, Iman. The stats didn't faze Dionne. They simply made her more determined.

Rather than trying to fit in, to become a clone of one of the aloof-looking, effortlessly groomed French girls, Dionne embraced her differences. If she couldn't compete with the others, she had to set herself apart, make her diversity her advantage. She didn't intend to compromise who she was for anyone, and she knew that every job she got was because the designer really bought into her whole style and vibe.

Not that many people *had* been booking her. The easy acceptance she'd hoped for when she'd moved from Detroit hadn't exactly happened. Dionne had imagined that she'd be feted by the whole of Paris, instantly proclaimed the Next Big Thing and snapped up by a world-renowned name such as IMG or Elite. Instead, she'd signed with a bog-standard agency that no one outside the industry had heard of and become a jobbing model, spending her life at go-sees and castings in the hope that the next one would turn out to be her big break.

She was constantly aware that she had only a finite amount of time to break out and make a name for herself before she became just another has-been, an also-ran, doing the rounds on low-grade jobs without a hope in hell of making it to the next level. Dionne was a child of the nineties, the era of the supermodel – of Cindy, Linda, Claudia, Naomi, Kate. Her goal was to become a household name, referred to by her first name alone. Nothing less would do. But she was nineteen years old and time was running out.

'Salomé Valentin?'

A woman emerged from the casting room, clipboard in hand, as she called out the name of the next model. Salomé stood up – she was ultra-thin, white, with mousy-brown hair – and tottered through on legs that looked too frail to carry her. Then the door banged shut, and the others resumed their habitual bored expressions. It wasn't done to look too enthusiastic about anything. Designers still overwhelmingly went for the dead-eyed, spaced-out look, particularly for runway work, lest any personality should detract from the clothes. Commercial was a little better – there at least you could inject some individuality, play a character. And it was where the big money was.

Like most girls who dreamed of being a model, Dionne's ambition was to do high fashion: edgy, editorial work. The pay was shit – an embarrassment almost – but it was a stepping stone to higher things. Having a *Vogue* cover or an *Elle* editorial gave you kudos and meant your face was seen by top designers, who in turn might use you in their big money ad campaigns – the holy grail of the modelling world, and one which was increasingly being muscled in on by celebrities.

Yet in spite of everything, all the schlepping around and the kicks in the teeth from the jobs you never got, Dionne still loved it. The thrill of being in the French capital hadn't dimmed; every time she turned a corner and saw the Eiffel Tower rearing up over the city, her heart skipped a beat. She couldn't believe that little Dionne Summers from downtown Detroit was running around Paris, working as a model and partying with some of the richest and most glamorous people on the planet.

She wondered what Dash Ramón would think if he could see her now. It made her laugh to think how she'd revered him. He might have been a big shot in her neighbourhood, but he was nothing to the people she hung around with now. They were players on an international stage, part of the exclusive jet set. And Dionne intended to be one of them.

The door opened again and Dionne looked up. Salomé Valentin sloped out without speaking to anyone, her face impassive as she walked out of the door. The woman checked her list. 'Dionne Summers?'

Showtime!

Dionne got up and went in, where she was introduced to the designer himself, Pierre Gavroche. Obviously gay, he was a short, wiry man dressed all in black and wearing black-rimmed glasses.

The clothes were a little boring for Dionne's tastes – a muted palate of greys, taupes and creams. Yet she had to admit that they were well made, and the fabric was high quality.

'I want her in the pencil skirt and the ruffle blouse,' Pierre muttered to his assistant. Addressing the models directly was not his thing, apparently.

There was no separate changing area, so Dionne dropped her clothes without batting an eyelid and slid on a camel-coloured pencil skirt, beautifully cut and lined. This was paired with a dramatic white blouse, slit in a deep V-neck to below the breasts, then wrapped around bandage-style to create a cinched-in waist. Dionne was bra-less, the edge of the fabric skirting her nipples, her collarbone standing out prominently.

'Wear these,' the woman told her, throwing her a pair of dark-brown Charles Jourdan heels. They were a size too small, but Dionne squeezed them on without complaint.

She looked good and she knew it. The pale colours contrasted beautifully with her dark, glistening skin, and the whole look was fierce.

The female assistant raised a camera to take a Polaroid. When it had developed, she scribbled Dionne's name underneath and attached it to her modelling card.

'Can we see you walk?'

Dionne obliged. The shoes were pinching her feet, but she kept her face set, moving with sass and attitude. Dionne had an excellent walk – she was always amazed by the amount of girls that couldn't put one foot in front of another.

Pierre and his assistant watched her in silence.

'And again please,' they said when she'd finished.

As Dionne set off, they began to confer amongst themselves in fast, low French, perhaps thinking Dionne couldn't understand. Her French wasn't the greatest, but she understood enough.

'Is she a little on the heavy side?' asked Pierre.

'We could make her drop a few pounds,' the woman assured him.

Dionne pursed her lips. She turned at the end of the imaginary runway and began to walk back.

'I'm not sure . . .' she heard Pierre Gavroche deliberate. 'Maybe we should go with a white girl. Are ethnics in this season?'

Dionne nearly fell off her heels. She was so fucking furious, she couldn't even speak.

'That will be all, thank you,' the woman called out.

Damn right, that was all, thought Dionne, humiliation burning through her as she pulled off the skirt. The white shirt was a little tight as she tried to drag it over her head. Perhaps they were right; perhaps she did need to lose a few pounds. She heard the tiniest rip as she pulled it a little bit too hard. That gave her an idea. Glancing over, she saw that Pierre and his assistant were deep in conversation, scanning over the list to see who was next. Dionne took hold of the sleeve and yanked it. The fabric fell away sharply with a satisfying tearing sound.

Pierre Gavroche looked up sharply. 'What the hell are you doing? *Putain!*' he swore, rushing over to find several hundred euros' worth of ruined shirt. The rip was small, but it was in the fabric, not along the seam where it could be easily repaired.

Dionne slipped on her own clothes, giving him the most innocent look. 'I'm so sorry. You know us *ethnics*,' she smiled, emphasizing the word. 'We're just so clumsy.'

Then she swung her bag over her shoulder and walked out, leaving Pierre Gavroche and his flunky gaping after her.

She knew that was one job she wasn't getting, but she didn't care. No one treated Dionne Summers like that and got away with it. The world would just have to learn.

6

Alyson was having a bad day.

'*Oui, j'arrive . . .*' she called over her shoulder, as she raced past the crammed tables in Chez Paddy. They were already short-staffed, and a sudden downpour meant everyone had abandoned their usual lunchtime terrace tables at the nearby cafés and headed for the cosy interior of the Irish pub.

It didn't help that Alyson had slept badly the night before. Her new flatmates, Dionne and CeCe, didn't appear to need sleep. Ever. Oh, they were sweet girls, and the apartment was gorgeous, but the way they lived their lives was crazy. Alyson had been there almost two weeks now and discovered that most nights the pair stayed out until dawn, finally rolling in with a large group of 'friends' they'd acquired over the course of the evening, before cranking the music up loud, breaking out the champagne and partying until they passed out.

She didn't understand how they managed to hold down their jobs in the boutique. If Alyson turned up late, exhausted and hungover every day, she'd be fired for sure. She guessed they were just those kinds of people – the beautiful ones, who breezed easily through life with everyone smoothing their path. Life had never been like that for Alyson. She'd always had to work damned hard for everything.

But no, that wasn't fair, she told herself. It was the lack of sleep making her irritable. CeCe and Dionne had been nothing but kind to her ever since she'd moved in, always inviting her out with them even though she declined every time. Clubbing just wasn't her scene. She had no interest in going out, getting drunk and making a fool of herself. She saw enough people doing that while she was at work. Perhaps it made her uptight, but she didn't like that loss of control.

'You okay?' Aidan asked, in that lilting Irish accent.

Alyson forced a smile as she rushed past him. The bar was a bomb site, the tables piled high with dirty plates and empty glasses.

'Alyson,' Aidan called. He caught her by the shoulders, forcing her to stand still for a moment. 'Don't worry about it,' he said easily. 'It's quietening down now. We'll have this place sorted in no time.'

'Thanks, Aidan.' Alyson gazed up at him, her blue eyes meeting his. Her skin was flushed from the exertion, wisps of fine, blonde hair snaking loose from her ponytail. She looked incredible.

Quickly, Aidan let go of her shoulders and dropped his gaze, not wanting her to see the look in his eyes. He'd worked hard to win her trust, and Alyson had never given him any indication that she thought of him as anything other than a friend. He valued that too much to spoil it with some clumsy come-on.

'I'll head down to the kitchen, help finish up there.' He cleared his throat, eager to get away.

'No problem.' Alyson was oblivious to his odd behaviour.

65

As she turned round, she realized Aidan was right – the pub was emptying out, and there was no longer a queue at the bar. Only a few customers were left now – a couple of English girls, giggling as they studied the happy hour cocktail menu; an old Irish guy, one of the Chez Paddy regulars, watching RTÉ on a wall-mounted flat screen; a smart-looking man in an expensive suit, taking his time over a whiskey and soda on the rocks.

'Busy day?'

Alyson was collecting empty glasses, and didn't hear the man speak.

'Busy day?' he tried again.

She turned, startled, breaking into a self-conscious smile. 'You could say that.'

It was the guy in the suit who had spoken to her. He was tall, well built and Gallic-looking, with handsome features and penetrating brown eyes. His hair was dark, flecked with grey; Alyson aged him at late thirties.

'Can I help you with anything?' he asked, spreading his hands in an open gesture.

Alyson took in his expensive clothes and immaculate appearance. He didn't look as though he'd ever done a menial job in his life.

'Have you worked in a bar before?' she couldn't resist asking.

His lips twitched, aware he was being teased. 'No, but I . . . I know a lot of people who do,' he finished with a smile, aware of how ridiculous that sounded. When he laughed, the skin around his eyes crinkled into fine lines.

'I'll be fine,' Alyson assured him, feeling caught off-guard somehow. She continued to clear away the leftover plates, aware that he was watching her.

As she carried them over to the bar, he got up from

his seat and joined her, settling his empty glass on the counter.

'Would you like another?' Alyson asked.

He nodded. 'Please. Whiskey soda, with ice.' He had a French accent, and Alyson was surprised. They didn't get many natives in Chez Paddy, especially not ones who looked like him – executives, in hand-tailored suits.

'Your accent is very unusual,' he commented. 'Where are you from?'

Alyson hesitated. She didn't like talking about her background. 'I'm from Manchester,' she replied eventually, answering with only the bare facts. 'The north of England.'

'Ah,' he explained passionately. 'Yes, I know it! You have a wonderful football team, of course.'

Alyson smiled in amusement. 'So I'm told.'

'But it is a beautiful part of the country,' he added quickly, sensing her lack of interest in the subject. 'There is the Peak District, no?'

'Yes, that's right,' Alyson replied in surprise, not expecting him to know the area so well.

'I have been to the north, two, perhaps three times. Manchester, the countryside, the Lake District . . . so beautiful,' he sighed, closing his eyes for a moment as though to re-live the memory.

'Were you there on holiday?' Alyson asked, slipping into the easy rhythm she'd learned at Chez Paddy – if the customer wanted to talk, ask them lots of questions about themselves.

'No, I visited for work. I am very lucky with my job – it allows me to travel often.'

Alyson pushed the whiskey and soda across the counter towards him. 'What do you do?'

There was a slight pause and she glanced up at him,

worried that she'd overstepped the boundaries. 'I'm in business,' he told her, taking a slug from his glass. 'And you?' He changed the subject. 'Have you travelled much?'

Alyson looked down at the counter and shook her head. 'This is the first time I've left England.'

'Yes?' The man raised his dark eyebrows, seeming surprised. 'And now you are living here? That is a big decision – when you have never travelled overseas before, to move somewhere completely different . . . You have friends here?'

'No,' Alyson confessed, her voice growing quieter. 'I didn't know anyone before I came.'

The man seemed to sense that something was wrong, smoothly changing the subject. 'And now you are here, what do you think of Paris?'

'Oh, I love it!' Alyson exclaimed, her face lighting up. 'I knew I would. I love the language, the architecture, the sense of freedom. It just seems like the most beautiful, romantic place in the world.'

'It is,' the man agreed, enjoying her enthusiasm. 'It is very beautiful. And very romantic.'

He stared hard at her, and Alyson suddenly found that she couldn't meet his gaze. There was something about the way he was looking at her with those intense brown eyes. It made her heart beat faster and she suddenly had the overwhelming urge to run away in terror, the fight-or-flight instinct kicking in—

'Philippe.' He reached out across the counter, offering his hand.

It took Alyson a second to realize what he meant. 'Oh! Alyson,' she burst out, feeling stupid.

'*Enchanté de faire votre connaissance.*'

'*Et vous aussi.*'

'You speak excellent French,' Philippe complimented her.

'Thank you,' Alyson managed to stammer. He still hadn't let go of her hand.

'Man, this place is a mess!' Aidan exclaimed as he emerged from the back. He stopped short as he took in the scene before him – Alyson, flushed and breathless, shaking the hand of some sleazy-looking guy almost twice her age.

His eyes narrowed and Alyson instinctively pulled back, as though caught doing something she shouldn't. She didn't know why she felt so guilty – Aidan never minded her talking to the customers.

'Sorry,' she apologized quickly. 'I started tidying up but then . . .' She stopped, unsure of what to say next.

Philippe stood up and turned to Aidan. 'It is all my fault,' he said easily. 'I have been distracting your staff, and I apologize.'

Aidan stared at him coolly for a moment, taking an instant dislike to this arrogant prick. 'No problem,' he said through clenched teeth.

Alyson watched the two men nervously, sensing the animosity that crackled between them.

Philippe knocked back his drink then threw a twenty-euro note on the counter. 'Keep the change. Nice to speak with you, Alyson.'

He walked out of the door without looking back.

Music pounded from the stereo speakers, a David Guetta track that was storming the charts all over Europe. The volume was turned up to max and the tiny apartment began to vibrate like a nightclub.

Alyson was sitting at the dining table eating her dinner, surrounded by piles of CeCe's sketches and half-finished garments.

Dionne and CeCe were getting ready for yet another night out in their usual flamboyant fashion. As Alyson

69

ate, Dionne let out a whoop and grabbed a deodorant can from where it had been flung on the coffee table before mounting the sofa, her legs wide apart in an attempt to keep her balance on the squashy cushions. She was fresh out of the shower and naked apart from a black lace thong that left nothing to the imagination. Using the can as a microphone she posed like a rock star, waving her arms in the air and thrusting out her crotch as she sang along with the music, her breasts swaying as she danced.

Alyson looked down at her plate. She tried to avoid seeing her own body naked, and had no desire to see anyone else's grinding in front of her.

'Why don't you come out with us tonight?' Dionne suggested, as she jumped down from the sofa and poured herself a glass of champagne. The question was becoming a constant refrain. Dionne always asked, and Alyson always said no.

'I have to work.'

'So call in sick,' CeCe shrugged. She was lying on the floor, smoking a cigarette and watching Dionne.

'I can't,' Alyson insisted.

'Come on, live a little!' Dionne chided, as Alyson flushed. Then Dionne changed tactics. 'Please,' she begged, her lips obscenely large as she pouted. 'I'm celebrating! I got me a modelling job and I want you to come celebrate with me.'

'Congratulations, Dionne,' Alyson smiled, genuinely pleased for her.

'Thank you.' Dionne made a sweeping bow, a movement that sent her bare breasts swinging.

Alyson averted her eyes. 'What is it for?'

'Catalogue work.' Dionne made a face. 'Not exactly high fashion, but the pay's pretty awesome.' Of course, she hadn't got the job for Pierre Gavroche. They'd even rung up her agency to complain about her – yeah, like *she* was the one with the attitude problem. But a day spent hauling her ass around town from one casting to the next had finally paid off. 'So are you gonna come?'

'I'd love to,' Alyson lied, 'but I really can't let Aidan down. Friday nights are always so busy, and we're short-staffed as it is.'

'Oooh, who's Aidan?' Dionne squealed. 'He sounds hot.'

'He's my boss.'

'And is he hot?' Dionne pressed.

'I . . .' Alyson faltered, unsure of what to say. She hated it when Dionne put her on the spot like that. '. . . He's a really nice guy.'

Dionne burst into peals of laughter. 'Come out with us, honey – we'll introduce you to some *hot* guys. We know all the cutest men in Paris. We'd find you someone, no problem.'

Alyson looked away uncomfortably as CeCe watched her curiously, blowing smoke up to the ceiling. 'Have you ever had a boyfriend, Alyson?' she asked casually.

Alyson glanced up sharply, feeling as if she'd been caught out. 'No,' she admitted, feeling hot with embarrassment as she saw the surreptitious glance that passed between Dionne and CeCe. She suddenly felt an overwhelming urge to fit in, to confide in someone about the man she'd met at work today, and the feelings he'd evoked. 'There is someone I like though . . .'

Dionne let out a whoop. 'Yeah, go, Alyson!' she cried. 'So come on, who is he?'

'He's . . . I met him at work . . .' she began hesitantly.

'I knew it!' Dionne exclaimed triumphantly. 'I knew this Aidan guy sounded cute! So you have a little crush on your boss, huh?'

Alyson opened her mouth to correct her, but Dionne was in full flow. 'Hell, go for it, girl. You've got to have a little fun while you're at work. Makes the day go faster. Hey, we're both gonna be on missions tonight!'

Alyson looked at her in confusion as Dionne carried on. 'While you're working your charms on the delectable Aidan, I also have my sights set on a guy and tonight's the night he's gonna be mine,' she growled. 'He's handsome, charming – and rich as fuck. Everything I want in a man. I am gonna go for him, and I am gonna get him!'

Alyson believed her. She couldn't imagine anyone turning Dionne down: she was an unstoppable force, the sort of woman who got whatever she set her mind to.

'Perhaps you can meet us after your shift,' CeCe suggested, turning to Alyson.

'Yeah, maybe . . .'

'Cool. You have my number, yes? Just jump in a taxi after work and call one of us.' CeCe stubbed out her cigarette.

Alyson made a noncommittal noise and carried her empty plate through to the kitchen, suddenly eager to get away.

She knew they meant well, but it wasn't for her. She couldn't think of anything worse than spending the evening in a noisy nightclub, trussed up in some ridiculous outfit while you were judged by a group of strangers who didn't give a damn about you.

Alyson sighed as she picked up a dishcloth – neither Dionne nor CeCe had done the washing up, as usual, and there was a pile of empty glasses in the sink left from last night's impromptu party.

If she was being honest with herself, she knew that part of her was scared – scared to go out, get drunk, meet a guy . . . *have fun*, a voice in her head chided.

That was the real reason it was easier to keep saying no. She wasn't like Dionne. Maybe it was something to do with being American, having that innate self-confidence, but Dionne seemed so at ease with herself. Okay, so she was also loud, irresponsible and unreliable, but she wasn't racked with doubts and insecurities about everything, the way that Alyson was.

Alyson couldn't imagine knowing her rent was due but blowing her last hundred euros on a bottle of champagne. She couldn't see herself turning up for work three hours late because she'd got so out of it the night before that she'd slept through her alarm. And she certainly couldn't envisage having a one-night stand with a guy she didn't know – let alone love.

She thought about the man who'd come into Chez Paddy today. Philippe. If she closed her eyes she could still picture his face – warm, dark eyes, a few laughter lines creasing at the edges, and full lips pursed in a Gallic pout. Just the thought of him made her pulse race faster, an excited, nervous sensation flooding through her belly, moving lower . . . Was this what the other girls at school had meant when they talked about having a crush on some boy? Or what Dionne felt when she staggered home after a night out and declared she'd met some honey of a guy she wanted to fuck until she couldn't see straight?

Oh, it was ridiculous, Alyson thought, waving the thought away. He was just one customer, passing through. She'd never seen him before and she'd probably never see him again, so it was in everybody's interests if she just forgot about him.

But she couldn't do that, and she knew it. He'd awakened something in her, something she'd never felt before. It was exciting and new and she wanted to see where it took her.

Idly, she wondered what the girls would say if they knew – if she'd announced to Dionne and CeCe that she'd fallen for a customer, a handsome, older man that made her heart pound and her insides fizz like a million tiny fireworks exploding throughout her body. What would Dionne do in that situation? There was no question – she wouldn't be mooning around the apartment, kicking herself for the fact that she knew nothing more about him than his first name. She'd have gone for it, seduced him with her clever lines and perfect body and smouldering gaze, until he was begging for her phone number, desperate to take her on a date.

Alyson exhaled in frustration, annoyed at herself for being so reserved and unadventurous. Dionne might have many faults, but Alyson couldn't help admire her headfirst approach to the world. Deep down inside, there was a small part of her that wondered what it would be like to lead Dionne's life, just for a day. To be so outrageous and unselfconscious, to be the centre of attention, dance naked on the sofa if you felt like it and do exactly what you damn well pleased without having to worry about money or work or your sick mother back home—

Alyson slammed the final plate down and dried her hands, hurrying through to her room to get ready. Her shift at Chez Paddy started in half an hour, and she couldn't afford to be late.

7

'Everything's under control, sir. No problems to report.'

'Glad to hear it.' Philippe Rochefort nodded curtly at Alain Lefèvre, his immaculately presented head of security, who was prowling round his sumptuous office. The man was six feet four inches of burly muscularity encased in a black Hugo Boss suit, and he was the kind of guy you didn't fuck around with.

'The club's filling up nicely, sir,' he commented, glancing at the bank of monitor screens.

'Yes, business has been extremely good since we opened.' Philippe allowed himself a smile. 'And I intend to keep it that way.'

He glanced at the Georg Jensen clock on the wall. It was just after midnight, the time when the beautiful people of Paris started to drift away from the early night bars and move on to their main clubbing venue. Since Bijou had opened three months ago, it had quickly become one of the most popular venues on the *branché* circuit, the well-heeled and well-connected loving its heady mix of funky interior, international DJs and gorgeous people.

'Do we have any VIPs due tonight?' Philippe asked, scanning the guest list.

Alain didn't miss a beat. 'Ophélie Winter is here already with a group of friends. Christophe Benoit and Nicolas Duchamp rang ahead to make sure their usual tables would be reserved for them,' Alain informed him, naming some of Philippe's business contacts. 'And there's a rumour that Leonardo DiCaprio's in town, so I've warned my people to keep alert for that.'

'Very good. Excellent.' Philippe stood up, pulling on his jacket. He was dressed in a business-casual combination of stone-coloured trousers and a pale-blue Roland Mouret shirt, a relaxed, trademark style that came from spending much of his time in the South of France. 'I'd better go down and make sure my guests are happy.'

Respectfully Alain stood aside, holding open the door as Philippe passed through, before speaking rapidly into his walkie-talkie to tell the rest of his team that Monsieur Rochefort was on his way to the main floor.

Philippe jogged steadily down the stairs. He was thirty-eight years old and in excellent shape. Three times a week – schedule permitting – he worked out at the gym with a personal trainer and kept a careful eye on what he ate. Since his father died of a heart attack in his early fifties, Philippe had tried to calm things down a little. Hitting thirty had been a turning point – he'd spent his twenties living the life of the idle playboy, taking full advantage of the fact that, thanks to a thriving champagne empire, his father was one of France's wealthiest men.

Yes, it had been a decade of debauchery and excess, Philippe reflected fondly. Ten years of clubs and yachts, models and cocaine, of gambling and recklessness with no thought to the future. Then, one morning, following a high stakes game of poker, Philippe woke up with a pounding head, a set of keys clutched in his hand and the vague recollection that he had won a nightclub called La Boîte. After some deliberation he had decided to keep it, more with the notion that it would be a great place to entertain his friends after hours than with any coherent business plan in mind.

But to his surprise he'd found that he enjoyed running the club. Benefiting from his natural sense of showmanship and self-promotion, La Boîte was soon rivalling Les Caves du Roy as the hottest spot on the French Riviera. Other nightspots soon followed, including the addition of a chain of high-class strip joints, La Mauvaise Pomme.

Bijou was the latest addition to Rochefort Enterprises, his first nightclub in the French capital, and looked set to be just as lucrative as his other ventures. But Philippe didn't take his achievements for granted. Initially somewhat surprised to find he had stepped out of the shadow of his father and was now a successful entrepreneur in his own right, he dedicated himself to his business, living out the maxim of working hard and playing hard. He had fantastic instincts when it came to striking a deal, and was proud of his 'hands-on' approach to running Rochefort Enterprises.

He was twenty-nine when his father died suddenly, making him the largest shareholder in the family company, Rochefort Champagne. It was worth at least twenty times more than his own fledgling business, but he was happy to appoint a CEO from the experienced board and leave the day-to-day running to his father's associates, popping in occasionally to glance over the books or inspect the vineyards.

Rochefort Enterprises was his own baby, the one he had tended and nurtured. This was where he had made his name, and it was what he enjoyed, allowing him to successfully combine business with pleasure. Handsome, charming and suave, he was a popular figure amongst his patrons – less so amongst his rivals, who saw him as a ruthless, controlling character.

They reached the door separating the nightclub from the private offices upstairs. Alain held it open and stepped aside to allow Monsieur Rochefort through.

It was time for Philippe to meet his public.

'*Bonsoir*, good to see you, have a great evening . . .' Heads turned as soon as he walked in, and Philippe worked the room like the professional he was, effortlessly circulating and chatting, complimenting and charming. He'd been doing this for so long that he could make it through the night on autopilot – which was fortunate, as Philippe's mind was elsewhere this evening.

He couldn't stop thinking about the girl he'd met yesterday. Alyson, she'd said her name was. He didn't even know her surname.

It was crazy, but he couldn't get her out of his head.

Yesterday morning he'd been working in his office in Bijou, trying to finalize the details of his American business plan. He was planning to expand to the US and was flying out on business for a few days, first to New York and then on to Las Vegas, where he would meet with realtors and view potential venues. While working through the proposals, he'd come up against some particularly complex contractual clauses and had decided he needed to get some air and clear his head.

So Philippe had set off walking. Bijou was in the 4th arrondissement, on the Right Bank, and he'd made his way aimlessly across the Ile de la Cité, over the Seine into the 5th, enjoying the freedom, the sense of clarity that being away from the office gave him. Then the heavens had opened, the rain had come down, and Philippe had stepped into the first bar he'd come across. It was the kind of place he'd usually avoid like the plague – a tourist trap, tacky and downmarket. But he hadn't cared. He needed alcohol and he needed to be anonymous.

Philippe didn't notice her at first. It was only when the customers began to thin out and he looked round properly at his surroundings that he saw her. He felt as though he'd had the breath knocked out of him, sure that his heart must be beating loud enough to attract the attention of the other customers. It was what the romantics might call a *coup de foudre* – love at first sight.

She was absolutely stunning, beautiful in a completely natural way. She wore no make-up, her undyed hair scraped back in a ponytail, her nails short and functional. She was the polar opposite of the girls who came to his club, the ones who were overstyled and over-made-up, their faces taut and frozen from too much plastic surgery. This girl looked human, she looked real. Even the shapeless black trousers and an unflattering T-shirt couldn't hide that amazing figure, all long limbs and slim curves.

She was clearly under pressure as she dashed from one table to the next, her cheeks flushed with colour. But she still took time to be polite and courteous to everyone, even the two awkward German customers who insisted on sampling a little of each beer before they finally ordered. Philippe was impressed – no, 'captivated' would have been a better word. He couldn't take his eyes off her. She was obviously very young – far younger than him, he realized with a pang – but that only added to the wholesome, naïve quality she exuded. For someone like Philippe, who had seen some of the most sordid parts of human nature, that innocence was enchanting. He would have put money on the fact that she was still a virgin.

And then he, the great Philippe Rochefort, the notorious lady-killer and epitome of Gallic charm, had been too nervous to speak to her. He hadn't known what to say; he'd been afraid to shatter the illusion he had already built up in his head. What if she turned out to be rude and unpleasant, cold and uninterested in him? Or if she already had a boyfriend? Philippe wanted to break his neck, whoever he was. Perhaps it was the guy she worked with, the one behind the bar. He certainly paid her enough attention, making little jokes and glancing at her when he thought she wasn't looking.

The guy disappeared into the back and the girl was left alone, looking vulnerable and beautiful and, before he could stop himself, Philippe had spoken to her, some crap about how busy it was. Hell, he was really losing his touch. But she had been wonderfully gracious and given him the most radiant smile. He was aware that he'd been selective about what he told her, saying that he was a businessman but leaving out the specifics. He watched her carefully for any flicker of recognition, any suggestion that she might have realized who he was, that she'd seen him in the pages of one of the glossy lifestyle magazines he often featured in, a glamorous woman on each arm. But he saw nothing. She clearly wasn't one of these girls obsessed with gossip magazines, scouring the pages for rich men they could target.

Then that idiot of a manager had come back and ruined the moment. Philippe had left hastily, before his temper overwhelmed him, and returned to his office more confused than ever. The walk that had been meant to clear his head had done nothing of the sort. He couldn't stop thinking about Alyson. She was in his head, under his skin, impossible to get rid of.

Earlier today he'd gone back to Chez Paddy. He'd told himself that he needed to see her just once, to set his mind at rest. She was probably nothing special – he'd exaggerated it in his mind, placed too much significance on a trivial meeting. But, even as he had the thought, Philippe knew that he was lying to himself. He remembered Alyson's smile, the way she moved, the way she had looked up coyly from underneath her wispy fringe, and he knew he had to see her again. He was helpless, drawn like a moth to a candle.

But she hadn't been there, and her jumped-up little boss had taken great delight in telling him she wasn't working that day.

'Tell her I passed by,' Philippe said.

Aidan had merely raised his eyebrows, with no intention of doing anything of the sort.

And tomorrow Philippe was leaving. He would be in the States for over a week and it was an important trip. He needed to concentrate, to ensure he was focused. He needed to forget about Alyson. He was Philippe Rochefort, internationally respected business magnate and legendary womanizer, not some love-struck adolescent.

'Philippe!'

Now, some woman was screeching at him from across the club. He vaguely recognized her, but she could have been any one of that identikit breed. Her surgically enhanced cleavage was poured into a clinging animal-print minidress, her bleached blonde hair dry and brittle. She came at him with unnaturally large Botoxed lips as she kissed the air at the side of his ears, once, twice and then an overfriendly third time.

He hated her for not being Alyson. He hated everything she stood for, all the superficiality, the falseness. He could almost see the euro signs in her eyes as she smiled at him, mentally calculating his bank balance.

The truth was that Philippe was tiring of this lifestyle. He had a yearning for something different – something more real, more fulfilling than the way he'd been living until now.

Resignedly, he pasted a smile on his face. '*Chérie!* Ah, how good to see you!' he lied, as he kissed her hand and the woman simpered like a little girl.

This was the only life he knew, and he had to get on with it.

8

Across the city, Dionne was finishing her third glass of Veuve Clicquot, generously provided by Saeed Al-Assad, one of her rich Arab friends. David, her regular date at the moment, was away working in Singapore, but Dionne had lots of male contacts in her phone.

Saeed had just flown back into Paris after three weeks away on business in Saudi Arabia. Young and good-looking, he was the stereotypical international jet-setter. Dionne saw him whenever he was in town, and now she and CeCe were out with him and his entourage in Kasbah, a Moroccan themed bar just off the *rue St Honoré*.

Saeed raised his glass. 'To Dionne, the next super-model!'

'Yes, to Dionne,' CeCe chimed in, grinning at her friend.

Dionne giggled as she toasted herself, loving being the centre of attention. This was definitely something she could get used to.

'What catalogue did you say it was again?' Katerina asked pointedly. A stunning Latvian model/actress, her biggest claim to fame was that she'd had a walk-on role in the last James Bond movie.

'Bonprix,' Dionne smiled, determined not to let Katerina rile her. They'd met a few times on the circuit. Dionne thought she was a bitch, but Saeed was paying, so he got to decide who came along for the ride.

Katerina sniffed. 'It's hardly a *Vogue* editorial, is it?'

'Six thousand euros, baby,' Dionne grinned.

'I think it's vulgar to talk about money,' Katerina drawled disapprovingly, in her thick, Eastern European accent.

Saeed watched the two girls with interest. 'I *love* to talk about money,' he declared, 'as long as it's big numbers. Anything less than a million doesn't interest me.' He laughed loudly, a booming, self-satisfied sound.

'I'll be making that soon,' Dionne declared, as Katerina rolled her eyes.

'So, where are you ladies taking me tonight? Where's hot?' Saeed changed the subject, placing a friendly hand on Dionne's knee. She was wearing the tiniest denim mini, which showed off her endless legs as she relaxed back onto the sofa.

'VIP Room?' suggested Katerina, referring to the exclusive club.

Dionne wrinkled her nose. 'No. No one fun goes there any more,' she told her dismissively, gently placing a hand over Saeed's to stop it from wandering any further up her thigh.

'How about Bijou?' CeCe suggested. She was dressed in a typically eccentric outfit; black Balmain harem pants that she'd picked up in a thrift shop, and an oversized, sequinned crop top, accessorized with chunky gold heels, enormous hoop earrings and a pair of deliberately geekish spectacles. 'I haven't been, but Dionne said it's incredible.'

Dionne stiffened, an unexpected surge of excitement pulsing through her. 'Totally!' she exclaimed, trying to suppress how badly she wanted to go there. Bijou meant Philippe Rochefort – the hottest guy in the city, as far as Dionne was concerned, and the man she'd set her sights on. With David out of town, this would be the perfect opportunity to get to know Bijou's owner a little better. 'I love it there – it's where it's at right now. Saeed, honey, you'll just adore it,' Dionne purred persuasively.

Saeed nodded thoughtfully. 'Where is it?'

'The Marais.'

'Fine, then let's go there,' he agreed easily, finishing his drink and pausing only to take a brief glimpse up Dionne's skirt as she stood up in front of him.

'I know the owner,' she commented casually, oblivious to what had just happened and unable to resist bragging. The statement was an exaggeration – she'd been introduced to Philippe once, on her first night in Bijou, but Dionne had learned that you didn't get anywhere in life without a little embellishment of the facts.

'Philippe? I met him in St Trop,' said Katerina airily. 'I was a guest at his club there. He is very handsome and he liked me very much.'

Dionne felt the implicit challenge in Katerina's statement, and relished the competition. *Back off, bitch. He's mine.*

'Yeah, he's a great guy,' Dionne agreed nonchalantly. 'Takes the time to be friendly to *everyone*. Even the little people.'

She shot Katerina a dazzling smile, then climbed into the blacked-out SUV, pulling CeCe in beside her. When they got to the club she would ditch Saeed and see who else was around – Katerina was welcome to his over-friendly advances. The rumour was she was little better than a prostitute and would sleep with anyone for the right price.

Dionne wasn't into that scene, but a lot of the girls she knew maintained their lifestyle that way – when they realized they were never going to make it big in modelling, they soon turned their hand to a much more lucrative trade. Even the world-famous Fashion Week could be little more than a flesh fest, with a whole seedy underbelly operating on the sidelines of the main event. Girls who hadn't been selected for the shows instead competed to make it into the beds of rich and powerful men – all for the right price, of course.

But while Dionne was happy to party, she wouldn't sleep with just anyone. It was a fine line, but she knew damn well which side she was on. Dionne was going to make it, and when she did it would be on her own terms.

Right now, she was going to have a little fun, and Philippe Rochefort was the perfect guy to be by her side – handsome, rich, well connected. Power like that was sexy, a real turn-on, and together they would make a spectacular couple. It wouldn't be easy, but Dionne loved a challenge. She was confident she could get any guy she wanted.

Smiling to herself in the darkness, she settled back into the luxurious seats of the SUV, watching in anticipation as the bright lights of Paris flashed by.

'Thanks, have a great night. Enjoy the rest of your holiday . . .'

Aidan closed the door and locked it, the bolts making a satisfying clunk as they slid into place. He'd already turned the music off, and the late-night silence was striking.

Alyson had begun clearing up, rinsing the drip trays and wiping down the tables ready for tomorrow.

'Take five minutes, if you want,' Aidan suggested. 'Get yourself a drink.'

'Thanks,' Alyson said gratefully. She poured herself an orange juice, then sat down at one of the tables, where she slipped off her shoes and began to massage her feet. The long shifts were always a killer.

Aidan fixed himself a neat Jameson's for Dutch courage and came over to join her. He watched her as she leaned forwards, her long, slim fingers making sweeping movements along the soles of her feet. Even after a gruelling shift she still looked incredible, the dark circles under her eyes highlighting her fragility.

Aidan took a slug of the whiskey, feeling the warming sensation as it hit the back of his throat. Shit, he had to get a handle on the situation. This girl was really starting to get to him.

As the manager of Chez Paddy, there'd been countless young women passing through, all far from home and looking for a friendly face. Aidan wasn't stupid – he was a good-looking guy, and could have taken advantage on dozens of occasions. But he'd always made it a rule not to get involved with the staff. It caused too many problems.

But Alyson was different. He couldn't stop thinking about her. She was different to all the rest, with a real sense of class, a vulnerability that brought out his protective side and a smoking body that brought out another side entirely.

He was ashamed to admit that he'd done something completely out of character the other day. It had been Alyson's day off and that French guy had come in looking for her – the older, smarmy creep. Aidan couldn't stand him. He'd asked for Alyson, and Aidan had coldly told him she wasn't working.

'Tell her I passed by,' Philippe had said, looking at Aidan with a cool, level gaze. There was something triumphant in his expression, as though he knew that Aidan couldn't compete with him – his power, his wealth.

Aidan had been furious, jealousy pumping through him. For the first time he'd felt his humble status, embarrassed of working in a tourist bar when this guy looked and behaved like he owned the world.

Aidan hadn't told Alyson about her visitor. He insisted to himself that he was just looking out for her, but deep down he knew his behaviour was born out of envy. He'd seen the way Alyson was with this guy, the way her eyes had lit up when she was speaking to him. He'd never seen her behave like that with anyone else – letting her guard drop completely, hanging off his every word.

Aidan gripped the glass tightly at the memory, his fingertips turning white with pressure as he threw back his head and downed the last of the Jameson's. It was do or die, and he was about to break his own golden rule.

'So, how's everything going with your new flat-mates?' he asked cheerily. As soon as the words were out of his mouth, he could have kicked himself. *Bloody coward.* It wasn't what he'd wanted to ask at all.

But then Alyson lazily opened her eyes – they were luminous blue and huge, framed by long, pale lashes – and gave him the most divine smile. Aidan felt as though the breath had been knocked out of him.

'They're great,' she replied tiredly. 'Really sweet girls. Kind of crazy, but fun.'

Aidan nodded, struggling to keep his focus. He took a deep breath and tried again.

'Good. Great. Look, I um . . . sorted out the rotas for the next two weeks. I don't know if you've looked at them?'

'No, I haven't had a chance yet, I'm afraid.'

'No problem.' Aidan paused, uncertain of where to go next. He cleared his throat awkwardly. 'It's just . . . it's worked out that we both have this Saturday night off. I was wondering if you fancied . . . if you wanted to do something. I know you said you hadn't seen much of the city, so I thought it might be fun to explore . . .'

Alyson broke into a wide smile. 'Yeah, that sounds great. I'd love to.'

'Really? Fantastic!' Aidan had to stop himself from punching the air. 'Right, well . . .' He cleared his throat, businesslike once more, as he tried to hide his delight. 'I guess we'd better get cleaned up in here.'

The music was pumping loudly as the DJ segued effortlessly from a remixed R&B track into electronic dance. A wash of coloured lights swept the room, bouncing off the mirrors and reflecting from the polished glass tables.

Saeed Al-Assad was seated in Bijou's VIP area, the exclusive roped-off section. The table in front of him was piled high with bottles of spirits and mixers, Rochefort champagne stacked in silver ice buckets. Saeed sat like a king surveying his harem, surrounded by a posse of black-clad friends, mostly Arabs, and short-skirted, beautiful girls – the ones he'd arrived with, and the ones he'd picked out of the crowd and invited to join him.

Behind the banquette seating was a recessed area, like a luxurious cave, the size of a double kingsize bed and with sheer gauze drapes that could be pulled across when the occupants wanted a little privacy. Already a number of girls were lying languidly on the oversized cushions, sipping drinks and artfully arranging themselves to show off their assets to best advantage. They would start off chatting to Saeed's friends, then slowly move closer to the man himself, each hoping to land the big fish.

Dionne had no interest in lying around being decorative – she was here to have fun. She and CeCe were dancing with abandon, the men around them watching with interest as they rolled their bodies, hips grinding, booty shaking. From time to time the pair got tantalizingly close, as Dionne flung her arms around CeCe and their bodies pressed together, leaving everyone watching and wondering: *will they or won't they?* Each of them loved the spotlight, craving the attention. Dionne, especially, fed off it, needing all eyes on her.

Wiggling her way past his entourage, Dionne leaned over to Saeed. 'I'm just heading to the bathroom, honey. Back soon.'

Saeed nodded easily, reaching over to give Dionne a playful slap on her behind as she walked off. Dionne span round, giggling, before grabbing CeCe's hand and pulling her away.

'Let's go have some fun,' Dionne whispered in her ear.

They wound their way through the crowd, Dionne ever alert for Philippe Rochefort. She hadn't seen him yet and hoped he'd put in an appearance tonight. She knew she'd be pissed if she didn't get an opportunity to speak to him.

But, even if he didn't show, she and CeCe were getting more than enough attention to make up for it. As they moved through the club, the men all checked them out, while the women narrowed their eyes jealously. Their attitude made Dionne laugh, all the uptight bitches standing around trying to bag a rich guy, not daring to do or say anything that might put off a potential sugar daddy. As far as Dionne was concerned, life was too short. She was all about having a good time, about drinking, dancing and enjoying herself. In her experience, men loved a wild girl – it made them imagine what she'd be like in bed.

The pair made their way to the bathroom where Dionne repaired her make-up, dabbing under her eyes where her mascara had streaked. She wanted to make sure she looked good. You never knew who was around – a lot of the top photographers and big model agents hung out here.

She spritzed on some perfume – Poison, by Dior – and readjusted her top. It was a loose gold halterneck, made from a silk mix that draped provocatively around her body, gaping open and showing her breasts whenever she leaned forward. Dionne was well aware of that. It never happened accidentally.

She turned to CeCe beside her, who was slicking on her trademark red lipstick.

'Okay, baby girl,' Dionne grinned. 'Let's go see what we can find.'

Philippe was making his way through Bijou, squeezing past the mass of bodies pressed up tightly together as they danced and drank. There was a good vibe in the club and they were at capacity, operating a strict one-out one-in policy. It didn't seem to deter the crowds outside, huddled on the pavement and hoping that they might get lucky, picked out of the mob and allowed inside to join the chosen few.

Philippe stopped briefly to pose for a photo with an up-and-coming pop starlet, then headed for the DJ booth. He wanted to ensure that the DJ had everything she wanted; he'd spent a lot of money flying her in from LA for the night and intended to keep her happy.

'Philippe! Philippe, honey!'

Out of the corner of his eye, Philippe saw some girl making a beeline for him. Tall, black, with an incredible body, she was barrelling towards him like a heat-seeking missile locked onto her target. He'd met her before, he thought – in his line of work it was necessary to have a photographic memory. His recollections of her weren't good. He remembered her as loud, attention-seeking and trashy. And she was American, he realized with distaste, pronouncing his name in a grating, nasal accent.

His mind was working quickly; perhaps he could still get away. The music was pounding and he could pretend he hadn't heard her. Changing course, he headed for the bar. He needed a stiff drink if he was going to survive this evening. As soon as the bar girl saw him approaching, she immediately began pouring a large whiskey with a dash of soda and not too much ice. Exactly how he liked it. The staff had been well trained in how to keep Monsieur Rochefort happy.

He drank it straight down and nodded to the girl to make him another as he felt a predatory hand clamp on his arm.

'Philippe, honey!' Dionne kissed him ostentatiously on both cheeks, thrilled to have finally tracked him down. She glanced around quickly to see if Katerina was watching – she'd show that dumb-ass clothes horse that there was only one woman Philippe Rochefort was interested in. 'Baby, how *are* you?' she demanded.

'Fine, thank you.' Philippe fought to be polite. He wasn't in the mood for this tonight. After he got rid of this girl, he would go home, take a shower and prepare for his trip tomorrow.

'Your club is amazing, I'm having a fabulous time,' Dionne gushed, going for the full-on charm offensive. She was a firm believer that the way to a man's bed was via his ego. 'And you're looking so incredibly handsome,' she murmured, leaning in close as she slid a hand along his torso. His shirt was open at the neck, showing the thick, dark hair on his chest.

'Thank you. You're very kind,' he muttered, as the bar girl handed him another drink. He downed it in one and felt it hit the spot that the first one hadn't.

Dionne sensed his distraction and upped her game. 'You know, I'd love to come here every night if I could. Are you here every night? That would totally be worth coming back for . . .'

'I'm afraid I go away on business tomorrow. I will be out of the country for at least a week.'

'A whole week! How'm I gonna survive that long without you?'

'You will manage.'

'It sounds so exciting,' Dionne persevered in a low, breathy voice. 'It must be awesome to fly all over the world the whole time.'

'It is not always so *awesome*,' Philippe pronounced the word distastefully, 'when it is work.'

'Oh, but you must have a lil' fun sometimes too, y'know what I'm saying?'

Philippe gave a tight smile but didn't reply.

Dionne pressed on, unfazed. 'So, are you going somewhere glamorous and exotic?'

'Perhaps you may think so. I must fly to the US.'

'The States!' Dionne exclaimed. 'Oh, I wish I was there! I miss my home country. Hey, maybe I could go in your suitcase?' she suggested mischievously.

Involuntarily, Philippe glanced at her full breasts

and well-rounded butt on her skinny frame. 'I don't think you'd fit.'

Dionne saw him look her over, noticed the expression on his face as he registered her spectacular body. It gave her an idea.

'Have you met my housemate, Cécile?' she cooed, dragging CeCe over from where she was chatting with friends. 'She's a designer, and *sooo* talented.'

Philippe smiled automatically, kissing CeCe's cheeks in greeting. Physically she was nothing special, not in the way that Dionne was, but her dress sense was striking and she undoubtedly had something about her – that indefinable *je ne sais quoi*.

'We do everything together,' Dionne continued, adding with a grin, 'And I mean *everything* . . .' She giggled as CeCe slipped an arm around her waist and leaned in, beginning to nuzzle her neck. Dionne turned and kissed her softly as CeCe responded, reaching up to pull Dionne's face down to hers. Their mouths were open, eyes closed. All around them, people began to stare.

Philippe shifted uncomfortably. He could feel the stirring in his crotch, the bulge growing in his trousers as he watched them, hands caressing each other's bodies. For Christ's sake, he reprimanded himself, he was thirty-eight years old and his dick still had a mind of its own.

Dionne came up for air, looking across to Philippe to ensure she had his attention. He was staring at her, that familiar look on his face that she recognized from so many men. It was almost funny, how easy they were to manipulate.

Dionne moved across to him, eager to seal the deal. She was tall, an inch or two above him in heels, and she bowed her head to whisper in his ear. 'How about we all get together before you leave,' she breathed. 'Give you something to remember us by.'

Philippe looked over at her, taking her in properly this time. She was stunning, no doubt about that – stacked, sexy, and with huge lips that would look great round his cock. The other girl looked wild, totally uninhibited.

What the hell, maybe he should go home with them. Perhaps this would be the way to get Alyson out of his system – by banging some meaningless women that he didn't give a shit about. They obviously didn't give a damn about him – other than as some kind of trophy fuck.

Breaking into a charming smile, Philippe turned to them. 'Ladies,' he began solicitously, his arm snaking round Dionne's waist. 'Can I buy you a bottle of champagne?'

9

It was still dark as Alyson rolled over and stirred grog-
gily, wondering what had jolted her awake. It didn't
take her long to realize. As she lay with her eyes tightly
shut, hoping to sink back into blissful sleep, she heard
the unmistakeable sound of Dionne and CeCe as they
clattered through the front door, drunk and giggling.
The door closed with a slam, and Alyson pulled the
duvet up around her ears in frustration.

'Please shut up . . .' she whispered into the darkness.
But whichever way she turned she couldn't block out
the sound of Dionne's flirtatious laughter, or the low
rumble of a man's voice, speaking in accented English.

Great, so they'd brought some guy back with them.
That meant at some point in the next couple of hours,
Alyson would have to endure the sound of Dionne or
CeCe – or possibly both – having extremely loud and
vocal sex, while Alyson irritably clamped a pillow
over her ears and waited impatiently for it all to finish.

Dionne seemed to be as uninhibited about sex as
she was about everything else in her life, and would
groan and scream with complete disregard for anyone
within earshot. Alyson sometimes wondered if she did

it on purpose, to spite her virginal and frustrated flat-mate lying awake in the room next door. She knew that wasn't really the case – it was simply that Dionne rarely stopped to consider anyone else – but Alyson couldn't help but think that way every time she lay alone in the darkness, unable to drown out Dionne's ecstatic moans.

She wondered if that would ever happen to her – if she would scale the dizzy heights of pleasure that Dionne seemed to reach night after night. If she would ever let her guard down enough to trust a man to make love to her, without fearing that he might laugh at her obvious inexperience, or her small breasts and boyish figure. She wasn't like Dionne, with an enormous cleavage and curves that went on forever. What man would ever find her attractive when he could have someone like that?

Alyson jumped guiltily as she realized Dionne was right outside her door.

'Sssshhhhh,' Dionne hissed, in a loud, ineffectual whisper. 'Don't wake my flatmate. She'll be really mad. She works, like, *all the time*,' Dionne said seriously, before she and CeCe collapsed into helpless laughter once more.

Miserably, Alyson turned over and burrowed down beneath the duvet, wedging it firmly around her ears. But as she heard the girls and their 'friend' move through to the lounge, heard the fridge being opened and a champagne cork being popped – *did Dionne ever drink anything else?* – Alyson knew she was in for another sleepless night.

Philippe Rochefort stumbled into the living room and sat down heavily on the sofa. The room seemed to swim before him. He knew he'd drunk far more than he should have; he'd been feeling a little low this evening and hit the whiskey hard. It was unusual for him to let his emotions rule him like this, but these last couple of days he'd been acting completely out of character.

Somewhere, at the back of his mind, he registered the thought that he was flying to the States tomorrow – today, in fact, he realized hazily. He had a flight to catch in a few hours and already he felt like shit. But then all thoughts were forgotten as the girl appeared in front of him – *What was her name again? The hot, black one? It didn't matter* . . . – and held out a champagne flute for him. Her friend hovered in the background, sipping her drink and watching the pair of them.

Philippe relaxed back into the soft cushions, spreading his legs and stretching an arm along the back of the sofa. If he was lucky, these girls might put on a little floor show for him – finish what they'd started in the club. They'd been all over him in the back of the car on the way here – kissing him, kissing each other, hands groping everywhere . . .

'So, Philippe, honey . . .' Dionne began. She sashayed across the floor towards him and tripped over the rug, landing on the sofa beside him in a jumble of long, brown limbs. The glass she was holding tipped and the pale-yellow liquid slopped over the top where it splashed on to Philippe's trousers.

'Sorry 'bout that,' she drawled, collapsing into giggles.

'It's . . . no problem . . .' Philippe waved a hand dismissively. His words were slurred, and the movement was an effort.

'Here, let me get it for you,' Dionne offered as she pulled herself upright and leaned towards him, rubbing at his trousers. Her hands gradually slid upwards, the movements becoming slower and more controlled as her long, slim fingers stroked his crotch. She was gratified to feel the large bulge steadily uncoil until it became hard and rigid, pressed tight and straining against his zipper.

Philippe closed his eyes and groaned. It felt good, dammit.

Dionne's eyes widened as she took in Philippe's reaction. 'Yeah?' she whispered, her lips warm and wet against his ear. 'You like that, huh? You like that, baby?'

CeCe took the lead from Dionne – they'd done this before – and the pair of them made a formidable team. She moved round to the back of the sofa behind Philippe and slipped her hands over his shoulders, running them down his chest. Her fingertips slid beneath his shirt, finding the tanned skin with its light covering of hair, feeling the taut muscles of his stomach.

'So strong . . . so masculine . . .' she murmured.

'You're so sexy, you could make a girl lose control,' Dionne whispered huskily as she began to nuzzle his neck, gently nibbling his ear lobe. CeCe continued to stroke his chest, her hands moving downwards to where Dionne was running her long nails teasingly across his lap.

'Ladies, I . . .' Philippe began.

'What is it, baby?' Dionne encouraged him. In a well-practised move, she swung her leg across his lap so that she was straddling him, her face inches from his. Her skirt rucked up around her waist as she pressed her body against him. She was wearing the skimpiest of panties and he could clearly feel her, warm and ready for him, through the light material of his trousers. Involuntarily, he groaned once again.

'Yeah . . .' Dionne smiled, pleased, as she winked at CeCe before turning her attention back to Philippe. 'Do you find me sexy, huh? Do you want me? 'Cos you are one beautiful honey of a guy . . .'

Philippe swallowed. He'd drunk a lot of alcohol before they'd left Bijou, and now his mouth was dry and sour tasting. He looked up to find Dionne's magnificent breasts level with his eye line, her young, supple body writhing against his. There was no doubt about it – she'd be a wildcat in bed. But she wasn't what he wanted. Not this evening.

'I . . .' he faltered.

'Say it, baby,' she whispered, her eyes half-closed as she caressed his body. CeCe was massaging his shoulders, two sets of hands caressing him, willing to administer to his every need. Philippe felt his resolve weaken.

'Tell me you want to fuck me,' Dionne insisted. She grabbed at his shirt, her fingers scrabbling to undo the buttons.

Blearily, Philippe tried to focus. Dionne was all over him, writhing and thrashing about. One of his buttons pinged off, rolling onto the floor and underneath the sofa.

'*Chérie*,' he began, trying to take hold of Dionne's wrists to keep her still. But she misinterpreted this as some kind of game and began to moan even more intensely.

'Yeah, that's right . . . Do you want me?' she demanded, her voice getting louder with every word. 'Tell me you want me. Tell me in French – it sounds *so* sexy!'

The one thing Philippe was becoming increasingly certain of was that he *didn't* want Dionne. In fact, he just wanted to get out of here, to get away. It had been a stupid, rash decision, coming home with these two girls who clearly had their own agenda.

Philippe tried to sit up and felt his erection wilt. Dionne felt it too and pulled away from him. For a second she faltered, then recovered her usual bravado.

'Don't worry about *that*,' she purred. 'That's just a lil' too much of the old whiskey. We can fix that in no time,' she promised, as she began furiously rubbing away at his crotch.

Philippe was becoming increasingly irritable. *Christ, did this girl ever give up?* Roughly, he pushed her hand away in an aggressive gesture.

'What is it?' Dionne asked. She sat back uncertainly, sounding increasingly unsure of herself. 'Do you want to see us together, is that it? You liked that, didn't you? Before, in the club?'

She signalled for CeCe to come over as she climbed off Philippe and they took up their place on the floor in front of him. Dionne stepped out of her heels, bringing her nearer to CeCe's height, as the two of them leaned closer, beginning with little butterfly kisses which quickly progressed to something more intense.

Dionne sneaked a sideways glance at Philippe, then raised her hands above her head as CeCe pulled off her top, the silky material sliding over her soft skin, leaving her breasts exposed.

Philippe exhaled heavily, his right knee bouncing in agitation. He knew they were doing it for his benefit, so he supposed he should pay more attention, but there was something so deliberate, so staged in their actions, that it rendered the show completely unsexy. He wasn't remotely attracted to either of them, he realized. In fact, his overwhelming sensation was now one of boredom.

Stifling a yawn, he checked his watch – a Patek Philippe, naturally – and wondered once again just what the hell he was doing here. His plane was in four hours, and there was no way he could land in New York exhausted and hungover. It was completely unprofessional. He would leave now, grab some Paracetamol washed down with a large bottle of Badoit, then catch a few hours' sleep on the plane before waking in time to go over the American proposals one last time before they landed.

Yeah, he needed to get out of here right now, he realized, wishing he'd listened to his first instincts in the club. The two girls were writhing around in front of him, desperate to elicit a reaction. It was pathetic. The shorter girl, the one with the freaky haircut, she was clearly into it, but the other girl just looked a mess, her skirt pulled up around her waist and her tits hanging out.

She was evidently from the wrong side of the tracks, obviously fame-hungry and money-grabbing. It didn't matter how many designer labels you dressed her up in, or how much she spent on her hair and make-up, she was still no better than trash. All the money in the world couldn't buy you class, Philippe thought with a sneer, his in-built snobbery coming to the surface. When you were from one of France's richest families, it was hard to avoid.

He drained his champagne flute in a parting gesture, slamming it down on the coffee table before climbing unsteadily to his feet.

Dionne looked round in confusion. 'Philippe?' she questioned. 'Where are you going?'

'Home,' he said shortly. He didn't even look at her.

'No, stay,' Dionne insisted, bolting across the room towards him. She pressed herself against him, running her body up and down his, her naked breasts trailing over his half-open shirt.

'Get away from me,' Philippe hissed. His tone was like ice and he lashed out at her, pushing her away from him.

Dionne fell, sprawling onto the floor.

Philippe stared at her in disgust, his lip curling. She looked like some kind of beetle, writhing on her back.

'I don't understand,' Dionne faltered, pulling herself upright. She was sitting at his feet, staring up at him while he towered above her.

'Don't you?' Philippe was drunk and tired, his irritation making him cruel. 'You disgust me,' he sneered. 'Look at you, at the way you live your life. You're worse than a whore – at least a whore is honest about what she wants.'

Dionne opened her mouth to speak, but he cut her off, jerking his chin in an arrogant gesture. 'You want money, yes?' He dragged a money clip from his pocket and pulled out a handful of notes. There must have been around two thousand euros in bills of a hundred, and he threw them at Dionne, prostrate on the floor. It fell around her like rain. 'Take it. I don't need it.'

'Fuck you,' Dionne spat, scrabbling to sit upright. She grabbed at the money, ineffectually throwing it back at him. It bounced off his legs and fluttered to the ground. 'Get the fuck out of my apartment, you bastard.'

'Oh yes, now you're showing your true colours. What a nice mouth you have on you.' He leaned over her, his face contorted with cruelty. 'Black trash, that's all you are. Why don't you go back to where you belong?'

Dionne sat, rigid with shock. For once in her life she found herself unable to reply. She could only watch helplessly as Philippe grabbed his jacket and walked out of the door.

Alyson sat up in bed and licked her dry lips. Her throat was parched, and all she could think about was getting a glass of water.

Silently, she pulled back the duvet and slipped out of bed, her bare feet landing on the carpet. She slept in an oversized Guinness T-shirt – free from a promotion at Chez Paddy – and the voluminous top only served to emphasize her slim body and delicate features. Her long, alabaster limbs stretched forever out of the black cotton shirt, her pale-blonde hair cascading down her back.

She padded across her room and stopped at the door, listening carefully. She wondered if she could get to the kitchen and back without being seen. It sounded as though everyone was in the lounge. The last thing Alyson wanted to do was walk in on some kind of orgy, a scene that wouldn't look out of place during the last days of Rome. Alyson had no idea what Dionne and CeCe did with the guys they brought home, but her imagination was running wild.

But then, it was *her* flat too, wasn't it? Alyson reasoned. She shouldn't be hiding in her room like a prisoner, afraid to step outside. She would dash out and hope they were all too caught up in what they were doing to notice her.

Alyson grabbed the door handle and opened it a fraction, when a sudden noise made her jump. She froze, her heart pounding in her chest. It sounded like shouting. Then a door opened and a man stormed out, hurrying down the corridor. Alyson shrank back into the darkness as he rushed past her room. He didn't turn the light on and it was too dark to see his features;

104

all Alyson could make out was the curve of a powerful shoulder, silhouetted against the blackness. His tread was heavy on the wooden floor, and he pulled a mobile phone out of his pocket as he went. Then the door slammed shut and he was gone.

Quietly, Alyson closed her bedroom door and climbed back into bed, her heart still thumping. Perhaps she didn't need a drink as badly as she'd thought. She would wait until the morning. She was pretty sure she'd heard only one man arrive, but the thought of running into any more of Dionne and CeCe's guests was mortifying.

She wondered if Dionne was lying in her bed next door, blissed out and satiated, bathed in a post-orgasmic glow. Did Dionne care that the guy hadn't stayed around to hold her, or was she fast asleep, satisfied now that she'd got what she wanted?

Alyson sighed and turned over, realizing in frustration that she was now wide awake. Her mind was racing, her body slowly coming to life. There would be no more sleep for her tonight.

Lying on the floor, Dionne was in shock. 'What the fuck . . .?' she managed.

'Are you okay?' CeCe came out of her stupor first, rushing across the room and kneeling down beside Dionne.

'Yeah, I'm fine.' Dionne wiped her face and was shocked to find her cheeks were wet. Embarrassed, she brushed the tears away. Dionne Summers did not cry over guys – especially not arrogant, racist jackasses. She sat up, shivering with shock. 'What did I do?' she asked CeCe in desperation.

'You didn't do anything,' CeCe assured her. 'You didn't deserve that. He's an asshole.'

Dionne was still stunned. 'I really liked him, CeCe. I went out on a limb for him. Now I just look like a total moron.'

'No, you don't. *He*'s the idiot,' CeCe assured her. '*Sale con*,' she swore, as she reached for her bag and pulled out the vintage cigarette case she always carried. Extracting one, she lit it and passed it to Dionne.

'What are people gonna say?' Dionne whispered suddenly. 'What about Katerina? When she finds out, the whole of Paris'll know. I'll never be able to show my face anywhere again.'

'Dionne, you have nothing to be ashamed of,' CeCe said softly, struck by how vulnerable Dionne suddenly seemed. 'He's the one who should be ashamed. *Fils de pute.*'

Dionne took a long drag on the cigarette, then handed it back, slumping miserably onto the floor. She felt drunk, tired and deflated suddenly, with an overwhelming desire to sleep.

'I'm cold,' she said miserably, to no one in particular. She was still naked from the waist down, her skin covered in goose bumps as she shivered uncontrollably.

CeCe glanced at Dionne's top, lying discarded on the floor. It was barely larger than a handkerchief. Instead, she stubbed out the cigarette and lay down on the enormous rug, spooning around Dionne. She pulled the other half of the rug over them, like a bed sheet, as Dionne snuggled back into CeCe's embrace, grateful for the comforting warmth.

She felt as though she was sixteen again, screwed over by Luis Fernandez and feeling utterly humiliated. Flashes of what Philippe had said replayed over and over in her mind . . . *Black trash* . . . *Worse than a whore* . . .

Dionne had vowed to put all that insecurity behind

her when she moved to Paris, but now she'd allowed it to happen again – she'd let a man take advantage of her, judging her own self-worth by the way he made her feel. Well, it would be for the last time, Dionne thought furiously. One day she would get her revenge on Philippe Rochefort; she wanted to humiliate him like he'd humiliated her, to make him feel small and stupid and worthless. Yeah, the time would come when he would regret the day he'd ever messed with Dionne Summers. She would make sure of it.

10

The *marché aux puces St-Ouen de Clignancourt* was the largest, most famous flea market in Paris. It sprawled over an area the size of seven football pitches, crammed with everything from antiques to children's toys, jewellery to books to bric-a-brac to furniture. The atmosphere was lively – curious tourists jostled with serious dealers, world music blasted out from stereos, while shifty-looking guys sold pirate DVDs displayed on blankets, ready to gather them up and run if the *gendarmerie* came sniffing around.

The market's popularity had made it over-commercialized, but there were still bargains to be had if you knew where to look. And CeCe knew exactly where to go.

It was a beautiful early summer's day as she strolled along, drifting through the crowds and soaking up everything that she could. The area was less than salubrious, but for CeCe it was a constant source of inspiration: a dusty old painting could trigger the design for a Napoleonic military-style jacket, an ornate mirror inspiring a revolutionary-era ball gown.

There were long-limbed bohemian girls browsing

the vintage stalls in flippy summer dresses and quirky headwear; skinny North African guys in jeans and T-shirts, barefoot in sandals with chequered scarves slung round their necks. The smell of food permeated the air, drifting out from the cramped cafés that bordered the streets and mixing with the pungent aromas from the road-side vendors.

CeCe took a left down a narrow, graffiti-covered alleyway that looked as though it led nowhere, and emerged in the heart of Malik market, the ultimate treasure-trove for secondhand clothing. CeCe kept an open mind, never looking for anything in particular, but she always left with something fabulous.

She loved this time by herself. Usually CeCe hated to be alone, surrounding herself with people and noise. But whenever she sat down to work she needed the solitude, the lack of any sort of distraction, while she immersed herself completely in her designs. The Sunday visits to St-Ouen were all part of that. It was the one morning when she dragged herself out of bed, regardless of what she'd been doing the night before, and caught the métro out to the north of the city, all the way outside the *périphérique*.

Dionne would still be asleep at this time of day, nursing a hangover or a broken heart – or both, if she was feeling particularly melodramatic, CeCe thought uncharitably, then immediately felt bad. Last night had been awful – the things that guy had said . . . It broke CeCe's heart to see Dionne spoken to like that. Why did she always have to go for the bad guys, leaving CeCe behind to pick up the pieces?

But she could never stay mad at Dionne for long. That was the whole problem. The balance of power in their relationship was completely unbalanced – fucked up, some might say. She hated the way Dionne used her to pull men, to put on a little girl-on-girl floor show to entertain the guys and lure them home. Oh, it had been fun at first – a game to play to tease the guys, to get attention . . . and CeCe certainly wasn't averse to getting up close and personal with Dionne. But recently it had started to matter more. Not to Dionne, she was sure of that. But to her.

CeCe's problem was that she was in love with being in love. It inspired her, made her happy, helped her to create. She firmly believed that her designs were better when she had a fantastic muse, a beautiful, glamorous creature – male or female – whom she could adore. It didn't have to be a sexual thing. She simply needed someone to idolize. And right now she was hopelessly, utterly, devoted to Dionne.

CeCe sighed. It was hard being in love with your best friend.

Distractedly, CeCe browsed the stalls, her hands trailing over a tantalizing mix of fabrics as she raked through the rails, picking discarded garments out of cardboard boxes and holding them up to the light. She found a stunning Eighties cocktail dress by Ungaro in dazzling sunburned orange, replete with shoulder pads and the designer's trademark draping, and haggled it down to fifty euros. CeCe didn't intend to wear it, just keep it for her inspiration rail, the collection of beautiful garments she'd built up to get her creative juices flowing.

Gradually she made her way through the market, heading towards the one stall where she always found something incredible.

'Cécile!'

The stallholder, Claude Legrand, greeted her like a long-lost granddaughter. '*Tu vas bien?*' he asked delightedly, standing up to kiss her on both cheeks, before settling back down on his stool. He smiled broadly, showing the gaps in his teeth.

Claude was in his sixties, and had been working as a garment trader all his life. He wore a tattered old polo shirt and his face was covered with white bristles. '*Alors, mon chou*, when are you going to be putting on your first collection?'

CeCe smiled ruefully. Claude asked her the same question every time, and she always gave him the same reply. 'Soon, I hope.'

'But you will show at Fashion Week this time, *non?*'

'I don't know,' CeCe shrugged. 'It's so expensive – I need to get the financing together, have my application approved. I really need to find a business partner so that I can concentrate on the designing. My brain wasn't made to deal with money.'

Claude raised an eyebrow disapprovingly. 'You waste too much time on things that do not matter. Always, you are in the clubs or at a party.'

'I'm networking,' CeCe replied sullenly.

'*Ah bon!* And how many orders has it got you? How many dresses have you produced because of this *networking?*'

CeCe didn't reply. Claude knew he'd made his point and decided not to press her any further. Instead he shuffled round in his seat, reaching for a carrier bag buried beneath a pile of clothes. 'I saved this for you. *Voilà! Tenez . . .*'

'Claude, it's magnificent!' CeCe gasped, as she unravelled the package and let the material slip through her fingers, holding it out so she could see it fully. It was a beautiful piece of silk in a rich petrol-blue, approximately three metres long and hand-painted with a design of peacock feathers.

'You like it?'

'I love it!' CeCe twisted it in the light so that the colours shimmered. She could visualize the finished design already – a beautiful halterneck evening dress with a daringly low-cut back and a full-length skirt that fell from the waist, tapering off into a small train.

'Good. It's yours,' Claude told her, as he began to fold it back up.

'How much?'

Claude passed her the bag, his large, gnarled hands closing over her own. 'For you, it is free.'

'Claude, I can't—'

'Yes, you can.' His eyes were twinkling. 'And you must make something incredible with it.'

'Oh, I will,' CeCe breathed. 'I can imagine it already.'

'Good.' Claude seemed pleased. 'And then you must show it at Fashion Week.'

'Eventually . . .'

Claude shrugged, trying to imply that he didn't care one way or the other. 'As you wish.' He stared hard at her, his watery blue eyes holding her own until she dropped her gaze uncomfortably. 'You are so talented, Cécile, but you must prove that you have the dedication. You are the only one who can make this happen, you understand?'

CeCe nodded, her fingers closing over the bag in her hands. It felt as though she carried something precious, something that she alone could bring to life.

'The most important thing for you should be your work – not the parties or the nightclubs. Once you prioritize that, then everything else will fall into place.'

'Thanks Claude.' CeCe flushed, knowing that what he said was right.

'*Bon*,' he muttered, settling back in his chair once more. 'Now, go home and start work. Next time you see me, I want to hear that you are the toast of Paris, and that Carine Roitfeld herself has commissioned a gown from you.'

His positivity was infectious, and CeCe couldn't help laughing. 'Watch this space,' she promised him.

'Oh my God, you have a date!' Dionne squealed. 'I knew this Aidan guy sounded hot.'

'It's not a date,' Alyson protested, feeling her face flush with embarrassment. 'It's just worked out that we have the same night off so we're going to explore the city together.'

Dionne shook her head, looking pityingly at Alyson. 'It's a date, honey,' she said firmly. 'Does he treat any of the other staff like this? *Exactly,*' she rushed on, before Alyson had a chance to respond. 'You're a girl, he's a guy and he knows that damn well. Do you like him?'

'I . . . He's a lovely guy but—'

'Are you planning on sleeping with him?'

'Dionne!' Alyson exclaimed in shock, wishing the ground would just open up and swallow her.

'Okay, okay,' Dionne grinned, finding Alyson's discomfort hilarious. 'Look, what are you gonna wear?'

'Um . . .' Alyson shrugged helplessly. 'This?' She was wearing the same black trousers she wore for work and a shapeless blue top with a floral design.

Dionne raised an eyebrow, looking distinctly unimpressed.

'It's not a date so it doesn't matter!' Alyson burst out.

'Girl, there is no way you're leaving this apartment looking like you stole your outfit from some retirement home. Dionne's gonna help you out, loan you some clothes.'

'I'm fine, thanks,' Alyson replied, a little too quickly.

But instead of being pissed off, Dionne looked amused. 'Nothing too outrageous, I promise. Maybe just some tight jeans to show off your figure, a cute little top . . .' Her gaze swept over Alyson, gauging her body type and planning what to put her in. They were roughly the same height – Alyson had similar proportions to Dionne, the only difference being that Alyson's figure came naturally, whereas Dionne had to watch every morsel she put in her mouth.

'Here, come with me.' Dionne held out her hand and dragged Alyson through to her bedroom. 'Don't mind the mess,' she apologized distractedly, throwing open the nearest wardrobe and riffling through.

Dionne's room looked like an explosion in a department store. It was pretty much impossible to keep tidy, as there were just too many things for the tiny space. Bags were spilling out of the closet, with clothes hung on the back of the door, the mirror, and from the curtain rail. At least two dozen perfume bottles fought for space on top of the chest of drawers, surrounded by a mountain of discarded jewellery boxes, their contents strewn across the surface. Shoes were hastily shoved in boxes and crammed under the bed, on top of the wardrobe – anywhere Dionne could find space – and the floor was carpeted with discarded underwear.

'Right . . .' Dionne began pulling items out. 'Try these.' She threw a pair of light denim skinny jeans at Alyson.

'They'll never fit me, they're tiny.'

'*You're* tiny,' Dionne assured her. 'Just try them, they stretch.'

Self-consciously Alyson unzipped her trousers, trying to hide her body as she did so. God, this was awful, like getting changed for gym class at school.

She dragged the jeans over her ankles, feeling them clamp around her calves.

'I don't think this is a good idea, Dionne. I'll never get them off again.'

'You'll be fine.' Dionne's voice was muffled, her head buried deep in the wardrobe. 'Just pull them.'

Sucking in her stomach, Alyson pulled, surprised to find that they slid easily over her thighs and buttoned up without a problem.

'Oh my God, your legs look amazing!' Dionne screeched as she emerged. 'Like a baby giraffe or something! Seriously, go look.'

She steered Alyson in the direction of the mirror. Alyson stared at her reflection and cringed. The jeans left nothing to the imagination, clinging like a second skin to show the sinewy shape of her legs, the gentle curve of her butt.

'They're so tight!' she exclaimed in horror. 'Dionne, I—'

'Now try this,' Dionne cut her off, throwing her a Breton-striped top.

'But—'

'No buts. Just do it.'

Resignedly, Alyson did as she was told.

'See? It looks fantastic on you!' Dionne enthused. 'Blue is totally your colour. It goes with your eyes.' She stood back to assess Alyson. 'Do you have another bra? Maybe white lace, or . . . You know what, you don't really need a bra, do you?'

'I don't?'

'No. Take it off.'

Feeling like she was in the hands of some particularly merciless bully, Alyson unhooked her functional T-shirt bra and slid it off.

'Perfect!' Dionne squealed. 'Hon, you are looking sexy as hell!'

Alyson turned back to the mirror. 'You can see my nipples!' she exclaimed, horrified.

'Oh trust me. He'll like that,' Dionne smirked. 'And if you add these,' she scrabbled around the floor, pulling a pair of vertiginous heels out from behind a bucket chair, 'your legs will look insane.'

'No chance,' Alyson shook her head. 'There's no way I can walk in those. I'll break my neck.' She'd gone along with Dionne so far, but she drew the line at stilettos. Resolutely, she stepped back into her thong sandals.

Dionne shrugged. 'Your call, I guess. Now, make-up! Just a little, I promise,' Dionne pleaded, as Alyson opened her mouth to protest. 'I've been dying to do this since you moved in! Honestly, with a touch of mascara to bring out your eyes, maybe some smoky eyeliner, a dab of lip gloss . . . Come on, don't you want to look nice for a change?'

Alyson raised an eyebrow, noting the implicit criticism of her appearance, but said nothing.

Dionne took her silence for acquiescence and dragged her over to the window, seating her beside the vanity table where the light was better.

'Now, we'll have to use your own base, as I don't have any that's gonna suit your skin tone,' Dionne explained.

Alyson looked blank.

'Foundation. Oh, shit, do you have a different word for it in Britain? Erm . . .' Dionne picked up a bottle of Bobbi Brown foundation and waved it in front of her.

'I don't have any of that,' Alyson explained apologetically. 'I don't really wear make-up . . .' Dionne's expression made her want to giggle.

'You don't . . . But I thought . . .? Your skin is flawless, I thought you at least wore a base. What do you do when you get a break-out?' Dionne asked suspiciously.

'I never . . . well, I don't really get spots.'

'Aren't you the lucky one,' Dionne said, somewhat tartly. 'So, no base . . . I guess we'll just start on the eyes then,' she shrugged, reaching for a chocolate-brown eye pencil.

The process went on for fifteen tortuous minutes, with Alyson banned from looking in the mirror and her imagination running increasingly wild. She remembered the girls back home in Manchester, dressed up for a night out with some of them resembling circus performers – all sweeping fake eyelashes, brightly painted lips and glow-in-the-dark blusher. If Dionne made her look like that, she would cry.

'Okay, I'm done,' Dionne announced, as she carefully dabbed underneath Alyson's eyelashes with a cotton bud and stepped back, satisfied.

Hesitantly, Alyson stood up and approached the mirror. As her reflection came into focus, she inhaled sharply. 'Oh wow,' she exclaimed. 'I look . . . I look so different! Like me, but—'

'But better,' Dionne said firmly. 'Hotter. Sexier. You like?'

'Yeah, I . . . I think so,' Alyson admitted. She reached up and gently touched her cheek, as though afraid it might disintegrate beneath her fingertips. It was stained with a pink colour – not in a harsh, brash way, but subtly, to bring out her cheekbones and give her a healthy, attractive glow. Her eyes looked huge – wide and fresh – and her lips had grown, giving her an unmistakeable pout. She looked like a polished, glossier version of herself, as though all the best parts of her had somehow been brought to the fore.

117

'Stand up straight,' Dionne instructed her, as she brushed Alyson's hair out over her shoulders and spritzed her with Chanel Allure. 'Let's get the full effect. Oh, and wear this,' she added, handing Alyson a chic, white blazer. 'It'll draw the whole outfit together – and keep you warm if it gets chilly later.'

Alyson stared at herself in the mirror once more. No doubt about it, Dionne had done a fantastic job. She looked like someone from a magazine – a fashionista, or one of the chic young Parisian women she saw on the Avenue Montaigne.

'What if people laugh at me?' Alyson asked nervously, looking up at Dionne with huge, luminous eyes that had been made even bigger with the help of Shu Uemera curlers and lashings of Lancôme mascara.

'Why the hell they gonna laugh at you, baby girl?' Dionne asked. 'You look beautiful. The men are gonna fall at your feet.'

Alyson bit her lip. Dionne didn't understand – her *raison d'être* was to have people look at her, but Alyson preferred to blend into the background. This new look made her feel like a fraud, a child dressing up in her mother's clothes.

Dionne reached over to hug her, struck by the sudden display of vulnerability. With an ache she remembered the younger sisters she'd left back in Detroit, all the moments she'd missed out on since she'd left – helping them get ready for their first date or choose a dress for junior prom.

'Honey, you see that girl in the mirror?' she began softly. 'Now she is beautiful, she is smart, but she gotta start believing in herself. She can do anything she wants, you know what I'm saying?'

Alyson nodded dumbly.

'Now this Aidan guy ain't gonna know what's hit

him. So you get out there and you work it, and you go *knock his socks off*,' she finished, mimicking Alyson's Lancashire accent.

In spite of herself, Alyson smiled, knowing deep down that Dionne was right. It was time to stop hiding behind the little-girl-lost act, and show the world exactly what Alyson Wakefield was capable of.

11

'Wow,' Aidan said before he could stop himself, as Alyson emerged from the métro at Pigalle and walked towards him. She was early – Alyson hated to be late for anything – but Aidan was already there waiting for her.

'You look . . . incredible,' he told her honestly, feeling a knot of desire and frustration start to build in his stomach. She was easily the most beautiful sight on the street, completely out of place amongst the sex shops and the seedy bars. She looked as though she should be boarding a private jet to some exotic island.

Alyson smiled shyly, her cheeks flushing pink. 'Thanks,' she replied, biting her lip nervously. But she was learning; Dionne had told her to accept any compliments she was offered with a simple thank you, and to never apologize for herself.

'I mean it – you look amazing,' Aidan repeated, unable to keep his eyes off her.

'Thank you,' Alyson said again, wondering why everyone seemed fixated with her appearance at the moment. She sneaked a sideways glance at Aidan; he was freshly shaved, his skin pale and smooth. His thick, dark hair was cropped close, and he wore jeans and a casual short-sleeved shirt. He looked good, Alyson realized. Different, somehow, to the way he looked at work.

'Are you ready to go?' he asked easily.

'Sure.'

They set off walking, Alyson falling into step beside him as they turned off the Boulevard de Clichy and into a maze of narrow streets, all heading sharply uphill. Alyson was thankful she'd turned down the heels.

'I can't believe you've never been up here before,' Aidan said incredulously.

'I haven't had time,' Alyson admitted, adding slyly, 'My slave-driver boss never lets me have a day off.'

'He sounds terrible,' Aidan teased.

'He's not so bad once you get to know him.'

They grinned at each other, and Alyson felt herself begin to relax. Dionne's suggestion that it was a date, along with the unfamiliar clothes she was wearing, had put her on edge. But Aidan was as friendly and laid-back as ever.

They chatted easily as he led them effortlessly through the rabbit warren of streets until Alyson was completely disoriented.

'How do you know where you're going?' she marvelled.

'I'll let you into a secret – I don't. But I have pretty good instincts, and if I'm right it should be somewhere around . . .'

They turned a corner and right in front of them stood the magnificent white-stone basilica of Sacré Cœur, dominating the skyline above them. Leading up the steep slope towards it was a crisscross of stone steps, winding through the flower-filled gardens on the hillside. There were people everywhere, chatting in every conceivable language, relaxing on the grass or seated on benches. Children ran around, shrieking excitedly, and at the bottom of the steps was an old-fashioned, brightly painted carousel.

'Pretty spectacular, isn't it?' Aidan asked, watching the delight on Alyson's face.

'It's beautiful,' she breathed, shading her eyes as she stared up at the dramatic white dome. She'd seen the church from a distance, naturally – it stood at the top of the Montmartre hill, the highest point in the city – but hadn't realized until she was up close quite how magnificent it was.

They rode the funicular to the top of the slope and made their way to the Place du Tertre, the famous square crammed with dozens of street artists. Alyson watched intently as they sketched portraits of the never-ending supply of tourists, charcoal dancing over the paper to provide a speedy souvenir.

'Have your picture drawn,' Aidan suggested, as the artists called out to them, trying to entice Alyson to sit and pose. But she shrank back, appalled at the idea.

'No, I'm too shy.' She shook her head bashfully as Aidan laughed.

'Should we find somewhere to eat?' he asked. The cobbled square was surrounded by restaurants, each with a waiter outside, who called to passers-by in a multitude of languages, trying to lure them inside with the promise of good food and good times.

'Yeah, that sounds great. Where do you recommend?'

Aidan shrugged. 'Take your pick. I think they're all pretty similar – it's more about the atmosphere than the incredible cooking. Do you want to sit outside?'

The evening was still balmy, exceptionally warm for early summer. 'That'd be lovely.' Alyson chose a place with red canopies and a traditional menu, where a pretty young waitress seated them.

'What would you like to drink?' Aidan asked.

'Just water, thanks.'

Aidan ordered red wine for himself, speaking briefly to the waitress before she giggled, then bustled away. 'Your French is really good,' Alyson told him, genuinely impressed. 'How long have you been over here?'

'Three years. I finished university in Dublin and didn't have a clue what I wanted to do, so I came to stay with a friend who was studying out here and never left. I got the job in Chez Paddy – just behind the bar at first – and now I'm managing the place.'

'And is that what . . . I mean, do you plan to . . .' Alyson trailed off, unsure how to phrase the question.

'Do I want to be a barman all my life?' Aidan looked amused as he finished the sentence for her. 'No, not for ever. But I figure I'm good at doing this. I'd like to open my own place eventually. Well, more than one would be great – a whole empire of bars and restaurants,' he smiled wistfully. 'But it's a question of finding a backer, raising the finance. I've got a business plan, y'know, but I can't afford to do it on my own . . . Anyway, enough about me.' Aidan reached for a piece of bread and popped it in his mouth. 'What about you? Are you planning to stay in Paris?'

'I'm not sure . . .' Alyson began uncertainly. 'It depends. I mean, I'm happy at the moment. My original plan was to get a job with a big company – somewhere like BNP Paribas or Masson International would have been perfect. Not that I don't enjoy Chez Paddy,' she added quickly.

'Hey, it's hardly a career,' Aidan said with feeling. 'So what's your real passion?'

'I'm interested in business,' Alyson confessed. 'If I could get an entry-level job with a large firm, learn the ropes, see how everything works and make my way up – that would be perfect. I tried when I first got here, but didn't get anything. I mean, I'm not a French native, I didn't go to university . . . Believe me, I've heard every rejection line there is.'

'Don't give up,' Aidan urged her. 'You're eighteen, right?' he said with a pang, realizing how young that sounded. 'You've got so much time. Maybe you should go back and study, if that's what the problem is?'

'No,' Alyson shook her head. 'I don't want to do that. It would feel like a step back. And besides—'

She was about to say something else, but then the waitress arrived with their starters. Aidan was annoyed at the interruption but tried not to show it. Alyson had told him more about herself tonight than she ever had at Chez Paddy, and it felt as if she was about to really open up.

Silently, Aidan took a bite of toasted bread smothered with pâté. He chewed slowly, then swallowed. 'It's good,' he told Alyson. 'Do you want to try some?'

'Okay,' she agreed, as Aidan held out the bread across the table and Alyson bit into it, brushing her mouth with her fingertips as it flaked on her lips. 'It's delicious,' she confirmed.

Aidan watched her as he swirled his wine in its glass. 'Do you ever drink?'

Alyson shook her head.

'Why not?'

She stopped eating for a moment, a thoughtful expression crossing her face. 'I guess . . . I don't like the thought of being out of control in that way,' she said eventually, thinking of her mother, of the empty vodka bottles and the horrific mood swings that would inevitably follow.

124

Aidan nodded, considering her reply. 'That's a very British way of thinking. You don't have to drink to get drunk, y'know. In France, they really appreciate the alcohol – you drink it with a meal to enhance the food.'

'That doesn't sound a very Irish way of thinking either,' Alyson teased.

Aidan smiled. 'Here, try a sip,' he offered, the rich burgundy catching the light as he held it out.

Alyson hesitated for a moment then reached for the glass. 'It's strong!' she exclaimed, as the flavours suffused her mouth. 'It tastes peppery almost . . . but fruity at the same time.'

'Very good,' Aidan grinned. 'I'll make a sommelier of you yet. Now, take another bite of the pâté . . . and a sip of wine . . . You see how the tastes complement each other?'

'Yeah,' Alyson nodded, breaking into a smile. 'You're a good teacher.'

She sat back in her chair, the warmth of the alcohol lingering in her mouth. Around them, the bustle of people continued, an incessant hum of background noise. The waitress brought over their main course, smiling and flirting with Aidan once again. He was a good-looking guy, Alyson realized, watching the pair with interest. She felt something stir within her, a proprietorial, jealous sensation.

'So why Paris?' Aidan asked as the waitress left. 'Why not London, or New York even?'

'Paris just seemed a good first step,' she said simply. 'Abroad, not too far.' *But far enough*, she thought to herself. 'I remember when I was younger, there was a school trip to Paris but we . . . we didn't have a lot of money,' she explained awkwardly. 'I couldn't afford to go, and then the other kids came back with their little replica Eiffel Towers, and all the girls had bought berets . . . I suppose it held a fascination for me after that. I studied French in school and loved it, so Paris just seemed the natural choice. Like you said, I'm still young. I can travel in a few years if the opportunities come my way.'

'I bet your parents miss you,' Aidan commented casually.

Alyson didn't look at him, dropping her gaze and keeping her eyes firmly fixed on the plate in front of her. 'They're . . . not together any more. My father left when I was nine. I came home from school one day and . . . he'd gone. He took my little brother with him.'

Aidan exhaled slowly, his eyes never leaving her face. 'Have you seen him since?' he asked gently.

'No,' Alyson replied coldly. 'Well, once actually. Right before I left . . .'

Alyson paused. She'd never told anyone all this before, but now she'd started she couldn't stop. It felt good to get it off her chest, as though coming clean would herald a new beginning for her. And there was something trustworthy about Aidan. She felt she could tell him anything and he wouldn't judge her on it.

'My mother had . . . issues,' Alyson continued, as Aidan sat quietly. 'Her behaviour was pretty erratic, right from when I was a kid. I guess one day my dad just couldn't deal with it any more. I was basically the adult after that. Mum had . . . she'd been diagnosed with schizophrenia, but she was pretty lax on taking her medication. I was terrified they were going to take me away . . .'

Alyson trailed off, fighting to regain her composure. Aidan looked at her encouragingly, willing her to continue.

'It must have been hard,' he said lightly.

'It was,' she agreed. 'I was working as soon as I was old enough, trying to keep everything together. I got a job waitressing, in a restaurant. It was decent money.

Then one night I came home and Mum . . .' Alyson's voice cracked, and she struggled to carry on. 'Mum was passed out on the floor. She'd taken an overdose. My dad turned up at the hospital – I hadn't seen him in years. He and the doctor decided . . . they said that it would be better if Mum went into a home, then she could get the proper care she needed. Dad suggested I get away, that I leave Manchester and do something for me, go where I wanted to go. But, Aidan, I – I feel so guilty . . .' Alyson's eyes began to fill with tears.

'Don't,' Aidan insisted. 'Don't feel guilty. You did as much as you could – more than that. Your dad was right. You have to start living your life.'

'I found out that she'd seen him,' Alyson continued. 'Dad had been round to visit Mum a few times, while I was at school, but she never told me. And he never asked to see me. I didn't find out until Mum was in hospital and . . . I don't know. I guess I was angry. I left because I was mad at her. And I left because I wanted – *needed* – to get out. I thought it was best for both of us – that me leaving might give her the kick she needed to start taking care of herself. But maybe I should never have gone . . .'

Alyson broke off, biting her lip to try and stop the tears that threatened to fall.

'Shall I get the bill?' Aidan asked gently. Alyson nodded, not trusting herself to speak. She reached for her purse but Aidan shook his head. 'I'll get this.'

He left fifty euros on the table and they stood up, making their way out of the restaurant. Aidan reached out to take her hand, and Alyson didn't object. It didn't feel forced or unnatural – it just felt right. They walked in companionable silence, each lost in their own thoughts as they headed back towards

127

Sacré Cœur, its smooth stone walls lit by white spotlights.

As they followed the flow of people round to the front of the building, Alyson gasped. The whole of Paris was spread out before her, dazzlingly illuminated against the blackness of the night. She walked up to the guardrail, her eyes sweeping over the view as she gradually began to pick out the famous landmarks. A line of lights directly ahead marked the Louvre museum; to the left, the distinctive twin towers of Notre Dame thrusting into the dark sky.

Alyson didn't think she'd ever seen anything quite so beautiful. She sank down onto the stone steps, feeling as though she never wanted to leave. Around her the crowds moved slowly, the low hum of conversation carrying on the night air. The atmosphere was relaxed and friendly; somewhere nearby a young guy was playing a guitar and singing softly.

Aidan sat down beside her, and she suddenly felt embarrassed about her earlier outburst. What on earth had made her share such personal information with a guy she'd known for only a few weeks? Now he would think she was some crazy woman, on the verge of falling apart at any moment.

'I'm sorry about tonight,' she began. 'I haven't . . . I've never told anyone all that before. I'm not sure why I dumped it all on you . . .'

'Hey, it's fine,' Aidan assured her. 'If ever you need to talk, I'm here. And I bet your mum's really proud of you. You did the right thing coming here.'

Cautiously, he wrapped an arm around her shoulders, pulling her to him. To anyone watching they would have looked like just another pair of young lovers, one of the many dotted around the steps of Sacré Cœur, enjoying the romance of the setting.

Alyson let her head rest on his shoulder, trying to force herself to relax, but the situation felt so alien. She'd never been this close to a man before, and every sensation seemed to be magnified – the masculine smell of soap and musky aftershave, the warmth of his body, the gentle press of his muscles against her.

Her heart was beating fast, her stomach churning with excitement as a delicious tingling spread through her whole body. But rather than enjoying the feeling, it left her confused, unnerved. Overwhelmed by a sudden sense of panic, she pulled away from Aidan and scrambled to her feet.

'What time is it?' she demanded, her cheeks blazing red. 'I think I have to go. I don't want to miss the last métro.' The words came out in a rush.

Aidan got slowly to his feet, disappointment rushing through him. 'I'll walk you back. We'll go to Abbesses – it's closer.'

Alyson set off quickly, Aidan quickening his step to catch up. This time there was no hand-holding, and they walked in awkward silence. The easy intimacy that had existed between them was well and truly shattered.

Aidan could have kicked himself. He'd promised himself he'd go slowly with Alyson. She was so vulnerable, she felt like glass in his hands. He'd finally broken through the walls she surrounded herself with, but now the boundaries were back up and higher than ever.

Well, from now on their relationship would be on her terms, Aidan told himself. Alyson saw him as nothing more than a friend and that was just fine – he would do his damnedest to protect her and not lose that friendship. He would do whatever it took to keep her in his life.

12

Philippe stared out at the Las Vegas Strip, the dazzling neon stretching as far as the eye could see before receding into silent, black desert. It was late at night and he was in a sumptuous suite at Azur, one of the new hotels in the CityCenter complex. In the morning he would sign a contract with Joel Steinberg, manager of Azur, to open a nightclub in the hotel. It would be Rochefort Enterprises' second site in the States; three days ago he'd inked a deal on a place in Manhattan, cementing his international expansion. When Philippe saw something he wanted, he moved fast.

Yeah, his US takeover was just beginning and life was good, Philippe reflected, as he glanced down at the woman kneeling on the floor in front of him, expertly sucking his cock. Her head was bent forward, her bleached blonde hair falling into her face as she bobbed back and forth, little choking noises escaping from her mouth as she took him deeper.

She'd been sent up by the manager of the hotel, a little sweetener for the deal. Steinberg was eager for Philippe to sign – that's why he'd installed him in the 2,000 square foot Presidential Suite with its own private butler, given him twenty-four-hour access to a limo and half a million dollars' worth of gambling credit to keep him entertained during his short stay.

Philippe was impressed with what he saw. By the time the girl turned up at his door, he'd already made up his mind to sign. But he didn't turn her away. Refusing a gift was simply bad manners.

He reached out and gripped the window ledge, feeling the pressure of his orgasm start to build. The girl flicked her tongue teasingly around the tip of his penis, her hands working his balls and shaft. *Was there such a thing as being too good at giving head?* Philippe wondered idly. This woman was too practised, too professional, he noted, wondering how many others she'd sucked off before him. It was a depressing thought.

Unwillingly, his thoughts came back to Alyson, as they had done the whole way through his trip. He couldn't stop thinking about her. He'd met some amazing women this past week – a particular highlight being the prim-looking Park Avenue princess whose immaculately presented exterior belied some filthy predilections between the sheets. But it was still Alyson he wanted.

He wondered what it would be like if it was her kneeling between his legs right now, untouched and virginal. She would be hesitant, uncertain, but he could teach her everything. Philippe shivered, feeling a frisson of excitement at the thought of being the first. The view of Vegas began to blur and Philippe closed his eyes, imagining that slim, beautiful body naked in front of him, her innocent expression gazing up at him as she took him in her mouth and sucked softly, tentatively, the pressure steadily increasing, his cock growing harder, thrusting faster, more urgently, until he couldn't hold back any longer and . . .

Philippe came powerfully, letting out a cry. He groped for the girl's head, holding her tightly between his hands so that she couldn't move. She tilted her mouth slightly to accommodate the full length of him and he felt his cock hit the back of her throat, pulsing in the final throes.

Finally he released her and she stood up, wiping her mouth. Philippe opened his eyes and the illusion shattered. The girl in front of him was nothing like Alyson: her tits were fake and her face was hard, unattractive. Philippe pulled on his trousers, feeling disgusted with himself.

'Mind if I take a shower?' she asked.

Philippe's lip curled. He just wanted rid of her. 'Quickly, yes?' he snapped.

The girl trotted obediently towards the bathroom as Philippe reached for his wallet and tossed a $500 tip on the coffee table.

Guilt money.

He strode across to the dining room and shut the double doors. By the time he emerged, the girl would be gone. The pages of the contract were spread over the enormous mahogany table and he glanced over them to keep himself occupied. Tomorrow he would conclude his business with Joel Steinberg, then fly home, where he would shower, nap, then go back to that shoddy bar to find Alyson.

He wanted her, badly. And Philippe Rochefort always got what he wanted.

David Mouret studied the leather-bound menu, his eyes scanning over the delectable choices. He was a strikingly good-looking man: black skin, chocolate-brown eyes and closely cropped dark hair. He wore a black Armani shirt with platinum-and-diamond cufflinks, and a chunky platinum Rolex adorned his wrist. He was not a man who believed in being discreet about his wealth.

'I missed you, Dionne.' He put down his menu and took Dionne's hand across the table. They were in Les Champs on the Avenue George V, an opulently decorated, ultra-exclusive restaurant with a ridiculously long waiting list. Unless, of course, you were David Mouret. Aged only twenty-nine, he was the phenomenally successful MD of a company that specialized in providing high-class, luxury cars to a discerning clientele. A self-made entrepreneur, his company had established branches throughout the country, and David had discovered that being handsome, charming and filthy rich opened a lot of doors – doors that would usually have been firmly closed to a young black kid from the suburb of Saint-Denis.

'Did you?' Dionne shifted uncomfortably. He was a great guy, but she didn't want him getting too attached. After all, it wasn't as if they were dating. She enjoyed his company, and his ready desire to spend large amounts of money on her. And he was dynamite in bed, she thought, unable to hide a wicked grin.

'Yes, I did,' he repeated. 'And I brought you a present.' David reached into his jacket pocket and handed across a small Cartier bag. Dionne looked up at him in excitement, her eyes shining. She reached inside the bag and took out a chunky box with the distinctive script across the top, catching her breath as she opened it. Inside was a stunning Cartier Tank watch in white gold, the strap set with diamonds.

'David . . .' she breathed, mentally calculating how much it must have cost. Ten thousand euros at least. 'It's beautiful.' She was stunned. She'd received presents from lovers before but nothing as extravagant as this.

David shrugged, as though it was nothing. 'I saw it at the airport. I thought you might like it.'

'I love it,' she assured him.

'Perhaps it will help you keep the time better,' he smiled wryly. Dionne was notorious for being late.

'Perhaps . . .'

'Put it on,' David encouraged her.

Feeling like a child at Christmas, she unclasped the bracelet and slid it onto her wrist. David watched her. As Dionne felt the cool metal clamp onto her arm, she realized that no one had ever bought her anything quite so incredible before. And certainly no one had ever bought her anything quite this special just for the hell of it, just because they were missing her. Sure, her momma always scrimped and saved to get her something nice for her birthday, but she could never have afforded anything like this. It probably cost more than Natalie Summers earned in a year.

Thoughtfully, Dionne fingered the gold chain she still wore round her neck, the gift from her parents when she turned sixteen. At the time Dionne had thought it was so classy, so elegant. Now it looked cheap and insignificant, the colour clashing with the white gold of the watch. Almost without thinking, Dionne unhooked the chain from around her neck and placed it in the empty box.

'It doesn't match,' she explained casually to David, not wanting him to know the significance of what she had just done. It seemed symbolic almost – the end of her old life, where she had battled just to achieve mediocrity, and the beginning of a new era where she was beautiful, successful and spoiled by a rich man. Just like she had dreamed, back in Luis Fernandez's studio . . .

Dionne snapped the box shut and sat upright, pushing

out the memories. She was a different girl now, and the watch was proof of that.

'I had some good news today,' she announced brightly, keen to change the subject.

'Yes?'

'I got a new contract – a big one. I'm the face – or should I say the legs – of DIM,' she giggled, naming the French hosiery company.

'That's wonderful,' David beamed. He looked genuinely pleased for her.

'It's a six-month contract,' Dionne rushed on excitedly. Her dark eyes were dancing, her face radiant with happiness. 'Although they can renew, of course, if they love me. I'm gonna be everywhere! Billboards, the métro, even bus stops . . . and my legs'll be on the packaging!'

David grinned, unable to help himself. It was no secret that he had dated a lot of girls, but they rarely held his interest for as long as Dionne had. She was a fireball of energy, and her zest for life was infectious. She was always out – doing things, seeing people, living life to the full. It was hard not to be swept away by her natural charm and enthusiasm, however frustrating she could be at times. And, on top of all that, she had a killer body that she wasn't afraid to use. David loved her tiny waist with the full, heavy breasts and a black girl's ass that could make him come within seconds when he rode her from behind and felt the firm, smooth skin of her butt rubbing against his balls . . .

'We need a bottle of champagne over here,' David summoned a passing waiter.

'*Tout de suite, monsieur.*' Seconds later, he was back with a perfectly chilled bottle of vintage Krug, set in an ice bucket. 'Are you ready to order now?'

135

'Dionne?' David looked across at her.

'I'll have the salmon. No potatoes, just a little salad. And no dressing.'

'You're sure?' David asked, as Dionne nodded reluctantly. Raising an eyebrow, David ordered his food and the waiter discreetly disappeared.

'I shouldn't even be eating at all,' Dionne sighed. 'I've got a shoot in five days and I've *got* to look perfect.'

David looked amused. 'Dionne,' he told her gently. 'Your figure is already perfect.'

'Yeah, well, you would say that,' Dionne responded testily, although his compliment had the desired effect. 'You're a man – and a straight one.'

David held his hands up. 'It's true. I cannot deny it.'

'What I mean,' Dionne explained in exasperation, 'is that you want different things in a woman to the designers. For a man, the more T&A the better. But then clothes don't hang right, see? Not if you've got too much booty going on.'

'Ah, but champagne, it has no calories so it is allowed, yes?'

'I'm not sure I believe you,' Dionne pouted, but she didn't protest as he refilled her glass.

Dionne took a sip and watched as David tucked into the bread basket, spreading the warm rolls with fresh, salty butter and devouring three without a break. When her food came, she picked at it delicately, trying to make it last as David ate his way through a full three courses. But the thought of what her new employers or her agent would say if she looked too big for the photoshoot steeled her willpower, so she even refused a mouthful of David's divine-looking *mousse au chocolat*.

When he had finished, David sat back in his chair

and sighed contently. 'That was delicious,' he smiled. 'A meal fit for the gods.'

'I will punch you if you order the cheese plate,' Dionne threatened. She felt light-headed, having drunk three glasses of champagne and eaten very little. She didn't think she could stand to see him plough his way through another divine-looking course.

'Okay then. No cheese,' David agreed. 'Just a coffee.'

Dionne narrowed her eyes. It was all right for him, he would work it off in the gym later, she thought, admiring his superb body. He was in great shape, with a powerfully built chest and shoulders and strong, toned thighs. He looked amazing naked, Dionne recalled, feeling the first stirrings in her groin as she watched him wipe his mouth roughly on the white linen napkin and throw it down on the table.

'So, what shall we do with the rest of the evening?' he asked, looking at her thoughtfully. 'Perhaps you would like to go out to celebrate your new contract? Perhaps to Bijou?'

Dionne's head snapped up. 'No,' she said, a little too quickly. 'No, I don't want to go there.'

'No?' David feigned surprise. 'I thought it was your favourite club?'

'Not any more.' She stared right at him, her gaze defiant, as though daring him to say what he was thinking.

David called her bluff. 'Is it because you have been sleeping with Philippe Rochefort?' His tone was casual but his eyes never left her face.

'Screw you!' Dionne retorted hotly. 'That's bullshit.'

'That's not what I have heard. I heard that you were flirting outrageously with him. That half the club was watching and that you left Bijou with him.'

'Had your spies keeping an eye on me, did you?'

she spat accusingly. She was backed into a corner and she would fight.

David kept his voice carefully controlled. 'People talk, Dionne. When you draw so much attention to yourself, you cannot expect it to go unnoticed.'

'I didn't sleep with him,' she repeated, the humiliation of what had happened that night rushing back to her. She wondered what other rumours had been going round. 'Yes, he came home with us. CeCe was flirting with him and—'

David snorted. 'CeCe's not interested in him.'

'Well, what does it matter anyway?' Dionne challenged him. 'I'm not your girlfriend. I can do whatever I want.'

'That is true,' he admitted.

'I didn't think we were exclusive. And I bet you weren't a saint while you were away.'

The look on David's face told her all she needed to know, and for a second she felt triumphant. But the feeling didn't last. After all David's kind words and the beautiful watch that now sat on her wrist, she didn't mean any more to him than she did to Saeed or any of the other men who took her out and paid for her drinks, simply because they liked to be seen with a gorgeous girl on their arm.

'So you think that makes us even? Like some kind of tit for tat?' David said angrily, the phrase sounding odd in his accent.

'Believe what you want, I don't give a shit. Like you said, we're not exclusive.'

'I didn't say that. You did,' David responded quietly.

Dionne didn't reply, and the silence hung heavily between them. Around them they could hear low conversation, silver clinking against china and the discreet sound of piano music.

'Look, I'm not interested in him,' Dionne repeated, feeling the anger rise as she remembered how he had treated her, the things he had said. 'He's too old, too sleazy. He's been with a million girls, everyone knows that, and I don't want to be another. I don't even know what they see in him,' she ranted, her tone venomous. 'He's pretty gross when you think about it.'

'I hear you were very drunk,' David stated.

She didn't know if he was giving her a get-out or criticizing her lifestyle choice. She decided to give him the benefit of the doubt. 'Yeah, well, you'd have to be drunk to go home with that dirty old bastard.'

David smiled, and Dionne felt the tension start to ease. She began to play with her watch, twisting it anxiously round her wrist. 'Thanks for my present,' she began awkwardly. 'It's amazing, I love it, and . . .' Dionne swallowed hard. 'I missed you too, David.'

13

It was a quiet day in Chez Paddy. Outside it was drizzling lightly, and the streets lacked their usual bustle.

Aidan was taking advantage of the downtime to catch up on some paperwork. He was upstairs in the office, while Alyson was alone at the bar, keeping herself busy to pass the time. She'd already removed all the optics to soak them in soda water, and was contemplating scrubbing the back bar when she heard the door clang.

She turned round, expecting to see a group of weary tourists tramp in demanding lunch. But what she saw made her heart skip a beat.

'Philippe!' she exclaimed, calling out his name before she could stop herself. Her eyes lit up as she saw him, her pulse beginning to race.

He was less put-together than she remembered. His tie was loose and the top button of his shirt was undone. He looked as if he'd been rushing.

'Alyson.' He smiled and his eyes crinkled at the corners, his face taking on a softness. '*Ça va?*'

'*Oui, ça va très bien, merci,*' she replied shyly, unable to stop smiling. '*Et vous?*'

'Yes.' He looked calmer. 'Now, I am very well. I have been away, for work,' he explained. 'In the States. That is why I have not come here.'

'Right,' Alyson nodded. She was embarrassed to admit it, but she'd been thinking about him. When he hadn't returned to the bar, she'd dismissed their meeting as something insignificant, telling herself not to be so ridiculous. She'd buried her feelings and got on with her life, the way she always did. Now she knew he'd been thinking about her too.

They stood in silence. Alyson realized she was staring at him. 'Can I get you a drink?' she asked quickly, trying to cover her nerves.

Philippe hesitated. 'No. No, thank you. When . . .' He paused, rubbing his brow. 'When do you next have time off from here?'

Confusion flickered across Alyson's face, unsure of where he was leading. 'I have Saturday daytime free, but I have to work in the evening. Then I have Monday night off . . .'

Philippe thought for a moment. 'Saturday. Would you like to come out with me? We could have lunch . . .?'

'Yes,' Alyson said quickly, surprising herself. 'Yes, I'd like that.'

'Good.' Relief flooded across his face. 'Good. I'll be in touch.' He threw her that smile once again, and dashed out of the door.

Alyson watched as he left, staring after him for the longest time. She bit her lip to stop herself from grinning like an idiot, a knot of excitement building in her stomach. She felt as though she had a secret; something exhilarating that made her light up inside.

She'd never really been interested in men before – never even had a boyfriend – but there was something about this guy that was different. He was handsome, naturally, but it was more than that. He had a self-assured quality that was unlike anyone she'd ever met. They way he moved, spoke, behaved – he seemed utterly confident and in control. He was a different nationality, clearly older than her, and yet . . . he'd asked her out. Alyson exhaled, a long, shaky breath, as her heart began to race once more. It was terrifying, but thrilling.

With a pang, she thought of Aidan. She wondered what he would say if he knew – he hadn't seemed to like Philippe the last time he came in. Alyson shrugged off the thought, telling herself that it was nothing to do with him. Aidan was her boss and they were friends – that was all. Sure, she'd had a good time the other night, but that was what friends did, wasn't it?

Picking up a dishcloth she turned back to the bar, pushing the feelings of guilt to the back of her mind. Aidan was her manager, and what she did in her private life was none of his business.

'Man, it's beautiful,' Dionne breathed, as she pushed open the wrought-iron gate and stepped into the over-grown garden. It was like entering a secret world.

'*C'est parfait!*' CeCe exclaimed in delight.

Her friend, François, followed them in through the gate, his camera equipment slung casually over his shoulder. He was typically French looking, with striking cheekbones that hinted at aristocratic roots, dark-blond hair growing past his shoulders, and a sexy covering of stubble. He was tall and slim, dressed in skinny jeans and a grey shirt. The whole look was deliberately laid-back, but the clothes were designer – a rich kid playing at dressing down.

Like most of CeCe's friends, he was from the moneyed, Eurotrash set; society kids who were drifting through life trying out whichever career they felt like. Photography was François' latest fad, but he knew if it didn't work out, he wouldn't be on the breadline. His parents would bail him out, and he would simply drift into whatever next took his fancy.

'Very impressive.' He whistled under his breath. 'The pictures will be *incroyable*.'

CeCe put a hand to her eyes to shade them from the early morning sun as she stared up at the house in front of them. It was glorious – a three-storey mansion in the 16th arrondissement, built from the distinctive cream-coloured Parisian stone and wreathed in climbing ivy. It had high-arched windows, ornately carved balconies and tall pillars either side of the cast-iron studded wooden door. The whole property was surrounded by a high stone wall; tall trees and unruly bushes had sprung up around it, making it almost impossible to see in from the street outside. You could walk past and not even notice the house was there.

A property developer friend of CeCe's had let them borrow it for the day. A former embassy for an Eastern European country that no longer existed, it had been on his books for some time and had fallen into a state of disrepair. Part of the stone wall was crumbling, a couple of windows had been smashed, and what had once been a formal, well-ordered garden had been left to grow wild.

CeCe fell in love with it instantly. It had a timeless quality and a wild beauty – the perfect place to shoot her lookbook. Inspired by Claude's advice, she had seized the moment and kicked her career up a gear. It was all very well sitting in her bedroom designing, running up samples of the clothes on the sewing machine in the lounge, but it was hardly going to turn her into the next Coco Chanel. She needed to take the leap – try and sell her designs, drum up interest in her label.

So she'd called in some favours. Dionne modelling and François taking photos were just the beginning. She hadn't lied when she'd told Claude she was well connected. She knew bloggers, writers, editors of hip, underground magazines, girls-about-town who would wear her dresses and create some buzz around her – make sure everyone knew CeCe was the up-and-coming designer to wear. After all, everyone loved to be first with a trend.

She'd even christened her new label – Capucine. It was the name of a flower, and also the stage name of a beautiful French model and actress from the 1960s who tragically took her own life. Capucine's story fascinated CeCe, and she felt that the name was the perfect tribute – glamorous and elegant, with an air of mystery.

'Okay.' She clapped her hands together in excitement. 'Let's get started.'

They made their way over the cracked flagstones towards the imposing entrance. CeCe fished the key out of her handbag. It stuck a little in the lock, then gradually turned, the door creaking as it swung open.

Dionne's jaw dropped. CeCe broke into a wide grin as François stared round, taking everything in. The entrance hall was enormous, tiled in black-and-white flagstones with a dramatic vaulted ceiling. A wide, sweeping staircase curled away to the left, with an intricately carved wrought-iron banister.

'Does this place have any electricity?' Dionne wondered.

CeCe flicked the switch beside her, and the place was flooded with a dingy light from the colossal crystal chandelier above. Not all of the bulbs worked; the glass was dusty and covered in cobwebs. It looked like something from a gothic horror novel, but CeCe knew it would look fantastic on camera.

'Come on, let's explore,' Dionne squealed, dumping the bag she was carrying. The three of them were like children as they raced from room to room, exclaiming over what they saw. At an upstairs window they found heavy damask curtains in rich burgundy shot through with gold, damp and stained with mildew. A moth-eaten flag drooped sadly beside a solid mahogany desk. Mounted near the entrance was an enormous bust of some long-forgotten leader, and what had once been the ballroom shimmered with an entire wall of floor-to-ceiling mirrors, edged in gilt and tarnished with black speckles. It was the ultimate in faded grandeur, and it was fabulous.

They based themselves in the ballroom and began to set up. CeCe found a dubious-looking power point, the plug socket hanging from the wall and the wires sprawling out from behind. She crossed her fingers and plugged in the iron. The clothes needed to look perfect, and she was willing to risk a little electrocution to ensure they did.

Dionne plopped down on the floor in front of one of the huge mirrors, and began unrolling her make-up kit. She was styling herself for the shoot – she did it so regularly she was practically a professional. She'd even spent last night putting in a new weave, sewing in extensions so that her hair was long and glossy, with infinite possibilities.

Outside in the hallway, François began to set up

for the first shot. He'd found a dramatic recessed arch with sweeping lines and intricate carving. Even with the overhead lights on, the building was dark; the high windows let in little daylight, obstructed by the thick bushes and tall trees. Quickly, he rigged up two powerful soft-box lights and set the camera on a tripod. He was using an old-fashioned camera with 35mm film, preferring the effect to digital. François knew exactly what CeCe wanted, and he planned for the shots to be glossy yet timeless, an old-school elegance with a hint of smouldering sex appeal.

Back in the ballroom, CeCe was helping Dionne into the first dress – a form-fitting creation in nude satin overlaid with black silk Chantilly lace. High-necked, with an Elizabeth I-inspired ruff to emphasize an elegant neck, it followed the line of Dionne's curves like a persistent stalker, blossoming out at the bottom to a wide fishtail in layers of ruffled lace.

'Dionne, you look amazing,' CeCe marvelled, as she hooked the dress and stepped back to admire her work. The clothes were perfectly tailored to fit Dionne's body, and she wore her hair up to give full effect to the dramatic neckline, a few strands hanging loose and curled. Her eyes were made up in shimmering emerald, her lips smudged with berry.

She saw that CeCe was staring critically at her. 'What's the matter?'

'It needs something,' she frowned. 'I don't know what . . .'

'You want accessories?' asked Dionne, grinning as she tipped out the bag she had brought with her. Dozens of scarves, jewellery and shoes clattered onto the parquet floor.

'Holy shit, Dionne. Where did you get all this stuff from?'

'Rivoli Couture.' Dionne was smiling like the Cheshire cat. 'I borrowed it.'

'Khalid is going to *kill* you,' CeCe exclaimed. 'You can get away with the odd item, but he'll notice if this much stock is missing. Although these *are* pretty spectacular,' CeCe marvelled, holding up a pair of hand-painted Erdem wedges.

Dionne shrugged. 'I couldn't give a fuck if he fires me. I'm planning on leaving anyway. I just haven't got around to telling him.'

'Really?' CeCe wondered if Dionne was serious. Every time she had a bad day she threatened to walk out. But this time there was something different in her tone.

'Totally. I've got enough money from modelling to cover me for a few months so I'm gonna go for it and hope the work keeps flowing in. Just be grateful you've got me today – you won't be able to afford me in a few weeks,' Dionne teased.

'Then I feel very lucky,' CeCe laughed, as she rummaged through her jewellery box and picked out an elegant pair of pearl earrings. She tried to keep her tone light, but inside she felt unsettled. So Dionne had made enough money to leave her job and model full time? The news only increased CeCe's determination to get her own career underway. She didn't know how she'd cope at Rivoli Couture without Dionne. She was the one who made it bearable, and now she was leaving. CeCe had the uncomfortable sensation of being left behind.

She pushed the negative thoughts to the back of her mind and handed the earrings to Dionne. The sight of her in the beautiful dress made CeCe swell with pride. She *was* talented, she insisted to herself; the rack of incredible dresses waiting to be photographed was proof of that. And she *was* going to succeed.

François stalked into the room, brushing his long hair away from his face. He looked perfectly handsome, perfectly put together. 'Ready?' he asked, as CeCe nodded. 'My God, Dionne, you look magnificent,' he said genuinely, his eyes roaming over her body.

Dionne smiled, pleased with his reaction. She twirled in front of the mirror, taking in her appearance. The dress was cut perfectly for her hour-glass figure, the high neck emphasizing her jaw line and giving her an almost regal air. She looked like a dark princess, a gothic queen.

'*Allez, viens,*' François said, taking her by the hand. 'Together, you and I are going to create something wonderful for CeCe.'

Dionne giggled, following him out of the room. CeCe came behind, ensuring the fishtail train didn't snag on anything. As they reached the alcove, François made final adjustments to the light while CeCe fussed around, making sure the lace draped as it was supposed to, that the ruff stood up stiff and even. Then she stepped back and left them to get on with what they did best.

Dionne shone. There was no other word for it. She came alive in front of the camera, dazzling with energy. She flirted with François and he lapped it up, the two of them sparking off each other's creativity. CeCe knew that a lot of designers didn't like such overt sexuality, but for her it worked. She loved the way Dionne gave her clothes a real sense of personality, bringing them to life in front of the camera.

They worked without stopping. As soon as one outfit was shot, François would set down and move the equipment to the next location while Dionne rapidly changed her hair and make-up. One moment she was a painted courtesan, the next a bare-faced ingénue. She could transform in minutes from old-school Hollywood glamour to innocent schoolgirl.

CeCe ran around being general dogsbody: pressing the clothes, doing last-minute stitching, helping François lug his gear and pampering Dionne's ego. At lunchtime she ran out and grabbed food for them all. Dionne barely ate, existing on black coffee and a banana, which she ate in small bites throughout the day.

In spite of everything, CeCe was excited. She raced through the day on adrenaline, and she could feel in her bones that the photos would be fantastic.

Dionne was a fire-cracker, never switching off. They shot her reclining on the dark mahogany desk, her skirt hitched up and a look of sexual promise in her eyes. Then alone in the garden, vulnerable amongst the undergrowth, as though captured off guard in a private moment. There was a dramatic pose in the ballroom, the mirrored wall being used to show Dionne's front and rear simultaneously; the back of the dress was cut strikingly low, with criss-cross lacing like a reverse corset, and the picture captured it perfectly.

The whole shoot had the vibe of a glossy magazine editorial, a deliberate decision by CeCe. She wasn't just selling the clothes – she was selling the lifestyle. The Capucine woman was aspirational, sexually confident and in control, and the photos needed to reflect that.

The sun had set by the time François finally called time. They had shot for eighteen hours straight and were all exhausted, but CeCe was elated. She cracked open a bottle of champagne and they sank down on the dusty floor of the ballroom, toasting each other with plastic cups in the dingy light.

'To CeCe,' said François, raising his cup.

'CeCe,' Dionne echoed.

CeCe grinned at the pair of them, so grateful for everything they'd done. She had a good feeling about today and this was just the start, she was sure of it. CeCe Bouvier was on her way.

14

Alyson was seated in the back of a sleek black chauffeur-driven Mercedes that purred like a kitten as it made its way through the Parisian traffic.

She crossed her long, slim legs – since the weather had turned warmer, she'd been living in shorts, and her pale northern skin was now lightly tanned – and looked over her outfit. She couldn't help it. Everyone else was taking such an interest in what she was wearing and it was starting to rub off on her. Besides, she wanted to look nice for Philippe, to feel confident in her appearance instead of being shy, inhibited Alyson who longed to blend into the background.

She'd told the girls she had another date and they'd squealed with excitement, fussing round as if she was making her debut at the Crillon Ball. They assumed it was a second date with Aidan and Alyson hadn't bothered to correct them. It just seemed easier that way.

She'd declined Dionne's enthusiastic offer of help, fearing another excruciating makeover session. Instead, Alyson had been shopping. She'd found a cute floral-print dress that flattered her body shape without being overtly sexy, and teamed it with her old denim jacket and strappy sandals, a small tan bag slung across her body. She looked both cute and effortlessly stylish.

She'd even bought a little make-up. Nothing too over the top – just brown mascara and a pale-pink lip gloss that tasted of marzipan. She took it out of her handbag and reapplied it, using the window to see her reflection. She hadn't thought to bring a mirror.

They were travelling along the Champs-Élysées and the tourists were out in force, browsing in the chain stores or paying extortionate prices to eat at the pavement cafés. Alyson could hardly believe that she was there at all – the whole experience was surreal. She'd arranged to meet Philippe in the Luxembourg Gardens and he'd offered to send a car for her. She'd almost fallen over when the Mercedes had shown up, the uniformed chauffeur alighting and smoothly opening the door for her. Monsieur Rochefort would meet her there, he'd informed her. She assumed they were going for a picnic. The idea was sweet, romantic.

They crossed the Seine at Pont de la Concorde and the magnificent Assemblée Nationale rose up ahead. Alyson stared at it longingly. She would have loved to work there – perhaps as a translator in one of the government departments or, as an intern, learning about French politics at the very heart of the system. She couldn't stay at Chez Paddy for ever. Aidan was great, but the need to move on was becoming ever more pressing.

Aidan. Alyson felt a fresh swathe of guilt at the thought of him. She hadn't told him where she was going. She didn't think he'd approve.

But there was no time to think about that now as they pulled up to the gates of the Jardin du Luxembourg and the driver came round to open her door.

'Please follow me, Mademoiselle.'

Alyson climbed out elegantly, trying to disguise the way her heart was pounding, and walked beside him through the ornate iron gates. The gardens were beautiful, immaculately kept lawns stretching as far as the eye could see, bordered by brilliantly coloured flowers. Stone statues kept guard over wide, sweeping walkways, and the whole park was dominated by the magnificent Luxembourg Palace.

Then she saw Philippe walking towards her. Alyson caught her breath, shocked at how handsome he looked. He was dressed, off-duty, in a dark-blue polo shirt and Ralph Lauren chinos, his skin tanned and his expression relaxed.

'Alyson!' Philippe exclaimed, breaking into a warm smile. As he bent down to kiss her on both cheeks, Alyson closed her eyes, inhaling the delicious scent of him, feeling the light graze of his stubble against her cheek. The chauffeur discreetly disappeared, leaving them alone. Philippe let his gaze run casually over her and Alyson felt glad she'd made an effort. She didn't want to disappoint him.

'Shall we go?' he asked, resting his hand on her lower back as he steered her further into the park. Alyson could feel the warmth of him through her thin cotton dress and she shivered, her skin breaking out in goose bumps. She willed herself to stay calm – she didn't want a repeat of the incident with Aidan, where she'd taken fright and run.

They strolled together down one of the wide avenues. Alyson watched the couples walk towards them, arms wrapped around one another, and wondered if she and

Philippe looked like that – just another couple enjoying the beauty of the gardens.

Suddenly there was a loud whirring noise from above, a deafening thwack-thwack-thwack of rotors. Alyson's head snapped up, shading her eyes as she tried to pinpoint where it was coming from. Other people were doing the same, gaping upwards as a gleaming black helicopter descended from the cloudless sky, the rotating blades making the chestnut trees tremble. People stood back, giving it room as it came in to land. Alyson watched in disbelief as it touched down and the rotor blades were switched off, shuddering to a halt.

'Come on,' Philippe told her, heading towards it.

Alyson followed him in confusion, watching uncertainly as he opened the door and greeted the pilot. He turned back to Alyson, his dark eyes gleaming. 'Are you coming?'

'It's . . . for us?' Alyson managed to stammer. A small crowd had gathered and the onlookers were watching her curiously. She felt self-conscious under their gaze, suddenly wishing she was anywhere but there. The idea of getting in a helicopter was terrifying – she'd never flown in a plane, let alone a chopper. And how well did she even know this guy?

She looked up and saw Philippe smiling encouragingly.

'Where are we going?' she asked, stunned.

'As I promised you – for lunch.'

Alyson wanted to burst out laughing, the situation was so absurd. She wondered what Dionne would do if she was here. It wasn't even a question – she would climb in without a second thought.

Steeling her nerve, Alyson stepped towards the helicopter. Philippe held out his hand to help her, then climbed in beside her, showing her how to adjust her seatbelt and headset.

'You can speak to me through the mouthpiece,' he explained. 'But Guy can hear everything you say,' he added, indicating the pilot. 'Ready?'

Alyson nodded, dumbstruck.

Guy started up the helicopter and the blades began to rotate once more, the grass beneath them flattened by the rushing air. They lifted up and swung heavily to the left. Alyson let out a cry, and clung on to Philippe's arm. He smiled reassuringly, covering her hand with his own as the chopper righted itself and they ascended directly upwards, leaving the gardens far below. The people looked tiny, the Palais du Luxembourg like a doll's house.

She stared, mesmerized, out of the window as Paris shrank and fell away beneath them. Heading east, they flew over the distinctive rooftops, the streets laid out in a jumble of curving streets and sweeping avenues, the boulevards running like arteries through the city. Alyson twisted in her seat, craning her neck to see the Eiffel Tower jutting proudly into the sky behind her. To her left was Sacré Cœur, where she'd been with Aidan . . .

'It's beautiful, no?' Philippe's voice crackled over the headset. Alyson could only nod, too self-conscious to speak in case she unwittingly said something stupid that the pilot heard.

Gradually they left the city behind, the smart houses giving way to the sprawling suburbs and finally petering out into the rural landscape of the Champagne-Ardenne. A rich carpet of fields spread out below them, green and yellow, bisected by river tributaries and patches of forest.

They flew for around forty-five minutes before

they began to descend, passing over vineyards where thousands of grape vines were planted row upon row along the banks of the Marne River. In the distance, Alyson could see a huge property rising up out of the fields, more like a château than an ordinary house. It was built in grey stone, turreted and imposing, and as the chopper moved lower, she realized they were heading straight for it.

They flew directly overhead, so close she felt sure they would land on the roof, but at the back of property was a flagstone courtyard where Guy expertly brought the chopper down to land. Just beyond was a large, rectangular lake, a statue of Poseidon reclining in the centre. The whirring blades of the helicopter created deep ripples on the surface of the water, shallow waves lapping at the weather-beaten stone.

As the rotors slowed, Philippe indicated that Alyson should remove her headphones and unclip her seatbelt. Then he opened the door and jumped out, his hands around Alyson's waist as he helped her down. She felt dizzy to be back on solid ground and clung to him for a moment, his arms strong and reassuring.

'Where are we?' she asked breathlessly.

'Château de Marne. My house.'

'You *live* here?' Alyson squeaked incredulously, as she took in the vastness of the property. It must have had forty rooms at least.

'Occasionally.' Philippe seemed amused by her reaction. 'This is my family's home. I live most of the time in Paris, or St Tropez – when I'm not travelling.'

Alyson burst out laughing. 'This is madness,' she cried in disbelief, wondering what on earth she was doing there. She was so far out of her comfort zone it wasn't funny.

'I think lunch will be almost ready,' Philippe told her easily. She expected them to go into the château but Philippe led her away, along a winding path that stretched down towards the riverbank. *'Et voilà!'*

On the grass beside the river, a red-and-white chequered blanket had been spread out, an old-fashioned wicker picnic basket in the centre. Philippe knelt down and began to unpack: baguette, olives, cheese, smoked salmon, salad, a bottle of champagne.

Alyson sat down tentatively beside him, tucking her long legs underneath her. The location couldn't have been more perfect. 'This is incredible. Thank you,' she said softly.

'You're pleased? Truly?' Philippe's eyes searched her face anxiously. 'Good.'

The champagne cork flew out with a pop, and Philippe poured two glasses.

'No thank you . . .' Alyson faltered, shaking her head as he held one out to her.

'Oh, but you must. This is my family's champagne – see?' He turned the bottle round for Alyson to read the label. Rochefort Champagne, emblazoned in gold with the traditional family crest.

'Rochefort Champagne is *your* company?'

'Yes. It was founded by my grandfather. The grapes are grown on the land around here. I can show you the vineyards later, if you would like to see them.'

'I'd love to,' Alyson breathed, hardly able to take in what she was hearing. 'I can't believe you own Rochefort Champagne,' she finished incredulously.

'Well, strictly speaking it belongs to the shareholders – it's a public company. But I'm a major shareholder, and we still think of it as the family business.'

'That's amazing. I . . . I find business really interesting,' Alyson admitted shyly. 'I studied it in school, and I just find that whole world fascinating – how people found a company, why they succeed . . .' She trailed off, worried that she'd said too much and made herself look ridiculous.

But Philippe was nodding in agreement. 'You are very perceptive, I think. Most people do not find business so interesting. They are interested in the money, yes,' he smiled wryly, 'but not the process behind it. So how come you are working a bar?' he asked bluntly.

Alyson flushed. 'It's not what I want to do,' she explained, telling him the same story she'd told Aidan – how she'd tried to find an entry-level office job when she first came to Paris but every door seemed firmly closed, and how, struggling for money, she'd fallen back on bar work. She felt awkward and childish, confiding her ambitions to this incredibly successful man who quite clearly had everything – a beautiful house, a dream career, and enough money to make Croesus look like small fry. But Philippe didn't laugh at her or belittle her. Instead, he handed her a champagne glass and raised his own.

'Then I hope that one day you will get what you want,' he said softly, tilting his flute against hers.

Hesitantly, Alyson took a sip, tasting the sharp, bubbling liquid for the first time.

'It's good, yes?'

'It's delicious,' Alyson told him honestly.

'I'm glad.' Philippe smiled at her once again. Alyson looked away, feeling the familiar sensation of nerves building in her stomach. Her skin felt warm, an unexpected rush of heat low in her belly. She took another sip of champagne, feeling reckless.

'Shall we?' he asked, indicating the food.

Alyson forked a little salad onto a bone-china plate, as Philippe helped himself and told her more about his life. Alyson watched him as he spoke. She'd never met anyone like him before, someone so well travelled and cultured. He'd seen and experienced so much in his life – all the things she wanted to do – and he made her feel a part of it. She felt significant speaking to him, no longer the lonely, scared girl she'd been back in Manchester. He made her feel as though she had something valuable to offer the world.

She didn't want to talk about herself but Philippe didn't seem to mind. He didn't pressure her into anything or force her to answer any questions. She felt comfortable with him, she realized. Such was his charisma that simply being around him made her feel special too. He was intelligent, charming . . . and incredibly handsome.

He stretched out on the rug in front of her, a relaxed posture that showed off his body. Alyson couldn't help but check him out. His arms were muscular, with dark hair on his forearms, and his shoulders were broad, his body tapering down to a solid waist, strong thighs, an unmistakeable bulge between his legs . . . Alyson flushed and looked away.

'There's something very sensual about eating with your hands, don't you think?' Philippe asked casually, breaking into her thoughts. He held out a ripe strawberry, fat and juicy. 'Here, try one of these.'

Alyson leaned forward to take a bite and her lips brushed against his fingers. She sat up quickly, her cheeks flaming, but Philippe didn't take his eyes off her. She felt a pull deep within her stomach, a charge of electricity that shot through her whole body. She wanted him, she realized. She wanted him to kiss her. And then, the next moment, almost as though he'd read her thoughts, Philippe moved towards her and his mouth was on hers, her senses overwhelmed at the smell, feel, taste of him. She'd always imagined she'd be terrified when this moment came, but Philippe was so assured, taking charge completely. Gently, he pulled her in towards him, his body so large, his arms so strong. It was intoxicating.

'I've been wanting to do that since the first moment I saw you,' he murmured.

'I . . .' Alyson didn't know what to say. She couldn't seem to think straight. 'What time is it?' She checked her watch and was shocked to discover it was late afternoon. 'I'm so sorry,' she apologized. 'I have to get back . . . I have to work.'

'Do not worry about it – I will sort everything. If you would like to stay, you can stay. No pressure,' Philippe said evenly.

Alyson looked around her, at the beautiful landscape, so tranquil and still. Paris felt like a world away – out here she could do anything, be who she wanted to be. She felt as though she'd jumped from a ledge expecting to hit the ground, but instead she was flying.

'Would you like to stay?' Philippe repeated, his dark brown eyes intense as he looked at her.

'Yes,' she replied, her voice barely more than a whisper. 'I'll stay.'

Aidan was behind the bar at Chez Paddy, gearing up for the Saturday night rush. It was getting busy and Alyson hadn't turned up yet. Aidan hoped she was okay – she was never usually late.

The phone in the back began to ring. Quickly, Aidan finished serving the couple at the bar, then sprinted over to pick it up.

'*Allo?*'

'Aidan Kennedy?'

'Yes?'

'Good evening. My name is Philippe Rochefort. I believe I may have spoken with you when I came into your bar last week? I'm calling on behalf of Alyson Wakefield.'

Aidan instantly stiffened. He knew exactly who was calling. He'd recognized the man's voice straight away.

'I'm a . . . *friend* of hers. I'm calling to let you know that, unfortunately, she won't be able to make it into work this evening.'

'Where is she?' Aidan demanded.

He heard Philippe laugh softly on the other end of the line. 'Don't worry about her – she's fine. She's with me. I really am sorry if this causes any problem. Perhaps if there's a way we can settle this financially? I'd be happy to pay for any inconvenience this will cause—'

'I don't want your money,' Aidan spat.

There was a pause. Aidan could almost hear Philippe smirking. 'As you wish. Oh, and you might want to find cover for her shift tomorrow. I don't think she'll be in then either. But I'll try and have her back with you by Monday, *d'accord?*'

He chuckled softly and hung up. At the other end of the line, Aidan slammed the phone back into its cradle.

He was so mad he couldn't see straight. His fingers itched to punch something.

A queue was building up at the bar, but Aidan didn't care. He stayed out back, standing in the dingy corridor where he forced himself to breathe deeply, in through the nose and out through the mouth.

So Alyson was with this Philippe guy. He'd heard

of him of course – a rich society guy, part of the Rochefort Champagne dynasty. She'd gone away with him for the weekend and hadn't even had the decency to tell him herself. And she was staying overnight. They were on a romantic weekend together, sharing a bed. The idea was torture for Aidan, the image of Alyson in another man's arms. And not just any man – that arrogant, sleazy French guy.

He'd thought Alyson was different, but she was just like every other woman out there, her head turned by money and power. Aidan cursed himself for being so stupid, for being taken in by the sweet, innocent act. That's all it had been – an act. He'd almost fallen for it as well. Those huge doe eyes, wide and tearful as she confided in him about her mother's illness and her father leaving. She'd seemed so sweet, so genuine.

Aidan had told himself to take it slowly, that she wasn't ready for anything heavy, and all the time she was fucking another man behind his back. What an idiot he'd been.

He exhaled heavily as he looked around him – at the grimy walls that needed repainting, the out-of-date health-and-safety posters peeling off the walls, grotty old cleaning cloths piled in a corner. He'd been here too long, he saw that now. What did he have to offer a woman? He was coasting with his life. He had real ambitions, a business plan that was sitting, forgotten, in a drawer upstairs. He needed to get out of here to make sure he could look at himself with pride when he looked in the mirror.

Perhaps it wouldn't work out between Alyson and this guy. Perhaps Philippe was exaggerating.

Aidan wanted to see her again. He felt sure that, at heart, she was still the same, sweet Alyson he knew.

How could he have got it so badly wrong? He'd be able to tell as soon as he looked at her exactly what the true story was.

All he needed was to look into her eyes, just once, and he would know.

15

Alyson lay stretched out in a glorious bubble bath, filled liberally with L'Occitane bath foam. The water was hot and she'd filled the tub almost to the top, sinking down low so the bubbles covered her entire body. Through the steam she stared out at the bathroom; it was old-fashioned and decadent, sumptuously decorated in marble and gold. The claw-foot bath in which she was reclining stood in the centre of the room, and dramatic arched windows, draped with heavy curtains in cream and gold, looked out over the estate.

She should be halfway through her shift at Chez Paddy by now, Alyson realized guiltily, but she pushed the thought away, all regret washed down the drain with the lavender-scented bathwater. Paris seemed like another planet, far, far away. She felt as though she'd been here, in Château de Marne, forever.

She'd spent an unforgettable afternoon with Philippe, strolling in the vineyards as they looked over his grounds and property. He was fascinating to talk to, never tiring of showing her things that he thought might interest her. He'd barely left her side all day, his arm wrapped round her waist as they walked. She liked that. It felt strong, and protective.

They'd reached a secluded spot, low in the valley and hidden from view by a thicket of trees. The clouds were heavy and threatening, only the occasional shaft of sunlight piercing through to reach the ground below, but nothing could dent Alyson's good mood. They looked out over the glorious countryside, and Philippe had taken her in his arms and kissed her once again, Alyson recalled lazily, the memory of his lips on hers still fresh in her mind. She'd felt as though she was floating, drifting through some wonderful dream from which she never wanted to wake up.

When they'd finally returned to the house, faces glowing with exertion, Alyson found that a formal dinner had been set up for them in the vast dining room. Wood-panelled and hung with forbidding-looking portraits, the room was almost gothic in style and more than a little intimidating. Candles had been lit, with antique silverware and fine French china laid out on the twenty-foot-long polished mahogany table. For a moment, Alyson was speechless.

'I didn't bring a change of clothes,' she finally blurted out stupidly, indicating the simple cotton dress she was wearing, the sandals on her feet.

'I did not expect you to,' Philippe smiled. 'This was meant to be a surprise. Please, do not make yourself uncomfortable,' he added, seeing the awkwardness on her face. 'It will just be the two of us, no one else. Now, what would you like to eat? Anything you want.'

'I . . . I don't know,' she stammered. Presented with the choice of whatever she wanted, she couldn't seem to think of a single thing. How could she tell him that food was the last thing on her mind? That she was so deliriously happy just being around him that she might never need to eat again. 'I don't . . . Perhaps something light?' she suggested desperately. 'I ate so much at lunch and . . . It's beautiful, Philippe, but it's all so overwhelming.' She waved her arms to indicate the opulence of the room.

'That is not a problem,' Philippe said, instantly understanding her. 'Do not worry. Come, follow me.'

He led her down a spiral staircase to the kitchen and dismissed the half-dozen staff there, then told her to help herself to anything she wanted. They sat on bar stools at the counter, picking tubs out of the fridge and eating whatever they felt like. It suited Alyson far more than sitting stiffly at some straight-laced dinner. She began to relax once again, totally at ease in Philippe's company. When he opened another bottle of champagne, she didn't try to stop him.

It grew dark outside the tiny, leaded windows, and Philippe reached across to take her hand.

'If you would like to go home, I can call for a car,' he told her, his voice low and insistent. 'Or, if you would like to stay tonight . . .'

Alyson felt her stomach flip-flop, an exhilarating mix of nerves and anticipation. 'I'll stay,' she whispered. She didn't know what she had just agreed to, but she was excited about finding out.

Philippe had taken her hand and led her up the main staircase, a grand, sweeping affair.

'This is your room,' he told her, pushing open a heavy wooden door, deep within the stone walls of the château. The rich burgundy walls were hung with paintings – countryside scenes, and images of hunting. An enormous fireplace dominated the centre of the room, and directly opposite it stood a four-poster draped in white voile. Through a small open door beyond was the en-suite bathroom.

'Is everything satisfactory?' Philippe asked, watching her expression carefully.

'It's incredible,' Alyson told him genuinely. It seemed ridiculous that Philippe was worried about whether or not she liked his house, when she'd never stayed anywhere this beautiful in her whole life. It was a world away from the cramped terraced house in Oldham where she'd grown up.

'Good. I'll leave you to rest. There's a robe in your closet. Use anything that you need to, and any clothes you would like to have cleaned, leave them outside your door and they will be washed and returned to you before the morning.'

'Thank you, Philippe.' Alyson felt overwhelmed with gratitude at everything he'd done for her. It was almost magical, the way he'd taken her from her ordinary life and into this dreamlike existence. 'I've had such an amazing day – you've been so good to me.'

Philippe shook his head. 'Not at all. I feel privileged that you're here with me. You're such a joy to be around, Alyson, simply beautiful – not just physically, but in spirit. I'm glad you're happy to be here. I would not wish to be with anyone else.'

He bent down to kiss her once again and Alyson responded. She loved the feel of his kisses, the touch of his rough stubble against her skin, the lingering smell of the Acqua di Parma cologne he wore. More than anything, she adored the way her whole body trembled when he kissed her, little pulses of electricity firing through her lips, her stomach, all the way down to her groin.

He pulled away and she took a moment to catch her breath, her eyes wide, pupils dilated.

'Goodnight, Alyson,' Philippe said finally. He looked as though he wanted to say something else, as if he was wrestling with himself in some way. Then he turned on his heel and walked quickly out of the door.

Alyson remained motionless, trying to gather her thoughts. Her mind was racing and she knew there was no way she could sleep just yet. Perhaps a bath would help her relax.

She'd emptied almost half a bottle of L'Occitane foam into the churning water, and now lay in the scented bubbles, her mind replaying her incredible day. She didn't know whether she was disappointed or relieved that she'd been put in a guest bedroom, instead of in the master bedroom with Philippe lying beside her. It was incredibly considerate, of course, that he'd given her privacy and hadn't taken anything for granted. But there was still a part of her that wanted to know . . . to experience what it felt like to . . .

Gently, Alyson traced her lips with her fingers, recalling how Philippe had kissed her earlier. He was so powerful, so assured. He was obviously a man used to getting what he wanted. She couldn't imagine how anyone could refuse him anything.

Brushing away the bubbles, Alyson looked down at her body. Her limbs were long and lightly tanned. The skin on her stomach was paler, where it hadn't been exposed to the sun, and her small breasts were the same milky-white. She brushed her fingers over them experimentally; her nipples tightened, two small, hard buds on her childlike chest.

Was it possible that Philippe found her attractive? she wondered curiously, staring at her body. He was obviously a man of the world, clearly experienced. Maybe he'd had his fill of girls like Dionne, with their ripe, curvaceous bodies and their confident, come-hither stares. Maybe he saw something in her that no one else ever had. Something special. Something beautiful . . .

The water had turned tepid, the bubbles had dissolved into an oily layer on top of the water. Alyson told herself not to be silly and pulled herself out of the bath, wrapping her body in the luxuriously thick cotton robe. She padded through to the bedroom, towelling her hair dry, when there was a knock at the door. She opened it cautiously, conscious of how she looked.

Philippe stood there. He took in her state of undress, the robe wrapped loosely around her body. When he spoke, his voice sounded thick. 'May I come in? There is something I'd like to discuss with you.'

Alyson nodded breathlessly, standing aside to let him in.

Philippe paced the room anxiously. 'I've been thinking,' he began, his forehead furrowing into a deep rivet. 'You shouldn't be working in that bar, Alyson. You're better than that. You need something that stretches you, that pushes you.'

'I don't have a choice,' Alyson started to protest. But Philippe cut her off.

'Yes you do. Come and work for me.'

Alyson stared at him, wondering if he was joking. 'Doing what?'

'In the offices of Rochefort Champagne. Of course, it would be starting from the bottom. A lot of filing, taking minutes and so on, but we could see how you progress.'

Alyson could hardly breathe. It was perfect! 'Seriously?' she burst out.

'Of course.'

'That's . . . I mean . . . I won't let you down,' she finally finished, her eyes shining with excitement.

'I'm sure you won't,' Philippe smiled. 'Now, how much notice do you have to give for this . . . little job?' His tone was dismissive.

'I'm not sure. I'll have to ask . . .' Alyson trailed off. She was about to say 'ask Aidan', but she didn't want to think about him now. 'Is that where you work?' she changed the subject.

'No. I will be there from time to time, but I have other business to attend to. The head of the company is a man named Richard Duval. He's a good man – I've known him for a long time. He was a friend of my father's.'

'Right . . .'

'Besides, I couldn't be around you all the time. It would be too . . . distracting,' Philippe smiled, raising an eyebrow.

Alyson blushed. She knew exactly what he meant. Suddenly she felt very vulnerable in just the cotton robe, her body naked underneath.

As though he'd read her thoughts, Philippe stepped closer, gently brushing her damp hair back over her shoulders. 'I promised myself I wouldn't do this,' he murmured. 'That I would come up here only to talk to you . . .'

'Do what . . .?' Alyson stammered. She could hardly get the words out. Her throat felt thick suddenly, her heart hammering so loud she felt certain he could hear it.

'This.' Philippe bent down towards her, his mouth crushing down on hers. Alyson moaned and kissed him back, her legs feeling as though they might give way.

He kissed her harder, deeper, his tongue moving roughly round her mouth. Philippe's hands were roaming over her body, brushing against her breasts, sliding under her robe. She felt the warmth of his skin against the flat of her belly and pulled away nervously.

'I'm sorry,' she apologized helplessly. 'I just haven't . . .

I mean, I've never . . .' Alyson looked away in embarrassment.

Philippe's eyes never left her face. 'Do you want to?' he whispered.

Alyson hesitated. Her body was on fire, a burning point of heat between her legs. She longed to know what it felt like to be with a man, to have him inside of her. Philippe was just so special, so perfect. He'd made all her dreams come true. She stared at his face, at those intense dark eyes fringed by thick black lashes, at that sensual, cruel mouth and strong jaw line. There was no use denying it. She'd fallen for him, and fallen hard.

'Yes,' she murmured. 'I want to.'

'Alyson,' Philippe breathed in delight. He kissed her as gently as though she was made of porcelain, then tugged lightly at the cord of her robe and slipped it off her shoulders, letting it fall to the floor.

Alyson inhaled sharply as his lips softly touched the hollow at the base of her throat. Slowly he moved lower, working down to her breasts as he took the tiny, pale-pink nipples in his mouth and sucked. Alyson heard herself moan but didn't care, lost in the sensations. She shuddered as Philippe kissed her belly button, the sensitive skin on her stomach, before he knelt down in front of her and moved between her legs, letting his hands slide up her thighs, all the way to that perfectly trimmed blonde bush. It was so refreshing – all the girls he knew were waxed, following the fashionable trend of looking like porn stars. It reminded him of just how innocent Alyson was.

He was on his knees in front of her, eager to bury himself inside of her. Philippe parted her legs gently, lowering his head, his tongue caressing the most intimate parts of her. Above him he heard Alyson

171

moan, and he sighed in satisfaction, marvelling at how responsive she was. She tasted so delicious, so sweet. It gave him a sense of power, knowing that he was going where no man had been before. She was uncharted territory. None of the women he'd had over the years could give him this – this purity, this complete trust.

His tongue was relentless, taking her to the brink. He felt her clutch at his shoulders, his hair, but he didn't intend to stop. Then Alyson pulled away, her skin mottled, her eyes wide.

'No,' she whispered shyly. 'I want to see you.'

Philippe stood up, his arms flexing powerfully as he pulled his shirt over his head. His skin was tanned, the hair on his chest thick and dark. Alyson watched him as he undressed and stood naked before her, completely confident, completely at ease with himself. His cock was hard and straining. Alyson stared, unable to take her eyes away. He looked so big that she wondered how he would ever fit inside of her. Would she know what to do? Would she bleed? Philippe was obviously so experienced, he would think she was ridiculous.

Alyson tried to push the worries out of her mind. She was sick of being shy and timid. She approached Philippe slowly, running her hands over him experimentally. His body felt different from hers; it was harder, stronger. She let her fingers trail lightly through the thick hair on his chest, heading lower, over his stomach. Finally, with shaking hands, she moved downwards, lightly running her fingers up and down his cock, over his balls. She heard him groan, and wrapped her fingers around his shaft. He felt huge between her hands, long and thick.

'You can squeeze harder,' Philippe told her, taking

her hands and guiding her. 'Don't be afraid – you won't hurt me.'

Alyson followed his lead, her hands stroking up and down in a firm, steady rhythm. Philippe's eyes were closed, his breathing coming faster. Alyson watched him, fascinated, the thick shaft moving between her hands as she began to pump faster. Philippe threw back his head, an agonized expression on his face, and reached out to stop her.

'Did I do something wrong?' she asked, mortified.

Philippe smiled. 'No. You've done everything right. But I want to wait.'

He led Alyson over to the bed where she lay down, reclining against the pillows with her long, alabaster limbs outstretched. She looked like a pre-Raphaelite painting, thought Philippe, her skin creamy and sensual, long blonde hair spilling over the sheets.

For a moment he simply stared at her, taking in that delicious body. Then he climbed onto the bed, his powerful body towering above her. Alyson looked up at him, her eyes wide as she took in his broad chest so close to her, his body so dominating. She opened her legs a little, nervous but determined.

'Don't worry,' Philippe murmured, seeing her anxiety. 'I'll go slow and you'll be safe, I promise.'

Closing her eyes, Alyson sensed him above her, his hot body bearing down on her. She wrapped her arms around his back, her nails brushing his skin as she parted her legs and felt him pushing against her, gently but insistently. He thrust harder and she cried out, biting down on her lip.

Philippe stopped instantly. 'Are you okay?' he asked in concern.

'I'm fine,' Alyson reassured him. He bent down to kiss her, his hands sliding over her body. Lost in his embrace, Alyson felt him slide deeper inside her, filling her up, and then he began to move against her. She moved with him, unable to help herself, pushing her hips against him. Her body responded to his movements, every nerve ending tingling as the rhythm got faster. It began to hurt a little, but Alyson ignored the pain, pulling Philippe closer to her until his cries got louder and he called out her name, collapsing against her. He lay heavily on top of her, his breathing slowing, as she caressed his back and kissed his damp skin. She felt him go slack inside of her and pull out, rolling over to lie beside her.

'Are you okay?' he asked softly, brushing the stray wisps of hair away from her forehead.

'Never better,' Alyson smiled. It was the truth. She let her gaze slide over his handsome face, hardly able to believe how her life had changed in twenty-four hours – from a virginal young girl who'd never even been kissed, to a vibrant, sexual woman. Her boyfriend was the most handsome man she'd ever seen, and he'd just offered her an incredible new job. Life couldn't get any better.

'Will you stay with me?' Alyson asked quietly, snuggling against him. She didn't want him to go back to his own room. She wanted him there with her in the morning when she woke up.

'Of course I will.' Philippe kissed her tenderly, wrapping an arm around her and pulling her close. 'Now I've found you, I won't ever leave you.'

16

CeCe and Dionne were in Galeries Lafayette, the largest and most glamorous department store in Paris. It boasted ten floors across three different buildings, crammed with designer labels, fabulous clothes and sumptuous food. But the two women weren't there to shop.

CeCe had a meeting with Danièle Marceau, head buyer for womenswear. It was a prestigious appointment, and one she'd only got through her friend Sasha, a junior buyer who was well respected by her powerful boss.

CeCe was nervous as hell, knowing that a break like this could catapult her to the next level. If a store like Galeries Lafayette agreed to stock Capucine, the rewards would be insane. She would be a serious player with a foot on the ladder. It would be the start she'd been dreaming about for so long.

Nervously, she glanced up at the clock on the wall. They'd only been allocated ten minutes with Danièle. The appointment was for eleven a.m.; it was already eleven fifteen, and they hadn't even seen her yet. CeCe hoped Danièle wasn't on some kind of power trip, making them wait around to assert her own authority.

Dionne leaned across, placing a reassuring hand over CeCe's. 'Don't worry. You'll be amazing.'

'Thanks,' CeCe replied gratefully. Dionne was sitting beside her, looking stunning in one of CeCe's designs. It was the peacock dress, the one she'd created from the material Claude had given her. It was one of the most beautiful yet wearable designs in her collection, perfect for this showcase.

That was exactly the reason she had brought Dionne along to the meeting – partly to act as moral support, but also to showcase the clothes. She hoped that if Danièle Marceau could actually see the work that had gone into them, the craftsmanship and attention to detail, see how they flattered Dionne's shape, it would have far more of an impact than simply seeing the photos.

Not that François hadn't done a fabulous job, CeCe reflected as she picked up her white leather-bound lookbook. She flicked through slowly, unable to suppress a feeling of pride at just how fantastic the shots appeared. It looked like a high-fashion editorial. The dilapidated state of the house contrasted perfectly with the luxurious clothes, and Dionne looked stunning in every frame: regal on the staircase like an African queen, as the layers of fabric flowed around her; knowing and sexual as she draped herself over a wingback armchair. Her skin was sleek and supple, her body fierce, and her face killed it every time.

The door opened and CeCe quickly snapped the book shut, jumping to her feet as Danièle Marceau emerged from her office.

'Thank you so much for seeing me,' CeCe said, as they shook hands.

'Not at all.' Her tone was cool but professional, much like the woman herself. She was in her forties and impeccably dressed, wearing YSL wide-legged trousers in soft fawn, a cream silk pussy-bow blouse and mid-heeled court shoes. She was rail-thin, her brunette hair swept up, her face beautifully made-up in neutral shades.

CeCe had made even more of an effort with her own appearance than usual matching grey, slim-leg trousers with a pinstriped shirt and a military jacket. She wanted to look businesslike, but not lose her individuality.

'Please, come through to my office,' Danièle offered.

CeCe and Dionne followed her. The office was neat and classic, clutter-free, with an elegant wooden desk and pale walls that were broken up with the occasional framed photo of Danièle with Carla Bruni, Catherine Deneuve, Karl Lagerfeld. They were on the seventh floor, and the windows looked out over the Parisian rooftops towards the spectacular Opéra Garnier.

'Take a seat,' Danièle signalled. There was only one chair, and Dionne continued to stand, aware that she was there to show off the dress and not sit crumpled in the corner.

'Again, thank you so much for taking the time to see me,' CeCe began. Danièle didn't respond; she simply looked at her expectantly, so CeCe continued, 'I'd like to introduce my new label, Capucine.'

She handed Danièle her lookbook; Danièle began flicking through as CeCe carried on speaking. Her pitch had been written and redrafted to perfection – she was confident that she had it nailed.

'. . . I use high-quality fabrics to give a true feeling of luxury,' CeCe continued effortlessly, 'working primarily with silk, satin, crêpe de chine and chiffon. And I love to use embellishment – sequins or embroidery – to ensure that each piece has a unique, individual feel, and that the Capucine woman feels truly special, just as she deserves . . .'

Her delivery was clear and confident as she spoke about her vision for the Capucine woman, her inspiration and her hopes for the brand.

The speech came to a close as Danièle stayed silent, giving no indication of what she was thinking. Her attention remained on the book, the pages held lightly between her thumb and forefinger as though it was a dirty nappy giving off a bad stench.

'It's very . . . *bold*, isn't it?' From the way she said the word, CeCe knew that wasn't a good thing.

'Capucine is for the woman who likes to stand out,' CeCe recovered, remembering her spiel. 'She's a confident woman, from the boardroom to the bedroom. She's in control, and she knows what she wants out of life.'

'Indeed.' Danièle pursed her thin lips. 'Well, she will certainly stand out in these designs.' She snapped the book shut and looked directly at CeCe. 'Forgive me, Mademoiselle . . .' she checked her notes, '. . . Bouvier, but I am a very busy woman, and I hope you are not wasting my time.'

'No,' CeCe exclaimed in horror. 'Not at all.'

'Good. It's simply that all I see before me is a young – *very* young – woman, with some rather abstract ideas, a dress that she's run up in her bedroom and a handful of pretty pictures.'

'But . . .' CeCe floundered, 'this is just the beginning. Yes, the collection is small at the moment, but it will grow. And if Galeries Lafayette were to invest in me, then—'

'That will not be happening,' Danièle interjected. Her tone wasn't cruel, simply matter-of-fact. She scanned over CeCe's résumé. 'You didn't train, did you?'

'No, Madame, I am self-taught.'

'Nowadays, in ninety-nine per cent of cases, that is

simply not enough. You must learn not only about the design, but also about the business side, what tools you will need, how to present yourself. I am sorry, but I have seen young students, fresh out of university, with better pitches than this.

'Yes, you are talented,' she conceded grudgingly. 'There is the occasional glimpse of flair, and the clothes are well made. But this is simply not a serious proposal to me.'

CeCe swallowed, feeling ridiculous.

'If I placed an order today, how would you fulfil it, hmm? Do you have pattern cutters, seamstresses, manufacturers at your disposal?'

CeCe flushed. It was all the answer Danièle needed. For CeCe, the situation was Catch 22 – until she had a large, confirmed order of the type that Danièle might place, she couldn't engage a whole production line to develop a collection that might never be bought. She simply couldn't afford it.

'No, but I—'

'But what?' Danièle demanded.

CeCe didn't reply. There was nothing she could say.

Beside her, Dionne had seen enough. She could feel CeCe's humiliation burning from her and she was furious at Danièle's condescending attitude. More than anyone, Dionne understood what it felt like to be looked down on, to have your whole self-belief undermined.

'Do you know how goddamn hard she's worked on this?' Dionne burst out, unable to stay quiet any longer. 'You're shittin' yourself at the thought of taking a risk but, lady, you wouldn't know talent if it jumped up and bit you on the ass.'

A shocked silence descended on the room. Danièle didn't even acknowledge Dionne. She kept her gaze directed at CeCe, only the tightness of her expression betraying the fact that she'd taken in every word Dionne said. 'It's very sweet of your friend to defend you like this, but I'm afraid it only serves to make you seem even more . . . unprofessional,' she finished in ice-cold tones. 'Now, if you'll excuse me . . .'

She didn't need to say any more. The meeting was over. CeCe was mortified. She felt as if she'd blown her chance before she'd even started, her dreams burned to ashes. She'd be a laughing stock within the industry.

She picked up her lookbook from Danièle's desk. Her cheeks were flaming, and she was desperate to simply scuttle away. But she was determined to retain some dignity. She stood up and extended her hand. 'Thank you for taking the time to see me.'

For a moment, she thought Danièle was going to ignore her. Finally, she looked up and threw CeCe a tight smile before turning back to her PC, seemingly engrossed in whatever was on her screen.

CeCe let her hand drop, gathering up her bag and bolting out of the door. She and Dionne clattered along the corridor, racing out of the store as fast as they could. CeCe just wanted to be away, and Dionne was struggling to keep up in her towering five-inch heels.

Neither of them spoke until they hit the safety of a café a few streets away, sinking down at a table and ordering two coffees.

'What a bitch!' Dionne burst out. She was in full evening dress and people were staring at her. 'CeCe, honey, I'm so sorry I opened my big mouth, but I just couldn't let her speak to you like that. Man, she was so uptight it was like she had a stick up her ass.'

In spite of herself, CeCe smiled. 'It's okay. It was pretty clear the answer was no – I don't think you could have made it any worse. I just feel so embarrassed. What was I thinking?' she moaned, burying her head in her hands to hide her face as the memory of what had just happened came rushing back.

'Don't be stupid, you were amazing in there. That pitch was so confident, and so brave. Life's all about taking risks, right?'

'I made such a fool of myself. She's right – I'm just not at that level yet. I felt like a ten-year-old, going in there with the pictures I drew for homework.'

'CeCe, you are fabulous. It's just one "no" out of the many hundreds of "yes's" you're going to get. Trust me.'

The waiter brought over their coffees, and CeCe sipped hers thoughtfully.

'I got a letter this morning – I didn't tell you because I didn't want to think about it myself. I wanted to push it out of my mind until this meeting was over . . .'

'Yeah?' Dionne was looking at her in concern.

'My application to show at Fashion Week was turned down.'

'Aw, shit,' Dionne swore. She slumped back in her chair looking pissed off. 'Shit,' she repeated with feeling.

CeCe shrugged. 'Same story, I suppose. No one knows me, I'm not established enough, I haven't come out of an accredited school. I'm a risk, Dionne, and they can't afford to take that chance.'

'God, this business is so frustrating!' Dionne burst out.

But CeCe looked utterly beaten. 'I don't know what to do. My head is everywhere right now. Maybe I should give up. You know, if everyone says no, they're saying it for a reason.'

'CeCe, you can't—'

'I mean, it's good to be ambitious,' CeCe carried on as though Dionne hadn't spoken. 'But there comes a point when you have to be realistic. Understand what is ambition, and what is self-delusion. Accept that if everybody says no, then perhaps they are right.'

'*No!*' Dionne's tone was fierce. She hated seeing her friend like this, so cowed and dejected. '*I* am saying yes, and I say you have to believe in yourself. Look at this dress,' she demanded, grabbing handfuls of the material she was wearing. 'It's stunning. Absolutely incredible. Everyone in here is staring at it. *You* created it, CeCe. Only you could have done it.'

CeCe smiled weakly. She appreciated Dionne's efforts, but it was going to take more than a pep talk to get her enthusiasm burning again. She could feel herself sinking into depression, a debilitating lethargy descending on her like a dark cloud that she remembered so well from her teenage years. It seemed easier to simply surrender to it. The meeting with Danièle had been her last chance and all CeCe could do now was give in to the horrible, soul-destroying sensations of hopelessness and helplessness that threatened to overwhelm her. It was like hurtling at full speed into a dark tunnel, the light rapidly growing further and further away until it was almost impossible to find your way back.

'Look at me,' Dionne continued anxiously, seeing the defeated expression on CeCe's face. 'I've been schlepping around Paris for two years now, fighting like crazy to get my modelling career off the ground. I've had more doors slammed in my face than you've had glasses of champagne – and we both know that's a lot,' she grinned, trying to lighten the mood. 'And suddenly – bang – it starts happening. The work's piling in. Did I tell you I've been booked for a shoot in Argentina next week? They're flying me out there, putting me up in an amazing hotel, paying for everything. I'm planning to bag an upgrade,' she smirked.

'That's great. Congratulations.' CeCe's voice was flat.

'Aw, shit, I wasn't showing off, hon.' Dionne suddenly realized how she must have sounded. 'I was just trying to say, these things turn around, y'know?'

CeCe drained her coffee. 'Maybe we should get going.'

'Look,' Dionne began desperately, racking her brains as she sensed CeCe withdrawing from the conversation. 'You want your designs to be seen, right? By everyone in the industry, the whole fucking world media, and to get maximum publicity?'

'Yes, of course. That would be incredible. But it's not that easy . . .'

Dionne simply grinned, a wolfish smile that implied she knew something CeCe didn't. 'Trust me. I have an idea.'

Aidan had just opened up at Chez Paddy when Alyson walked through the door. As soon as he saw her, he knew; knew that arrogant French arsehole had had his slimy hands all over her. She was positively glowing, her skin radiant, her eyes alive and vital. There was a self-confidence there that hadn't existed previously, as though she'd grown up over the course of the weekend. She looked ten times more beautiful, and ten times more unobtainable. Aidan knew immediately that he'd lost her.

'Hi,' she said nervously, looking up at him with those luminous blue eyes.

They stood in awkward silence.

'Aidan,' Alyson began, as she stepped towards him. 'I'm so sorry about this weekend. I really am.' She wondered what had happened to her; she felt as if she'd lost her mind. She would never normally be so unreliable, but being away from Paris and with Philippe had made her lose all sense of responsibility.

Aidan shrugged, feeling like a petulant child. 'Where were you?' he demanded.

Alyson wondered what Philippe had told him. She hadn't even asked. 'I—'

'You know I could fire you for this?' Aidan cut her off.

Alyson flinched at his harshness. She'd never seen this side to him, hurt and lashing out. 'Aidan,' she began gently, 'there's something I need to talk to you about.'

'Go ahead.' His hands were on the bar, gripping it tightly. It was like a physical barrier between them.

This wasn't how Alyson had imagined the conversation. She'd pictured them sitting down together, sharing a drink as they had done so many times at the end of a long shift. But it was too late to stop now.

'I've been offered a job,' she began. 'Working for a big company. It's exactly what I wanted—'

'Is that why you've been sneaking off? To go for interviews? Alyson, I'd have given you the time off if you'd asked. I know this place isn't permanent for you, and I want to see you do well—'

'I haven't been going for interviews,' Alyson interrupted him. 'I didn't . . . It's for Rochefort Champagne.'

She let the words sink in, watching Aidan's face as he put two and two together. Philippe Rochefort. Rochefort Champagne. She didn't think she'd ever felt more ashamed, knowing exactly how it must look.

'Oh, right. It was *that* kind of interview.' Aidan's features took on a hardness as Alyson bowed her head, cheeks flaming. 'Well, I guess you passed with flying colours.'

'Aidan—'

'You know, I always thought you were the kind of girl who wanted to get by on your own merit – not on your own back.'

Alyson gasped in shock. The words were like a slap in the face.

'I thought you had more self-respect,' he continued relentlessly. 'But look at you. You've turned into some walking cliché – your dad walked out so you're throwing yourself at the first man who comes along, looking for a father figure to replace him.'

Alyson winced in pain, stunned by how cruel Aidan was being. She had expected him to be mad, but not like this. She'd trusted him, confided in him about her family, and he'd thrown it back in her face. 'I thought you were my friend,' she burst out. 'I thought you'd be happy for me.'

'I can't be happy about this. I think you're making the worst decision of your life.'

'Do you?' Alyson said uncertainly, wondering why Aidan was so against it. Was she really making such a terrible choice? Everything had happened so fast, she'd had no time to think it through. And now that she was back in Chez Paddy, away from Philippe's arms and the heady glamour of Château de Marne, maybe her decision had been a little hasty . . .

She mustered her dignity, determined to put the doubts out of her mind. This was everything she wanted, her opportunity to make a better life for herself, and she wasn't about to let Aidan's bitterness put her off. 'How long's my notice period?' she asked coldly.

Aidan looked back at her, his blue eyes steely. 'You know what? Just forget it. You can leave now. You've already let me down twice this week. Brianna covered

185

for you and she's looking for extra shifts – I'll give her yours.'

'Okay . . .' Alyson suddenly felt close to tears. He'd called her bluff, but she didn't want to leave it like this. 'Aidan, please . . . Look, thanks for everything.' She swallowed hard, trying to keep her composure. 'I'd really love it if we could stay friends . . .'

Aidan laughed harshly. *Friends.* That's all they'd ever been. He'd been kidding himself if he thought there was anything more. 'Enjoy your new life, Alyson. I hope it brings you everything you want.'

Alyson stood helplessly, looking at the stranger in front of her. She simply didn't recognize the look on Aidan's face.

She opened her mouth to speak, but realized there was nothing more to be said. Turning on her heel, she walked out of the door without looking back.

PART TWO

17

Paris, France
Three months later

CeCe's life had done a complete one-eighty in a matter of weeks. Gone were the late-night parties and the debilitating hangovers. In their place were crack-of-dawn alarm calls and nothing stronger than freshly ground espresso. She was up with the sunrise, working until her fingers bled, putting together her new designs. Inspiration was coming so thick and fast that she barely had enough time to note down one idea before her brain moved furiously onto the next. Her days were one crazy, exhausting whirl of sketching, designing and creating.

She was throwing everything she had – physically, mentally and financially – into this reckless idea of Dionne's. But it would work. It *had* to work. CeCe was through with wasting time sucking up to people in the hope that they would take an interest in her clothes, dragging herself from one independent boutique to the next, practically begging the owners to take her stuff on a sale or return basis. She wanted something bigger, and this time she was going all out. If Dionne's plan worked, it would put Capucine on the fashion map instantly – bang, explosion, overnight sensation. If it didn't . . . well, that didn't bear thinking about.

She would be broke, certainly. Did she even have any other options? She would rather get kicked out onto the streets than go crawling back to her parents and admit they were right. She could always try and get a job as a fashion reporter, or start her own blog, but really, that would break her heart. The idea of spending her days commenting on other people's successes, writing about other designers' collections, when she knew instinctively that she could do so much better . . . The thought made her feel sick to her stomach.

CeCe had left Rivoli Couture a few weeks ago. She and Dionne had resigned on the same day, leaving Khalid apoplectic with rage and demanding to know where he was going to find two more staff members at such short notice. CeCe didn't care. He'd be fine, and he wasn't her concern.

Since then it had been difficult financially. No, more than difficult. CeCe had sacrificed everything. The meagre savings she had in her account had gone towards the rent, and she was living on boiled rice and tinned chickpeas, whatever was cheap, to try and eke out the little money she had left. From time to time, when things were getting desperate, she helped out her old friends in the clubs – hostessing, or working the door. She'd had her half-head of hair chopped into a chin-length bob, and some of the people she used to hang out with didn't even recognize her. As the girl checking their coat, she didn't merit a second glance. It hurt, but CeCe was too wrapped up in her designs to care. She was about to take the biggest gamble of her life, and if it paid off it would all be worth it.

Dionne had been amazing, CeCe reflected. Her career

had suddenly taken off and she was being flown all over the world, booked for shoots and winning contracts right, left and centre. Currently, she was plastered over the buses and billboards of Paris as the face of skincare brand Diadermine. It made CeCe smile every time she saw it, proud of how well Dionne was doing. She looked more beautiful than ever, and if anyone deserved it, Dionne did.

She'd helped CeCe out as much as she could, covering the rent one time and stocking up the cupboards when she was home. CeCe had told her not to, insisting that this was something she needed to do on her own.

'Uh uh, we're a team, boo.' Dionne was adamant. 'I'm doing this because I believe in you. When Fashion Week's over, you're gonna be the hottest name on everybody's lips, and that's when you can pay me back with a nice, fat contract . . .'

CeCe heard a noise in the kitchen and looked up, startled, from where she was stitching beads onto a red tulle dress. There were hundreds of them, and she was planning to hand-sew every single one. She glanced up at the clock. Seven-thirty a.m. Alyson would be leaving for work. She was another one who was always busy these days; she had a new job, and a boyfriend, if you could believe that. She'd never brought him back to the flat, and he'd been the subject of much speculation amongst CeCe and Dionne. He was bound to be a geek, they decided: shy and awkward.

'Alyson, is that you?' CeCe shouted.

Alyson wandered through, spooning honey-drizzled porridge into her mouth. 'Yeah. Are you okay, CeCe? You look shattered.'

CeCe paused, wondering when she'd last looked in a mirror. She rubbed a hand tiredly across her eyes, and noticed that her face felt greasy. 'Yeah . . . I haven't been to bed yet. I didn't realize the time. I will do just a little more, then have a short nap.'

Alyson frowned. 'Make sure you take care of yourself, okay? Can I get you anything before I go? Toast? Coffee?'

'I'm fine, thank you. Have a good day, Alyson.'

'I will.'

The door banged shut, and CeCe was alone once more. She took a deep, revitalizing breath, blinking rapidly to try and keep herself awake. Alyson was a sweet girl, CeCe had decided. She was simply more reserved than her and Dionne; she had different interests, different priorities to the two of them. But she was changing. She had this brand-new job she was so excited about, and she left the apartment every day in a suit and heels. She was actually taking time over her appearance, getting up early to blow-dry her hair and apply a little make-up.

CeCe let out a yawn, and stretched her arms to the ceiling, feeling the temporary relief in her shoulder blades as her muscles relaxed. What with Alyson's new job and Dionne's whirlwind career, it felt as though everyone's lives were changing.

CeCe just hoped hers was too.

Walking through the gleaming wood and brass doors into the foyer of Rochefort Champagne, Alyson still felt that same rush of excitement she'd experienced every day since she started. She could hardly believe that she, Alyson Wakefield from a small town in Lancashire, was actually working for this prestigious multinational company. She practically had to pinch herself every time she stepped into the magnificent old building near Montparnasse.

'Bonjour, Franck,' she greeted the security man on the door.

'Bonjour, Mademoiselle Alyson,' he replied, with a deferential nod.

Alyson headed for the stairs – she worked on the second floor so there was no need to take the lift, and besides, she loved walking up the old-fashioned sweeping staircase and hearing her kitten heels clack on the marble floor.

It was eight a.m., and only a handful of people were in the office already. Alyson didn't officially start until nine, but she loved to be in early to gear up for the day ahead. There was always something to learn, always something new to discover.

'Bonjour, Matthieu,' she called to one of her colleagues as she switched on her PC. He gave a little wave in reply.

Alyson was well liked amongst the other staff. She worked hard and did everything that was asked of her, taking the initiative to troubleshoot problems before they got out of control. The advantage of being the office dogsbody was that it gave you the opportunity to help out everyone – you could soon ingratiate yourself by doing the tedious, boring jobs that no one else wanted to do, whether it was mountains of filing or the afternoon coffee run.

There was also a tiny part of her that felt as if she had to prove herself. She had no idea whether or not the others knew about her relationship with Philippe. She suspected they did. The managing director, Richard Duval, was certainly aware, and information like this had a habit of being filtered down via the gossip network.

It didn't bother Alyson unnecessarily. She felt confident that her standard of work would speak for itself, without needing to make reference to who she was dating. Besides, Philippe was rarely in the office.

193

Alyson had discovered that he had a number of other business interests – mainly bars and clubs – and Rochefort Champagne was only one of them. In fact, he'd confessed to owning a slew of unsavoury sounding properties, including a chain of strip joints. *High class*, he'd assured her.

Alyson had snorted in derision. *If you were naked, you were naked*, she thought sourly. *It didn't matter how much men were paying to see it.*

She'd been furious when she'd found out – in fact, they'd had their first and only row on the subject. Okay, so he hadn't exactly lied, but surely keeping it from her deliberately was just as bad? Philippe had insisted that the clubs were an old part of his portfolio, that he planned to sell them as soon as the market came right. Alyson wanted to believe him. After all, she had her own secrets. The things she'd told Aidan – about her mother's illness, her father walking out – there still didn't seem to be a right time to tell Philippe.

He was a busy guy, obviously. He had the American expansion to oversee, and Alyson was slowly coming to realize just how important he was. She'd read a profile of him in *Les Échos*, the financial daily, and he'd been named as one of France's most eligible bachelors in *Point de Vue*. A quick Google search brought up thousands of entries – and not all work related. He'd had a pretty prolific dating life before meeting Alyson.

One evening he'd taken her to a benefit gala, a black-tie event at the Palais Garnier, and she'd been shocked to find that the photographers outside wanted pictures of the pair of them. They'd posed together on the red carpet; Alyson had been mortified. Yes, Philippe was obviously very powerful, very well connected, and extremely good at what he did.

And he adored her.

He'd already asked her to move in with him, and she was sorely tempted. His apartment in Faubourg Saint-Germain was stunning, and she spent a lot of time there after work. Dionne was rarely in their shared apartment these days, but CeCe was working like a demon on some new project and the flat was constantly overrun with her designs; dresses draped everywhere that she got mad if you even touched. It was impossible to relax there, and Philippe's place had become a sanctuary, a refuge from the rest of the world. Even if he was working late, Alyson would stay over, curled up in his study reading, or watching old French films in the screening room. But she'd declined his offer to make it permanent. It was too soon, and Alyson wanted to retain some of her independence.

Her heart still raced when she saw Philippe, but more than anything she admired his confidence, his charisma. She loved being around him, loved watching the stylish way he lived his life. She'd learned so much from him over the past few months. He'd taught her about business, about people, about sex . . . Their relationship was almost one of mentor and student, as she soaked up everything he had to offer. Uncomfortably, Alyson recalled what Aidan had said about Philippe being a father figure. But that wasn't true, was it?

No, she thought firmly, pushing the doubts to the back of her mind. If their sex life was anything to go by, his relationship with her definitely wasn't paternal. It made her blush to even think of it. The things they did together . . . The way he touched her . . . Alyson bit her lip, trying to stop herself from smiling. She felt sure that everyone in the office must be able to tell what she was thinking, to see the way she was squirming in her seat at just the thought of him.

She was glad she'd waited to have sex – that she

hadn't just given it up to some guy during a quick fumble in the back of a car, or in a stranger's bedroom at a party, the way most of her classmates at school had done. And she was proud that she didn't sleep around with any man that crossed her path, like Dionne. Alyson had bided her time waiting for someone special, someone who knew how to treat her, and it had been the right decision. She loved the closeness and the affection of making love, the way she would curl up on Philippe's warm chest afterwards and listen to his heartbeat, while he held her close and stroked her hair. He would cover her with kisses, whispering in her ear as he told her how beautiful she was, how perfect . . .

Focus! she reprimanded herself, as her inbox popped up and she began to scroll through her emails. She needed to concentrate – she couldn't spend all day dreaming like some love-struck schoolgirl. Other than Philippe, her job was the most important thing in her life right now, the one area where she knew she had the potential to really make a difference.

When she'd started, she'd known nothing about the business, but she was learning quickly – where the main markets were, who were the key players and rivals. Every day there was something new to learn, a fresh challenge that she had to overcome. Since starting work three months ago, Alyson lived and breathed Rochefort Champagne. Richard hadn't tried to box her into any one area; instead, he'd let her find her own way, developing her strengths and focusing on the areas that really interested her. Alyson could feel that she was growing in confidence, trusting her instincts and not being afraid to speak up. She believed that the points she made were valid, that she wouldn't simply be laughed at and dismissed.

'Good morning, Alyson. How are you today?' Richard Duval had left his private office and passed by her desk, stopping briefly to speak with her as he did most mornings. He was a short, grey-haired man in his early sixties, balding and a little paunchy, the executive lifestyle finally catching up with him.

'Good morning, Monsieur Duval. I'm very well, thank you. And yourself?'

'Excellent, yes. Listen, I'd like you to come and take minutes at the senior management meeting today. It'll be held in the boardroom at ten. Are you free? No other projects on the go?'

'No, that's fine. No problem,' Alyson assured him.

'Very good.' He turned to go, and then thought better of it. 'You really are doing an excellent job, Alyson. I'm very pleased with your progress.'

'Thank you, sir.' As he walked away, Alyson found that she was beaming with delight.

A few hours later, and Alyson had stopped smiling.

The meeting had droned on into the early afternoon and everyone was flagging. Alyson was doing her best not to stare out of the window. She'd practically given up taking minutes; it felt as if everyone was repeating the same points over and over.

'. . . if we can incentivize the consumer in some way . . .'

'. . . yes, but with these revenue constraints . . .'

'. . . need to manage the expectations of our client base . . .'

As far as Alyson could see, it was less of a meeting and more an exercise in self-aggrandizement by a group of people who loved the sound of their own voices.

Her immediate manager was one of the worst – Bernadette Sauvage, a dragon-faced woman who seemed to have taken a strong dislike to Alyson and never said anything positive to her.

They were discussing the new marketing strategy, and reviewing the effectiveness of their six-month plan. Sales had been down recently, and most of the middle-aged men and women around the table were convinced that youth was the answer. Like every other brand, they were obsessed with seeming young and hip, and capturing the lucrative under-thirty market.

To Alyson, the solution seemed perfectly obvious. She knew from her research that Rochefort Champagne was a classic, well-respected brand, known for its sophistication and elegance. They needed to rediscover that image, to make it the luxury brand of choice for the connoisseur, not an expensive fizzy drink to be thrown down the necks of rap artists, or the likes of Dionne and CeCe on a night out; those who were more concerned with style over substance.

'. . . and as our sales remain static in the over-fifties sector—'

'Actually they're not.'

A dozen pairs of eyes swivelled to look at Alyson. Shit, had she really just spoken out loud? Yes, she had, and she'd just contradicted her boss.

Bernadette Sauvage was looking at her like she wanted to insert her Mont Blanc roller-ball pen somewhere rather unpleasant.

'What did you say?' she demanded, her face turning puce.

'Nothing.' Alyson looked mortified. 'Sorry, forget I spoke.'

Richard Duval, seated at the head of the table, smiled at her kindly. 'No, Alyson. What did you want to say?'

Alyson hesitated for a second, wondering what to do for the best. But she'd already opened her mouth.

She took a deep breath, deciding to go for it. 'The sales figures might be the same for the over-fifties, but that's not in real terms. There's an ageing population, so if the figures remain static, in actual fact our market share is declining.'

A deafening silence greeted her statement. Everyone was staring at her, a mixture of bemusement and outright hostility on their faces. Alyson caught the eye of Richard Duval. He nodded encouragingly. The sight gave her confidence to carry on speaking.

'In fact, I don't believe the strategy *should* be to focus on the younger market – it's what everyone does and there's already too much competition in that sector. We're not Cristal or Moët. We don't want Scarlett Johansson advertising our product. I believe that would be doing a real disservice to Rochefort Champagne's heritage.'

Alyson cleared her throat. 'The age group with the most disposable income is the over-fifties – once their children have left home they are time and cash rich. We should focus on this core client base, with a new campaign emphasizing the quality and tradition of our product. Above all, Rochefort Champagne should be very luxurious, very classic and very French.'

No one spoke. Alyson sat back in her chair, feeling her cheeks flush bright red. She wondered if she was about to get sacked.

'Thank you, Alyson,' Duval said finally. He was scribbling notes on the pad in front of him. 'Very interesting. Now, the next item on the agenda . . .'

18

Dionne lay back on the pristine white beach, digging her heels into the sand as she extended one leg and arched her back. Above her the sky was a dazzling azure blue, cloudless and perfect, the scorching sun beating down on her body. A few metres away she could hear the gentle lap of waves as the crystal-clear waters of the Indian Ocean kissed the shoreline. It was like heaven.

Distantly, Dionne registered the click of a camera. She moved again, elongating her neck as she clawed at the sand. This time, she looked right down the lens of the camera.

'Beautiful, Dionne. *Bellissima!*'

She was the new face of Etam Swimwear, and this was her first shoot for them. They had flown out to Bali and Dionne felt like the luckiest girl alive. The weather was perfect, the five-star hotel was stunning, and – the best part – she had a whole crew dedicated to her every need. Hair, make-up, stylist, photographer, a runner to get her a cold drink when she needed to cool down, or a slice of fruit if she felt hungry. The whole thing revolved around Dionne, and she revelled in it.

Right now she was wearing a fuchsia-pink bandeau bikini with a cute little ruffle around the top. The colour combination looked incredible – white sand, blue sky and the hot-pink bikini against her black skin, which she knew would just pop on camera. Her hair was long and wavy, sprayed liberally with Bumble and bumble surf spray to give it that perfect sun-kissed look.

'Yes, Dionne, you are like a tiger! A gorgeous, sensual animal! And again . . .'

Dionne played up to the camera, pouting and fixing the lens with a provocative stare. She twisted her body a little – tiny movements, ensuring every shot gave something different. She knew just how to angle her arm so it looked slim and taut, how to stretch out her legs to make them toned and long.

Marco, the photographer, was hilarious. An arrogant, womanizing Italian, he knew how to get the best out of the women he worked with. Playful teasing kept the shoot light, while an endless stream of compliments made the girls feel sexy.

Now he was up close to Dionne, kneeling in the sand beside her as he continued to shoot. He was gorgeous, with olive skin and dark hair pulled back in a ponytail. Okay, so his nose was a little on the large sign, but in Dionne's book that was a good sign.

'Make looove to the camera, Dionne,' he instructed in that flowing Italian accent.

Their bodies were so close they were almost touching, the whisper of skin on skin. Dionne was starting to feel horny as she rolled around in the sand, her breasts crushed beneath her, her face smouldering as she stared straight down the lens.

'Okay, we've got it,' Marco announced as he stood up and winked at Dionne. She smiled back, her eyes full of promise as he reached out a hand to help her up. She took it gratefully, throwing her arms around him and pressing her body against his.

'Thanks, Marco, that was awesome,' she purred.

'And you were divine, darling . . .'

They held the embrace for just a little too long, Marco's hands roaming over the bare skin of Dionne's lower back before his assistant ran over to take the camera from him and they broke apart.

Dionne grinned to herself as she walked off across the beach. They would probably sleep together later – *definitely*, if Dionne had her way. Okay, so he was a total player and unbelievably arrogant. But hey, he was hot, with a great reputation in the sack, and neither of them was looking for a relationship.

It was the transitory nature of the lifestyle, and it suited Dionne perfectly. There you were, trapped in paradise with a small team of beautiful, narcissistic people, all working closely together . . . it was like a pressure cooker waiting to explode. Casual sex was everywhere and no-strings hook-ups were inevitable. Photographers and models was the obvious stereotype – but stereotypes existed for a reason, Dionne had realized.

Besides, she was hardly ever home these days. Her career had taken off and she spent her days crossing the oceans, flying from one continent to the next. She was still seeing David off and on, but hell, a girl had needs, and Skype sex could only get you so far.

The past few weeks had been even more manic due to the shows: New York and then London. It had been Dionne's first time in the UK capital and she'd loved it. Of course the weather was awful, but the vibe was so fashionable and the nightlife was awesome. She wished she'd had more time to soak up the city, but her schedule had been intense, a never-ending merry-go-round of fittings, castings, walking. No sleeping, no eating.

Next was Milan, but Dionne had blown it off in order to do this photo shoot. Everyone knew the Italians never took black girls anyway. Being out in Bali was a much better proposition, and gave her time for a little R&R. She'd be back in Paris soon enough. CeCe was working like a demon in preparation for Fashion Week, and Dionne had promised to give her all the help she could.

But for now she was here, beneath the blazing sun and the sweeping palm trees. She strutted across the beach, making sure that everyone got an eyeful of her high, round booty. She knew Marco would be watching, as well as the holiday-makers who couldn't take their eyes off her. The Sands was a high-end, luxury resort, and she'd noticed some hot, loaded guys hanging around. Maybe Marco might have some competition after all . . .

Dionne flopped down in a director's chair beneath a large parasol. A young guy handed her a bottle of iced water, and she took a sip. Then she relaxed back into her chair as the hair and make-up team got to work, ready to transform her look for the next outfit. Jeanne, the hair stylist, began adding a cute little braid to her tangled locks.

Dionne picked up a copy of *Paris Match* magazine that was lying around, gratified to find her own face staring back at her from the inside cover. It was her Diadermine commercial. She was practically unrecognizable from her current beach-goddess look with her hair scraped back, skin supposedly free of make-up, healthy and glowing. Any pores or flaws had been airbrushed away, and her eyes were brown and liquid, her lips enormous. She stared at herself for a moment, then turned the page, coming to rest on *la vie parisienne* – the weekly column of who had been spotted out and about in Paris that week.

Skimming over the pictures of celebrities and society names, Dionne saw something that nearly made her fall off her seat.

'Holy shit!' she swore, as Jeanne looked over in concern.

'Are you okay?' she asked. But Dionne didn't answer. She was staring intently at the page, wondering if she'd made a mistake. But no. There was definitely no mistake.

Dionne hesitated for just a second, then picked up her phone to call CeCe.

Philippe lay in his king-size bed with Alyson, their bodies twined together in post-coital bliss. The Egyptian cotton sheets were dishevelled, their skin lightly matted with sweat.

Philippe was propped up on the pillows, his arms spread wide as Alyson curled up to him, her head resting against his chest as he breathed in the fresh, clean scent of her hair. He leaned down to kiss the top of her head and she stirred, moving against him. He loved the way she was so responsive, so utterly adoring. It made him feel like a god.

Philippe gazed in satisfaction around his bedroom – at the soft lighting, the top-of-the-range technology, the smattering of antiques that the interior designer had sourced. He had what he considered to be one of the best apartments money could buy, and a stunning girl in his arms who was willing to do anything to please him. Yes, life was working out pretty well for Philippe Rochefort.

'I spoke to Richard Duval earlier,' he commented casually.

'Oh really?' Philippe felt Alyson's body tense beside him, and he smiled in amusement. He knew she'd be worried about what Richard had said.

'Yes.' Philippe waited a beat before putting her out of her misery. 'He's very impressed with you. He thinks you're doing an excellent job.'

'Oh,' Alyson sighed in relief. 'I was worried . . . I might have spoken out of line,' she finished, not wanting to go into details.

'Not at all. He's very pleased with how you're doing. In fact, it's been suggested that you accompany the management team to Zurich next week, to present to the money men. The board are getting a little anxious about the direction the company is taking, and we need to explain our strategy, calm any nerves. Richard tells me he thinks it would be an excellent experience for you to attend.'

'Really?' Alyson turned over, sitting up and looking straight at Philippe to see if he was joking. 'He wants me to be part of that?'

'Exactly. I don't know the details of what Richard expects, how much of a role you will play . . .'

'That's incredible!' Alyson couldn't keep the smile from her face. 'Thank you so much, Philippe.'

He shrugged dismissively. 'Not at all. It was all down to you.'

'But you gave me the break,' Alyson insisted. 'You believed in me enough to give me that opportunity, and now . . .' She broke off, her eyes shining.

Philippe smiled indulgently as Alyson leaned over to kiss him. He drew her closer, feeling those small, sharp nipples press against him. She parted her legs willingly, and Philippe's erection stirred. But no, he

205

wanted to keep control of himself. Pulling away, he glanced at his watch. Eight p.m.

'How about we go out for dinner, hmm?' he suggested. 'To celebrate.'

'Okay,' she agreed easily. 'I'll go and grab a shower.' She kissed him once more, then climbed out of bed.

Philippe watched in appreciation as she walked away. Those long, toned legs that went on forever, right up to that tight bottom. Her precision-cut blonde hair shimmered down her back, stopping just below her shoulder blades. Before she'd started work with Rochefort Champagne, Philippe had taken her to a discreet, exclusive salon where they'd taught her the basics – good haircut, a few subtle highlights, leg wax and a mani-pedi. She was quick to learn, eager to appear groomed and professional.

Shopping had been the next thing. They'd hit the Avenue Montaigne for work clothes, and a handful of evening dresses that she'd left at Philippe's apartment.

He got out of bed and headed to the closet. For himself, he selected an Yves St Laurent suit in dark grey, with a bespoke Charvet shirt. Next, he moved to the end of the rail, to the few dresses that belonged to Alyson. Philippe always liked her to look sophisticated; nothing too slutty or obvious. He picked out a rather plain, black silk Lanvin dress and hung it on the front of the wardrobe, pleased with his choice. She would wear that tonight.

It was essential that she looked good at all times, and didn't do anything to embarrass him. She didn't know it yet, but Alyson was auditioning for the role of Madame Philippe Rochefort, and so far she was giving a stellar performance. He wasn't getting any younger, Philippe reflected, and he needed someone like her. Alyson was gorgeous – cool and elegant, like a Hitchcock blonde – and she was pliable too. In her eyes, Philippe could do no wrong.

Of course, he'd had to tell her about the other side to his business. The nightclubs and the strip joints – gentleman's clubs, as he preferred to think of them. He'd kept it from her as long as was feasible. She was his little innocent and he wanted to protect her, didn't want her to know that seedy world existed, or that he was such an integral part of it.

Alyson had been mad as hell when she'd first found out, but Philippe had soon won her round. Unlike most women, Alyson wasn't particularly materialistic. If he'd offered her expensive presents, she'd have taken it as an insult. No, he'd had to play it smarter than that. A little grovelling, a few apologies delivered with a sad face and puppy-dog eyes, the reassurance he really was a man of high morals and would get shot of them as soon as he could – she was soon eating out of his hand again.

He'd managed to lure her away from that grotty little pub, and once she moved in with him his mastery over her really would be complete. Of course, she spent most of her time at his apartment, but she still insisted on keeping her rental place. A hankering for independence, or some such bullshit.

Which reminded him, he really had to speak to Richard Duval about her. Sure, working at Rochefort Champagne was a nice diversion for her, a pleasant way for her to pass the time somewhere he could keep an eye on her. But it couldn't be for ever. He needed to keep her expectations realistic – that way, she wouldn't be too disappointed when being a wife and mother to the Rochefort heir became her new vocation.

Yes, he would call Richard very soon. It was sweet of him to encourage her, but Philippe didn't want it to get out of hand. There was no way he could allow Alyson to get too serious about her work. That simply wasn't the plan.

Alyson was soaping her body in Philippe's spectacular shower. Made from Carrara marble, the walk-in wet room was easily large enough for two people and boasted a carved seat running the length of the wall. Water fell like rain from a huge circular panel in the ceiling, while tiny jets spurted out from the walls. Alyson turned slowly through three hundred and sixty degrees, feeling the water gently massaging her whole body. It was pure luxury.

As she washed, her mind turned to Zurich, excitement coursing through her at the very thought of it. She was really doing this! Climbing the corporate ladder, making a name for herself. And Philippe was behind it all, driving her on, forcing her to believe in herself and do better. There'd been nothing but good ever since he came into her life. Every time she was around him, another dream came true.

Of course, it was a little odd working for Philippe's company. Maybe in the future she would work elsewhere, gain experience with Rochefort Champagne and move on. But for now she owed Philippe everything. She was well aware of that.

She'd come so far since working at Chez Paddy. Everything had happened so fast, and her stint at the pub seemed like a lifetime ago. She'd always meant to go back when a little time had passed, to see Aidan and make things right between them. Maybe even take him out for dinner now that she was earning a decent salary, to pay him back for their evening in Montmartre. But life these days was a whirlwind, and somehow Alyson just hadn't found the time.

She turned off the shower and stepped out, wrapping herself in a thick white towel. She caught sight of herself in the mirror, kept clear due to the anti-fog system, and briefly studied her reflection. Her face was bare of make-up, her cheeks lightly flushed from the steam. She looked young, fresh and beautiful.

She padded through to Philippe's bedroom, where he looked up from checking his phone. 'I thought you could wear this,' he said, indicating the dress hanging from the wardrobe.

'Sure,' Alyson agreed, happy to defer to Philippe in these matters. She had little interest in fashion, and even less awareness of what looks suited her body shape. She wanted to look good for him, but that was the extent of her involvement. Besides, he was a worldly, cultured man, and she trusted his judgement implicitly.

She slipped into the exquisitely lined dress, the material sliding over her body like water, and turned around, allowing Philippe to zip her up. He took his time, drawing it out, planting little kisses on the flawless skin of her back as he went. Alyson shuddered. Even the lightest touch of his fingers on her body made her skin tingle.

As Philippe headed for the shower, Alyson sat down at the low desk she'd commandeered as a vanity table, quickly blow-drying her hair, then applying a little make-up. If it had been up to her, she would have gone *au naturel*, but Philippe had insisted on buying her the quality basics – Chanel foundation and blush, Lancôme mascara, a choice of lipsticks in subtle colours. She spritzed herself with the Coco Mademoiselle he'd bought her, and added discreet diamond earrings – a present for their three-month anniversary.

She turned as Philippe strode into the room, a towel

wrapped around his waist. His hair was wet and dripping, his naked stomach tanned and taut, the dark hair
on his chest matted with water.

Alyson stood up, presenting herself to him. 'How
do I look?' she asked shyly.

She watched as Philippe's practised gaze ran over
her, his eyes moving from the smooth, shiny curtain
of hair, all the way down her body to her Carven court
shoes. They were black, mid-height – Philippe didn't
like her in anything too suggestive.

His face creased into an expression of approval. She
was sophisticated, elegant and beautiful – everything
the future Madame Rochefort should be.

'Perfect,' he replied, breaking into a wide smile. 'Just
perfect.'

19

'Do you really think it's her?'

'Just look at her! She's the total spit of Alyson.'

'But why the hell would she be with Philippe Rochefort?'

Dionne shook her head at CeCe's question. 'Damned if I know. I mean, in what universe does that timid, mousy little British girl run into someone like Philippe Rochefort? She's hardly gonna be getting her groove on at Bijou, is she? It totally blows my mind to even think about it.'

Dionne and CeCe stared at the photo once more. A well-thumbed copy of *Paris Match* was open on the kitchen counter in front of them. It was the only surface in the flat that wasn't covered in fabric or sketches or any of CeCe's other paraphernalia.

'And you really think it's her?' CeCe mused.

'Of *course* it is. If not, then she's got some doppelgänger walking round the city.'

'So you think it was a one-off, or are they dating?'

'They couldn't be dating,' Dionne scoffed. 'He wants someone with money and class, remember? And she ain't from no high-society background.'

'Fucking, then?'

'What, Lil' Miss Virgin? No way.'

'So what do you think it was all about?'

Dionne paused. 'Maybe he's working his way round the city. Hell, he's fucked every other girl in Paris.' *Except me . . .* The thought came unbidden to Dionne as she remembered that horrible night, remembered Philippe Rochefort calling her every name under the sun before walking out on her. She'd offered herself to him on a plate and he'd rejected her.

CeCe shifted uncomfortably, realizing exactly what Dionne must be thinking.

'Maybe we should forget about it. Just pretend we never saw it,' she suggested.

But Dionne's dark eyes were glittering with excitement, her beautiful face animated, as though something had just occurred to her. 'No, I don't think I'm gonna do that,' she said thoughtfully. 'I mean, something like this is hard to forget, don'tcha think?'

'Dionne—' CeCe began, but broke off as the front door slammed. She shot a warning look at her as the kitchen door opened and Alyson bounced in.

'Hey,' she smiled at the pair of them, dumping her Prada work bag – another present from Philippe – on the tiny breakfast bar.

'Hey, Alyson, what's up?' Dionne greeted her brightly. Beside her, CeCe discreetly closed the copy of *Paris Match*, angling her body to try and hide it.

'Ooh, hot bag,' cooed Dionne, with a pointed glance at CeCe. It was the kind of thing Alyson would never buy for herself.

'Oh, thanks.' She looked faintly embarrassed. 'It was a present.'

'Wow, who from?' Dionne asked instantly.

'I . . . Just a friend . . .'

'Man, I wish I had friends like that,' Dionne said deliberately. There was a touch of malice in her tone, a bitterness in her response that Alyson couldn't understand.

'So, how's things?' Dionne tried a new tack. 'Are you still seeing that cute bar manager?'

'Aidan?' Alyson flushed, startled that his name should have come up. 'No, I'm not . . . We were never really—'

'Shame. He sounded sweet,' Dionne cut her off abruptly. 'And what about work? How's that new job workin' out for ya?'

'It's great,' Alyson nodded, thinking that Dionne was behaving extremely oddly. She was probably still wired from the night before — that was usually the case. 'Really great, actually. They're sending me on a business trip to Zurich tomorrow so . . . that's exciting . . .' she trailed off awkwardly as Dionne stared at her.

'Sounds amazing,' Dionne replied sarcastically. 'You must be impressing somebody. Where is it you're working again? A drinks company, you said. What, like Coca-Cola?'

'Not exactly . . .' Alyson hesitated. She'd avoided telling them exactly where she worked. Dionne and CeCe went through champagne like most people went through water, and she couldn't take the constant demand for her to bring home 'freebies' and 'samples'. She'd simply told them she'd started work for a drinks company and let them make their own assumptions. 'It's a champagne house, actually,' she admitted. 'Rochefort Champagne.'

'*Really?*' Dionne arched her eyebrows so high they nearly reached her hairline. 'Well . . . Doesn't that sound like fun? I guess you need to go pack for your trip tomorrow. I wouldn't want to hold you up . . .'

'Yeah, I'd better go. See you guys later.' Alyson seized

the opportunity to leave, grabbing her bag and scuttling out of the room, grateful to be away from Dionne's inquisition.

'Have an awesome time,' Dionne called after her, before turning to CeCe in triumph. 'I told you! She's fucking dating him,' she hissed.

'She didn't say that,' CeCe protested. 'Maybe they're just colleagues.'

'Yeah, right. Who else is gonna be buying her Prada bags and Armani suits?'

'Perhaps the job is well paid?' CeCe offered.

But it did little to dampen the fury in Dionne's eyes. 'I can't believe he's dating *her*,' she raged. 'Like, taking her out in public, letting them be photographed together.' She picked up the copy of *Paris Match* and shook it at CeCe. 'What has *she* got that I haven't, huh? Apart from a flat chest and a whiny little Brit voice?'

CeCe could only shrug her shoulders while Dionne ranted.

'You remember what he said to me, CeCe? He spoke to me like I was nothing. Like I was a piece of shit.' Her voice sounded choked. 'Why the fuck is *she* so special?'

'Do you think she knows?' CeCe asked gently. 'About his reputation, I mean.'

Dionne shrugged. Her eyes were blazing, her chest rising and falling in anger. 'Who knows? Who cares?'

'But shouldn't we tell her? We need to warn her or something.'

'I'm not her mom. She can learn her own lessons.' Dionne snatched up an apple from the fruit bowl and bit into it, her teeth crunching down fiercely on the tangy flesh. She chewed silently for a moment, thinking back to how Philippe Rochefort had treated her that night. Humiliation flooded through her at the memory, a sick feeling in her guts as she remembered what he'd said to her. *Black trash. Worse than a whore.* No guy spoke to Dionne Summers like that. She wouldn't let him get away with it.

But if he *was* dating Alyson . . . Dionne smiled suddenly, flinging the apple aside as the first stirrings of an idea began to form. The information could be useful – she just wasn't sure how. Not yet.

'What are you thinking?' CeCe asked suspiciously, recognizing Dionne's expression.

'Maybe we *should* tell her,' Dionne mused thoughtfully. 'Just not right away. I mean, we wouldn't want to ruin her little business trip, would we? Don't worry,' she added, seeing CeCe's sceptical expression. 'I'll tell her soon. I just need to find the right moment.'

Zurich was exhilarating.

Even though the day was grey and overcast, the Swiss city was beautiful, with its quaint old buildings standing on the edge of Lake Zurich. For Alyson, it was overwhelming. She felt as though she'd finally arrived.

The people in the streets were smart; there was the scent of money in the air. A small fleet of private cars had delivered them from the airport, driving to their hotel in the heart of the financial district. Alyson had shared a car with two of her colleagues – Tobias Venn and Marc Lasalle – as well as Richard Duval. She'd been nervous at first, but they'd soon made her feel at ease. Richard had shown a particular interest in her, chatting about her background and asking her opinions, without ever getting too personal. Alyson was flattered.

And now she was in the hotel, preparing for the big meeting. When she'd first seen her room at the Park Hyatt she'd wanted to dance around and jump up and down on the bed with excitement. It was superb – simple and modern, neutrally decorated in browns and creams. There were fresh flowers on the table, and gorgeous little Blaise Mautin toiletries in the bathroom. Her window looked out over the city itself; she could see the suited workers hurrying past below.

On the glass-topped desk, Alyson's company laptop stood open, the first page of today's presentation displayed on the screen. Alyson wasn't going to be presenting – she was merely there as part of the team, to support and learn – but it would be a great opportunity, Richard had assured her. There would be the chance to network, to meet investors and to get to know the senior managers a little better. Alyson was nervous; she knew they'd be watching her to see how she conducted herself and determine whether or not she had what it took to progress. She intended to grab this chance with both hands.

She smoothed down her skirt, checking her appearance in the full-length mirror. Yes, she was definitely learning, she thought with satisfaction, staring at the beautifully cut designer suit that Philippe had bought her. Alyson had purchased a lot of new work clothes with her first pay check, but Philippe had insisted on buying her this for Zurich and she'd acquiesced. The last thing she wanted was to let the team down by turning up in some cheap, high-street outfit.

Usually, Alyson favoured shift dresses with matching jackets; the shape flattered her long, lean body, emphasizing the slight swell of her small breasts, skimming over the gentle curve of her bottom. She teamed them with a skinny belt, creating the illusion of a waist on her boyish figure. But today she'd gone old school: a simple grey pencil skirt that fell just below the knee, paired with a crisp white Michael Kors blouse and the exquisitely tailored jacket. No modern dresses or ball-busting trouser suits. Her hair was pulled back, just a light dusting of powder and a slick of pale lip colour by way of make-up. She wanted to look unobtrusive and unthreatening – nothing to alarm the staid money men.

There was a sharp knock at the door and she quickly smoothed down her hair, unplugging her laptop and tucking it under her arm. She was ready.

Alyson opened the door to find Bernadette Sauvage standing there. She looked uncomfortable in an ill-fitting suit that might once have been the right size but was now pulled taut with strain. Her dyed mahogany hair was trying to escape from the French pleat she'd attempted to pin it in, and her face was red from too much blusher.

'Are you ready?' she asked shortly. Her gaze ran over Alyson with a flicker of distaste.

'Yes,' Alyson smiled brightly, stepping towards her. But something in Bernadette's face stopped her.

'Oh dear, then perhaps I should have told you earlier. I'm afraid we've decided that you won't be needed after all. Sorry about that.' Bernadette didn't sound at all sorry.

'But I thought—'

'Yes. There's been a change of plan. It's been agreed that it should be senior management only.'

'Okay.' Alyson's heart was thumping, and she was struggling to take it all in. She knew her face must be betraying how she felt, and she fought to keep herself composed. *Stay cool. Be professional. Don't let this old battleaxe know she's rattled you.* 'Is there anything I can do?'

'No,' Bernadette said shortly. 'You should make the most of it while you're here. Perhaps go for a walk. Or ride on a tram.' Pointedly, she checked her watch. 'I'd better go. I don't want to be late.'

She marched off down the corridor, swaying with self-importance. Alyson let the door swing shut and sat down on her bed, her body crumpling in despair.

I haven't come all the way to Zurich to go for a bloody walk!

She caught a glimpse of her reflection in the mirror – spots of colour had appeared high on her cheeks; her lips were tightly pursed. It was rare for her to get this angry, but she felt as though she'd been set up. Who was Bernadette to tell her that and why hadn't Richard overruled her? Had Alyson displeased him in some way? Did he even know what had happened?

Alyson picked up her phone and instinctively scrolled to Philippe's number. She would speak to him, find out what had happened, make sure Bernadette got carpeted for what she had just done, and—

Alyson threw her phone down on the bed in frustration. She couldn't do that. There was no way she could go running to Philippe – she didn't want him to think she couldn't hack it. More than that, she'd be an object of derision amongst the others. Running to her boyfriend, the big boss, at the first sign of trouble. It was pathetic. No, she had to do this herself, otherwise she wouldn't earn any respect.

She was in this on her own.

It was late evening and Alyson had spent the day in her room, browsing the Internet and trying to read. She hadn't dared leave the hotel in case she was suddenly needed for something; she didn't want everyone to think she'd swanned off shopping on company time.

But she'd heard nothing.

She wondered for the thousandth time that day why Richard had changed his mind. It was humiliating, and she was dreading facing everyone again. The team would all know, all be looking at her and laughing behind her back – the girl who wasn't judged competent enough even to sit quietly in the corner while the big boys got on with the important stuff.

She wished she'd been able to talk things through with Philippe, but she knew it was a bad idea. Besides, he was on a business trip in the States and she didn't want to disturb him. He'd left yesterday, and wasn't expected back for over a week. It would be the longest they'd gone without seeing each other. Oh well, she knew he was busy setting up the American side of Rochefort Enterprises and she was proud of him for that. At least it was night-clubs and not strip joints, she thought darkly.

Distractedly, Alyson reached out and picked up the printed itinerary for the day, from where it lay on the coffee table. The plan for this evening was cocktails at seven, followed by a private dinner. It was a dressy affair and she'd brought a beautiful deep-blue Halston Heritage number. She didn't know if she was still invited, but to be on the safe side she had showered and changed, zipping herself into the dazzling dress. She'd gone stronger on the make-up side, wearing a bold Chanel red lipstick. Philippe had bought it for her, saying that every woman should own one, and now she was glad he had. She didn't know why she'd brought it with her, but as she slicked it on she realized it was perfect.

Screw them, Alyson thought, in an uncharacteristic display of rebellion.

Her hair was freshly washed, shimmering over her shoulders. The red lipstick brought out the colour in her cheeks, emphasizing her pale skin and making her blue eyes sparkle. Next to her, Bernadette Sauvage would look like a menopausal bag lady, Alyson thought with satisfaction.

For the first time she was realizing the power of her beauty. She'd never been interested in clothes and make-up, but now she was beginning to understand how they could make a difference to your confidence, and to the way people perceived you. In Giambattista Valli heels, with her Miu Miu clutch, Alyson felt like player. She could take on anyone, from Bernadette Sauvage to the most powerful investor.

Alyson checked her watch. Ten minutes to seven. She sat down on the corner of the bed, ready to wait. If she hadn't heard anything by ten past she would take off the dress, remove every last scrap of make-up and curl up in bed with her pyjamas on, hiding under the duvet. She would order something nice from room service, watch an old movie and feel glad that it was all on Rochefort Champagne's bill.

The minutes ticked by. At two minutes to seven, there was a knock on the door. Alyson steeled herself and opened it. Richard Duval stood there, looking surprisingly dapper in a black tux. She towered over him in heels and he looked up at her, his expression remorseful.

'I'm very sorry about earlier,' he apologized. 'There was no choice. But I am aware that is no consolation.' He tried to keep his eyes fixed on her face. She looked incredible – haughty and imperious, yet young and vulnerable. He could see exactly what Philippe saw in her; he'd done very well for himself. Richard was less sure what Alyson saw in Philippe – she didn't seem to be the gold-digger type. Yes, he was handsome, but a man with Philippe's reputation needed to be handled by someone with more experience than this naïve young girl.

Richard smiled kindly. 'Are you coming to dinner?'

'I didn't know if I was still invited.' Alyson wasn't being petulant, simply honest.

Richard held out his arm for her to take. 'Well, you are. Come, walk with me.'

Alyson let the door shut behind her, and together they made their way down the corridor.

'Alyson, I want you to know that you are very talented, and you exhibit a great deal of potential. You are smart, logical and you should have the credit you deserve. If it had been up to me, you would have been in there today.'

Alyson's forehead creased in confusion and she spoke without thinking. 'But surely you can overrule what Bernadette says?'

'Yes, I can.' Richard hesitated. 'But it wasn't her decision.'

'No? Then whose?'

There was a pause. Richard reached out and pressed the button for the lift. 'Look, I really shouldn't say any more. Already, I have said too much.'

Alyson fell silent. She didn't understand what Richard meant. If neither he nor Bernadette had authorized the decision, then who had? Richard was the MD, for Christ's sake. Perhaps the others had got together, en masse, to complain at her inclusion. Yeah, maybe the guys who'd worked there for years didn't appreciate having their thunder stolen by some little upstart who'd barely been there for five minutes. But that didn't make any sense – they'd never been anything but polite to her face, and it wasn't as if she was going to do anything more than sit in the corner and observe anyway.

Unexpectedly, Richard began to speak again. 'Look, Philippe is an old friend of mine – I've known him since he was born – but he does have something of a ruthless reputation. Just be absolutely sure you know what you're getting yourself into, *d'accord?*'

Alyson turned to look at him, but Richard wouldn't meet her gaze. In front of them, the elevator doors pinged open. 'Shall we?' he asked neutrally, indicating that she should go ahead.

In a daze, Alyson walked into the lift. Her mind was whirling. What the hell was that supposed to mean? Was he implying that *Philippe* was behind the decision? But that was ludicrous. Why would he stop her going to the meeting when he knew she wanted it so badly? And he'd seemed so supportive. He'd bought her the suit, the dress – he'd even taken her out for dinner to celebrate . . .

She caught sight of her reflection in the lift mirror and realized how shocked she looked. Oh God, the last thing she wanted to do now was to walk out there and face all of her colleagues – especially Bernadette. They would all be laughing at her, knowing she hadn't made the cut. Did they know that Philippe was behind the decision? It was just too awful. She began to wish she'd just locked her door and gone for the pyjamas and room-service option.

The numbers counted down swiftly and the lift doors opened. Once again, Richard offered her his arm. He seemed to understand what she was feeling. As they approached the bar, he spoke to her in low tones. 'Keep your chin up; don't let them see what you're thinking. You know the key to this game? Bravado. Always brazen it out. You have ability, yes, but that's only half the battle. You need the confidence too, perhaps even a little arrogance. Once you have that, you'll be a more dangerous prospect than any of those fat cats out there.'

'Thanks, Richard.' Alyson gave him a half-smile, then composed her face. She lifted her chin, a steely glint appearing in her blue eyes. She looked beautiful, confident, more than a match for any of them.

Alyson stepped into the lion's den.

20

It was the beginning of Paris Fashion Week and CeCe's flat was in chaos. She had lost ten pounds, was main-lining black coffee and cigarettes, and couldn't remember the last time she'd slept. She looked like a vampire. She was living in her pyjamas and her only source of fresh air was the sash window, open a crack in the living room.

All her energy, all her creativity, was being driven into making sure this venture was a success. Real life could be dealt with afterwards. Right now, everything was on hold as she threw herself into securing Capucine's future.

Girls had been traipsing in and out of the flat all week for fittings and last-minute adjustments. CeCe had been calling in favours all over town, trying to find thirty-two women with model proportions who were willing to work for nothing more than free coffee, a credit on their résumé and the potential for some fabulous exposure. It wasn't the easiest task CeCe had ever undertaken.

Anyone who was any good had already been snapped up for Fashion Week, or was keeping their options open for the slew of last-minute castings. Working for no pay on some no-name show was simply not an option. The girls who *were* willing to do it were largely unusable – too short, too chunky, too unreliable, or simply unable to put one foot in front of the other without looking like a carthorse. It had been a fucking nightmare, but after weeks of arm-twisting and unashamed begging, CeCe had finally managed to find a full complement of models to show off her stunning designs.

Dionne had turned down the prestigious YSL show in order to model for Capucine, and CeCe was immeasurably grateful, but in return, Dionne had demanded that she close the show – to walk last and be the very final thing the crowds saw, the grand climax to the whole daring shebang.

She'd also insisted on wearing a divine white silk-organza dress. Most designers these days didn't bother with the traditional wedding dress finale, and CeCe hadn't intended to either. But she had a gorgeous white creation, a full-length column dress with a soft boat neckline and an audacious plunging back, shimmering with crystals. It looked stunning against Dionne's dark skin, and CeCe knew it would make a huge impact. So, in homage to the old tradition, she'd agreed to put this dress right at the end.

Now all she needed to confirm was the styling for the show; she'd roped in a couple of make-up student friends of hers, and her regular hairdresser, Laurent, had agreed to swing by with his team. François had been commandeered to take photos on the day, and—

CeCe's phone began to ring, for probably the hundredth time that day, and she snatched it up. '*Allo?* Oh, hi, Natalia, *ça va?* What? Shit, tell me that's not true . . . Well, is she going to be okay? Yeah . . . Yeah,

I understand . . . Okay, well, give her my best.' CeCe hung up. 'Fuck,' she swore. 'Fuck fuck fuck!'

'CeCe?' Alyson asked hesitantly as she walked into the room. She was eating a bowl of Caesar salad, and she looked nervously at her flatmate. 'Is everything okay?'

'No, actually. One of my models just dropped out.'

'Oh no!' Alyson looked genuinely devastated. She'd seen how hard CeCe had worked over the past few months, bringing this whole project together. 'That's such a shame.'

'Tell me about it. She's had a nervous breakdown or something, gone to rehab. Usual story. Her flatmate just called to let me know.'

'Oh, the poor girl. Is she going to be all right?'

'She'll be fine,' CeCe managed, through pursed lips. 'She just needs to get off the drugs and start eating something. Fuck!' she swore once again, as she began riffling through the mounds of paper and sketches on the dining-room table, trying to find her list of potential models. She finally located it crumpled beneath a swatch of fabric samples and quickly scanned the names, grabbing her phone.

Alyson, apparently forgotten, sat down on the sofa as CeCe began making calls, each one more frustrating than the last. Not interested, not available, deported due to visa expiry.

Jesus, this was like Mission: Impossible.

CeCe stabbed angrily at her phone, hanging up on the last girl she'd tried. The silence was deafening, the only sound coming from Alyson quietly crunching her salad. Even that almost caused CeCe to explode; her nerves were jangling, taut and pushed to breaking point. The slightest thing could push her over the edge. She span round in her seat, about to ask Alyson as

225

pleasantly as she could to shut the hell up, when suddenly she stopped dead.

Alyson's head was bowed as she leafed through some papers for work, her long legs tucked beneath her. Even though she was sitting down, dressed casually in jogging pants and a sweater, CeCe could clearly make out her slender shape. She must have been five ten or five eleven easily, all long, slim limbs, her body lean and healthy. And she was beautiful – ethereal almost – yet quirky enough for high fashion with that amazing bone structure and fine, blonde hair.

CeCe continued to stare as Alyson, oblivious, speared a forkful of her food. CeCe cleared her throat.

'Alyson . . .'

'Yeah?'

'Have you ever thought of modelling?'

Alyson stopped mid-chew. She looked at CeCe as if she was crazy. 'Me?'

'Yes.'

'No.' Alyson shook her head vehemently. 'No, that's not for me at all. I'm not . . . I mean, I couldn't do . . . That's more Dionne's thing, isn't it?'

'Yes, but you'd be great at it too.'

'I don't think so.' The idea sounded crazy to Alyson. 'I'm happy doing what I'm doing.'

'Well you wouldn't have to change career . . .'

Alyson frowned, and CeCe decided to lay her cards on the table. 'Look, I'm one model down and I'm desperate. I think you'd be perfect, and, really, you'd be doing me such an enormous favour, I cannot say how grateful I would be . . .'

'I'm so sorry, CeCe.' Alyson looked stricken. 'There's no way I could do it. It sounds terrifying. All those people looking at you. What if I slipped, or fell over? I'm sure you'll find someone, and I honestly think you're better off not having me in the show – I'd probably just do something to ruin it . . .'

CeCe remained silent, her disappointment evident.

'If there's anything else I can do to help . . . Maybe behind the scenes, you know – organization or something?'

'Don't worry about it,' CeCe said shortly. 'I'd better get on with this.'

'Okay.'

Alyson looked upset, and CeCe felt bad about the way she was behaving. 'Thanks anyway, and . . . let me know if you change your mind.'

Alyson smiled ruefully, confident that wasn't going to happen. There was more chance of Dionne taking a vow of abstinence than there was of Alyson agreeing to model.

Philippe was in New York, looking out through floor-to-ceiling windows at the vastness of Central Park far below. The city skyline was astonishing, his view stretching past the enormous skyscrapers as far as the Hudson River. A sense of exhilaration rushed through him, a heady feeling of power. Yes, New York was the place to be. Europe felt like small fry – the States was where the big boys came to play. Like the song said, if you could make it here . . .

Philippe turned around, his back to the window. Come to think of it, the view in here was pretty incredible too, he thought smugly. Mindy Lieberman, the wife of one of Rochefort Enterprises' US investors, stood in front of him wearing nothing more than a scrap of La Perla lace – black, sheer and slutty. Philippe thought of Alyson, with her sensible T-shirt bras in white or nude, her plain white cotton panties. At first it had been a turn-on – coupled with her youth, it made Philippe think of some naughty schoolgirl – but lately he'd begun to wish she would spice it up now and again.

That was why Philippe was here. To get himself a little excitement. This woman had about twenty years on Alyson and from the way she was looking at him now, she'd picked up a trick or two along the way. Hell, she looked as if she'd been right the way through the *Kama Sutra* and back again.

Sex with Alyson was fine – she was eager, responsive, never turned him down. But she was kind of, well, *vanilla* for his tastes. They rarely got out of missionary; Alyson had a tendency to lie back and let him get on with it. That was fine in its own way – Philippe made sure he always got his rocks off, and besides, he was judging Alyson on her potential as a wife and mother, not on her skill between the sheets. There were plenty of other ways Philippe could get what he was looking for. His father had always had mistresses, he remembered. It was just the way things were.

And Mindy seemed more than happy to oblige. He'd met her at dinner last night and she'd flirted heavily with him, inviting him round to her apartment today with the assurance that her husband would be working. As a general rule, Philippe didn't like screwing around on another man's territory, but on this trip he was feeling reckless. The new club was coming along nicely, and he had the fragrant Alyson covering his needs back home.

Philippe stared at Mindy, feeling his cock stir and harden. She looked good, in that generic New York way: blonde hair perfectly highlighted; body kept unnaturally thin through strict dieting and a punishing exercise regime; age impossible to determine thanks to a subtle yet skilful surgeon. As Philippe unbuckled his belt, he felt the phone in his pocket vibrate. Irritably he pulled it out. Alyson. Philippe grinned slyly, pulling off his trousers as he answered the call.

'Alyson, darling! *Comment ça va?*'

'I'm okay,' Alyson told him. She sounded a little down.

'That's good,' Philippe replied distractedly. He crooked his finger, beckoning Mindy over. She strutted across the room towards him, discarding her bra and parties on the way. She was freshly waxed, Philippe noted with amusement. New York women and their obsession with grooming. 'Listen, *chérie*, I cannot talk for long. I am very busy right now.'

'Oh, right. I can call back later if you like?'

In front of Philippe, Mindy turned round so her back was to him. Then she bent straight over, hands flat on the floor in front of her feet. Man, that was some party trick. All those hours of yoga must have really paid off.

'Actually,' Philippe smiled, 'now's a perfect time.'

That skinny little bottom was staring up at him, her hairless pussy beautifully inviting. Philippe moved towards her, inching himself inside of her. Shit, that felt good. She was wet and tight – so tight, he wondered if she'd had surgery. Either that, or she was religious about her Kegels. 'So how was Zurich?' Philippe tried hard to control his breathing, hoping Alyson couldn't hear the way he was practically panting down the phone.

'Not great.'

'No?' Philippe feigned surprise.

'No. I wasn't allowed to take part in the end. I had to stay in my room.'

'What? Why not?' Philippe turned his head, seeing

himself in the full-length mirrors that lined the far wall. He pulled his belly in, watching as he thrust in and out, his cock sliding smoothly between those splayed legs. Mindy's hair was messed up and hanging in her face, her tits swaying freely.

'I don't know.'

'Darling, don't worry about it. You are only young and your time will come.' Experimentally, he slipped a finger inside Mindy's ass.

But Alyson wouldn't let the subject drop. 'It was very odd. I spoke to Richard about it, and he implied the decision was out of his hands. But I thought he was the MD, so how could that happen?'

There was a pause. Philippe continued to thrust, but his mind wasn't on the job. When he spoke again, his voice was tight with anger. 'He said that, did he? I can't think what he meant.'

'Can't you?' It was a challenge and they both knew it.

In front of him, Mindy began to cry out, pushing herself back against his balls. Philippe covered the speaker with his palm, worried that Alyson would hear. He could feel the pressure of his own orgasm building.

'Darling, look, I'm very busy right now,' he told her shortly, glancing down at Mindy bucking and writhing beneath him. 'We'll talk more when I get back, okay?'

Philippe hung up, not giving Alyson the chance to respond. He threw his phone to the floor, removing his finger and reaching round to grab Mindy's breasts. She spread her legs wider and he reached down between them, sliding his fingers over the slick nub of her clitoris, stroking her relentlessly until her cries grew louder and he felt her clench around him, her body shuddering to climax.

Distantly, Philippe thought back to what Alyson had said. He wouldn't be spoken to in that way; wouldn't have his authority challenged like that. Everything she had, she had because of him – the job, the clothes, the lifestyle. He had made her, and he could break her.

In front of him, Mindy tried to stand up, but Philippe held her down. She would stay where she was until he was good and ready. He began to move faster, harder until the blinding light overtook him and he exploded in release. He stayed inside her, continuing to move until his cock stopped twitching and he'd squeezed out every last drop. Finally, the sensations faded and he pulled out with a groan, his dick limp and sated.

Now he'd finished, he just wanted to get out of the apartment. Mindy was gushing, telling him what a fantastic lay he was, but Philippe wasn't listening. The conversation with Alyson had disturbed him. She was getting a little headstrong – that damn independent streak coming out again. Well she would just have to learn. They did things his way, or she would suffer the consequences.

At the other end of the phone, Alyson was furious. Had Philippe really just hung up on her? Something was going on, and she didn't like it.

He seemed to be brushing her off, disregarding her feelings. She thought back to that day at Château de Marne, all the effort he'd gone to, how charming and solicitous he'd been. She guessed that meant the honeymoon period was over.

Alyson stared at the blank screen of her mobile, feeling the anger rise in her chest. Well, she wasn't going to call him back – there was no way she'd give him the satisfaction.

Instead, she stomped through to the kitchen, slamming

cupboards and banging her mug down on the counter. She needed a cup of tea, the quick-fix solution for every Brit abroad.

'Are you okay, Alyson?' It was CeCe.

Embarrassed about the noise she was making, Alyson walked through to the living room to apologize. CeCe was kneeling on the floor, pinning a dress on a beautiful girl. She was tall and slim, her expression bored. She looked Slavic, with cheekbones you could slalom down and sultry, hooded eyes.

'Oh, sorry.' Alyson was caught off guard.

'No problem.' But CeCe looked stressed. 'You sounded angry.'

'Yeah.' Alyson took a deep breath, forcing herself to smile. 'I'm fine now. Thanks.'

'Are you a model too?' It was the girl that had spoken to her, her accent strong and Eastern European.

'No,' Alyson flushed. 'I just live here.'

'You look like a model,' she said, studying Alyson so intently it was disconcerting.

'That's what I've been telling her,' CeCe agreed eagerly. 'Are you sure you don't want to change your mind about the show? I'm still looking for someone . . .'

Alyson shook her head, but stayed where she was. CeCe sensed an opportunity. She got up from where she was kneeling and unhooked the peacock dress from the picture rail, holding it up so Alyson could get the full effect. 'This is the dress I need someone to wear. It will be such a shame if it doesn't go in the show . . .'

In spite of herself, Alyson moved across to look at it. 'CeCe, it's gorgeous.' Her voice sounded awestruck. She'd never really paid much attention to CeCe's designs before — besides, CeCe shouted if you got too near. But now Alyson saw how much work had gone into it; the fine stitching, the exquisite material. It was full length and backless, with real peacock feathers that had been used to create a dramatic train.

'You should wear it,' the girl told her bluntly. 'You will look spectacular.'

Alyson bit her lip. She reached out to touch it, letting her fingers trail over the silk, feeling the way it slipped like water through her hands. Even though Philippe had bought her some nice clothes, she didn't think she'd ever seen anything this stunning. Everything he chose for her was dark and old-fashioned, in sludgy browns or dull greys. This was young, bright, vibrant. Alyson's heart began to race.

'*Please*,' CeCe asked beseechingly. 'I've called everyone. You would be doing me such a huge favour, you can't imagine how grateful I would be.'

Alyson thought about it. She was still mad with Philippe over the way he'd treated her, feeling that, in some twisted way, this would be payback. He wouldn't want her to do it, she was sure of that. But he was away. He would never know. Besides, why shouldn't she do a favour for a friend?

In a moment of clarity, Alyson suddenly saw how much control Philippe had over her life. He dictated almost every aspect, she realized, flushing with embarrassment – where she worked, how she dressed, even what she ate. In restaurants he always ordered for her, a gesture she used to think of as romantic but which now seemed more disturbing, a blatant statement of the power he wielded. Since the beginning of their relationship she'd always deferred to him, respecting his knowledge and experience, but maybe she'd let it go too far. She was her own person, not some rich man's puppet.

With a rush of excitement Alyson stared at the peacock dress, imagining herself wearing it. She could almost feel the rich material clinging to her body, the cool, slippery sensation of the silk on her bare skin. She felt giddy, light-headed almost.

'Okay, I'll do it.' The words were out of her mouth before she even knew what she'd said.

'*Vraiment*?' CeCe looked stunned.

Alyson nodded quickly before she changed her mind.

'Oh, thank you so much!' CeCe exclaimed, throwing her arms around Alyson. 'You don't know how pleased I am, I'm so happy, Alyson!'

Alyson smiled in bemusement, wondering what on earth she'd just agreed to. 'When's the show?'

'Wednesday,' CeCe informed her. 'Can you get time off work?'

Alyson shrugged. 'Maybe I'll just call in sick.' She was starting to feel rebellious, and she liked it.

21

The Tuileries gardens in central Paris were beautiful. It was the end of summer, just creeping into autumn, and the leaves on the trees were beginning to turn. The first winter chill was evident in the cool breeze, an unmistakeable change after the long, summer days.

Outside the *espace ephémère,* the vast temporary marquee erected in the heart of the gardens, the fashionistas were waiting. It was the last day of the Paris shows – the final day of the season – and everyone was getting a little antsy. The atmosphere felt like the last day of school, with the fashion hacks exhausted from four weeks of shows, partying and champagne, and everyone rather looking forward to the whole thing being over.

The YSL show was due to begin at three p.m., and the invitees were growing impatient. The hierarchy was strict, with the celebrities ushered inside and seated first on the all-important front row – Emma Watson, Clémence Poésy, Alexa Chung and Kristin Scott Thomas had all been snapped arriving. Outside, the press and bloggers were left in the holding pen, huddling self-importantly behind enormous black sunglasses, latte in one hand, cigarette in the other.

Outfits were judged and reviewed, praised or condemned. For the fash pack, the first chill in the air was an excuse to throw on the most covetable items from their new winter wardrobe; despite the mild temperatures, skinny bodies were poured into knee-high boots and cashmere knits, oversized yeti coats and the occasional fur for those who dared to brave the animal rights protesters.

Gossip was swapped, and points were scored over who'd blagged the best seats, or who'd skipped the waiting list for this season's 'it' bag. Designer watches were anxiously checked. An over-running show had a knock-on effect, meaning you might be late for Dior on the other side of town, and the traffic was bound to be murder.

But the overriding sensation was one of boredom, killing time until the action started. A photographer snapped a few shots for atmosphere, knowing they would never get used. Curious members of the public loitered nearby, drinking in the excitement, then drifting away when they realized no one famous was in the crowd. Pigeons pecked at the ground while, high overhead, aeroplanes crisscrossed the sky.

Everything was calm and quiet, with no sense that anything out of the ordinary was about to happen.

Alyson was seated in the back of a huge, black, seven-seater Range Rover, trying not to be sick. She didn't think she'd ever felt so nervous in her life.

But she looked incredible, there was no denying that. She'd been literally sewn into the peacock dress and it fitted her to perfection. Looking in the mirror, she was almost unrecognizable. Her hair was slicked back and piled on top of her head, her eyes painted silver and her lips rubbed with a berry shade. The make-up artist had used black blusher, applied in thick streaks along the line of her cheekbones. Alyson thought she looked like a corpse, but hey, that was fashion for you.

They turned onto the *rue de Rivoli*, and Alyson's heart lurched. She leaned against the window, feeling the cool glass on her forehead. Could she even do this?

CeCe had wanted the peacock dress to lead the collection, but Alyson had begged her to change her mind. There was no way she could go first. She wanted to be somewhere in the middle, in the safety of the pack.

She'd barely slept last night. She'd lain awake, thinking of all the things that could go wrong. Her number one fear was falling over. The heels she was wearing were higher than anything she'd worn in her life, and she hadn't even been able to walk in them at first. Dionne had given her an aptly named crash course yesterday in the apartment, her feet sliding all over the polished wooden floor as she struggled to keep her balance. It was like learning to walk all over again, trying to capture the distinctive model strut; long strides, upright posture, chin tilted slightly down, one foot almost crossing the other. There was so much to remember, and surely it would be almost impossible on the uneven ground of the Tuileries? Alyson swallowed. It didn't bear thinking about.

She turned to look at the other girls, wondering if they were as terrified as she was. There were four models in the back with her, another one riding up front with the driver. They all stared straight ahead impassively, their faces blank. None of them spoke to each other. Alyson got the impression they weren't very friendly. Dionne was in a different car. They'd been put in the order they were going to walk, and as Dionne was last she was in the final vehicle.

Alyson knew it must be an impressive sight. Six brand-new gleaming Range Rovers, all in black, travelling in convoy through the centre of Paris. Pedestrians were stopping to stare, trying to peer in when the cars slowed down. *They must think we're the President or something*, Alyson realized.

The cars had been provided by David Mouret, one of Dionne's friends. Alyson wasn't sure if Dionne and David were dating, and didn't like to ask. He'd been round to the apartment enough times, but Dionne often had guys round. David ran a car-hire company, and had provided the vehicles free of charge. She knew CeCe was immeasurably grateful, and they certainly looked pretty cool, with gleaming chrome alloys and tinted windows.

They pulled alongside the cast-iron railings on the north-facing side of the Tuileries, and Alyson felt her stomach lurch. She had to fight an overwhelming urge to scramble out of the car, pull off those ridiculous shoes, and run at full pelt along the street, never to be seen again. Or maybe she would just open the door and be sick straight into the gutter. Either way, it wouldn't be pretty.

Alyson closed her eyes, taking a few calming breaths. She was doing this for CeCe, she reminded herself. It wasn't about her; it was about doing a favour for a friend. In less than an hour it would all be over, and then she could go back to her ordinary life and be plain, uninteresting Alyson Wakefield. Just the way she liked it.

CeCe was standing behind the trunk of a large chestnut tree, trying to look unobtrusive in a vintage velvet wide-brimmed hat and oversized sunglasses. Her heart was pounding as she waited for the fleet of cars to arrive, hoping no one would recognize her and blow the whole thing.

This was make-or-break time. In just a few minutes she would find out whether all her hard work had paid off, whether it had been worth taking the gamble and – most terrifying of all – whether she really was good enough.

Dionne thought she should drum up publicity – ring round the news agencies, maybe get a PR company involved – but CeCe didn't want to. She wanted it to be a complete shock, a bolt from the blue, like a flash mob. She just hoped she could pull it off.

The event had been an utter nightmare to organize. From six a.m. this morning she'd had girls arriving at the shared apartment – thirty-two of them all together, all stroppy and long-limbed, bitchy and competitive. She'd tried in vain to organize some kind of production line, where they had their make-up applied in her bedroom, their hair styled in Dionne's, with the rest waiting in the living room. It had been carnage. The girls had done exactly what they wanted to, floating round the flat and out into the corridor in different states of readiness, and constantly seeking out CeCe with an endless barrage of complaints that, quite frankly, she just didn't have the time to care about. Soothing thirty-two outrageous egos was not at the top of her to-do list for the day. Well, thirty-one egos. Alyson just sat quietly in the corner, looking as if she was about to throw up.

CeCe had ordered in some food – nothing too heavy, just small sandwiches, salad and a fruit platter. She didn't want any of the girls fainting on her. But they only seemed interested in the champagne and coffee.

The food remained largely untouched, with the hair and make-up team wolfing the majority when they had a spare second.

One girl, Irène, was even thinner than she had been when they'd done the final fitting two days ago, and CeCe had had to make emergency last-minute alterations with a needle and thread. Irène was so thin that you could count her ribs in the revealing dress, her stomach concave and the muscle mass on her upper arms eaten away. Rumour had it she was existing on B12 shots and little else but, callous as it sounded, that wasn't CeCe's concern right now. The girl was obviously sick, but as long as she could make it down the runway and show off the dress, then that was all CeCe needed.

She stared round the magnificent gardens, taking in the lovers ambling along the chalky white paths, small children sailing boats in the pond as their parents looked on. It felt like a good omen that she was making her debut here, right in the heart of the city and just across from the *rue de Rivoli*. They were only a few hundred metres down the road from where Dionne and CeCe had worked together in Rivoli Couture, but the hideous clothing and incessant demands of Khalid Hossein felt like a lifetime ago. She'd come so far since then, CeCe thought proudly, daring to take risks and chase her dreams. She was minutes away from a career-defining moment, one that had the potential to launch her into the big time.

And right around the corner was where she wanted to be – the designer boutiques of the *rue du Faubourg Saint-Honoré*, where the *beau monde* of Paris went to shop, and where anyone who was anyone had a store. Past, present and future were represented right here, CeCe reflected, feeling the significance of the moment.

Out of nowhere, the line of black SUVs suddenly pulled up alongside the railings near CeCe's hiding place and she felt her stomach leap, seeming to jump right up into her throat. This was it. She tried to gauge the impact from the reactions of passers-by. People were staring curiously, some even stopping to watch. It was a good sign.

CeCe pressed closer to the tree, hoping to blend in as she watched. In sync, the six drivers got out of their vehicles and walked round to the passenger side. They wore identical black suits and dark glasses, lined up along the pavement like Secret Service agents. Then, at exactly the same time, they moved forward to open the doors.

Suddenly there were beautiful girls everywhere, flooding the sidewalk. They were tall and stunning, other-worldly almost, as they towered over the tourists, dressed in the most incredible clothes. It was a dazzling sea of colour – gold, silver, magenta, topaz, ruby, indigo, white. People took photos as the girls swarmed onto the pavement, a few onlookers even filming on their camera phones. Passing cars honked their horns, tourists spontaneously applauding at the extraordinary sight. It was like a flash mob – exactly what CeCe had intended.

The models paid no attention to the stir they were creating, keeping their gaze fixed firmly ahead. Then one by one they began to walk, up the short flight of steps and into the gardens. Katerina, the Latvian model CeCe had met on her first night in Bijou, was in the lead, loving every minute. She wore an astonishing aquamarine gown, with layers of diaphanous chiffon and a plunging, jewelled bodice. Behind her, the other girls followed in perfect formation, like a flock of arrogant swans who knew just how beautiful they were.

CeCe watched as they walked the prearranged route, first heading towards Place de la Concorde, then circling round to come back right past the *espace ephémère.* She could see Dionne at the back, looking amazing in the white evening gown as she strode confidently through the park.

It was so different to an ordinary fashion show, with all its razzamatazz. Usually there would be music pumping and lights flashing, all manner of special effects. Out here, CeCe had nothing – no props and no distractions. It was all about the clothes, and she would be judged purely on her designs. She didn't think she could stand the tension. Would this work? Would anyone even pay attention?

CeCe watched anxiously, singling out each girl in turn. Irène was still managing to stay upright, and the heavy make-up hid the fact that she looked like death. A few of the girls had been on the coke already this morning, and CeCe had heard every excuse under the sun – *It calms me down, It wakes me up, As long as I'm on the jazz I don't need to eat . . .* CeCe had shrugged and turned a blind eye. She wasn't there to mother them; she was there to ensure her clothes looked immaculate and the show kick-started her career.

The girls were approaching the fashion tent area now, where everyone was waiting. CeCe could almost see the buzz, like it was a physical thing. One by one, the hacks turned to look, the excited chatter growing louder. Katerina walked towards them, almost to the very edge of the enclosure, then turned sharply, moving along the side of the press pen and back the way she had come from.

Gradually the journalists realized what was happening. The Tuileries were being treated like one giant runway.

'Bite, damn you,' CeCe whispered under her breath. All they were doing was watching, their eyes hidden behind dark glasses. None of them spoke – they just stared, silently. It was impossible to tell what anyone was thinking.

Then – bang – a flashbulb went off. It was followed by another, and then another, and the next minute there was a surge as the photographers ran forward, each one trying to get the money shot. Television cameras followed, and within seconds it was chaos. Everyone wanted to see what was happening, to know what was going on.

One of the reporters thrust a microphone towards the girls. 'Whose designs are these?' he demanded. 'Who's behind this?'

None of them responded, or even reacted. They simply kept walking, looking straight ahead as they'd been instructed to do.

The press went wild, shouting questions and chasing them through the park as they headed towards the exit. Reporters got on their phones to their editors, trying to work out if anyone knew what was going on. It was mayhem.

Quickly, CeCe left the gardens. She'd seen enough. Heart thumping, she slipped into the final car, grateful for the blacked-out windows, and waited for the girls to return.

Katerina had reached the steps and filed out of the park, the others following behind her. A camera crew were filming everything, the models pursued by a mob of photographers and fashion hacks.

Dionne was the last to get into the car, the scrum around her separating to let her through. The reporters shouted after her, sounding desperate. 'Who organized this show? Who's the designer behind it?'

Dionne hesitated for a fraction of a second, as though she was going to give them an answer. Then she slammed the door shut and the car drove off into the Paris traffic, leaving the bedlam behind.

22

Dionne settled back into the luxurious buttercream leather seat of the Gulfstream 200, running her hands over the soft fabric and enjoying the vast amount of space. She stretched her endless legs out in front of her, admiring how slim and sleek they looked in the denim cut-offs she was wearing.

A young stewardess, immaculately presented in a custom-made navy blue suit, approached the party. 'Would you like a drink, madam?'

'Yes. Champagne,' Dionne requested.

Moments later, the woman came back with a bubbling flute and a deferential smile. Yeah, she could definitely get used to this lifestyle, Dionne reflected. There was no tedious check-in or humiliating security procedures when you were flying private. No crying babies or screaming children to ruin the flight. Just straight out to the airport at Le Bourget and directly onto the plane.

Twisting round in her seat, Dionne raised her glass at Saeed. He'd been so generous, lending them his jet like this. A couple of days in St Tropez, partying hard to let her hair down, was exactly what Dionne needed. She'd been working nonstop for weeks — New York,

London, Bali, Paris – and now that the season was over she was looking forward to getting a little crazy.

She and CeCe had been planning this trip for weeks, and Saeed had kindly offered to facilitate their escape. They'd arranged to leave directly after the show, the thinking being that, whatever happened, triumph or disaster, they would escape the chaos of Paris for a hedonistic couple of days in the South of France. If the show was a success, what better way to celebrate than a night of partying in St Tropez? And if it went badly . . . Well, they could hit the clubs and drown their sorrows.

But the early indications were good and Dionne was on a high. She'd been the star, as she'd known she would be, and a high-profile gig like this could only boost her career.

She'd been the final girl to walk, the grand finale to the whole extravaganza. She'd been the last one to step into the car – she could barely reach it due to the crush of photographers surrounding her. They'd worked themselves into a frenzy, snapping her as she struggled to close the door on them, even trying to scramble into the car after her. They yelled incessantly, demanding to know who the girls were, who'd designed the clothes . . . Dionne had been beside herself with excitement, but said nothing, just as CeCe had instructed. She'd stared out through the tinted windows as the cars pulled away in convoy, the crush of tourists on the pavement watching them leave as the paps raced down the road after them, still snapping furiously. The film cameras continued to roll, reporters frantically texting, making phone calls, in an effort to discover who lay behind it all . . .

'Have you found anything yet?' Dionne leaned across to CeCe, who was tapping away on her laptop.

CeCe's hazel eyes were shining with excitement.

'We're everywhere! The bloggers are on it; it's all over the Internet. We've featured in some of the early press round-ups. Every time I hit refresh there's something new. Listen,' she continued, quoting:

'*The Yves Saint Laurent collection was today upstaged by an impromptu show that took place outside the venue itself . . .*

'*Using the Tuileries as one giant runway, the fashion world looks set to be shaken up by the arrival of this exciting new talent . . .*

'*The designs were subversive and daring, the show itself unquestionably a coup. Whoever the designer is, with such boldness and genius, they're undoubtedly set for a great future . . .*'

CeCe clutched Dionne's arm in excitement. 'Oh my God, we've even got a mention on Style.com!' It was scrolling across the top of the page, breaking news. 'Look, there you are,' she squealed, thrusting the laptop across to Dionne.

It was open on the 'Slave to Fashion' blogspot, the huge picture showing Dionne stalking across the gardens with the beautiful white dress billowing around her. Her bearing was haughty, regal almost, her shoulders square, her back tall and upright. And the setting was stunning, the photo capturing the clipped chestnut trees and bubbling fountains in the background.

CeCe leaned over and clicked a couple of buttons. 'These are the shots François emailed to me. He's planning to release them to the press, to try and sell them. I hope he does well out of it – he's helped me so much.'

'They're awesome,' Dionne agreed, scrolling through to find pictures of herself.

'Hey, Alyson,' yelled CeCe. 'Come and look at these.'

Across the aisle, Alyson was staring out of the plane window, watching the changing French landscape below her. The further south they flew, the more unfamiliar it became.

No one was more surprised than Alyson to find herself on a private jet heading to La Môle airport, but when CeCe and Dionne had asked her along at the last minute, she'd decided to go for it, throwing a few essentials into a suitcase and jumping into the car that Saeed had sent, along with her flatmates. She was still exhilarated following her modelling debut and suddenly anything seemed possible. Sure, the show had been terrifying, but the buzz afterwards was like nothing she'd ever experienced.

Yeah, she was definitely learning, Alyson reflected: daring to say yes to the new opportunities that came her way and following her instincts. So far it was working out pretty well.

Besides, she still hadn't heard from Philippe.

'Won't your boyfriend mind?' Dionne had asked, when she'd agreed to go with them. She had a strange expression on her face that Alyson couldn't quite read.

'He's out of the country,' Alyson had explained. 'Working overseas.'

Why not go for a couple of days away with her friends? She'd called the office, crossing her fingers as she explained she was still sick and unlikely to be back in the office before Monday. Philippe would never know – she'd be back before him anyway, Alyson thought, with a growing feeling of defiance.

She unclipped her seatbelt and padded over to CeCe. The Arab guys – friends of Saeed's – watched her as she went, muttering to each other then laughing. Alyson tried to ignore them, not wanting to speculate on what they might be saying. She was very grateful to Saeed for letting her tag along on their little getaway, but she didn't want any of his friends to get the wrong idea.

'What?' she asked, plopping down beside CeCe.

CeCe swivelled the laptop round so they could both see: an image of Alyson filled the screen. 'Oh, wow!' she exclaimed, feeling her cheeks flush.

It was embarrassing to see herself like that, all done up and strutting through the park as though she thought she was someone special. But there was part of her that was excited too, a fierce sensation of pride that refused to be smothered. She didn't pay a lot of attention to fashion – that was Dionne and CeCe's world – but she knew enough to know that she looked good.

CeCe clicked on the photo and a close-up shot of Alyson filled the screen. The photographer had caught her at the perfect moment, appearing to look right into the camera. Her gaze was confident, with something intriguing in her expression that invited the viewer in. Her lips were partly open, her head tilted just slightly to emphasize that superb bone structure.

'Not bad,' Dionne said coolly. 'Is that one of the shots François took?'

'Yeah, I think so,' CeCe replied. She had so many windows open on her desktop that she was getting confused. 'Oh, wait a minute. No, actually, they're from the *Stylista* website.' She checked again to make sure she hadn't made a mistake.

'*Stylista?*' Dionne asked in surprise. It was one of the most influential blogs in the fashion world. 'Are you sure?'

'What does that mean?' Alyson asked innocently, not noticing as Dionne pursed her lips in annoyance.

'Am I on there?' Dionne asked tightly, ignoring what Alyson had said.

'I don't think so . . .' CeCe sounded distracted as she tapped on the keyboard. 'Oh my God, they're calling you *l'Inconnue!*'

'Who?' Dionne demanded.

'Alyson! Look here . . .' CeCe pointed to the screen as she read the text out loud. *'But perhaps the biggest discovery of this show, even more than the clearly talented designer, is this unknown model. Stunning, youthful, and with a look that's both timeless and bang on trend. We've made some enquiries, and none of the major agencies represents her. Do you know who she is? The search is on.* Qui est l'Inconnue?'

Philippe stepped out onto the balcony of his villa, nestled high in the hills above St Tropez. The view from the property was incredible – out over the glorious blue Mediterranean Sea, the gleaming white boats bobbing on the water. It was early morning, but already it was shaping up to be a sizzling end-of-summer day, the warm breeze blowing gently through the cypress trees.

Philippe lit a cigarette, squinting in the light. He'd just showered and was wrapped in a Ralph Lauren robe, his dark hair slicked back from his face. His skin was tanned, his feet bare.

A pair of nut-brown arms wrapped themselves around his waist and Philippe smiled. 'Good morning, Luciana.'

She reached for his cigarette, took a drag, then stubbed it out beneath her Gucci heels. Philippe didn't think he'd ever seen her without heels, not even now, first thing in the morning when she was wearing nothing more than a wisp of silk and lace.

Luciana was his latest recruit at La Boîte, his St Tropez nightclub. He'd poached her from a casino in

Monte Carlo where she was working as a croupier and made her assistant manager. She was good, and she knew the most important thing of all – how to keep her boss happy.

Hailing from Brazil, Luciana was dark-haired and petite, with a hard, compact body and ridiculous curves. Her butt was high and round; her boobs were fake, but they'd been well done. She was the complete opposite of Alyson, in every way.

Alyson. Hmm, she'd been pissed at him when they'd last spoken, Philippe remembered. Richard Duval had said more than he was supposed to. He would deal with him when he got back. For now, he had to keep Alyson sweet. Maybe he would propose very soon. Just to seal the deal.

Of course, she still thought he was in New York. He hadn't lied to her, exactly. He'd just changed his mind and decided to stop off in St Tropez on the way back, to see how Luciana was settling into La Boîte. It seemed she was working out very well indeed.

There was a discreet knock on the balcony door, then it slid open. Georges, a member of Philippe's housekeeping staff, wheeled in a breakfast tray.

'Would you like to eat out here, sir?'

'Yes, thank you.'

Georges began setting down the plates on the cast-iron table – fresh fruit, pastries, orange juice and a pot of freshly ground coffee. On the corner of the table, he laid out Philippe's newspapers – *Les Échos*, *Le Figaro* and the *Wall Street Journal*.

Luciana sat down coquettishly, making eyes at him across the table and picking delicately at a piece of grapefruit.

Philippe ignored her. He would take her back to bed a little later. Right now, he had his morning routine to

251

attend to, and he didn't like to be disturbed. He picked up *Les Échos* to scan the financial news, but the front of *Le Figaro* caught his attention.

He opened it out fully, gasping in shock.

'*Qu'est-ce qu'il y a?*' Luciana demanded, in heavily accented French.

Philippe didn't reply. Dominating the front page was a huge picture of a woman. She was stunningly beautiful, dressed in a dazzling emerald peacock-print dress that fitted her slender body to perfection. She could have been a movie star or a supermodel. She looked like a goddess.

Across the top ran the bold, black headline: *Qui est l'Inconnue?*

Philippe knew exactly who it was. It was Alyson.

Only a few miles away, in the heart of St Tropez itself, Alyson was stretched out on a sun lounger beside the pool at the Hotel Byblos. She didn't think she'd ever been somewhere so luxurious, and it was making her head swim.

She was wearing her ancient swimming costume – plain black and classic – and felt a little self-conscious with so much flesh on show, but comforted herself with the fact that no one would be looking at her. Beside her, Dionne was posing in a tiny gold bikini, the top half fighting to restrain her ample breasts, the bottom half little more than a glorified thong. The waiter had almost fallen in the pool when he brought over their drinks; he'd been so busy gawping at Dionne's body.

Spread around them on the sun loungers were today's papers. It made Alyson feel ill to look at them. Her face was everywhere, staring out from the papers beneath gigantic headlines. *Qui est l'Inconnue?* That was all the fashion world seemed to be asking right now. It was insane. She was pretty sure Richard Duval would have realized she wasn't really off sick, given that her photo was plastered all over the front of *Le Figaro*.

CeCe sat next to her, her phone permanently clamped to her ear. She looked cute, in a retro Fifties polka-dot swimsuit, but right now tanning was the last thing on her mind. Her BlackBerry had been ringing nonstop all morning. Word of her identity had begun to leak out, with reports of who was the designer behind the collection appearing on numerous websites. CeCe didn't mind – after all, the whole point of the Tuileries stunt was to put her on the radar. She'd established a profile and made the impact she wanted. Right now, she needed to capitalize on that.

Katerina had already done a gushing interview with online *Vogue*, praising CeCe's 'awesome talent and unsurpassable genius'. Even more surprising was a quote from Danièle Marceau at Galeries Lafayette, saying she'd already been in talks with the young designer about producing an exclusive line for the store, and adding that she'd always been a huge admirer of CeCe's talent. CeCe had nearly choked on her mimosa when she'd read that. It seemed that when you were hot, everybody wanted to jump on the bandwagon.

Alyson shaded her eyes as she watched her friend, the phone glued to her ear while she gabbled away in French so fast that Alyson struggled to understand. She was so glad it was all working out for CeCe, thrilled that she'd been a part of it. She just didn't know if she was prepared for all the attention it seemed to have brought to her.

Suddenly Alyson's phone began to ring. She pulled it out from beneath her towel and saw Philippe's number flashing up. Her stomach lurched, a feeling of nerves sweeping through her. 'Hello?'

'Alyson?' Philippe sounded mad. In spite of herself, Alyson felt a surge of excitement, adrenaline pulsing through her as her body geared up for a fight.

'Yes?'

'What the hell is this?'

'What?' she asked innocently.

'You – all over the front of every newspaper in France.'

'I didn't think it was *every* one,' she answered insolently. There was a shocked silence. This was not the way Philippe imagined she would respond; he expected her to be apologetic and contrite. 'Philippe? Are you still there?' she asked in mock concern.

'Yes, I'm still here. And I'm waiting for an explanation. You've made me look like a fool, Alyson.'

'I don't see how—' she began. But Philippe cut her off.

'Why didn't I know about this? Since when have you spent your time strutting half naked through the Tuileries, pretending you're a model? Is this what you do when I'm not there, hmm?'

Stretching languorously on the sun lounger, Alyson smiled. She'd never heard Philippe like this before, and she was kind of enjoying it. She remembered Richard Duval's warning, about Philippe's ruthless reputation. Well, two could play at that game.

'Darling, I'm very busy right now,' she said sweetly, trying not to laugh as she parodied the way he'd brushed her off during their last phone call. 'We'll talk more when you get back, okay?' Then she hung up on him, feeling the sweetness of revenge. Perhaps she had a ruthless side after all.

Almost immediately, the phone rang again. She

looked at it nervously, expecting it to be Philippe calling back to give her a dressing down. It was a number she didn't recognize, a Parisian dialling code. Alyson answered it cautiously. '*Allo?*'

She listened in astonishment to the voice on the other end, her face changing from confusion to joy to fear. After a few minutes she hung up, looking shell-shocked. She turned to Dionne beside her.

'Was that your boyfriend again?' Dionne asked smugly.

'No.' Alyson was too stunned to notice anything strange about the question. 'Dionne, have you ever heard of a modelling agency called IMG?'

'IMG?' Dionne sat bolt upright, her dark skin seeming to pale. 'Yes. Why?'

'That was them on the phone – a lady called Fabienne. I'm meeting with her when I get back to Paris. They want to represent me.'

Beside her, CeCe was hanging up her call. 'Alyson, that's incredible,' she burst out. 'They're one of the biggest agencies in the world. They've got offices in New York and London too, haven't they, Dionne?'

'That's right,' Dionne replied, through clenched teeth. Her body was tense, her jaw line tight. The upper half of her face was hidden by her huge Oliver Peoples sunglasses, but that was good. It meant Alyson couldn't see the way Dionne's eyes were burning with fury.

23

Dionne was applying her make-up in the sumptuous hotel room, looking out over the curving swimming pool. It was night now and the pool lights had been switched on, the water still and empty.

Saeed really was a darling for bringing them here, Dionne reflected, as she clamped the eyelash curler down onto her lashes. She'd have to make sure she was *very* appreciative later.

Although he and his friends seemed more interested in Alyson, Dionne thought resentfully. Everyone did. What was it about her? Dionne just didn't get the fascination. Alyson was mousy, boring, yet everyone was going crazy for her. Her phone had been ringing off the hook, and what did she do? Rather than making the most of it, Alyson had panicked and switched it off. Both IMG and Elite had rung. She'd arranged appointments with both of them, but then looked as if she was about to cry, talking some nonsense about how she didn't want to be a model, she wanted to be a businesswoman.

Puh-lease. Dionne wanted to slap her. These were opportunities she would have killed for, and yet Alyson was turning them away. She kept saying how she wanted a 'real' job, as though modelling wasn't. Surely every girl wanted to travel the world, to be photographed and be beautiful? Why the hell would you want to sit in an office all day every day, slaving away for the rest of your life in the hope that one day you might get promoted to some petty managerial position with a half-decent salary?

Angrily, Dionne swept blusher over her cheeks. Fashion Week had taken it out of her and her skin was suffering. As soon as she got back to Paris, she would go to the Plaza Athénée for a facial. Maybe even head to a spa for a few days. One of the fun ones, with delicious food and to-die-for massages – not one of those that put you on some spartan regime, with a piece of spelt bread, a cup of hot water and a beating with a birch stick before dawn.

Alyson would probably enjoy that, Dionne thought nastily. She seemed determined to do life the hard way, rather than having fun and making every second count, the way Dionne did. She'd already been onto her agent, telling her to capitalize on the publicity from the Capucine show. CeCe was doing well, and Dionne needed to be associated with that success.

Everyone thought modelling was easy, but it wasn't. The constant travelling was hard, the pressure to lose weight, the frequent rejection. Dionne had seen extreme things – models swallowing cotton balls to fill up their stomach without taking in calories. Girls who got through the day on little more than a few lines of coke and some vitamin shots. If you weren't strong, the industry would break you in a season.

Yeah, even if Alyson went for it, she would soon find out that she couldn't hack it. Dionne contented herself with that thought and selected a pair of earrings – large chandelier-style drops. Then she stepped in front of the mirror and checked her appearance. She was wearing a short, tight, citrus-yellow Hervé Léger dress that left nothing to the imagination. Her long hair was loose and wild, her skin glistening with cocoa butter. The whole look was sexy as hell, and perfect for St Tropez.

She picked up her purse and went to knock on CeCe's door. 'Hey, babe, you look cute.'

CeCe was wearing a striped playsuit with bright-red Mary Janes and a matching red flower in her hair.

They kissed on both cheeks. 'And you look like a streetwalker,' CeCe grinned.

'That's exactly the look I was going for.'

Dionne felt the first stirrings of amusement as she tottered along the corridor on vertiginous Louboutins, the pair making their way to Alyson's room. Earlier that day, Dionne had insisted on looking through Alyson's suitcase and declared all her clothes completely unsuitable. Cheap, flowery dresses that looked as though they came from Tati, prim cotton shorts more suited to a Girl Scout leader. Didn't she know this was St Tropez, darling? You couldn't dress as if it was a family barbecue in Nowheresville, Ohio.

So Dionne had invited Alyson to look through the clothes she'd brought: naturally, there was a huge selection. Flying private meant no weight restriction, and Dionne had had taken full advantage of that.

'Just don't touch the Hervé,' she warned, indicating the tiny, bandage dress she'd picked out.

Alyson couldn't imagine in what universe she might ever choose to wear the minuscule neon dress, and assured Dionne she'd stay well away. Almost reverentially, she worked her way through the beautiful collection, eventually settling on a white, full-length Valentino gown that Dionne had stolen from a shoot.

'Sure, wear that if you want,' Dionne said airily, as though it was no big deal.

Alyson had been so appreciative, and yet she'd look awful in it, thought Dionne smugly, feeling a delicious pang of *Schadenfreude*. St Trop was all about being young and hip, but the Valentino was more suited to a red-carpet premiere or a formal dinner. Alyson would look ridiculous. Plus the long gown would drown her, the light colour totally washing out her complexion.

They arrived outside Alyson's room and CeCe knocked on the door. She answered immediately and Dionne gasped in shock, a wave of fury washing over her. Alyson looked incredible. The one-shoulder, Grecian-style robe fitted her perfectly, gathering under the bust then falling to the floor in folds of fabric. Her slim figure and pale skin gave her an ethereal quality, like an angel or a classical goddess, while her blonde hair was swept back and secured in a simple bun.

'Do you like the accessories?' CeCe asked Dionne breathlessly, indicating the simple jewellery and silver clutch. 'I lent them to her. They really set off the dress, don't you think?'

'Gorgeous,' Dionne said tonelessly. She was still in a state of shock. She felt totally outclassed, like a hooker standing there in her little dress. Alyson possessed an innate sense of elegance and chic that Dionne never would. She looked like Grace Kelly.

'Do I look okay?' Alyson asked nervously. Dionne could have slapped her. She hated that breathy, little-girl tone that Alyson used. Why couldn't she just grow up? She wasn't a kid any more.

With a flash of clarity, Dionne realized that Alyson was the epitome of everything she hated, all the traits

she'd fought so hard against and would never be –
white, pretty, princessy. Life fell into place so easily
for girls like that. She looked like one of those
aristocratic Brits that Dionne had encountered on her
modelling shoots, the ones who brought out every
feeling of insecurity and inferiority that she'd tried so
hard to bury.

'You look fine,' Dionne said shortly. 'Come on,
let's go.'

The party on the boat was in full swing. The DJ was
on top of his game, pumping out a hot selection of
tracks as the beautiful people mingled. The backdrop
was the picture-perfect harbour of St Tropez where the
yacht was moored, the charming painted houses lit by
soft yellow lights.

Dionne didn't notice any of that. She was dancing,
drinking and flirting, her voice getting louder as the
night wore on. She was high too, helping herself to a
little of whatever was being passed around. Her inhib-
itions had gone, and she felt on top of the world. She
snuggled up to Saeed, sitting in his lap as she told him
repeatedly what a perfect host he was, then the next
moment she was gone, whirling from one group to the
next.

She was holding court with a group of guys – rich,
Eurotrash playboys vying for her attention – when she
spotted something that stopped her in her tracks.

'I have to go find my friend,' she told the men, as
she staggered into the tightly packed crowd in search
of CeCe.

She found her chatting to a cool-looking group, and
urgently grabbed her arm. 'Come with me,' she hissed,
dragging CeCe off.

'Dionne, what—'

'There,' Dionne hissed, as she pointed across the crowd. 'Isn't that—'

'Philippe Rochefort,' CeCe finished, her mouth dropping open.

He was standing with his arm wrapped casually around the waist of a woman that wasn't Alyson. He looked very attentive, leaning down to speak to her, his hand straying over her butt.

'I thought he was in New York,' CeCe managed to say.

'So did I. So did Alyson.'

'Where is she?' CeCe looked round in alarm. 'Should we tell her?'

'Maybe,' Dionne grinned.

CeCe glanced at her suspiciously. She didn't like her expression.

Dionne's mind was working quickly through the drunken fog, a knot of anxiety tearing through her gut as she stared at Philippe. She remembered the humiliation he'd put her through, the way she'd vowed to get back at him one day. Well, now was the perfect opportunity, and it looked as if she could bring Little Miss Priss down a peg or two into the bargain as well.

She gazed out across the crowd, seeing Alyson at the back of the boat talking to some guy she didn't recognize. *Look at her*, Dionne thought hazily, feeling an intense wave of dislike. *With her perfect looks, her perfect life and her rich, powerful boyfriend*. Dionne was the one who'd taught her everything. Months ago, when she'd been heading out on her first date, it had been Dionne that she'd turned to for advice, and Dionne had given it in good faith. Now look how Alyson repaid her – by stealing the limelight from her; taking all the attention from CeCe's show that should rightfully have been hers . . .

Dionne swiped a glass of champagne from a passing waiter and downed it in one. 'Yeah,' she grinned slyly. 'I think we should tell her.'

She made a move, but CeCe grabbed her arm to stop her.

'Don't worry, I'll be nice,' Dionne assured her, crossing her fingers behind her back. Then she disappeared into the crowd, heading directly for Alyson.

Alyson was standing against the railings at the far end of the boat, looking out over the dark water. It was such a beautiful, balmy night, she could hardly believe she was here. At first, she'd felt a little out of place, but the champagne had soon helped with that. She'd become something of a connoisseur during her time working for Rochefort Champagne, and appreciated a fine vintage. Tonight, after a couple of delicious glasses, she'd switched to orange juice, conscious of the fact that she didn't know these people. She didn't want to make a fool of herself in front of them, however outrageously some of them might be acting.

She'd started off talking to a small group – all of them clearly very rich and very important, with jet-set lifestyles and awe-inspiring careers. But gradually they'd drifted away, leaving Alyson alone with a gorgeous German guy. He was tall and blond, strappingly built and breathtakingly handsome in a black suit and crisp white shirt that was unbuttoned a little too low.

They spoke English together, and he'd introduced himself as Count Wilhelm von Niedersachsen-Holstein. Alyson wasn't sure whether to believe him. Did German counts with crazy names really exist, or were they just something out of fairytales?

'All my friends call me Willy,' he'd smiled lazily,

262

showing dazzling white teeth. Alyson wanted to giggle.

But Willy didn't seem to notice as he talked incessantly about himself. He told her about his interests – racing cars, racing boats, racing horses. Alyson smiled politely and tried to look interested. As he talked he relaxed, draping one arm along the side of the railing and around her waist. Alyson flinched at the intimacy but, she reasoned, the party was loud and it was hard to hear. That was the reason he was leaning in so close, she told herself.

'Alyson!'

She glanced up to see Dionne tottering towards her. For once, she was relieved to see her. Willy was getting a little too friendly and a little too boring. Alyson didn't know much about cars or boats or horses and they were running out of conversation.

'I brought you a drink,' Dionne told her brightly, holding out a champagne flute.

Alyson took it, not wanting to be rude. 'Thanks,' she smiled, thinking that Dionne seemed very drunk. Her eyes were glittering brightly, the pupils large and dark, and she didn't appear to be able to focus.

'Hi, I'm Dionne Summers,' she purred, leaning in to kiss Willy on the cheek. She pressed herself up against him, her breasts pushing into his chest.

'Wilhelm,' he said politely, looking a little bemused.

Alyson watched her friend in embarrassment, but she figured Dionne had been to more of these events than she had. Maybe that was just how everyone behaved.

'Would your boyfriend mind you talking to him?' Dionne practically yelled, apparently oblivious to the fact that Willy was still standing beside them.

'I—'

'But he seems like a nice guy,' Dionne cut her off. 'So many guys these days are total assholes, y'know what I'm saying? There's this one guy here tonight – I know him from Paris. CeCe and I took him home one night. We were planning to . . . well, you know. The three of us,' she giggled, in a loud stage whisper.

Alyson flushed. Willy looked amused.

'But, honey, it was *sooo* embarrassing. He was the most terrible lay, with the *tiniest* cock I have ever seen in my life. And he couldn't get it up! The impotent fucking jerk,' she spat venomously. 'But then he's dipped his dick in every girl in Paris. He's probably got something nasty.'

Alyson began to wonder why Dionne was telling her this.

'And he's got the worst reputation,' she continued relentlessly. 'Such a player. A total womanizer. Everyone knows it.'

'Who is this guy?' Willy asked curiously.

Dionne looked delighted, grinning like the cat that got the cream. 'Who *is* he?' she crowed triumphantly. 'He's over there. Look!' She extended one long, painted fingernail, pointing right across the crowd at Philippe Rochefort. He was standing side-on to them, his profile clearly visible and his arm around another woman as he held her tightly, his fingers splayed over her bottom.

'He's fucking disgusting. He makes me wanna hurl,' Dionne hissed gleefully as she melted away into the throng.

Alyson felt her blood run cold. Time seemed to stop. As though he could feel her gaze on him, Philippe turned round, the crowd seeming to part at that exact moment. They locked eyes and a cry escaped from Alyson's lips, a choking, strangled sound.

It's not possible, she thought in horror. Philippe

wasn't even supposed to be in the country; he was in New York. Wasn't he? And he had his arm round some other woman, their bodies close together in a way that suggested a prior intimacy . . . Oh God, it *was* him and he was walking towards her.

'What the hell are you doing? And who the fuck is this?' Philippe immediately went on the offensive. He yanked Wilhelm's arm away from her, squaring up to him. Willy was taller and broader, but Philippe was furious, acting instinctively. Alyson looked on in horror as Willy's friends intervened, pulling him away and placing themselves in front of Philippe.

'What are you doing here?' Alyson pleaded. 'You're not even supposed to *be* here.'

'And this is what you do, is it? When you think I'm not around. Flaunting yourself at every man in sight?'

'Philippe, please—'

'Who is this girl? I don't even know you. I wake up this morning to find you staring out at me from the front of the newspaper, and now you are here, cavorting at some party.'

'You were supposed to be in America,' Alyson repeated.

'And you were supposed to be in Paris. I flew here on the way back from New York as I had business to attend to.'

'Oh right. With *her?*' Alyson jerked her chin at the girl beside him. She was dark-haired, Latina, with a smug expression and outrageous curves poured into a dress so small that even Dionne would have thought twice about wearing it. Immediately, all of Alyson's insecurities resurfaced. Of course she wasn't good enough for Philippe. She looked like a boy, lanky and flat-chested. Who on earth would find her attractive?

'Don't be ridiculous.' His tone was dismissive. 'She works for me.'

'What, like *I* work for you?' Alyson shot back, her voice threatening to break. 'How many more of us are there, hmm? Tucked away in little jobs, where you can keep an eye on us and no one else can touch us?'

'Don't be ridiculous, Alyson. Stop being so childish.' But he looked rattled. 'Let's leave, now.'

'No.' Going anywhere with him was the last thing on her mind.

Philippe looked stunned, outraged that Alyson dared defy him like that in public. He lashed out, determined to hurt her. 'Is this how you are when you think I am away? Just another low-rent, euro-trash girl? Is that why you were parading yourself all over the media? *L'Inconnue*,' he scoffed.

'I – that wasn't supposed to happen . . .' Alyson shook her head, stunned by the way Philippe was behaving. What had happened to the kind, loving, charming guy she knew?

By now people were noticing the commotion, breaking off from their conversations and turning to stare. Saeed came over, his ever-present entourage behind him. 'Alyson, who is this man? Is he bothering you?'

'She's with me, my friend, so back off,' Philippe threatened.

'Alyson is a guest of mine.' Saeed's tone was calm, but menacing. 'If someone upsets her, that upsets me.'

Philippe turned round to look at him properly. Saeed was wearing traditional Arab dress, a long white dishdasha and headscarf. Philippe's lip curled.

'A guest of *his*.' The implication was clear. 'You're just like the rest, fucking anyone you can if you think you'll get something out of it. You little whore.'

Alyson slapped him. The crack was loud, audible above the music. 'How dare you? How dare you call me that?'

Philippe shook his head, unrepentant. 'You're not the girl I thought you were, Alyson.'

'No.' Alyson was furious now. 'I'm not the girl you *wanted* me to be. That's the difference. You tried so hard to keep me under your control, and all the time you were running round with every slut in Paris. All the late nights when you told me you were *working*. God, I was such an idiot!'

'Alyson . . .' Philippe reached out to her, his tone conciliatory.

'Get your hands off me,' Alyson spat, her Lancashire accent suddenly harsh. It made her feel sick to think how she'd trusted him. How she'd let him touch her, make love to her, when really she was just the latest in a long line. He'd even been with Dionne, for Christ's sake. CeCe too.

Alyson looked up, horrified, to see the group of people surrounding them. She caught sight of Dionne's face in the crowd, her expression ecstatic.

'You knew, didn't you?' Alyson whispered accusingly. Somehow Dionne had found out about her and Philippe, and used it to cause maximum humiliation.

'Alyson, don't be ridiculous,' Philippe said sharply, grabbing her arm. 'Come with me. We can talk about it and—'

'Don't touch me,' she yelled. 'Don't ever come near me again. You tried to make me into something I'm not – into what *you* wanted. But I'm my own person. And from now on I do what *I* want, not what anyone else tells me to.'

Her breath was coming fast, her eyes burning with

fury. A feeling of utter shame swept over her as she saw the scandalized faces of the guests, all staring in fascination at the pair of them. She felt an overwhelming sensation of being trapped, the crowd seeming to press in on her, mocking faces everywhere she looked.

With a strangled cry she turned and ran, pushing her way blindly through the crowd as she sprinted off the boat and back down the wooden pier to the dock. Her white gown billowed out behind her; she looked like a ghost against the night sky. Then the darkness swallowed her up, and she was gone.

PART THREE

24

Eighteen months later

Aidan Kennedy was sweltering in the simmering Dubai sun. For an Irish boy like him, such heat was unfamiliar.

He strolled along the waterfront at the Madinat Jumeirah, enjoying the laid-back vibe. It was incredibly peaceful, only a handful of tourists passing him as he walked, and the view was amazing – right across to the Burj al Arab, the instantly recognizable symbol of Dubai. A hotel shaped like an enormous sail, built on a man-made island – an incredible feat of engineering. It boasted a seven-star rating, an interior decorated in gold leaf.

Aidan smiled wryly at the thought of it. He was doing well for himself, but he wasn't quite in that league yet.

He checked his watch and wandered back along the waterway, a water taxi steadily chugging past him. It was mid-afternoon, and the sun showed no signs of cooling yet. He stuck close to the buildings, taking advantage of the shade. The Madinat complex was built around a traditional souk, the heart of the community, to reflect its heritage, although like almost everything else in Dubai, it was thoroughly modern.

When Aidan had almost reached his destination, he stopped, looking from a distance at the property he had come to view. It was empty at the moment, but there were no metal shutters, no boarded-up windows with graffiti and fly-posters like you'd find in Paris or London. Just wooden shutters, which blended in beautifully with the surrounding buildings.

A man approached him. He was European looking, dressed in a suit. Aidan strode forward to meet him. 'Justin Fox?'

'Yes,' the man smiled, offering his hand.

'Aidan Kennedy.' He shook it firmly – Aidan had learned the importance of a good handshake.

'Well, it's great to finally meet you, Aidan.' They'd spoken on the phone already. 'Let's get down to business, shall we? As you can see, it's a superb property, in an unbeatable location . . .' The realtor launched into his speech as he unlocked the wooden shutters, pulling them aside and opening the door. Aidan wasn't listening to him. He blocked out the sound of the sales patter, making his own judgements as he looked around. Over the past couple of years, he'd learned to trust his gut.

His first instincts were that the place was perfect. Justin turned on the light and the room was brought to life. It was a little dusty, an old desk and some rubbish left over from the previous occupants. There was a bar in the corner, very Eighties with mirrors and neon. Aidan didn't care about that. He planned to gut the interior and put his own stamp on it. But it would match his other properties – corporate branding was key.

Yes, Aidan thought as he looked round, examining the kitchens out the back, the cellar downstairs. This was exactly what he wanted. He felt a growing sense of excitement at the thought of expanding out of Europe. This would make the perfect site for his third Kennedy's – his rapidly growing bar and restaurant chain.

Not long after Alyson had left Chez Paddy, Aidan had resigned. He'd been there long enough, coasting with his life. But he had no plan of what to do next; all he knew was that he wanted to get out of Paris, so he'd retreated across the Channel to London, crashing on a friend's sofa.

He'd spent a while not working, growing a beard, getting drunk and sleeping with as many women as possible. He would head to the tackiest bars in Leicester Square, where the alcohol was flowing and the women were easy – students, hen parties, all seduced by his alluring Irish accent and up for a good time.

When he woke up one morning in a poky hotel room near King's Cross, lying beside some girl he'd rather have chewed his own arm off than gone home with sober, he knew it was time to change his lifestyle.

Somewhere, at the back of his mind, a thought kept niggling away. The business plan he'd drawn up in Paris. His long-held dream of owning a bar and restaurant.

He found his rough scribbles, faded and creased, and drew it up properly. Thirty-five pages of well-researched charts and tables, goals and projections. It was clear, concise and ambitious. Aidan printed it off and dragged himself around all the major banks in London, trying to get a loan. It wasn't a good time. The markets were unstable and the banks were cautious, wary of investing such a large amount on such a risky project.

The friend he was staying with – Niall Hamilton, an old mate from uni – had a great job as a commodities broker and owned a beautiful apartment in South Kensington. He offered to put it up as collateral. Aidan said no, but Niall insisted – he had a lot of spare cash floating around and had been thinking of speculating, investing in property. This was his first punt. They negotiated a rate of interest – high enough so that Aidan felt he was being fair to his friend, low enough that he stood a hope in hell of paying it back if it all went pear-shaped. Combined with a small bank loan and Aidan's own meagre savings, his long-held dreams were about to become a reality.

Aidan worked like a dog to get Kennedy's London off the ground. He hired the best people he could afford and project-managed the whole venture himself. He hardly slept, rarely went home and frequently crashed out in the office. But Aidan was proud of himself and the way Kennedy's was shaping up. He worked with a great designer to get exactly the look he wanted – classic with a modern twist, all cream walls and soft lighting, Irish linen and Waterford crystal on the tables. None of the dark, faux-rustic look he'd grown to hate at Chez Paddy.

Five months later, the first Kennedy's officially opened, on Charlotte Street in central London. It had taken time to find the perfect location – Mayfair was deemed too pretentious, Islington too passé, Covent Garden too touristy. Aidan wanted Kennedy's to be a cut above the usual tourist traps, a destination venue for locals as well as visitors. The food was European, combining the best of British, French and Irish. The drinks list was extensive – but he made sure they didn't stock Rochefort Champagne.

After a high-profile launch, business was slow and

Aidan was worried. But word got around. The restaurant was regularly reviewed, always favourably. The bloggers praised it; foodie websites couldn't get enough of it. It became a firm favourite with the media set, who drifted up from Soho and, thanks to Niall's influence, it hosted its fair share of City folk. Kennedy's also began to acquire something of a celebrity following, especially amongst those performing in the nearby West End theatres. And where celebs went, rubbernecking fans inevitably followed, hoping to catch a glimpse of a famous face.

Within six months they'd begun to break even, a feat practically unheard of. By the eighth month, they were turning a small profit. Aidan didn't rest on his laurels and began searching for a second site, this time in Dublin. Ireland was in economic turmoil, but Aidan had confidence in his brand and was filled with an almost sentimental desire to return to his home town – the local boy made good. Niall suggested a partnership but, grateful though Aidan was for his support, he didn't want to be beholden to anyone. This time when he went knocking, with a positive balance sheet and some impressive figures, the banks were far more accommodating.

A few months later, Kennedy's Dublin opened, just off Harcourt Street in a fashionable part of the city. It could have been completed sooner, but Aidan was eager to do everything himself and commuted between the two locations, insisting that no major decisions could be made without him. He found the ideal venue almost immediately but held out, certain he could make the vendor drop his price. He was right.

In just over a year, Aidan had gone from sleeping on Niall's sofa, waking up hungover and uninspired, to owning two successful restaurants in two capital cities.

And he didn't intend to stop there. Like his customers, his appetite was insatiable. He planned to open a third Kennedy's as soon as possible, and considered numerous locations. He knew that this one would be outside of Europe – he wanted to begin his world domination as soon as possible. The US was in the running, as was the Far East. But Dubai was up and coming, thrusting and precocious, just like himself. Full of ex-pats, he had a ready-made clientele, and Aidan believed the sophisticated yet unpretentious atmosphere of Kennedy's would go down just as well there as it had in London and Dublin.

It wasn't just Kennedy's that was on the rise – the man behind it was too. The *Financial Times* had profiled him. Forbes mentioned him as one to watch, and he gave interviews to *GQ* and Irish *Tatler*. Aidan was young, stylish and rich. *And* he was single. Of course, there were women now and again. More regularly than that, if he was being honest. But when interviewers asked if he was looking to settle down, he simply smiled enigmatically and said he was too busy for that, or that he just hadn't met that someone special.

It was a lie. Aidan *had* met that someone special. He saw her every day, staring out at him from the cover of glossy magazines, on billboards, even in TV ads. Alyson. He couldn't get her out of his head. But she'd chosen Philippe Rochefort over him. Oh, he knew they'd split up ages ago, but it still hurt like hell. He remembered the way the guy had looked at him – like he was nothing. Lower than nothing. Well, no one was ever going to look at him like that again, Aidan vowed, balling up his fists so tightly that the veins on his arms stood out.

He walked out of the Dubai property as Justin Fox locked up behind him. He'd seen everything he needed to see. Aidan felt the hot sun beaming down, burning his skin after the shade of the interior.

'Send the details over to my lawyer,' Aidan instructed him. 'I'd like him to look through the papers.'

The two men shook hands and parted.

Aidan stood for a moment feeling the full force of the late afternoon heat, almost revelling in the discomfort. He'd just found his third Kennedy's, and a sense of invincibility pulsed through his blood. He was building an empire to rival Philippe Rochefort's. He wanted to ensure no one could ever look at him like that again.

Dionne walked into the studio, flung herself into the make-up chair and pulled off her dark sunglasses.

'You're late,' said a voice. It was Alexa Palmer, brand director of Armani Exchange, who Dionne was supposed to be shooting a campaign for today.

'And?' Dionne shot back. 'It's not like you can start without me.'

She shook her hair out behind her, closing her eyes as the make-up artist, Elise, got to work. She was the star and she knew it. After all, if it wasn't for her, they would never even sell their ridiculous little perfume or lipstick or whatever the hell it was she was supposed to be advertising today. She'd only flown into NY from Paris a couple of hours ago; they should be fucking grateful she was there at all, Dionne thought irritably.

'Nicolo's been here for hours,' said Alexa. Nicolo was the male model.

'So what. Nobody cares about him,' Dionne quipped. It was all the more infuriating because it was true. 'Let me go check him out,' Dionne announced. She got up out of the chair and walked off as Elise stared after her in exasperation. 'If he's a moose or a dork I'm not working with him.'

'She's a total fucking nightmare,' Elise hissed as Dionne flounced off.

'She's just as bad as everyone says she is,' agreed Alexa.

'What a diva,' said Gerard, the hair stylist. Gerard was gay, and his tone was awestruck.

Dionne barged into Nicolo's dressing room without knocking. 'Is he in here?' she yelled. 'Oh hel-*lo*,' she broke off, a lascivious look crossing her beautiful face. Nicolo was pulling on a pair of spotless white briefs. Dionne caught a glimpse of firm, tight buttocks as he stood up and whirled round. His skin was tanned and glistening. He had an incredible six-pack, an impressive bulge in his trunks. Dionne stared unashamedly.

'Is that all you, or have you got a roll of quarters down there?'

'*Scusi?*'

'Never mind, honey,' Dionne grinned wickedly. It didn't matter if they didn't speak the same language. Some things were universal. She let her eyes run languidly over him, leaving him in no doubt as to her intentions.

Then she walked right up to him, standing intimidatingly close. He was a few inches taller than her, and when he looked down, he couldn't help but stare directly at her cleavage. Dionne tilted her head upwards, as though she was about to kiss him. 'I'm Dionne, nice to meet you,' she purred, her voice breathy.

Nicolo looked intoxicated by her, absolutely under her spell. Elise, standing behind Dionne, was pissed off. Nicolo had been pretty friendly with *her* until Dionne had rocked up. It was like a form of racism, Elise thought bitterly. Models only stuck with their own breed – other beautiful people. It was as though they didn't want to pollute the gene pool. Five-foot-nothing make-up artists with out-of-control hair and a few extra pounds on the hips certainly didn't count.

'Well, I'm looking forward to working with you,' Dionne told him breathlessly. She turned and sashayed to the door, throwing him a look over her shoulder.

Elise followed her as she finally sat back down in the chair.

'Make sure I look hot,' Dionne snapped at her. Then she closed her eyes as Elise got to work, reflecting on the perfection of the butt cheeks she'd just seen. She wouldn't mind grabbing onto those later. And if Nicolo was lucky, she might suck him off before she made him go down on her.

Dionne felt confident she could have him. She could have any man she wanted.

Of course, David was still hanging around, but sometimes that wasn't enough. It was like everything in her life these days – she could have whatever she wanted. Dionne could make the most insane request and some underling would be despatched to find it, with instructions to return as fast as possible.

Eighteen months ago, when she'd walked for Capucine, her career had already been on the up. But that one show had sent her career skyrocketing. Dionne had shown no hesitation in dumping her small-time agent and signing with Elite as soon as she could. She hadn't stopped working since, catapulted into the big league. Armani, Marc Jacobs, Alexander McQueen, Louis Vuitton – you name them, she'd walked for them. She'd done ad campaigns for Versace, Gucci and Burberry, covers for French *Elle*, Brazilian *Vogue* and *i-D* magazine. There'd been a collaboration with MAC, and spokes-model roles for H&M and Revlon.

Ultimately, Dionne wanted to be a global brand, a multitasking super force. Heidi had the presenting, the Birkenstocks, the maternity line. Kate had the music, the high street collaborations, the perfumes. Dionne wanted to be bigger than any of them.

The only blight in her otherwise charmed existence was Alyson Wakefield. Perfect, pretty Alyson – or Ally, as she'd been rebranded. *L'Inconnue*, as the media sometimes fondly referred to her. She'd just walked straight into the career Dionne had been fighting for her whole life, and everyone loved her. She'd even stolen Dionne's guaranteed gig as the face of Capucine, and for that Dionne couldn't forgive her – or CeCe.

The two women had very different styles. Dionne was strong and brash, feisty and in-your-face. Her shots were always electric, full-of-energy action poses. You almost expected her to leap from the page and sock you in the face.

In comparison, Alyson was boring and insipid – according to Dionne, anyway. With her slim, pale body, she was perceived as vulnerable and waif-like, touted as the natural successor to Kate Moss. She'd been photographed dewy-eyed and flat-chested for Calvin Klein, WASP-y and precious for Ralph Lauren. Dionne couldn't stand her.

She'd tried to trash her career before it even got off the ground, but it hadn't worked. Alyson's rise had been too meteoric, and Dionne simply didn't have the clout.

The two hadn't spoken since that day on the yacht. Alyson had walked out, leaving without speaking to anyone. Dionne refused to feel guilty over what she'd done. Alyson needed to get with the real world. Men slept around. Hell, women slept around. Why couldn't Alyson just get out there and have a little fun?

According to tabloid reports, she was still single. She was never pictured out with guys. All she did was work that skinny butt off, and designers and the media all loved her.

Dionne pursed her lips in a way that made Elise sigh in frustration. Dionne didn't notice. She was too busy brooding about Alyson Wakefield. Well, she wasn't going to think about her any more. She was going to think about the gorgeous guy next door and what she was going to do to him after the shoot.

Fuck Alyson Wakefield, and her workaholic, virginal ways. Dionne was going to take over the world, and she was going to have a hell of a lot of fun doing it.

25

The club was dark. It was a narrow cavern of underground tunnels, the brickwork painted black and covered in posters for upcoming gigs. Music was playing loudly – French pop, occasionally mixed in with something edgier.

CeCe leaned against the wall, feeling the rough edge of the brickwork press into her back. She took a slug from her brandy and coke. She was starting to feel good – she'd taken a little MDMA to loosen her up, and it was beginning to kick in. Hazily, she stared around her. There were a lot of people on the dance floor and the sweat was dripping from the ceiling. Beside her, two girls were heavily making out, oblivious to everyone around them.

CeCe wondered if anyone recognized her. With her distinctive style, she rarely blended into the background. Her hair was still cropped short, but she'd grown out the other side and dyed the whole thing a vivid red. It was pretty noticeable. Then again, she wasn't on the radar for anyone outside the fashion world. The models were the public faces, and very few designers achieved household recognition unless they courted it. CeCe didn't court it. She had no interest in being a celebrity. She just wanted to be known for what she did.

She downed the brandy and coke, and felt the world begin to blur. That was good. That was how she wanted it to be. To dull the pain, and not to have to deal with reality.

The last eighteen months had been a roller coaster by anyone's standards. The Tuileries show had had the desired effect, catapulting her into the fashion industry's consciousness. Almost instantly she was the hottest new thing on the block, bigger than she'd dared to dream. Celebrities wanted to wear Capucine on the red carpet, requests tumbling in thick and fast for a bespoke gown for this event or that film premiere.

CeCe had gone from being a one-woman band to suddenly acquiring a huge team, each of whom claimed to be necessary for her future survival – agents, managers, publicists, spokespeople, not to mention a whole design team to help her produce the hugely anticipated next collection. CeCe had appointed quickly and well – young, hungry kids who were outside the established modes. She didn't want anyone safe or risk averse – those who'd trained in knitwear, or who favoured drab, 'classic' styles in grey and beige. CeCe took the talented and the eccentric, those who fitted her ethos and could share her vision.

Then there had been the endless flights. To the Far East to visit factories, to Italy to source materials. She'd hired a team of pattern-cutters in Poland, a PR agency in the States to promote Capucine over there. It was nonstop. CeCe wondered if she would ever find the time to design again.

But the fashion world was waiting with baited breath, eager to see her A/W collection, this time presented 'officially' at the Carrousel du Louvre. CeCe's feet had barely touched the ground in six months, and the second collection was built on adrenaline, enthusiasm and excitement. The critics adored it, falling over themselves to give it glowing reviews, each one more effusive than the last. Commercially, it was a huge success; Capucine A/W had been stocked by Printemps in Paris, Selfridges in London, by Saks and Neiman Marcus in New York, to name but a few.

Hand in hand with the rave reviews came the job offers. CeCe was approached to become head of womenswear at Hermès – a dream job by anyone's standards, let alone someone who'd been a complete unknown twelve months ago. But after agonized soul-searching and endless sleepless nights, CeCe turned it down. Her priority was to make a success of Capucine, to build the label and grow it – not to throw it all away and become immersed by some huge brand.

Then LVMH made an offer to buy her out. They were offering everything she needed on a plate – money, security, big-name backing, all dangled temptingly under her nose. CeCe bit the bullet and turned them down too, fearing outside interference and a loss of control. Everyone said she was crazy. Perhaps she was. All she knew was that she'd made it this far by herself, and selling out at the first opportunity would feel like failure. So she struggled on by herself, spending days on end kicking herself for not having succumbed to the billion-dollar pockets of LVMH. Life would be so easy, so much more secure . . . But in her heart, she knew she'd done the right thing.

And then the backlash started. The whispers had begun with her last S/S collection, a year after her fêted Tuileries debut. Most of the reviews had been positive. Just a few – that bitch Ana Rodzik on the

Slave to Fashion website, and that known dyke-hater, Stéphane Matthiae, who wrote for *Madame Figaro* – had voiced their dissent. Phrases like 'unoriginal', 'running out of steam' and 'one-season wonder' had been bandied about.

CeCe tried to ignore them, putting her head down and getting on with her designs, an A/W collection that would put her firmly back where she belonged and silence her detractors. But the pressure was getting to her, the stress of the situation undeniable.

The latest Paris Fashion Week had ended just over a fortnight ago, and CeCe had been roundly slated. This time, the critics hadn't been so limited – the consensus was that she'd lost it.

It happens to so many . . . commiserated *La Mode*. *After a promising start, Capucine turns out to be little more than a one-season wonder . . .*

CeCe Bouvier has become a victim of her own hype, bitched Stylista.com. *Her latest show proves that her much-heralded debut was nothing more than a clever PR stunt.*

CeCe had burned with fury when she read that. She was so annoyed, she could hardly see straight.

But it didn't just affect her – it crushed the team around her. They'd believed they were joining something new and exciting, looking forward to a bright future in a prestigious fashion house. CeCe could hardly bear to see the look of disappointment in their eyes. They were losing their belief in her, losing faith in the Capucine label. And that, for CeCe, was harder to bear than anything else.

She knew she needed to get back on the horse, rally the troops and dive headlong into her next collection. It needed to be incredible, something original, beautiful and coveted, to put her back on the map and prove her critics wrong. But she couldn't do it. CeCe hated to admit it, but she was terrified. She'd only been back in the studio once. The looks on everyone's faces, the accusation and blame in their eyes, had frightened her so badly that she'd locked herself in her private office, requesting not be disturbed. She'd spent a horrific afternoon staring at a blank piece of paper, unable to do anything. It was as though her brain had shut down. No inspiration came.

CeCe had fled, straight to a bar where she'd begun drinking. When it got later she'd moved on to a club where she'd picked up a girl. Anything to dull the pain, to not be alone when she woke up. When the girl left the next morning, CeCe threw on her clothes and headed out to a bar, where the cycle began again. This had been going on for two weeks now, and she hadn't been back to Capucine's offices since. The black mist had descended, the depression that CeCe knew from experience was so hard to battle her way out of. She didn't even have the energy to try; she wanted to lie back, wave a white flag and lose herself somewhere at the bottom of a brandy bottle.

Tonight she was at La Douceur, one of her less frequented haunts in the Marais. CeCe stared at her empty glass for a moment, then staggered to the bar for another. As she slumped against the counter, a girl approached her. CeCe turned her head to look, unashamedly checking her out. Her vision was blurred, but the girl was cute. Asian – Japanese maybe. Her face was pretty, with fine features and sloping, almond-shaped eyes; a long curtain of thick, dark hair fell straight down her back.

'Can I buy you a drink?' CeCe asked. Her words were slurred.

The girl shook her head, reaching for CeCe's hand

and pulling her onto the dance floor. It was totally unexpected. For a second, CeCe just stood there stupidly as the girl began to dance.

Her body was tiny. She wore black skinny jeans, slung low on her protruding hips, heavy biker boots and a white vest top with spaghetti straps. She had a flat chest, sharp nipples visible through the thin fabric, and a snake inked in black on her right shoulder blade. Her skin was creamy white, contrasting dramatically with the dark tattoo.

CeCe began to move, awkwardly at first. She didn't usually dance, and she'd been drinking heavily. Her body felt clumsy and uncoordinated. She started to move from side to side, swaying to the rhythm, feeling the beat. CeCe closed her eyes self-consciously, not wanting to see the girl watching her, trying to get lost inside herself.

She knew she couldn't go on like this – the drinking, the partying, the one-night stands – but she didn't know what else to do. She was paralysed by fear. It was weeks since she'd touched her designs; after that abortive attempt in the Capucine offices, she'd been too scared to even try. She knew what the real problem was. Her muse had deserted her.

CeCe needed to be in love to design. It didn't have to be a sexual thing, she just needed to adore someone, to give her all to them. For a long time that had been Dionne. She'd been crazy about her since the first night they met; she loved being around her, absorbing that energy and lust for life. It was no coincidence that she'd been at her most creative and most inspired in those early days, when she, Dionne and Alyson had shared an apartment in the 8th. Dionne had pushed her all the way – hell, she'd even been the one to suggest gate-crashing the Tuileries and putting on the flash-mob show that had launched Capucine globally.

It was after that Fashion Week that everything had begun to fall apart. The press had picked out Alyson as the star of the show – not Dionne, as everyone expected. They'd clamoured for interviews with CeCe and Alyson, 'the designer and her muse', as they'd been dubbed. *L'Inconnue* and the woman who'd discovered her.

Dionne had been livid, accusing CeCe of betraying her. Hadn't they agreed, all that time ago, that when one of them made it, they'd do whatever they could to help the other? They'd made a pact, Dionne reminded her furiously, and that pact couldn't be broken.

CeCe was torn. Had it been solely down to her, she'd have chosen Dionne in a heartbeat, but the situation was no longer that simple. The fact was that Alyson was now the one getting all the publicity. It was Alyson the press were clamouring to speak to. She and CeCe were the dream ticket as far as the media were concerned, and Dionne was just another of the jobbing models CeCe had booked for the day.

'You're a fool if you don't take her,' Jacques Perrot, CeCe's new second-in-command told her.

The rest of the team were equally enamoured: 'We want to work with Ally – she looks amazing in the clothes, she perfectly captures the spirit of Capucine, and everyone loves her.'

Her new investors were even plainer – 'Go with Ally, or we pull the funding.' The consensus was clear and CeCe was backed into a corner.

'It was out of my hands,' she told Dionne beseechingly, as she broke the news that Alyson had been chosen for Capucine's first campaign. 'I'll make it up to you, I promise.' She couldn't bear Dionne to be angry with her. They'd been friends for so long and CeCe worshipped her; she would walk over hot coals if Dionne demanded it.

Dionne looked at her long and hard. She drew herself up to her full height, a sneer forming on those bee-stung lips. 'Go fuck yourself,' Dionne told her bluntly.

They hadn't spoken since, and CeCe missed her more than she could possibly say, horrified to think that she'd put her career before their friendship. At first she'd tried to make up with her, but her phone calls went unanswered, emails ignored, and after a while she simply gave up. Dionne's career continued to flourish and the message was clear: *I can do this without you.* She was ferociously ambitious, willing to do whatever it took and trample on whomever she needed to in order to make it to the top. At times, the strength of her determination was frightening.

Any chance she got, Dionne would bad-mouth Capucine and Alyson, refusing to work with either of them. It was incredibly unprofessional, but the press loved a bad girl and rivalry like that sold magazines. Dionne got the fame she craved and became a gossip column staple, frequenting the world's hot spots with a veritable harem of eligible men – dining with David Mouret in Paris, partying with a hot young rock star in Miami, holidaying in the Turks and Caicos with a big-shot movie producer. CeCe papered over the cracks in her broken heart and tried to move on.

When Dionne packed her things and moved out of their shared apartment, CeCe couldn't stand to be there any longer. Everywhere she turned there were ghosts – of Dionne, of Alyson, of the good times the three of them had shared, the tears they'd cried and the ridiculous quantities of champagne they'd drunk. She handed in her notice for the tenancy and moved out the following day, not even staying until the end of the notice period. It felt like the end of an era. She bought her own place in Sentier, the textile district; a beautiful, high-ceilinged, two-hundred-square-metre apartment, a stone's throw from Capucine's offices. She intended it to be a new start, a way of proving to herself that she was grown up enough to live on her own.

She hated it.

She'd never really lived by herself before, and she couldn't handle it. The silence, the oppressive sound of nothing, the hell of being left alone with her own thoughts. Instead of going home she would work until the early hours at the studio, then crash out overnight on the cramped sofa in the office. She might go back to her apartment in the afternoon and grab a shower, before hurrying back to Capucine. The daytimes weren't so bad; it was the nights that were the worst, all alone with only the darkness and the silence for company.

Sometimes she would go out to a club and pick up a girl – it was a long time now since she'd been with a guy – and take them back with her. It meant there was someone to hold her in the night, and be there for her when she woke up.

At first, CeCe realized that all the women she was bringing home were carbon copies of Dionne – black, curvy, outrageous. So she began deliberately going against type. Short, busty blondes; butch-looking, masculine women; or Oriental, like the girl in front of her now. Delightfully androgynous, with slim bodies and skinny hips.

CeCe opened her eyes. The girl was dancing as if she didn't give a damn what anyone thought. Her arms were thrown above her head, her body moving in time to the music. She smiled at CeCe and moved closer. Then she wrapped her arms around her and leaned in to kiss her. Instinctively, CeCe responded. At the back of her mind she felt faintly embarrassed, knowing that she was drunk, that she must smell of brandy and cigarettes. The girl who was kissing her smelt divine. It wasn't perfume, just the scent of her skin – fresh and clean, like soap and moisturiser.

CeCe pulled her closer as their kisses grew harder, mouths open, tongues exploring. The girl tasted sweet, as though she'd been drinking something fruity. Her lips were soft, her body small and tight. CeCe let her hands roam across that flat, compact ass, around the tiny, almost nonexistent curve of her waist. She stroked the skin on her arm; it was hairless and soft, like a child's.

The girl broke the kiss, pulling away and leaning her cheek against CeCe's as she spoke in her ear.

'I'm Mayumi,' she told her, raising her voice to be heard over the noise of the music. 'What's your name?'

'Cécile,' CeCe told her. She was yelling in her ear, too drunk to make a good impression. 'I'm Cécile,' she repeated, unsure if Mayumi had heard her.

Mayumi looked at her and smiled, tossing her long, dark hair over her shoulders. 'Okay, Cécile. Let's get out of here.'

26

Alyson was sitting in her hotel room in Tokyo. It was situated on the forty-eighth floor of the Park Hyatt hotel, and the view was breathtaking, out over the dazzling skyscrapers and futuristic towers of Shinjuku, all the way to Mount Fuji on a clear day. Now it was dark, and the city below her was a sea of shimmering lights and glistening neon, the Tokyo Tower lit up brightly in the distance.

Right now, Alyson didn't care. She closed the shades and sank down onto the bed. She wasn't tired; she just felt listless, apathetic. She had no idea why she felt so down. It seemed ridiculously self-indulgent. Here she was, in this beautiful hotel suite, with the world at her feet – literally – and yet, for all its luxury, the room felt like a prison cell.

Alyson lay lifelessly on the bed. She knew she should do something, but she couldn't decide what. Bathe? Eat? Sleep?

Her phone began to ring. Lazily, Alyson rolled over and reached for it. It was her agency in New York.

'Hey, Ally, it's Donna.' The voice on the other end had a sharp, Brooklyn accent and talked at a mile a minute. 'So, I have your flights confirmed to JFK tomorrow. I've spoken with Keiko at Shiseido and told her that your shoot absolutely cannot overrun. There's a car coming for you at four p.m. Japanese time, and it *cannot* be delayed.'

In spite of herself, Alyson smiled. She couldn't imagine the mild-mannered, polite Keiko refusing anything of this abrasive Yank. 'Okay,' Alyson agreed resignedly.

There was a pause on the other end of the line. 'You okay, Ally?'

It's Alyson! She wanted to shout. *My name is Alyson!* Only her father had ever called her Ally, and for that reason she despised it. But she'd been rebranded, repackaged to make her palatable to the masses, and now everyone knew her as Ally. Sometimes, it felt as though the whole world wanted a piece of Ally, supermodel and supposed fashion icon. No one was interested in Alyson Wakefield, the shy, awkward girl from Manchester.

'Yes,' she replied. She hesitated for a moment. 'No, actually.'

Was that the tiniest sigh on the other end of the line? 'What is it?' Donna asked briskly.

Alyson paused. 'I don't know if I want to do this,' she said, in a small voice.

'Do what? The shoot?'

'The whole thing. The shoot. Modelling . . .' She'd just made it through another season. Four cities, endless aeroplanes, God alone knew how many shows. The intensity, the craziness, people talking about her as though she wasn't there, sticking pins in her, the complete loss of dignity . . . Even just the thought of it depressed her unbearably.

'Ally . . .' *Yes, Donna definitely sounded pissed off.*

293

'You're just tired, okay? *Everyone* hates the season,' she lied. 'I know it's long and stressful, but it's over now. Look, you've been working really hard, so how about I try and clear your diary for a few weeks' time and you can take a few days off, hmm? Book yourself in somewhere nice and just disappear. I know this fabulous place in the Maldives; all the girls here swear by it. You want me to give you the details?'

'No, thanks.' Tropical spas weren't exactly her thing. 'But maybe some time off does sound good . . .'

'Exactly,' Donna said crisply, sounding pleased that the crisis had been averted. One thing Ally Wakefield could always be relied on for was her professionalism. She turned up on time, did whatever was asked of her, and was unfailingly polite to everyone from the photographer right down to the work experience kid who fetched the coffee. She was never hungover, never threw a hissy fit, and always nailed the shot.

But there was something almost detached about her. She didn't seem interested in the whole fashion world, nor in the perks of celebrity. The rumour was that she'd never asked to keep anything from a shoot. She even turned down free stuff, sent it back with a polite note. Who the hell turned down a complimentary Marc Jacobs handbag with a six-month waiting list? But the way Ally saw it, she already had a handbag and was happy with it, so why would she need another?

To some, this aloofness made her even more fascinating. In an age where celebs spilled every detail about themselves, when everything from what they had for breakfast to what brand of toothpaste they preferred was documented and posted on a website somewhere, this sense of mystery was refreshing. As long as she kept bringing in a truck-load of cash for the agency, Donna didn't care what she did.

'You'll be fine. Have a bath, and an early night. You'll feel better in the morning. Better still, I have some friends out in Tokyo right now – John Forbes, the photographer. He shot Gisele for Italian *Vogue* last month,' she gabbled. 'And there's Ayako Takata, she's Head of Branding for Kenzo. Also Giuliana Petrucci, this divine little Italian model on our books who's working out there at the moment. Do you know any of them? I could give them a call, you could head out to dinner with them . . .'

'No, thank you,' Alyson said quickly. Fashion people. She couldn't think of anything worse. She hated all the bullshit that went with the industry. She didn't think she'd come across one genuine person the whole eighteen months she'd been part of it. They only wanted to know her while she was hot, she thought cynically. She couldn't think of one person she could really call a friend, who'd still want to be there after the buzz around her inevitably cooled.

'Okay, your call. I'll speak to you soon, Ally.'

'Bye.' But Donna had already rung off.

Alyson lay on her bed, staring at the ceiling. Donna didn't understand what she was talking about. No one did. How could she complain that she felt completely unfulfilled, empty inside, when everyone else thought she had the perfect life? After all, she got to travel the world, wear incredible clothes and make more money in a day than most people made in a year.

She knew she sounded ungrateful, like a spoilt child, but she couldn't help how she felt. Of course, there were perks to the job. She'd invested wisely with the money she'd made, and knew that if it all stopped tomorrow she'd be set for life. But Alyson had never wanted to be a model. Her ambitions lay in other directions, and right now she felt as if life was passing her by. She needed something to challenge her, to excite her senses and stimulate her mind.

Stop feeling sorry for yourself! Alyson reprimanded herself sharply. It was pathetic. She jumped up off the bed, pulling on her Burberry trench and tucking her hair up under a matching trilby. It was less of a fashion statement and more a way of trying to go incognito. Since making a name for herself, Alyson had learned the importance of hats and a large pair of sunglasses.

She grabbed her purse and headed to the elevator with a growing sense of excitement. She loved Tokyo. It was the third time she'd been here, and whilst the city was becoming familiar, there was still so much to see. She knew she'd barely scratched the surface.

She walked out of the hotel, slipping into the crush of people on the pavement, just another face in the crowd. She adored the energy and buzz of Tokyo, the way it forced her out of her comfort zone. Not everyone spoke English, and many of the signs were in Japanese only, so any solo outing was always an adventure. In a lot of ways, the city felt so Western and advanced, but the culture was completely alien to her, and if she stepped off the beaten track it felt as though she was in another world.

Tonight, that was exactly what Alyson needed. She just wanted to walk and explore, to be anonymous and unnoticed. She headed towards Shinjuku Station, past the flashy malls and the high-tech stores selling the latest must-have gadgets. Alyson kept walking. She wasn't here to shop.

No one seemed to recognize her. Oh, she attracted plenty of attention – at five foot eleven, with white-blonde hair, she felt like a different species, towering over both men and women. But with her hat pulled low, the brim of her collar turned up against the chilly

Tokyo spring, she could pass unnoticed through the busy streets.

As she reached Shinjuku Station, she stopped dead. Just above her was an enormous billboard, her own face plastered across it and staring down at her. For a moment, she didn't move. The crowds flowed around her, hurrying on their way. No one paid attention. It was like a clash of two worlds – up there was unreality: beautiful, untouchable Ally. Down in the street she was just Alyson, and no one gave a damn.

She put her head down and kept walking, past the station, skirting the edge of the red light district at Kabukicho. Her mind was racing, trying to work through the issues in her head. As she so often did, Alyson found herself going back to that night in St Tropez, the night that had changed everything for her.

She'd run from Philippe and fled back to her room, expecting someone to come after her. No one did. She was alone, she realized, completely reliant on herself – the way she always had been. There was no way she would trust anyone again – not friends, not a man. Trust was for fools who didn't mind having their hearts broken.

Quickly, Alyson had got her things together. It didn't take long. She packed her small suitcase and checked out, scribbling a brief note for Saeed on the hotel notepaper. She thanked him for his hospitality and apologized for leaving without saying goodbye. He probably didn't give a damn, but she prided herself on good manners. Then Alyson took a taxi to the airport. Not to Le Mole, where she'd arrived, but to Nice, with all the other holidaymakers who couldn't afford to fly private.

When she got back to the apartment, the first thing she did was email her resignation to Richard Duval.

She felt bad – he'd been nothing but kind to her – but she apologized for the short notice and said she was sure M. Rochefort would approve the decision. Richard had probably been expecting this email for a while, she realized.

After that, she packed and got the hell out of there. She couldn't bear to stay in the apartment another night, and wanted to make sure she was gone before Dionne and CeCe got back. What was it Dionne had said? That they'd both been with Philippe? Dionne and CeCe together, planning to have sex with her boyfriend.

Questions raced through Alyson's mind. When? How long ago? And where? Had they been in Philippe's beautiful apartment, the place where she'd spent so much of her time and regarded as a sanctuary from the rest of the world? His bed, where she'd slept with him night after night, where she'd let him touch her and do things to her no other man had done? Or had they been here, in the very flat she shared with the pair of them. Maybe she'd even overheard them, lain awake at night listening to Dionne groan and scream through the wall . . .

Alyson felt sick. No, she was never trusting anyone again, she vowed, as she threw her clothes into a suitcase. Tears stung at her eyes, but she blinked them furiously away. She called a taxi and drove straight to a cheap hotel, where she finally gave in to her misery, throwing herself down on the small, hard bed and sobbing. She felt as though she was back to square one. It was eerily reminiscent of when she'd first arrived in Paris – no job, no friends, just a shitty hotel room in an unsavoury area. She cried until she was exhausted, eventually falling asleep on top of the dirty counterpane.

She almost didn't make her appointment with IMG.

She overslept, depression making her drowsy, and when she finally woke up she barely had the energy to get out of bed. But she hated letting people down and dragged herself up. Alyson didn't make any effort with her appearance. The make-up Philippe had bought her for work lay untouched in her bag, and she simply threw on her old jeans and T-shirt. They'd soon see that they'd made a big mistake, that Alyson Wakefield was no model.

Incredibly, they hired her on the spot. They spoke to her briefly, took a few test photos and told her excitedly that she was going to be the Next Big Thing. Alyson wasn't impressed – she assumed they said that to everyone, and she'd had enough of bullshit promises to last her a lifetime.

They asked where she was living. When she told them, they moved her straight out into model accommodation. Five other girls, bitchy and competitive, all sharing a tiny space. It was hell. Alyson lasted two weeks before she moved out. By then it was clear she could afford her own place. The work was flying in, and everyone wanted to sign *l'Inconnue*, the hottest new model in town.

Magazines wanted to interview her, features were written about her. Alyson told reporters the bare minimum, then began to decline interview requests altogether. She didn't like the fact that what she said seemed to have changed by the time it made it into print. That the huge pull-out quotes they used didn't accurately reflect the way she'd expressed herself. That the media appeared to be trying to mould her into something she wasn't to fit the story they'd created.

More than anything, she hated the intrusion into her private life. Why did some nosy journalist she didn't know from Adam deserve to know every detail of where she'd grown up, where she liked to holiday, what her favourite skin-care product was? It was none of their damn business. So she kept quiet and continued to model. What else could she do? It wasn't as though she had a real job, something concrete that she could go back to. She'd been a barmaid, then a general dogsbody for her ex-boyfriend's company. Now she was bringing in good money. Most importantly, while she was forever working, travelling, moving, she had no time to think. She could block out all thoughts of Philippe, how she'd trusted him and how he'd betrayed her.

Blocking out thoughts of Dionne was more difficult. She was everywhere and, unlike Alyson, she wasn't shy about talking to the press. It wasn't long before the gossip rags began to get wind of some feud between the two women, and it seemed pretty obvious that Dionne had leaked it, hoping for more publicity. She wasn't exactly subtle. Usually, the two of them avoided each other as best they could, but Alyson had heard rumours of Dionne refusing to do shows if Alyson was already booked for them. Alyson didn't care. As far as she was concerned, that just meant Dionne lost out on work.

The fashion press were fascinated by the animosity between the two of them, and it spilled over into the wider media, with mainstream magazines picking up the story. No one knew what had caused the fall-out between them. Dionne dropped hints every now and again, alluding to an argument over a man, or a professional rivalry. Every season, designers tried to get the two of them on the runway together – it would be a huge coup for a design house to book the two warring models – but Dionne always refused. On one occasion, Burberry had shot the two of them separately, then Photoshopped them into the same ad for the inside foldout cover of Vogue. Dionne had threatened them with legal action.

Alyson couldn't see what she'd done wrong. Dionne was the one who'd got it on with her boyfriend, publicly rubbing her nose in it, so why was she acting as though *she* was the injured party? And okay, so Alyson had headed up the print campaign for Capucine's debut collection, a role that Dionne saw as rightfully hers due to some long-held pact with CeCe, but how was it Alyson's fault if CeCe changed her mind? As far as she was concerned, it was just work, nothing personal. CeCe had explained what happened that night with Philippe, and how sorry she was, but it was before Alyson had started dating him. Unlike Dionne, Alyson had got over it and moved on.

Her breath was coming fast as she walked and she could feel herself getting angry at the memories, her shoulders tightening with tension. Maybe she should have gone out for dinner after all. At least she'd be surrounded by people, forced to make conversation rather than brooding alone.

Alyson looked up to realize she'd unconsciously walked in a large circle. She was back in Nishi-Shinjuku, at the other end of the street from the hotel. Alyson set off towards it. She would order room service, just something light, then bathe and sleep. Hopefully tomorrow she'd feel better.

She entered the building and took the lift up to the hotel lobby. A male receptionist came rushing across as he saw her enter. His suit was smart, his manners polite.

'Miss Wakefield, you do not have your cell phone?' he asked.

Alyson checked her bag and realized she'd forgotten it.

'A lady has been calling for you, many, many times.

Donna-san, in New York. She left a message, asking that you would call her immediately.'

Inwardly, Alyson scowled. What did she want now? She was probably worried Alyson wasn't going to show up tomorrow. Or maybe she had booked her in for some more work, after promising she wouldn't. That was all they cared about – work and money. Alyson was nothing more than a commodity to them.

But she didn't let her frustration show. She simply thanked the receptionist and headed across the lobby to the elevator.

Back in her room, Alyson called Donna.

'What is it?' she asked shortly. 'Have you booked me in for another job?'

'No, nothing like that.' Donna sounded uncomfortable.

'Is everything okay?'

'Not exactly.' Donna hesitated. 'It's your father.'

Alyson felt her heart contract. Adrenaline shot through her, her pulse rate tripling. 'I don't have a father,' she stated, her voice hard.

'Well you do now, honey. He's spoken to the press. The *Mail on Sunday* are doing an exposé on you this Sunday. We've seen a proof copy and . . . it's not pretty.'

27

The beautiful people of Paris streamed up to the entrance of the Four Seasons George V. Sansôme, the famous French jewellery house, was throwing a dinner, and the great and good of Paris were invited. Photographers jostled outside as guests posed on the red carpet, tucked safely behind the security cordon. Everyone was impeccably dressed, the men handsome and distinguished in black tie, the women in their finest *haute couture*, dripping in Sansôme diamonds.

Inside, the Salon Vendôme looked spectacular. The round tables were covered in immaculate white linen, decorated with slim gold candles in flower-covered candelabras and French crystal tableware. The food was exquisite, but many of the guests didn't eat – the figure-conscious simply pushed the petite portions of beef medallion around their plates, perhaps taking a tiny mouthful of wilted spinach.

Dionne was seated across from David, sandwiched between André Renard, the gorgeous Marseilles-born Formula 1 driver who'd taken last season by storm, and Bertrand Benoit, Vice President of the French Fashion Council. Bertrand was a randy old goat, with swept-back silver hair and a deep mahogany tan. He kept leaning across and dribbling on Dionne's cleavage, telling her she should pay a visit to his place in Mustique. Dionne wasn't surprised. His wife was sitting next to David, covered in garish jewels, her expression severe. She didn't look as though she'd be much fun in the sack.

On David's other side was Esther Levy, a gorgeous Israeli model. She was gap-toothed and flat-chested, with long, blonde hair, and looked stunning in a sleek, peach silk dress. She was very feminine, very unthreatening. Just like Alyson Wakefield, Dionne frowned, noticing that David seemed engrossed in speaking to her.

He really was incredibly good looking, thought Dionne, looking at him objectively. That smooth, chocolate skin perfectly set off by the sharp white shirt and black jacket. His eyes were dark and warm, his body solid and powerful . . .

Dionne sighed. So why did she always feel as if she needed something more?

Maybe she'd just got used to David always being around and started taking him for granted. Their relationship had certainly had its ups and downs over the past few years. There were periods when both of them claimed to be faithful, really trying to make a go of things, but these were inevitably followed by stand-up rows and vicious arguments. Yet no matter how bad their bust-ups, David always came running back – then there would be expensive presents and making up in spectacular style . . . But still she wasn't satisfied.

Dionne turned to the guy next to her with a dazzling smile. André Renard. Man, but he was cute. Blonde and tanned, with perfectly styled hair and bewitching blue eyes. There was something arrogant in his face – a slight sneer to the lip, an overconfidence in his actions. It was sexy, thought Dionne, feeling herself start to get hot. It marked him out as a winner.

They'd been making polite conversation all the way through the meal and Dionne was tired of being polite.

'So, I hear you like to go fast,' Dionne purred, noticing with pleasure the way André's eyes roamed hungrily over her body. Her sumptuous Elie Saab dress was cut low, the tight bodice pushing up her breasts to eye-popping levels. She wasn't a believer in subtlety.

André smiled, amused by her forwardness. He liked it when women didn't play games.

'Yeah, and I'm the best there is,' he stated arrogantly. 'World number one.'

'At what?' Dionne asked breathlessly.

'Racing. Life. Sex.' He gave a Gallic shrug, raising an eyebrow suggestively. 'I have many talents.'

Dionne's chest was rising and falling, her breath coming fast. Yeah, this guy was definitely on the same page. She glanced briefly across the table to see if David was watching. He wasn't.

She leaned forward in a subtle movement, running her hand along André's muscular thigh beneath the table. His expression registered surprise, his blue eyes widening, and then he smiled. Dionne's fingers moved higher, dancing over his crotch. She could feel him through his trousers, hard and thick.

'That's quite a claim,' she whispered.

'Give me the chance and I'll prove it. I guarantee you won't be disappointed.'

Dionne broke into a wide grin, amused by his arrogance. She got off on stuff like this. It was a power kick. She loved risky sex – the riskier, the better – only now she was starting to need a bigger high each time.

She stood up, pushing back her chair. The other

diners at the table turned to look at her. 'Please excuse me, I need to use the bathroom,' she stated deliberately. David nodded, only half paying attention. Around him, the guests went back to their food.

Dionne turned to go, leaning down to speak to André. 'Meet me outside in five minutes,' she murmured. 'Take me for a test drive.'

Then she stood up and sashayed out of the room, a satisfied smirk on her face.

'My God,' breathed Alyson, as her car pulled up outside Lynn Wakefield's house. She'd boarded the next available flight from Tokyo to London, then taken a car service up to Manchester, a gruelling eighteen-hour journey in all, but the scene outside her mother's home was worse than anything she'd imagined. The usually quiet street was heaving with reporters, crammed onto the pavement and spilling out into the road.

'These all for you?' asked the driver, nodding at the swarm of photographers.

'Seems like it,' Alyson replied in disbelief.

'Good luck,' he offered.

'Thanks.' She was going to need it. She stared up at the house, a good-sized, new-build detached property in a nice area. It was the first time she'd seen it since she'd bought it for her mother a few months ago, and it was a far cry from the ramshackle terrace Alyson had grown up in.

She and her mother had been in touch, sporadically, over the last year or so, gradually rebuilding their relationship. They spoke on the phone, the conversations stilted and awkward, but Alyson told herself it was progress. She still didn't speak to her father.

Lynn had moved back into her house after more than a year spent living in the care home, and appeared to be doing well. Once she realized that Alyson was making serious money, she'd hesitantly asked for some – just small amounts at first. Enough for a new vacuum cleaner, or to cover the grocery bill. Alyson, wracked with guilt, had offered to buy her mother anything she wanted and suggested that she move out of the depressing terraced house where she'd lived since Alyson was a baby. Her mother hadn't wanted to go far – it was important to her to keep things familiar, to have her friends nearby – so Alyson bought the new property outright, a few streets away from the old place. All Lynn's bills were direct-debited from Alyson's account, and a monthly allowance landed in her mother's bank. She'd done as much as she could – although you wouldn't know that from the *Mail on Sunday* story, thought Alyson bitterly.

She stared out of the window one final time, pulling down her sunglasses and wrapping a scarf round her head. Taking a deep breath, Alyson stepped out of the car.

As soon as the reporters realized who it was, they swamped her, flashbulbs popping so brightly she could barely see. People were shouting questions, cameras being thrust in her face. It was terrifying.

'Ally, have you spoken to your dad?'

'Is there any truth in what he's saying?'

'When was the last time you visited your mother, Ally?'

Alyson ignored them all, her expression stony-faced. She battled her way down the path, physically pushing the paparazzi out of the way as she fought to get to the door. It opened in front of her and she scrambled over the step, then the next moment she was inside, safe in the hallway as the door slammed shut behind her.

It seemed startlingly quiet after the commotion outside. Instead of the hordes of photographers, it was suddenly just the two of them, mother and daughter alone for the first time in more than three years.

It was Lynn who broke the barrier first, cautiously opening her arms. Alyson embraced her, the sensation so strange and unfamiliar.

'You look tired,' Lynn said, breaking away and holding Alyson at arm's length.

'It was a long journey,' Alyson offered by way of explanation, brushing her face self-consciously. She'd barely slept on the flight and there were dark circles under her eyes, her body thinner than ever. 'You look good,' she told her mother. 'Everything does.'

And she meant it. The house was clean and tidy, and Lynn looked well presented; her skin was healthy and clear – it had lost the puffiness and dullness from when she'd been drinking – and she'd dyed her hair, the grey covered with a natural ash blonde.

'Would you . . . um, would you like a cup of tea?' Lynn asked awkwardly. They were little better than strangers.

'Please,' Alyson nodded. 'I'll help make it. You can show me round.'

Lynn led her through to the kitchen, pointing out the furniture Alyson had bought for her, the framed photos of Alyson and her brother that she had put up. As they walked into the kitchen, Lynn turned on the overhead light. All the curtains in the house had been closed to stop the paparazzi taking pictures through the windows, and the rooms were dark in spite of the daylight outside.

'How are you?' Alyson asked.

Lynn paused before answering. When she spoke, her words were guarded. 'I'm okay. You?'

'I've been better,' Alyson admitted truthfully. 'Have you seen the article?'

Lynn nodded. 'I've got it through there,' she said, indicating the living room.

'Did you know?' Alyson began, voicing the question she didn't want to ask. 'Did you know he was going to do that? What he was going to say?'

Lynn Wakefield looked nervous suddenly, a haunted look in her eyes. 'I didn't, Alyson, I swear I didn't know anything about it. But . . . it's complicated. Come on, let's sit down.'

Alyson picked up her mug and followed her mother through to the lounge. The *Mail on Sunday* was spread open on the coffee table, staring accusingly out at them. It made Alyson feel sick to look at it – the huge headlines, the sensationalized pull-out quotes, accompanied by pictures of her looking hard-faced and cold on the catwalk, aloof and untouchable in a fragrance ad.

The headline was *Ally's Secret.* Donna had faxed her a copy before she left Japan and she'd had the whole fourteen-hour flight to read it, digest it and grow furious. She couldn't believe what her father had said.

He'd made her sound like the worst kind of person, claiming she'd abandoned her sick mother to pursue her modelling career, hiding Lynn away from the world like a dirty little secret. It said Alyson was ashamed of her mother's illness, that she'd dumped her in a care home and run away to Paris, leaving her at the time when she needed her the most.

Even a suicide attempt couldn't persuade cold-hearted Ally Wakefield to stay with her mother, the article said. *Ally walked out as her mum begged her not to go.*

It claimed that Lynn Wakefield was forced to work as a cleaner just to make ends meet, whilst Alyson lived a life of luxury, a fabulous existence of glamorous parties and private jets. They brought up the feud with Dionne as proof of Alyson's 'unpopularity' within the industry, saying that she was bitchy and stuck-up, that she didn't socialize with the other girls and was obsessed with money. They even ran the photo of her outside the Palais Garnier with Philippe Rochefort, the caption stating: '*Even as a teenager, Ally used her stunning looks to snare one of France's richest bachelors.*'

The story was nothing but a hatchet job made up of lies and conjecture. Alyson didn't even know how to begin to refute it. Every single allegation was untrue, but she had no idea where to start. Yes, it was true that her mother was working as a cleaner, but that was her choice and it wasn't about the money – it got her out of the house, gave her a sense of routine that helped to stabilize her condition. As for the claims that Alyson had somehow tried to ensnare Philippe Rochefort . . . The very thought of it disgusted her. It was all she could do not to rip the paper into a million pieces, take it outside and burn it. But she knew it wouldn't do any good.

'Are you still in touch with him?' Alyson asked. There was no need to specify who she was talking about.

'I still see Terry . . .' Lynn admitted. 'From time to time. I can't just cut him off, Alyson,' she protested, seeing the look on her daughter's face. 'Legally, we're still married. There's so much history . . .'

'Do you miss him?' Alyson asked quietly, unable to tear her gaze away from her mother's anguished face.

Lynn wouldn't look at her. 'Sometimes,' she whispered. 'Not *him* exactly . . . But there's never been anyone else since he left. Sometimes I miss the company . . .'

Alyson exhaled slowly, trying to control her breathing. She didn't think it was possible to feel any guiltier than she did right now.

'But I didn't know he was planning to do this,' Lynn insisted, gesturing towards the newspaper. 'I promise you I didn't. He asked about you when he came round. Of course I talked about you, told him how well you were doing. Maybe I talked a bit more than I should have done, but I'm proud of you, love.'

A noise like a strangled sob escaped from Alyson as she tried to hold herself together.

'Then he got more personal – did you have a boyfriend, how much money were you making? I said that you were doing well, that you'd invested in some properties, bought this place for me . . .' Lynn's voice was getting quieter and quieter. She looked devastated. 'I never in a million years thought he would . . . that he'd go . . .'

Alyson put her mug down, resting her hand on her mother's as she fought back the tears that were forming.

'I should never have left you,' Alyson asserted, shaking her head.

Lynn Wakefield clung to her daughter's hand. 'Don't be silly. It gave me the kick I needed. Waking up in that hospital was terrifying – I knew straight away that I didn't want to die, that I needed to get my life sorted out. I hated it in the home, but I had to prove to them that I was okay before they'd let me come back. And I am okay. I sorted myself out,' she said, with more than a hint of pride in her voice.

'I shouldn't have gone,' Alyson repeated. 'I feel so guilty.'

'Don't,' Lynn said firmly. 'It was the best thing you could have done for both of us. What kind of life would it have been for you, spending your best years running round after me? No, you got out there and made something of yourself. Look at you now, how well you're doing. It's incredible.'

Alyson felt torn. Everyone thought that she had the perfect life, that she'd achieved more than most people even dream of and should be grateful for it. But it didn't feel like that at all. 'I'm not sure . . . It's not what I want to do,' she confessed, turning her wide, blue eyes on her mother. 'I just don't know any more. I feel so lost.'

Lynn Wakefield shrugged, reaching across to take her daughter in her arms. 'Do what makes you happy, love. You only get one chance at this life, and you have to make it count.'

Dionne was squeezed inside a tiny broom cupboard, a dull light flickering on and off overhead. Her back was rammed up against a stack of toilet roll, her feet straddling a plastic bucket. It wasn't the most glamorous location in the world, but right now she didn't care.

André's body was pressed up against hers, his breath hot on her neck. The door was unlocked, the whole situation risky as hell, but Dionne knew they were both getting off on it. André was talking dirty, a barrage of filth pouring out of his mouth as he described exactly what he was going to do to her. Dionne moaned, biting her lip as she scrabbled to undo his trousers. The sense of urgency was palpable, André's hands sliding up her thighs as he fought his way through layer after layer of chiffon that seemed determined to prevent him reaching his goal.

His bow tie had been dragged off, discarded somewhere on the floor, and his shirt was undone. Finally, Dionne unhooked his trousers, pulling down the zip and tugging down his pants, gratefully freeing his swollen penis.

He wasn't the biggest she'd ever seen, but now wasn't the time to be fussy. After all, it was what he could do with it that counted, she thought optimistically.

She hitched up one leg, bracing it against an industrial-sized container of bleach, as André grabbed her buttocks, tugging her towards him as he entered her. Dionne gasped, flailing with her arms and bringing half a dozen bottles of hand wash crashing from the shelves.

The sex was fast and urgent. Dionne clutched at André's smooth, muscular back, trying to keep her balance in her skyscraper Gucci heels. She heard a tearing sound, and realized it was the hem of her ridiculously expensive Elie Saab dress. She didn't care.

André thrust relentlessly, both of them hot and sweaty in the tiny cupboard. André groaned loudly as Dionne cried out, oblivious to who might hear her. She was close to climax, closing her eyes as she wrapped her legs around André's waist and rode him for all he was worth.

Outside the door, a waitress from the Sansôme function passed by. She heard the commotion and smiled to herself. At least someone was having a good time. She wondered if she should tell her manager, but decided against it. The staff at the hotel were known for their discretion, and she didn't want to cause a scene. No, she would leave them to it.

She quickened her step and moved on.

The cups of tea had gone cold.

Alyson and Lynn sat in silence, all talked out. Even the paps outside had gone quiet, with all but the hardy having left for the night. Alyson curled up on the sofa, a faux-fur throw draped over her body. She felt like a child again. She just wanted to go to sleep, and hope that when she woke up, life would be normal again.

Lynn stood up, collecting the mugs. 'I'll go and wash these, then I think it's time for bed.'

As she headed to the kitchen, Alyson heard her phone ringing inside her bag and groaned. She'd meant to switch that off. She dragged herself up off the sofa, grabbing her travel bag which she'd dumped by the door, and pulling out her mobile.

'Hello?'

'Alyson?' said a voice.

Alyson felt her stomach turn over, her heart rate suddenly tripling. She recognized the voice instantly. 'Yes?'

'It's Aidan. Aidan Kennedy.'

28

'Aidan?' Alyson let out a long, shaky breath. 'What . . . I mean, how are you?'

'I'm well, yeah . . .' There was an awkward pause. It was almost two years since they'd last spoken. 'Sorry for calling so late. I didn't know if you'd be up. I thought maybe I could just leave a message . . .'

'I'm still up,' Alyson told him, feeling stupid as soon as she'd said it.

'Right.' Another silence. 'I was just calling to see how you were, really. I mean, I saw the papers and . . .'

'I'm fine,' Alyson said instinctively.

She heard Aidan take a breath. It was incredible, how familiar his voice was after all this time. 'No you're not,' he said gently.

The unexpected kindness knocked her for six. Her eyes welled up, a lump balling in her throat. She'd spent so long battling, showing a strong face to the world, that someone seeing through the mask really got to her. 'You're right,' she admitted. 'Oh God, it's been a nightmare, Aidan. The things he said – that's not me. I'm not like that . . .' She broke off as her voice cracked, threatening to break.

'I know you're not,' Aidan assured her. 'I know. I remember what you told me – about your mum, and about your dad leaving . . . I just wanted to make sure you were okay . . .'

With a sudden flashback, Alyson remembered that night in Montmartre. How sweet and kind Aidan had been. He'd listened when she'd needed to talk, he'd been there for her. 'Aidan, I'm so sorry,' she began, the words tumbling out before she could stop them. 'For everything . . .'

'Alyson—' Aidan began, but Alyson needed to speak.

'I always meant to come and see you, I really did. But somehow it was never the right time. And then everything blew up and my life just got crazy.'

'I noticed,' Aidan said lightly.

'We're . . . we're not together any more.' There was no need to spell out who she was talking about.

Aidan stayed silent. He'd known, of course – there'd never been any mention of a boyfriend in the articles about her, and Philippe had been pictured with dozens of different women over the last couple of years – but he didn't say anything.

'You were right,' Alyson admitted. 'I made a huge mistake. Maybe I *was* looking for a father figure, I don't know. But I was young, and naïve, and—'

'I didn't call to talk about Philippe Rochefort,' Aidan interrupted. There was a harshness in his voice that he couldn't hide, and Alyson realized how badly she'd hurt him.

'No,' she agreed.

'I called because I was worried about you. Where are you now?'

'I'm . . . I'm with my mum.'

'Good,' Aidan nodded. 'That's good. Are you staying there?'

'I don't know,' Alyson admitted. 'It's crazy. There are so many photographers outside, and they won't leave as long as I'm here, but I don't know where else to go. They're staking out my flat in Paris and—'

'Come stay with me,' Aidan said simply. 'I'm in London right now. There's no reason for them to look for you here.'

'I can't,' she said automatically.

'Why not?'

'Because . . .' Alyson thought about it. 'I don't want to impose,' she finished lamely.

Aidan laughed, a rich, warm sound. 'Trust me, you won't be imposing. The offer's there if you want it.'

Alyson sank down onto the sofa, clutching her phone tightly. From the kitchen, she could hear the sound of her mother washing up, the clash of crockery on crockery. She knew she couldn't stay here much longer, but where else could she go? She didn't have any close friends she could turn to, and she didn't want to hole up in some anonymous hotel, playing cat and mouse games with the press as the staff inevitably sold her out and she had to move on to the next location.

Alyson took a deep breath. 'That's really nice of you, Aidan. That'd be great.' She was telling the truth. She'd been on her own for so long that it would be nice to be looked after, to have someone take care of her for a while.

'Fantastic,' Aidan sounded relieved. 'Rest for tonight, then catch a flight tomorrow. Don't go to Heathrow – the paps are horrendous. Fly into London City and I'll meet you at the airport.'

'Thanks, Aidan.' She wanted to say something more, but the moment seemed to have passed.

'Hey, no problem.'

* * *

David Mouret was enjoying speaking to the young woman he'd been seated next to. She was certainly a lot more inviting than that old dragon on his other side.

Her name was Esther, she'd told him, in a voice that was low and sensual, her accent unusual. She was a model too, but that was where the similarity with Dionne ended. Where Dionne was rash and impulsive, this girl seemed considered, thoughtful. And where Dionne said whatever came into her head, with no time for deeper issues, Esther had her own opinions on religion, literature and art – all the topics that bored Dionne. Not that Dionne wasn't intelligent – she was simply more instinctive, thought David. But talking to Esther was a refreshing change.

They were deep into a discussion about Middle Eastern politics when Dionne stumbled back into the dining room. Her dress was creased and her hair was a mess, her make-up streaked across her face. She took out her compact and slicked on some lipstick in an attempt to restore her dishevelled appearance. Then she slipped back into her seat, trying to keep the smirk off her face.

Across the table, David looked up at her, his face questioning and angry. Dionne simply smiled back at him, suddenly engrossed in the untouched dessert that sat on her plate. It was passion-fruit cheesecake with a mango coulis, and she had no intention of eating it.

Moments later, André sat down beside her. He was running his hands through his hair, and his shirt was uneven, as though it had been hastily tucked in. He and Dionne studiously ignored each other as he attacked his dessert with gusto, and Dionne sipped at her glass of champagne, tilting her body so her back was to him.

After André had finished eating, he leaned across to speak to her, his hand proprietorially slung round the back of her chair. Dionne turned round in delight, giggling as she spoke to him. She reached out to rest a hand on his shoulder, her fingers sensually stroking his neck. The gesture didn't go unnoticed by the guests around them; a few turned to look discreetly.

Dionne scooped up a spoonful of her untouched dessert and fed it to André, both of them laughing at her ineptitude. She was drunk, and her hand was unsteady. Some of the sauce dribbled down André's chin. Dionne caught it with her thumb and fed it to him like that. André sucked at her fingers, his gaze never leaving her face.

Conversation around the table had dwindled to almost nothing as everyone was distracted by their very public display of affection. There was a loud screech of chairs as David stood up, excusing himself to Esther. Fury blazed in his eyes as he marched round and grabbed Dionne by the arm, practically dragging her to her feet.

'Come on, we're leaving.'

'What are you doing?'

David didn't speak. He pulled her out of the room, and she stumbled after him, unsteady on her heels. David had a damn good idea what was going on, and it was all he could do not to punch that prick André on the way out of the door. But he knew Dionne was just as much to blame, and that taking it out on that pretty boy wasn't going to help.

'Where are we going?' Dionne demanded. She was wriggling like a kitten, trying to get away from him.

'Upstairs.' They'd taken a suite for the night.

'Oh, okay.' Dionne grinned wickedly, her manner instantly changing as she trotted after him obediently.

David didn't speak until they were safely inside the

room. As soon as the door slammed shut, Dionne threw her arms around him, trying to kiss him. He pulled sharply away, but Dionne wasn't discouraged.

'Oh come on, baby, I know how you like this.' She dropped to her knees, fumbling with his fly as she tried to unzip his trousers.

'Dionne, what the fuck are you doing?'

She looked up at him from her position on the floor. 'Isn't it obvious?'

David shook his head in disgust. 'Get up,' he told her furiously.

Dionne struggled to her feet. She stood there, swaying, her eyes half closed.

'What were you doing with him?'

'Who?'

'Don't play the innocent, Dionne. Tonight you've made me look like an idiot in front of hundreds of people. You are supposed to be with *me*, Dionne, and yet you are all over some other man.'

'Well what about you and that girl you were sitting with – Esther?' Dionne pouted. 'You looked pretty into her.'

'I was seated beside her, and we had a pleasant conversation like civilized adults. I was not feeding her with my fork, practically fucking her in the dining room.'

Dionne bit her lip to stop herself from giggling. If only David knew what she'd really been up to . . .

'David,' she murmured, in a singsong voice that was meant to appease. She wrapped her arms around him, pressing her body against his as she began to kiss his neck. 'Don't be mad with me, baby . . .'

David groaned, relenting in spite of himself. She could always do this to him; she knew exactly which buttons to press. When that incredible body was wrapped round him, promising exquisite things to come, he was helpless. 'Dionne . . .' he moaned, leaning in towards her.

Suddenly he pulled away, shoving her roughly so that she fell back onto the bed. She smelt of sex – that sweaty, musty, unmistakeable scent. 'I can smell him all over you,' David spat. 'Just get away from me.'

'David, baby . . .' Dionne pleaded, lying back against the pillows. She stared up at him seductively, running her fingertips lazily across the top of her cleavage.

'Did you fuck him?' David demanded. 'Did you bring him up here?'

Dionne muttered something incomprehensible. The bed was so comfortable that she couldn't muster the energy to move. Her eyes began to close, the endless champagne catching up with her.

'You're a mess, Dionne. Sort yourself out.'

Dionne didn't respond. She'd passed out.

David stared at her. Her beautiful dress was torn and rucked up around her thighs, exposing her long legs. She'd borrowed diamonds from Sansôme for the night, worth over a million euros, but one earring was missing, and a link on the bracelet was broken. She was trouble, David realized sadly. Whenever Dionne was around she brought him nothing but heartache and humiliation. He loved her, he'd given her chance after chance, but he couldn't do it any more. From now on, she was on her own.

David took one final look at her and walked out.

29

CeCe lay awake in her low-slung, king-size bed. Mayumi was sleeping beside her, her breathing slow and even. Both of them were naked, and CeCe let her gaze run over Mayumi's tiny body and milky white skin, the intricate snake tattoo twisting its way across her right shoulder blade. Her thick black hair was splayed out over the pillows, her tiny breasts almost covered by her arms as she curled in the foetal position. She was so young, thought CeCe: only eighteen to her own twenty-three.

CeCe moved closer, spooning round her, delighting in the warmth of Mayumi's body. She closed her eyes, letting herself relax. As long as Mayumi was here, in her arms, she felt safe. A remarkable sense of calm had descended on her ever since Mayumi had been in her life, and – most importantly – she was designing again. In fact, she'd hardly been able to stop. As soon as her pencil touched the paper, she would dash off a whole series of sketches, inspiration flooding through her. It was as if she was possessed by an unstoppable muse.

And the designs she was producing were good. They

were inspired, original, ground-breaking. The whole team was relieved; she could see it in their faces. It meant their jobs were safe, for another season at least.

She knew they'd been worried about her. Hell, she'd been worried about herself. The nonstop partying, the desire to drink herself into oblivion. It wasn't normal and it wasn't healthy. She'd slid into a deep depression, the black demons chasing her down like they had done in the past, but she'd got through it. No drugs, no doctors, no counselling, CeCe thought proudly. She'd come through it by herself, and it was all because of Mayumi.

She wrapped her arms around her, holding her tightly. Perhaps a little too tightly. Mayumi stirred in her sleep, but CeCe was terrified to let her go, too afraid of what might happen if she left. She couldn't bear to sink back into that zombie-like state, where the days passed in a blur and life didn't seem worth living. Mayumi had literally brought her back to life.

Despite having lived in the city for years, CeCe had never visited the usual Parisian tourist haunts. Mayumi changed all that, opening her eyes to a wealth of new experiences. They took a boat trip on the Seine, wandered hand-in-hand round Notre-Dame and queued for hours to see the *Mona Lisa*. They ate at Les Deux Magots, checked out museums, pop-up galleries, temporary exhibitions. She found inspiration everywhere, and Mayumi was on hand to document it all.

She was studying photography at Spéos, and was permanently attached to her camera. She shot in black and white, producing glorious stills of the city and its inhabitants, but some of her best pictures were of CeCe. Mayumi loved to photograph her when she was working, uninhibited and unselfconscious. Sometimes she took pictures in their more intimate moments, a range of explicit yet artistic monochrome stills. There was a beautiful photo hanging in the living room that she'd taken of CeCe, naked and leaning out of the window as she smoked a cigarette, her elbows resting on the window sill. Her hair was a mess, her nipples protracted in the cool breeze as the smoke curled away from her. She looked thoughtful yet focused as she stared wistfully over the city, the shot perfectly capturing CeCe's determination and vulnerability.

Photos of the two of them were everywhere throughout the apartment, blown up to poster size on cheap paper. CeCe's favourite was a picture Mayumi had taken by simply turning the camera round and snapping a close-up. Only their faces were visible, dominating the entire frame, but CeCe looked so happy and relaxed, Mayumi impossibly beautiful.

CeCe kissed her lightly on the shoulder, her lips gently brushing skin so pale it looked like marble. Mayumi stirred and woke, turning round to face CeCe. Her face was creased with sleep, her eyes heavy, but she smiled when she saw her, rolling across to kiss her good morning.

They held each other for a moment, kissing lazily, limbs entwined. CeCe let her hands slide over Mayumi's shoulder, to her breasts, then down to her stomach, but Mayumi pulled away.

'What time is it?' she asked.

'Almost ten.'

'I should get up. I have a class at eleven.'

'You don't have to get up now, do you?' CeCe tried hard to keep the frustration out of her voice. She didn't want to sound like a nag.

Mayumi kissed her again and climbed out of bed, padding naked around the apartment. CeCe heard her turn on the espresso machine in the kitchen before she

324

came back with her camera, snapping CeCe bundled up in the sheets. CeCe messed around for a while, pretending to look sultry or wide-eyed and innocent, but she quickly grew self-conscious.

'Don't take any more,' she pleaded, holding her hand up to the lens to shield herself. She climbed out of bed and walked across to Mayumi, gently pushing the camera out of the way and reaching for her.

'I have to take a shower,' Mayumi told her.

'Whatever.' This time, CeCe didn't bother to hide her disappointment. She pulled on her robe and wandered aimlessly around the apartment as the water began running in the bathroom. She drifted into the kitchen and made two cups of coffee, then sat down at her designs. She retraced the outline of a dress she'd drawn the previous night, before standing up again, unable to settle. Moving across to the window, she stared out at the city, watching the way the sun hit the rooftops and reflected dazzlingly off a hundred skylights.

Mayumi came out of the bedroom. She was fully dressed, her bag slung over her shoulder.

'Do you have to go?' CeCe asked. She walked over and wrapped her arms around Mayumi, pressing her body close.

'Yes,' Mayumi said firmly, disentangling herself. 'But I'll be back later, okay? Okay?' she repeated, as she briefly kissed CeCe.

CeCe tried to quell the rising sense of panic that always threatened to engulf her at the thought of being left on her own. 'Call me when you have a break, yes? Or I can come up and meet you, if you like. I don't mind.'

Mayumi stroked her cheek reassuringly. 'I'll see you later, baby.' She turned to walk out of the apartment.

'I love you,' CeCe called after her.

Mayumi didn't turn round. 'You too.'

The door slammed shut. CeCe stood for a moment, not knowing what to do. She felt utterly lost. Her gaze landed on the pictures of her and Mayumi and she walked over to the nearest one, studying Mayumi's face before reaching out to run her hands over the image, her fingers tracing Mayumi's eyes, her cheeks, her lips.

She knew she should get dressed. She needed to go to work, but any movement felt like too much effort. She dragged herself back to the bedroom and collapsed onto the still-warm mattress, the imprint of her and Mayumi's bodies almost visible in the tangled sheets. CeCe pulled the duvet over her head and lay absolutely still. She inhaled deeply, breathing out reluctantly. She could still smell Mayumi, her fresh scent all over the bedclothes.

Suddenly she sat up and reached for her phone, calling Mayumi's number. It took a few seconds to connect then went straight to voicemail. She was probably on the métro, CeCe reasoned, flinging her phone down in disappointment.

Her heart was thumping, the loudest noise in the apartment. Everything else was silent. Jesus, it was quiet. So damn quiet. CeCe had the overwhelming urge to scream at the top of her lungs, the noise threatening to bubble up in her throat. It was all she could do not to open her mouth and let it out, anything to break that horrible, oppressive silence.

Her breath was coming fast, the palms of her hands growing clammy. She reached out, gripping tightly onto the headboard to stop the world from spinning. She couldn't be here, she realized hazily. She couldn't stay by herself – she needed to be around people.

Quickly, she threw on some clothes, finding a denim

shirtdress with a chunky-knit cardigan, knee-high socks and men's brogues. She tied a scarf round her head then walked into the lounge, snatching up the sketches from the dining-room table. She'd done them last night while Mayumi worked beside her, quietly composing an essay on her laptop. CeCe glanced over them. They were good. She was pleased.

She stashed them in her bag, and looked round the silent apartment. No, there was no way she could stay here alone. She would go into the studio and call Mayumi from there.

Alyson dropped her travel bag in the hallway of Aidan's apartment. He followed behind her, carrying a small suitcase and closing the door quickly. It was dark outside; Alyson had taken an evening flight and arrived late in London. She was relieved to finally be there, but still unsure whether she was doing the right thing.

She looked around her, taking in her surroundings. Aidan was clearly doing well for himself: duplex apartments in the heart of Fulham didn't come cheap, and it was immaculately decorated.

'Your place is beautiful,' she told him.

'Thank you.'

They were still circling each other uncertainly, aware that there was so much that hadn't been said. On the ride from the airport they'd made small talk, careful to avoid anything controversial.

At least no one seemed to have followed them, Alyson thought gratefully. The press obviously weren't expecting her to fly to London – and why would she? She had no base there, no family. She'd called her agency in New York and told Donna she was taking a few days off, then hung up and switched off her phone. She was going off radar and it felt fantastic.

'Did you decorate it yourself?' Alyson asked, staring at the ornate mirrors and enormous vase of silk flowers. The apartment had some feminine touches. She wondered if he had a girlfriend.

'No,' Aidan admitted. 'I got someone in. I've met a lot of good people, so I thought . . . why not?'

'Right.' Alyson looked round thoughtfully.

'Would you like a glass of wine?' Aidan asked, and then checked himself. 'Oh, I mean, do you still not drink? I have juice, coke . . .'

'I'll have a wine, thank you,' Alyson smiled. 'I'm not a lush, but I do like the occasional glass.'

'Red?'

'Perfect.' She recalled the first time she'd drunk red wine – Aidan had made her try some of his that night in Montmartre. She wondered if he remembered it too. It felt like a lifetime ago. When she looked back, she barely recognized the shy, naïve girl she'd been.

She followed Aidan as he led her through to the lounge. He was dressed casually in a simple grey T-shirt and J Brand jeans. He'd always been good looking, but money had brought out the best in him. He obviously took care of himself – but not in a vain way. She remembered the hours Philippe put in at the gym, the way his bathroom cabinet contained more cosmetics than she owned. She couldn't imagine Aidan being like that.

He headed through to the kitchen and emerged with a bottle of Merlot and two glasses, his muscles flexing under his T-shirt as he pulled out the cork and poured, every gesture confident and controlled.

'Cheers,' Alyson said, raising her glass.

'What are we celebrating?'

Alyson thought about it. 'Getting away from it all,' she declared finally.

'I'll drink to that.'

They clinked glasses, and Alyson took a sip of her wine. It was strong – rich and fruity. 'Thanks so much for letting me stay here,' she said, sitting down on the sofa and curling her legs underneath her. She was still wearing the comfortable clothes she'd picked out for the flight – skinny jeans and a loose tunic top by Tory Burch. The outfit flattered her body, emphasizing her long legs and slim frame. She looked sensational.

'Hey, no problem,' Aidan said lightly.

But Alyson couldn't let it drop. 'I mean, after everything that happened . . .'

'Maybe I overreacted at the time . . . What can I say? You were one of my best employees so I took it hard when you left,' he teased.

Alyson laughed. She felt the tension lift, that same ease that had always been there between them. In spite of everything, he was the same old Aidan – albeit richer and better looking.

Alyson felt an unexpected shiver of excitement as she took in those sparkling blue eyes and that familiar smile. *It must be the wine*, she told herself. But the feeling wouldn't go. She daren't look at Aidan in case he could tell what she was thinking, sure that just one look would give her away.

If truth be told, she was scared. She'd kept that side of herself long buried, and hadn't dated anyone since Philippe. She didn't trust men, didn't trust their intentions, especially not in the industry she was in. Okay, so most of the guys in the modelling world were gay, but there were a lot of men out there who just wanted a gorgeous girl on their arm to feed their ego, look hot and keep quiet. *Modelizers*, the other girls had called them. Well, Alyson was no one's arm candy. So she'd shut herself off, thrown herself into her work.

Oh, she'd had all the usual clichés thrown at her – Ice Maiden, Virgin Queen. But she'd kept her head down and tried not to care.

'So how is everything?' Aidan asked carefully, settling into a chair opposite. Alyson was grateful for the distance. 'How are you doing?'

'Yeah, I'm all right . . .' she said slowly.

'And how's your mum? Is everything good between you two?'

Alyson sighed heavily. 'We had a talk, sorted some things out. She seems to be doing okay. It's crazy there, though – you should have seen all the reporters, clustered round her house like vultures. They've offered her insane amounts of money for her side of the story.'

'She hasn't talked?'

'No. At least one of my parents has some loyalty,' Alyson noted bitterly.

'Have you heard from your dad?'

Alyson's face hardened with a steeliness Aidan had never seen before. 'No. Even if he did try to get in contact, I wouldn't speak to him. Not now. But you know the worst thing? If he'd tried to get in touch before . . . I mean, even if he'd come to me and asked for money, I'd have given it to him. He's my dad, you know? I would have made the effort. But he didn't even try. He just went behind my back . . .'

She trailed off, afraid that she might not be able to hold back the tears. Aidan sat forward in his chair, reaching across the space and laying a reassuring hand on her arm. His touch was like fire, her skin white-hot where he held her.

'You know you can stay here as long as you like,' he said seriously. She caught a trace of his scent – clean and fresh, like soap and shaving foam. Not expensive aftershave, like Philippe had worn, cloying and over-whelming.

'Thanks, Aidan.'

'Stop thanking me. It's no trouble at all.'

Alyson smiled, in spite of herself. Aidan was still holding her arm, and she didn't trust herself to say anything more.

'And what, when this all blows over it'll be business as usual again?' Aidan asked. He sat back in his chair, picking up his wine glass and draining the contents.

'Maybe not,' Alyson shrugged, meeting his gaze. 'I've been thinking about quitting for some time.'

'Quitting?'

'Modelling,' Alyson clarified.

Aidan said nothing. He poured himself another glass and leaned across to top up Alyson's, waiting for her to carry on.

'I've been thinking about it for a while,' she explained. 'I know it sounds ungrateful – I've had so many opportunities. I've seen so many places, had experiences that other girls would kill for, but . . . It's not *me*, Aidan. I feel like a fraud. They dress me up and paint my face and I suppose I pretend pretty well, but I'm dying inside. No one gives a damn about me and everything's fake. There's no challenge, nothing to push me . . .' She trailed off, willing him to understand.

Aidan cleared his throat. 'I have to admit, I was surprised when I first heard about your new career. It didn't seem very . . . *you*. You were always so driven, so passionate about business. I remember that night in the Place du Tertre where you told me about your dreams, about what you wanted to do with your life.'

Alyson smiled in delight. 'I thought you'd forgotten about that.'

Aidan glanced away, refusing to meet her gaze. 'No . . . I haven't forgotten,' he said quietly.

The tension sat heavy in the air, the awkwardness that Alyson had feared returning. The room was largely dark, lit only by a pair of chrome, overhanging lamps. In spite of the contemporary decoration, the apartment was homely and comfortable. Alyson loved it already.

'So what are your plans?' Aidan asked, breaking the silence. 'Like I said, you can stay here as long as you need to.'

'Don't worry, I won't be around for ever,' she joked, although at that moment it was exactly what she felt like. No one knew where she was, and it was such a relief to be away from all the pressures of her real life. Even the thought of going back to modelling made her feel sick. But then, branching out on her own was equally terrifying. Much as she hated her profession, it was all she'd known for the last two years of her life. And, financially, it was extremely rewarding, giving her a badly needed feeling of security. For someone who'd struggled all her life, that was huge.

'I've told my agent to cancel all my appointments for the next couple of weeks and then I'll get back to them. I just need a bit of time out, you know? But after that . . .' Alyson sipped her wine thoughtfully, the alcohol warming her and lowering her guard. 'What I'm going to do with the rest of my life – I really don't know.'

30

Unbeknown to both women, Dionne and Alyson were now in the same city, just a few miles between them as Dionne attended a fitting for Vivienne Westwood in London. She was standing in the centre of the studio as Bianca, the stylist, moved around her, tucking and pulling. Dionne was scrolling through her iPhone, paying little attention.

'Jesus, for fuck's sake,' she burst out, as she felt a pin jab her sharply in the ribs.

'Sorry,' Bianca said irritably. She was a trendy Hoxton girl, with a bleached blonde Louise Brooks bob and eclectic taste in clothes. 'Could you keep still please? You keep moving.'

'Could you not fucking prick me? *Incompetent bitch,*' Dionne swore under her breath.

Bianca took a deep breath and considered walking out. She'd dealt with a lot of divas in her time, but Dionne was the worst of the lot.

'I can't get this to hang right,' Bianca complained. Dionne was wearing a rather eccentric lilac shirt, with ruffles and enormous puff sleeves, but it needed to fit flat over her stomach. Bianca tried smoothing it down, but it puckered and rippled. 'Have you put on a little weight?' she asked innocently.

'No I fucking haven't!' Dionne swore indignantly. 'How dare you!'

Inside, she was quietly seething. She'd been thinking the same thing herself. Right, from now on she would cut out milk in her coffee, stop eating fruit – didn't it have an insane amount of calories, or bloat you, or something? And she would haul her ass down the gym. She hated it, but it had to be done. A little discipline, and she would soon drop the extra couple of pounds.

She continued browsing through her phone, coming to land on Style.com. 'Breaking News' was the huge headline at the top, above a picture of Alyson Wakefield's face. It was the one used in her Shiseido commercial, and she looked cool, elegant and impossibly beautiful – the epitome of the English rose. Dionne's lip curled in distaste. Goddamn white girl, had everything handed to her on a plate. Life was easy when you looked like that. Well, at least she was having a tough time lately – her own father had sold a story on her, and the things he'd said were brutal. Now Alyson might understand just a fraction of what it was like to struggle, Dionne thought in satisfaction.

She scrolled down curiously, reading the story. Then her mouth fell open in shock and she let out a scream of delight, pulling away from Bianca who swore in frustration. She'd finally got the line to come right, and now Dionne was flitting off somewhere.

'Holy shit, have you seen this?'

'What is it?' Bianca asked irritably, as Dionne continued to whoop, fist-punching the air.

'Alyson Wakefield's retiring!'

'What?' Bianca burst out in disbelief. 'Ally?'

'Uh huh.' Dionne's dark eyes were glittering with

excitement. *'British supermodel Alyson Wakefield, known as "Ally", today announced her retirement from the world of modelling,'* Dionne read. *'In a brief statement issued by her agent, IMG, she said: "Due to recent events in my personal life, I am announcing my retirement from modelling with immediate effect. I never chose the attention that comes with this lifestyle, but it appears to be unavoidable, and I am no longer willing to risk my private life. I would ask that the media give my family and myself space at this difficult time."'*

'Poor girl,' Bianca said sadly, shaking her head.

'Poor girl? Dumb bitch, more like. What, someone sells a story on her and she runs like a frightened dog with her tail between her legs. Like anyone's even that interested in her boring private life,' Dionne scoffed.

Bianca stared at her incredulously. She'd had it with Dionne's bullshit attitude and opened her mouth to let loose a stinging retort when Dan Markovic, the photographer, walked in.

'Hey, boo, did you bring the champagne?' Dionne grinned.

'What are we celebrating?'

'The end of Alyson Wakefield's career,' she told him, with barely concealed glee.

'What?'

'She's left modelling,' Bianca filled him in. 'Over all that personal stuff.'

'Shit, no way.' Dan looked shocked.

'Hey, it's party time, right? The industry's better off without that pathetic excuse of a model. Leave it to the professionals, huh?' Dionne pirouetted on the spot, throwing her arms up in the air.

Dan exchanged glances with Bianca. 'You know what? You're a real bitch, Dionne.'

'Oh, fuck you, Dan.' She waved her hands dismissively.

'No, fuck *you*, Dionne. I've worked with Ally. She's a sweet girl and a great model. She doesn't deserve all this shit she's going through.'

'*Oh, she's so sweet and nice,*' Dionne mimicked him, putting on a baby voice. 'Well, maybe she's better off out of it then. There ain't no place in this business for anyone not strong enough to take it.'

'Yeah?' Dan was looking at her in disgust. 'Well, if you need to be a soulless tramp to make it, then you're on course to go right to the top.' He turned on his heel and walked out, his expression furious.

'Screw you, Dan,' Dionne yelled after him. Lowering her voice, she muttered, 'Fucking faggot.'

Her breath was coming fast, her chest rising and falling as adrenaline pulsed through her body. She stalked back across the room to Bianca, who was looking at her in horror.

'Sort this fucking thing out,' Dionne snapped, tugging the blouse around her midriff then throwing her hands up in exasperation. 'And don't go saying I'm goddamn fat.'

Bianca got to her knees, taking a pin out of her mouth as she tacked the fabric together. 'Oh, don't worry,' she said, her expression unexpectedly smug. 'You're not fat, Dionne. You're pregnant.'

'Where are we going?' asked Alyson, for about the tenth time that evening.

'You'll see,' Aidan smirked maddeningly. They were driving along Tottenham Court Road in his Audi R8.

Alyson sat back in frustration as Aidan grinned at her. 'Not long now.'

She'd been going stir crazy, holed up in his apartment for the past fortnight. No one had discovered her hiding place and the press had finally lost interest.

Since she'd released the statement, there'd been a flurry of activity and then she'd been forgotten about. The Next Big Thing was always just around the corner – in this case, some young Brit actress that was making waves in Hollywood.

Alyson had no idea what she was going to do next, but for once she was enjoying the luxury of free time. She spent her days pottering round Aidan's apartment, watching films, reading and occasionally speaking to her mother, then cooking for Aidan when he got back at night. They sat down over long meals, sharing a bottle or two of red, and talked about everything – life, art, politics. His interests were varied, and he was far more eloquent and informed than she'd given him credit for.

She was aware he was neglecting his work for her. He'd cancelled a trip to Dublin in favour of spending time at Kennedy's London, and while Alyson felt guilty, she was also grateful. More than that – she was flattered; secretly thrilled that he'd chosen to spend time with her over anything else.

Last night he'd asked her if she was ready to go out again. Alyson had hesitated at first – she'd grown so accustomed to living in their little bubble that the thought of heading back into the real world was terrifying.

'Low key, I promise,' Aidan told her. And she trusted him.

She'd dressed well, but casually, in jeans and a silk tank paired with a cropped blazer. Her make-up was neutral, and she wore no jewellery apart from a plain silver pendant. She didn't even bother to blow-dry her hair, just left it to dry naturally. It was such a relief after all that time spent caring about her appearance, having her hair sculpted into eccentric styles and paired with outrageous make-up.

The car swung left, then left again, coming to a stop outside a smart restaurant. Above it was a discreet sign, navy blue with white writing in a scroll font.

Alyson's eyes lit up in delight. 'Kennedy's?'

'Yeah . . .' Aidan looked embarrassed. 'I hope you don't mind. I wanted you to see it. And we're closed for the night, so you don't have to worry about other customers,' he explained, as Alyson visibly relaxed. 'The staff are all sworn to secrecy.'

'You've thought of everything,' Alyson smiled. Their eyes locked, and for a second Alyson felt a shudder of excitement clutch at her belly. Aidan looked so handsome, so mature in that grey suit and the dark-blue shirt which perfectly picked up the colour of his eyes.

Stop that, she told herself sharply. Aidan had been so good to her. She didn't want to spoil it by making things complicated.

Quickly, she climbed out of the car, checking the street for photographers. Aidan held the door open for her, ushering her into the restaurant.

'Do you like it?' he asked expectantly, watching her face carefully as she stared round for the first time.

'Aidan, it's wonderful. I love it,' she told him honestly. It was light and airy, the feel modern, but not brash. The walls were painted cream, the decoration in shades of taupe and mushroom, with beautiful crystal chandeliers overhead.

'It's so relaxing, really welcoming,' Alyson continued, running a practised eye over the room. 'Everything's luxurious, but understated.'

'Good.' Aidan looked thoughtful. 'I'm glad you like it. There's something I want to discuss with you later.'

'What's that?' Alyson began, but they were interrupted as the maître d' came over.

338

'May I show you to your table?' he asked politely.

'Thanks, Pawel,' Aidan grinned, as Alyson giggled nervously. She was aware of a waiter hovering discreetly in the background, the girl behind the bar standing to attention. It felt odd that all those staff were there for just the two of them.

Pawel showed them to a table at the back, away from the window. They sat down, and the waiter brought over a bottle of white wine and a jug of iced water. There were no menus on the table.

'What are we eating?' Alyson asked.

'A little of everything,' Aidan smiled. 'I've requested the tasting menu – with a few twists.'

'It sounds wonderful,' Alyson sighed, as she relaxed in her seat, taking a sip of deliciously chilled wine. Discreet music was playing in the background and the overhead lights had been dimmed, the restaurant illuminated by soft uplighters on the wall and candles on the tables.

'I'm glad you made me come out tonight,' she told Aidan.

'Good,' Aidan smiled. 'I was starting to worry.' He tried to keep his tone light, but he meant what he said. It had been great having her around all the time – better than great; he didn't know he'd function when she left – but this wasn't the Alyson he knew. She was smart, ambitious and determined. He knew she wouldn't be happy spending the rest of her life doing nothing.

Alyson understood him immediately. 'I just needed some time,' she explained.

'I know. But you're getting restless. I can sense it.'

'Maybe . . .' Alyson smiled, forgetting how well he knew her.

She was saved from saying anything more as their first course arrived – an *amuse-bouche* of mushroom velouté, served in a shot glass and drizzled with truffle oil. It tasted delicious.

'Aidan, that's amazing,' Alyson told him.

'Did you expect anything less?'

'Perfectionist,' she said accusingly.

'Sounds like someone I know,' Aidan countered, spinning the focus back onto her. 'So tell me, Miss Wakefield, what are your plans?'

'I don't know. What do unemployed, twenty-something ex-models *do*?'

'Whatever they want.'

'I don't know what I want,' she said uncomfortably.

'I think you do. What did you always talk about – going into business, working for a company . . .'

Alyson laughed hollowly. 'Who's going to employ me? Do you think I can get an entry-level job somewhere, doing the photocopying and making the tea?'

'You think it's beneath you?'

'No,' Alyson retorted hotly. 'It's just . . . complicated. And in any case, I do have *some* experience. I worked . . .' she hesitated '. . . at Rochefort Champagne for a few months.'

'Yes,' Aidan nodded, his expression grim, as Alyson looked away.

Fortunately, at that moment, the waiter arrived with their next course – scallops cooked in butter and garlic, served with grilled asparagus and a swirl of sweet potato puree. He poured fresh glasses of wine from a new bottle, then disappeared.

'God, this is divine,' Alyson gushed, as the perfectly cooked food dissolved in her mouth.

'Try some of the potato,' Aidan suggested.

Alyson did, closing her eyes in rapture.

'So . . .' Aidan began, trying to sound casual, as though he hadn't been turning the idea round in his mind every day for the past fortnight. 'How about working for me? My company's expanding. You could help me out, oversee the business when I'm not around. We could go into partnership . . .'

Alyson was shocked by the suggestion, but she instinctively felt his proposal wasn't right for her. 'Aidan—'

'It wouldn't be a vanity job,' he insisted quickly. 'You could invest cash – I'm always looking for backers to help finance new ventures. Then you'd have a vested interest.'

Alyson put her fork down and sighed. 'I'm sorry, Aidan, I can't. Not again . . .' Unwillingly, she thought of Philippe. The situation felt too similar, and there was no way she could have someone in control of her again.

'Right.' Aidan chewed thoughtfully, realizing what she meant. It felt as if the shadow of Philippe Rochefort was always hanging over them.

'I need to be independent,' Alyson explained. 'To do something on my own terms.'

'So start your own business.'

'Doing what? I don't want to just bring out a skin-care range, or a make-up line, or bloody yoga mats, the way every other retired model does.'

'Then don't,' Aidan said easily. 'Do something you really want to.' He took a long swallow of his wine, then stabbed an asparagus spear. 'What are you good at? What are your skills and interests?'

Alyson shrugged. 'I finished my education at eighteen, did a little bar work and a couple of months making the coffee in an office. Then I spent the next two years being really good at walking up and down and having my photo taken. What exactly does that qualify me for?'

To her surprise, Aidan burst out laughing. 'Wow, when you put it like that it sounds pretty bleak.'

Alyson flushed, realizing she sounded like a spoilt brat. 'I'm sorry,' she apologized. 'I'm being pretty negative, aren't I?'

'Yes,' Aidan said flatly. 'I'm not trying to hassle you, but I think you need pushing and I think now's the time. You're climbing the walls at my place, and it's not healthy. You need to think about what you're going to do next.'

'Why are you doing this for me?' she asked softly.

For a moment, Aidan didn't respond. Silence fell between them, just the gentle tinkle of background music audible. The soft candlelight flickered over Aidan, shaping the contours of his face. His cheekbones were sharp and defined, his lips thick and full. Alyson squirmed on her chair, feeling the first stirrings of something she'd suppressed for a very long time start to lick at her groin. *It's the alcohol*, she insisted to herself, hastily taking a sip from her water glass.

Aidan stared at her, those dazzling blue eyes unrelenting. 'When I first met you, all that time ago in Chez Paddy, you were so ambitious, so dynamic and motivated . . .' *And beautiful*, he added silently. 'I knew you were destined for better things than that crummy bar – and I don't mean modelling. That was incidental. It was never what you were meant for.'

'And what was I meant for?' she asked, her voice low.

'Whatever you want,' Aidan said simply. 'I honestly believe that you can do anything. Just decide what that is, and don't stop until you get there.'

'I wish it was that simple,' Alyson said helplessly. 'I wish I had your kind of self-belief.'

'You do. You just need to rediscover it.'

The next course arrived. They both sat in silence until the waiter had left.

'Right,' Aidan said briskly, ignoring the food on the table. 'Let's brainstorm. What are you good at? What are your key skills?'

'Well . . .' Alyson began, trying to stay positive. 'I have a pretty good brain. I'm very logical and organized.'

'Excellent start,' Aidan smiled encouragingly.

'And . . . I've travelled a lot?' Alyson offered hesitantly. 'I mean, I've met a lot of people, have a knowledge of a lot of different cultures. Whenever I have time off, I always try to get out into the city to see things and learn about the country . . .'

'Good. Languages?'

'French, obviously. My Italian and Spanish are pretty good. I've picked up little bits here and there – Japanese, Arabic.'

Aidan raised an eyebrow thoughtfully. 'That's great. What else?'

'Um . . .' Alyson was stuck.

'Great people skills.'

'No.' Alyson shook her head.

'Absolutely,' Aidan insisted. 'Even back in Chez Paddy I could see that. The customers loved you. You were really relaxed with everyone, easy to talk to. You still are. Look how polite you are to people.'

Alyson shrugged off his compliments. 'That's just manners.'

'Well, that's something a lot of people don't have these days, believe me. And you're real – not like so many of these fake bullshitters,' he said with feeling. 'Look at the tributes in the press when you announced your retirement. Everyone was falling over themselves to say nice things about you – how sweet you were; how much you'd be missed.'

'That's not what that *Mail on Sunday* journalist wrote,' Alyson muttered darkly.

Aidan waved his hand dismissively. 'Right, put it all together and what do we have? Languages, travel, people skills, a business brain—'

'Travel agent?' Alyson couldn't resist quipping, as Aidan glared at her.

'You know, maybe that's not too far off,' he said eventually. 'You could use your knowledge in a consultancy role – maybe some kind of travel advisory service . . .'

'Or business advisory,' Alyson spoke up suddenly. 'When businesses relocate. If they're moving to a territory they don't know – or even thinking about moving – I could let them know what it would entail, help them ensure that a move goes smoothly—'

'That they know the local customs, don't make any cultural faux pas,' Aidan cut in.

'Exactly!' Alyson exclaimed. She was starting to get excited in spite of herself. It sounded perfect. It meant she would get to travel, which she loved. She could use her languages and she would be running her own business. 'A consultancy firm, helping companies to expand and relocate overseas,' she clarified. 'Could I really do that?'

'Of course you could,' Aidan encouraged her, thrilled to see her old enthusiasm returning after two weeks of moping round on his sofa. 'We'll get on the Internet when we get back, start doing some research. I can help you put together a business plan. I guess you probably don't need to raise finance . . .'

'Well, I'd want to start small,' Alyson put in, terrified at the thought of gambling all her hard-earned cash on some insane business venture.

'Start small, think big,' Aidan grinned at her. He raised his glass and they clinked in celebration. Alyson was glowing, radiant with excitement. Aidan didn't think he'd ever seen her looking more beautiful – she just seemed to get better and better. But she would never feel the same way about him, she'd made that clear. He wasn't going to make a fool of himself like last time – this time around it was strictly professional.

Aidan broke the silence. 'In fact, I might have a proposal for you.'

'Oh yes?' Alyson looked at him, intrigued.

'Kennedy's Dubai. I'm setting it up at the moment and I need someone to help me. It would be a semi project manager role, but I need help with all the red tape out there. Is that something your new company might consider?'

Alyson smiled. 'Maybe . . .' She felt as though she'd been set up.

'Great. Well if your company – what is it called, by the way?'

Alyson thought for a second. 'Dante,' she said eventually, breaking into a smile. The name of the street she'd lived on when she first moved to Paris. 'Dante Consulting.'

'Dante.' Aidan nodded. 'Well, if Dante Consulting could give me a quote, I'll consider it and get back to you.'

Alyson wanted to hit him. 'Don't you dare turn me down after all this, Aidan Kennedy,' she threatened.

'You're right. I'll hire you unconditionally,' he grinned, the teasing look in his eyes making him more handsome than ever. 'Congratulations to the world's newest MD,' he toasted. 'Dante Consulting has its first customer.'

31

Dionne was sitting awkwardly on the ergonomic chair in her obstetrician's office. It was an exclusive clinic, the best in Paris, located on the Avenue Marceau.

'Yes,' Dr Anne-Sophie Vincent confirmed. 'You're pregnant. I'd say around five to six weeks. We'll be able to give you a more accurate date with your first scan. Congratulations,' she added unnecessarily. It was clear from Dionne's face that this wasn't a longed-for pregnancy.

'Right.' Dionne swallowed. She felt faint suddenly, a whole range of emotions rushing through her, impossible to take in.

'Are you okay?' Dr Vincent asked. 'Can I get you anything?'

'A glass of water, please.'

Dr Vincent picked up her phone and, within a few seconds, the door opened. An assistant ushered Dionne outside, seating her on a chair in the waiting room and returning with a glass of water.

'Thank you,' Dionne said stiffly. The assistant left and Dionne sipped at the water, trying to gather her thoughts.

She was pregnant. *Fuck.*

She hung her head, dizziness overwhelming her once more. Okay, so she hadn't had her period for a few weeks, but that was nothing new. Her cycle had always been erratic – extreme dieting and the stress of the job did that to you. And she went through so many different time zones, it was difficult to keep track of when exactly it was due.

But now . . . That was it. Confirmed. She was pregnant.

Whose was it? Her subconscious formed the question she didn't want to consider. She didn't even know. She'd initially assumed it must be David's but, thinking back, there'd been so many guys lately . . .

Oh God, Dionne thought, feeling nauseous. She didn't know whose it was. There'd been that photographer who'd shot her for some Russian magazine, the model from the Armani shoot, André the racing driver, and a couple of random guys she'd met in clubs – one a stockbroker, the other . . . a DJ? Dionne screwed up her face, trying to remember. Not that it mattered. They'd been brief encounters – hot and heavy, with instant gratification. She hadn't even caught the surname of most of them.

Man, she sounded like such a slut. It hadn't seemed that way at the time. As far as Dionne was concerned, she was just having fun, enjoying being young, gorgeous and single. But looking back on it . . . Damn, she'd been drinking heavily too. More than drinking – she'd indulged in a little coke here and there, done some of the party drugs that were going around . . . Whatever was available and made her feel good. Every night she'd been out getting trashed.

Instinctively, Dionne cradled her stomach. There was barely any difference yet – it was still toned and flat. It was so weird to think there was already a new person in there, a new life. What if she'd done some damage to it already? Could they test for that sort of thing? Hell, did she even want it in the first place? How could she be a mother, responsible for a whole other person, when she could barely take care of herself?

She was twenty-two years old and a top model, but she was still cementing her position – she wasn't yet established like Heidi or Gisele. Dionne didn't know if her career could cope with a year-long break. Besides, did she want to travel the world with a baby in tow? She hardly saw herself as an earth mother, popping out in the middle of a shoot to breast-feed before strutting her stuff in front of the camera. And she definitely wasn't the Angelina type, traipsing around the globe with a rainbow troupe following behind.

Shit, she didn't even know what colour this baby was going to be. The father could be black or white – she just couldn't remember . . .

Dionne let her head drop into her hands, wondering how the hell she'd ended up in this situation. She was a party girl, not a mom. She spent her nights having fun, not changing diapers.

But already there was a stirring of something deep inside, some deeply buried maternal instinct. Even now, Dionne felt fiercely protective of this baby. Poor little thing, only a few weeks old, its future entirely in Dionne's hands. She instantly identified with it – it reminded her of the way she'd had to battle and been written off by everyone. She still had a few weeks to make a decision, but this baby was a fighter, she sensed it.

Whatever happened, she was going to need support,

Dionne realized, pulling her phone out of her Mulberry bag. Taking a deep breath, she called David.

'What do you think?'

CeCe excitedly threw the stack of glossy prints down on the table. The rest of the team gathered round to look. No one spoke.

'Well?' CeCe demanded.

'This is the new autumn/winter ad campaign?' Jacques Perrot asked carefully. Jacques was second in command and worked closely with CeCe. He looked like a geek but possessed an incredible talent. For this shoot, however, he'd been excluded; CeCe had insisted on doing it by herself, with the help of Mayumi.

'Yes,' CeCe confirmed, her eyes shining. 'Aren't they amazing?'

There was a sceptical silence.

'They're . . . different,' someone said tactfully.

'Exactly! They're stunning. No one has ever seen anything like this before,' CeCe enthused. 'Mayumi's ideas are revolutionary. She's just so creative.'

'Aren't they a little extreme?' asked Gilles Boudin, Head of Marketing, doubtfully.

'That's exactly the point,' CeCe turned on him. 'Have a little vision, would you? These images are works of art in themselves. They're pushing the boundaries, subverting the whole notion of what fashion really means.'

'CeCe,' Jacques began carefully. 'There's no doubt that they're incredible images but . . .' he paused, looking round at the rest of his team for support. 'We're in this business to sell clothes.'

'Really?' CeCe's head snapped up. 'I thought we were in this to be innovative and daring, to make something beautiful. If the whole point of Capucine is to churn out sales units, then we might as well shut up shop and I'll go work for Pimkie.'

CeCe was fuming. The tension in the studio was obvious, and Jacques decided to proceed with caution.

'All I'm saying is that this collection has to appeal to women. It has to be covetable, aspirational. Women have to see these photos and be willing to kill to get their hands on the clothes. They have to believe that by wearing Capucine they'll be magically transported to some other world where they're richer, thinner, more beautiful, more glamorous. You have to build that world for them, CeCe.' Jacques paused, letting his words sink in. 'And we can't do that if the clothes are being modelled by *men*.'

There was a deathly silence in the studio. Everyone was looking at CeCe, waiting to see how she would react.

CeCe stared at the photos laid out on the table. One showed a muscled hunk wearing a blush-coloured lace shirt, his bulging, tattooed bicep straining against the delicate material. Another showcased a tight, sexy pencil skirt in a herringbone print. But instead of sliding smoothly over the rounded hips and slim waist of a woman, the photo showed the solid bottom, chunky thighs and wide calves of a well-built man, his legs tapering down into heels that had surely been designed for a drag queen.

All the pictures were taken in traditional advertising style, with men in the same sensual, submissive poses as the female models would usually be – draped over a four-poster bed, leaning seductively against a wrought-iron balcony. It blurred the boundaries, playing with the whole question of gender.

'It's ground-breaking,' CeCe burst out in frustration. 'The clothes will be investment items, collectors' pieces.

We'll generate so much buzz that stock will fly off the shelves, simply so women can say they own something from this Capucine collection.'

'And their bitchy girlfriends can say it looked much better on the male model than it does on them,' Gilles quipped, to smothered laughter.

'Mayumi adores it,' CeCe said hotly. 'And so do I.'

'You can't let your girlfriend dictate company policy,' Jacques insisted.

'She dictates it whether you like it or not,' CeCe was shouting now. 'Her influence is everywhere. How do you even think I came up with these designs? It's because I have Mayumi and she inspires me.'

'Sometimes you just have to take a step back,' Jacques said gently.

'You know, I kind of like them,' said Valérie Lemoine, another member of the design team.

CeCe turned to her gratefully. 'Thank you! Finally, someone with vision. Mayumi's tutor thought they were incredible, unlike anything he'd ever seen.'

'Mayumi's tutor has seen them?' Jacques' tone was suddenly harsh. 'He's seen our exclusive campaign that's not even out to trade yet?'

CeCe shrugged. 'It was Mayumi's coursework. He had to grade it. She got top marks, incidentally.'

Jacques looked as if he wanted to kill someone. 'Our new campaign is your girlfriend's fucking school project?' There was a stunned silence in the studio. 'CeCe, can we have a private word?'

'No,' CeCe retorted defiantly, her eyes blazing. 'Whatever you want to say to me, you can say it in front of the whole team.'

'Fine,' Jacques stated. She'd pushed him too far. 'It may be your name out there, but the rest of us here are working our arses off too, and we're not about to

351

see Capucine made to look ridiculous because of your childish obsession with this girl. I realize she's important to you—'

'I *love* her,' CeCe yelled.

Jacques ignored the interruption. 'But I'm worried about you, CeCe. You're too into her, it's like you're blind to anything else, and you're making Capucine into a joke. It's not healthy, CeCe, and quite honestly . . .' Jacques broke off, wondering if he had the nerve to say what he was thinking. 'I don't think it's going to have a happy ending.'

Dionne sat awkwardly in her apartment. David had arrived and was perched on the edge of an armchair looking decidedly uncomfortable. He hadn't taken his coat off. It was as if he already knew, thought Dionne. Something had changed already between them, she could feel it. The distance between them was painfully obvious, their usual familiarity nothing but a memory.

Dionne stifled a yawn. It was eight a.m. and she'd slept badly. David had insisted on coming over early, before he went into the office, telling her it was the only time he could spare.

'Thank you for coming,' Dionne said formally, settling herself on the sofa. She was wearing tight jeans and a flowing A-line top. Not that her bump was visible yet, but she didn't want to give him any opportunity to guess what she was going to tell him. He knew how hard she worked to stay in shape and a pot-belly would look suspicious.

David inclined his head. 'That's okay. You said it was important.'

'Yes, it is.' Dionne hesitated. 'Would you like a drink?'

'No, thank you. I'm good.'

'Right.' Dionne stared at him. He looked so handsome in his work suit, a classic trench slung over the top. Could he really be the father of her baby? Instinctively she clasped her hands to her stomach. David would make a good father. He'd been there for her so many times over the years, never letting her down. She just hoped he'd stand by her now.

'Dionne, I don't have time to play games,' David said irritably. 'I have somewhere I need to be. I came because you said it was important.' His muscles were tensed, as though he might get up and leave at any moment.

Dionne panicked. 'I'm pregnant,' she blurted out.

David's forehead creased in confusion. For a moment he just stared at her. 'What?'

'I'm pregnant.'

David's dark skin seemed to pale. He nodded, trying to take it in. Then he looked her straight in the eye. 'Is it mine?'

'David . . .' Dionne pleaded.

'Don't fuck with me, Dionne,' he snapped. 'I know what you're like. Let's face it, we've never been exclusive.' He sounded bitter. 'Is it mine?'

Dionne hung her head, feeling close to tears. 'I don't know,' she admitted.

'Oh Christ,' David sighed. 'And you invited me here today expecting . . . what?'

'I don't know,' Dionne said again in frustration. 'I just felt you should know.'

'Great, thanks.' David's tone was sarcastic. 'Me and how many others? Have you got appointments scheduled all morning, huh? Someone arriving straight after I leave?'

'Don't . . .' Dionne whispered, shaking her head.

'Why am I here?' David sounded angry now.

'I'm scared!' Dionne cried, turning on him, her eyes

wide and filled with tears. 'I don't know what to do. I just thought . . . you've always been there for me. You've been so good to me. I thought we could . . . try again?'

David shook his head sadly. When he spoke, his voice was thick. 'I can't, Dionne.'

Dionne tried to suppress a rising sense of panic. 'David, I love you,' she told him. 'I know I haven't always been the best person, but I'm trying to change. I *have* to change.'

David was torn. He'd never seen Dionne like this — so scared, so vulnerable. He knew it wasn't an act. This was real. But he had to stay strong. 'Do you know how long I've waited for you to say that to me? To tell me that you love me, you need me. Once upon a time it was all I wanted to hear.'

'Once?'

'It's too late,' David said quietly. 'I'll always be there for you if you need me. You only have to call me and I'll drop everything. But you and me — it's over.'

'Why?' Dionne asked desperately. 'What's changed?' Then the penny dropped, her eyes widening in alarm. 'You're seeing someone, aren't you?'

There was a pause. 'Yes,' David admitted finally. 'I really like her, and I want to see if we can make a go of it.'

'Who is it?' Dionne demanded. 'Do I know her?'

'You left me no choice,' David tried to explain. 'You pushed me away. Time after time, I was there for you. I would have done anything for you, you know that, but you flung it back in my face, humiliated me. I kept on coming back — I really thought we'd make it work in the end . . . But then I gave up. I had enough.'

Dionne stared at him. She knew every line on his face, every contour of his body, but she'd never seen him look at her like he was now – with coldness, with pity. 'Who is it?' she asked. 'You owe me that much at least.'

'Esther Levy,' David said finally, his voice little more than a whisper. 'She's . . . a sweet girl.'

Dionne closed her eyes, remembering the stunning model David had sat next to at the Sansôme dinner. The night she'd ignored him, too busy screwing André Renard – another one of the possible fathers – in the cleaning cupboard.

'Sweet girl,' she repeated. 'Not like me, huh? Well, I'm sure you'll be very happy together,' she finished sarcastically, unable to resist.

'Dionne—'

'What?' she shot back, eyes blazing.

'Look, if the baby's mine, I'll be there for you okay? I promise. I just need to know . . . You can't expect me to throw everything away when I don't even know if it's—'

'Yes David, I get the picture. I'm a slut, right? I know what you're saying . . .' The tears began to fall before she could stop them. She brushed them away, angry with herself for the display of weakness. *Fucking hormones*, she berated herself. She'd be crying at TV commercials next.

David stood up, resting a hand awkwardly on her shoulder. It was hard to believe they'd ever been lovers, as intimate as two people could get.

'I should probably go,' he offered. 'But if I can help you in any way . . . Financially or . . . Do you need money? Is that why you invited me over?'

Dionne lashed out, swiping his hand away. Memories of Philippe Rochefort returned unbidden – that night in the apartment where he'd utterly humiliated her, throwing euro bills in her face. Was that all anybody thought, even now? That she was just a gold-digging whore, out for what she could get. 'I don't want your money,' she hissed. 'Just leave me alone.'

David looked at her. For a moment it seemed as though he was about to say something else, then thought better of it. 'Call me if you need me, okay?'

Dionne didn't respond and he walked out of the apartment in silence, the door banging shut behind him. She listened to the sound of his steps retreating along the corridor, down the stairs and out of her life, before she lay down on the sofa and howled, letting the tears stream down her face until her eyes were swollen and her nose was bright red. It was cathartic, letting out all the emotions she'd kept bottled up since she'd found out she was pregnant.

This was it then. She was on her own.

The minutes ticked by as Dionne lay prostrate on the cushions, before she finally dragged herself upright and pulled a tissue from the box on the table, noisily blowing her nose. There was no doubt in her mind that she wanted to keep this baby, she realized, resting her hands on her belly. It might be the only thing she had left in this world, the two of them against everyone.

Dionne didn't need anyone else. She was going to have this baby, and she was going to do it on her own.

32

Alyson stepped out of Dubai International Airport. The automatic doors slid open, and a wave of heat washed over her. The shock almost took her breath away; she was totally unprepared for it.

'Wow,' she exclaimed, under her breath. She'd travelled all over the world during her modelling career, but never experienced anything like the wet, humid heat of Dubai. It was like walking into a steam room. Immediately all of Alyson's clothes felt clammy, sticking damply to her skin even though she was wearing just the lightest linen trousers and tunic top which she'd changed into just before they landed.

It was the middle of summer, and the mercury was touching 110°F. The Tarmac was shimmering, the locals looking laid-back in their white dishdashas and head-scarves, eyes hidden behind designer sunglasses.

Beside her, Aidan grinned. 'It's a little different to London, huh?'

'It's insane,' Alyson replied, feeling as though she might melt into a puddle on the floor at any second. She could feel her pale skin protesting at the very thought of exposure to the fierce desert sun.

A uniformed driver put their bags into the trunk of the black stretch limo that was waiting for them.

'Impressive,' Alyson commented wryly.

Aidan waved her away. 'You're lying. I know you're not the sort of girl to have her head turned by all of this.'

Alyson smiled at his teasing. 'Maybe not. But it's not a bad way to travel.'

She climbed inside, the air-conditioning deliciously cool after the scorching heat outside. Alyson sighed in relief as she seated herself in the cavernous interior.

'Would you like a drink?' Aidan asked, indicating the well-stocked mini-bar.

'Just a mineral water, thanks.'

'Nothing stronger?' he pressed, helping himself to a whiskey.

'No.' Alyson looked pointedly at his drink and grinned. 'I'm working.'

Aidan acknowledged the jibe with a tilt of his head, and gazed back at her admiringly. She was so focused, so professional, always cool and unflappable. Nothing seemed to faze her. She still looked elegant and serene, in spite of the searing heat they'd just come through.

He sipped at his whiskey, adding a little water and feeling like a naughty child as they turned onto Sheikh Zayed Road, one of the main highways running through the heart of the emirate.

'Wow,' Alyson said again, staring in disbelief out of the window. She felt as if she'd entered wonderland, as though she'd shrunk and everything around her had grown. The vast, largely empty motorway was six lanes wide, flanked on either side by colossal skyscrapers. Alyson had spent enough time in cities like New York and Hong Kong to be used to enormous towers, but these were something else. They lined the road as far as the eye could see, awe-inspiring in their dominance of the skyline. Most impressive of all was the Burj Khalifa, thrusting half a mile into the sky like a glittering spear. It was so tall that even when Alyson pressed up against the window and craned her neck, she still couldn't see the top as they passed by.

And it looked as if work was still going on. Not content with the mass of buildings they'd already erected, the signs of construction were everywhere. Dotted amongst the skyscrapers was a sea of cranes in red and green, swinging out over vast areas that were still, essentially, building sites. It was unbelievable to see all this rising from what had once been little more than sand, a small fishing village on the edge of the Arabian Desert.

'Crazy, isn't it?' Aidan seemed to voice what she was thinking. 'Anything you can dream of, they can build it here.'

'I've never seen anything like it,' Alyson marvelled. 'It's spectacular, but . . .' She hesitated. 'Isn't it kind of . . . trashy?'

Aidan burst out laughing. 'I never had you down as a snob.'

'I'm not,' Alyson retorted, flustered. 'It's just—'

'I know what you mean,' Aidan grinned. 'Maybe a little,' he conceded. 'But you go where the market is, and there's a huge expat community here. Most of them are earning generous salaries, they don't pay tax, they're away from home and it feels like one long holiday. That's the lifestyle out here. When they're not working, they just want to go out and party hard. The way I see it, they might as well spend some of that hard-earned cash in Kennedy's.'

Alyson nodded thoughtfully, unable to fault Aidan's logic. She sat quietly for the rest of the journey, watching the incredible sights as they passed by, trying to get a feel for the place and mentally planning how on earth she was going to do this.

It was six weeks now since Aidan had first floated the idea of them working together, and Dante Consulting was now official, registered at Companies House in London and with its own logo and freshly designed website. There was no mention, as yet, that Alyson was behind it. She thought that might work against her – that as a young ex-model she wouldn't be taken seriously in the business world. She wanted to work quietly, under the radar for a while, until she'd built up a portfolio and felt confident putting her name out there again.

So she'd thrown all her energy into working with Aidan, finding out exactly what he needed from her and planning her strategy for Kennedy's Dubai. She'd already learned vast amounts about the emirate, its exacting laws and unfamiliar customs, but this was her first trip to see the site itself. The launch was set at eight weeks from today, and Alyson sometimes wondered if she'd taken on the impossible.

She stared distractedly out of the window, the glittering blue of the Arabian Gulf dominating the view. It looked incredible, shimmering in the sunlight, so flat and calm. They were passing Jumeirah Beach, with the dramatic wave-shaped hotel on their right, and beyond that, the Burj al Arab rearing proudly out of the ocean, its brilliant whiteness gleaming against the cloudless azure sky.

They arrived at the Madinat shortly after and were shown directly to their respective suites, but Alyson had no time to appreciate the sumptuous view out over the winding waterways, or the opulence of her room with its twenty-four-hour butler who introduced himself as Ahmed. Within minutes, Aidan was knocking on her door, as excited as a child at Christmas, demanding that she come down and see his new property. Alyson protested, saying that she wanted to shower and change after the long flight, but Aidan wouldn't let her.

'You look great,' he insisted. 'Besides, you're here to work, not holiday.'

'I'm increasing my fee,' Alyson grumbled. But she accompanied him back through the hotel, out into the relentless sun and the beautiful, peaceful setting of the Madinat Souk. Aidan kept up a brisk pace past the old-fashioned buildings and the interlocking canals, crisscrossed by wooden bridges. It really was out of this world, Alyson marvelled. It would be easy to lose all sense of perspective here, to get swept up in the unreality of it all.

Aidan stopped in front of a shuttered property right on the waterfront, just a little further along from a row of bars and restaurants. He pulled up the shutters, his muscles flexing beneath his shirt, and unlocked the door, standing aside to let Alyson through. Some work had been done since the last time he was there – the rubbish left by the previous tenant had been cleared, and a wall had been knocked through in preparation for the new layout.

Aidan was buzzing with excitement as he showed Alyson round. 'This is where the bar's going to be, and I plan to put the reception *here*. Then this pillar is coming down to make the back more open, and I want the kitchen to be like Kennedy's Dublin – you haven't seen that, but I've shown you photos, right? And then I'm importing the same lights, as well as all the Irish linen and Waterford crystal, to keep a sense of continuity across the branches . . .' He turned to

Alyson, his enthusiasm impossible to hide. 'Well?' he asked breathlessly. 'What do you think?'

Aidan's excitement was infectious, his descriptions so detailed that Alyson could picture everything as it would be. It was a great space, exactly right for Aidan's needs, and it would look amazing when it was finished.

'Oh, Aidan,' Alyson breathed. 'It's perfect.'

Dionne was sitting on her couch, eating a huge bag of potato chips. She was just over four months' pregnant, and her bump was growing steadily. She hadn't worked for weeks – all of her jobs had dried up or been cancelled. She'd stopped bothering to ring her agent; the constant refrain – that there was nothing for her – wasn't what she wanted to hear. So she spent her days watching trash TV and eating crap; her body was craving Cheetos, which she had sent over from the States, and chocolate ice cream, which she ate by the bucket-load.

She'd stopped going out too. If she stepped out of her apartment, there was always some asshole with a camera demanding to know who the father of her baby was. She still didn't know the answer herself, so how could she be expected to tell anyone else? Instead she stayed in, gave up caring about her appearance and slobbed out in sweats and an old T-shirt. She couldn't remember the last time she'd exercised or done her hair. Besides, for the first trimester she'd had the worst morning sickness, which seemed to be exacerbated by everything – the smell of food, perfume, car fumes. Just the air on the Parisian streets was enough to make her feel nauseous and her apartment became her refuge.

Anyone could have told her she was depressed. The problem was, she didn't have anyone around to tell her that. Sure, her mom had been excited about the

362

news, once she got over the fact that Dionne wasn't marrying the baby's father. *I don't know who he is, Momma . . .*

'I don't want him to be a part of it,' Dionne told Natalie Summers, which wasn't entirely the truth.

'Honey, that's crazy, he gotta face up to his responsibilities,' her mom argued.

Dionne's tone was brittle. 'I've got enough money of my own, I'm going to do this by myself.'

'Come home,' Natalie said softly. 'You've been off gallivanting round the world for long enough: now it's time to stop. Come home, where I can look after you and my grandchild.'

For a second Dionne considered it, tempted by the ease with which she could just hide away from the world and let her mother look after her. But she knew it was a bad idea. After five minutes back home, she'd be climbing the walls, desperate to get out of Detroit, just like she'd been all those years ago.

'I'm fine, Momma,' she lied. 'I have people here. How's Daddy?' she asked casually, changing the subject.

'Oh, you know,' Natalie said lightly. 'Same old.'

Dionne knew exactly what that meant.

'How about if I fly out for a while?' Natalie suggested. 'I'd love to see your place, see what kind of life you have out there. I'm proud of you, honey.'

Dionne swallowed hard, blaming pregnancy hormones for the tears that pricked her eyes. Her momma had never told her she was proud of her before. 'Maybe nearer the due date,' she managed to say, her voice thick.

If Dionne was being honest, she was scared as hell. She didn't have anyone, and she was embarrassed for her mother to know that; desperate to keep up the appearance of the glamorous, sociable life she'd once led. She even attended her regular check-ups on her own, hiring a driver and wearing big black shades.

David had called, once or twice, to see how she was doing. He was a good guy, and Dionne believed him when he said he'd always be there for her, but she'd well and truly burned that bridge. There'd been photos in the gossip magazines of him and Esther, speculating on whether an engagement was likely. She knew the media always exaggerated these things, but still, their relationship seemed to be going well. If she tried hard enough, she could almost convince herself she was happy for him.

Even more surprisingly, CeCe had sent flowers when the news of Dionne's pregnancy had broken. It was a sweet gesture, the first step in a possible reconciliation. Dionne hadn't replied yet, uncertain whether she would. Her pride was still as fierce as ever, but there was part of her that was ashamed, knowing she didn't deserve CeCe's kindness after the way she'd treated her. CeCe was blind when she was in love – Dionne knew that better than anybody, and she had taken full advantage of it in the early days. She felt like a bitch just thinking about it.

And when CeCe had chosen Alyson as the face of Capucine, Dionne had gone ballistic, doing everything in her power to trash the brand in its infancy. She'd said some horrible things to the press and behaved appallingly, but back then she didn't care. Now she did, her conscience pricking as she looked back on what she'd done.

The rumours within the industry were that Capucine was struggling, but Dionne took no pleasure in that. It made her sad to think how drastically her relationship with CeCe had changed, from being as close as sisters to little better than enemies. She remembered how tight they'd been back when they were desperate to make it, both poor as dirt but stylish as hell and always able to afford a bottle of champagne even when they couldn't make the rent. They'd both achieved everything they'd dreamed of, and more, but Dionne wondered if either of them was truly happy with how their lives had turned out.

Dionne sighed, flicking through the channels on her enormous widescreen TV. She had cable, and liked to watch all the trashy American shows that reminded her of home.

She turned on to *E! News*, where they were rounding up some story about Mariah Carey. Then the presenter with the big hair and the tiny body turned to the camera, her expression grave.

'Now, an *E! News* exclusive. There are fresh rumours doing the rounds about model and mom-to-be, Dionne Summers, and they are not what she wants to hear, are they, Todd?' She turned to her co-anchor.

Dionne sat bolt upright, her eyes glued to the screen. What info could they possibly have? Even *she* didn't know who the baby's father was; any story about that had to be pure speculation.

'No, Ashley, they are not,' Todd said, his voice low and serious, his forehead creasing into a concerned frown.

Just get on with it, Dionne willed them, hating them for their fake sincerity.

'Within the last few minutes, reports have surfaced that explicit pictures exist of a sixteen-year-old Dionne Summers. It's claimed they were taken at the start of her career, and show the young model in a number of – let's say – "compromising" positions,' Todd smirked.

'That's right,' Ashley agreed cheerily. 'No one knows who's behind the deal, but the rumour is they're being shopped around and will be sold to the highest bidder. Several porn companies are said to be interested, including those behind Paris Hilton and Kim Kardashian's infamous sex tapes. Now, onto news of Victoria Beckham's latest outfit . . .'

Dionne sat motionless with shock, staring at the television. The colourful images flashed across the screen, but she couldn't take in a word. The pictures Luis Fernandez had taken, the ones she'd almost managed to forget about . . . *Almost*. She'd always told herself that if they were going to come out, they would have done so by now. But she was wrong, and now they were all over the news.

She felt sick, and it was nothing to do with the baby. She pushed the bag of chips to one side and tried to breathe.

Christ, what were people going to say? Sure, she'd done nude before, but it was kind of different when you were being shot by Mario Testino.

Tears burned at the corners of her eyes, her blood running hot in her veins. *Luis Fernandez was a piece of shit*, she thought furiously. The photos he'd taken were practically pornographic, right between her legs and leaving nothing to the imagination. And she'd been so young, barely more than a child . . .

Dionne choked back a sob. Sure, she'd been naïve, but also so optimistic and excited, eager to start her career and believing that Luis Fernandez could put her on the road to the big time.

But Dash Ramón had set her up and now *everyone* was going to see those photos – her parents, her family, her agent . . . She would be a laughing stock. Her reputation was already on the line – her agency had made it clear recently that her bolshy attitude didn't endear her to anyone – and now that she was pregnant it could be the kiss of death to her career. She'd planned to start working again as soon as she could after the birth, to plough straight into a full-on fitness regime and drop the excess pounds as fast as she could. But with these revelations, would anyone even want to hire her? And if not, what the hell was she going to do with her life?

She needed to call someone, to talk things over and get a little sympathy.

She had no one. The realization hit her like a sledge-hammer and her head dropped as the tears began to fall. She'd barely had time to wipe them away when her cell phone began to ring.

'Go away,' Dionne screamed at it. 'Fuck off!' She didn't even bother to see who was calling; she knew it wouldn't be good.

Then her landline began to ring, her laptop beeping as the emails came flooding in. All around, her lights were flashing, electronic noise demanding her attention as the world's media swamped her, trying to discover if the photos really existed and what she intended to do about them.

Dionne had no idea. She just wanted it all to go away.

She flung herself down, burying her head in the sofa cushions, and wept.

33

As soon as CeCe turned the key and walked into her apartment, she knew something was wrong. It was quiet. Far too quiet. It didn't just feel empty – it felt deserted.

Trying to push down the panic rising in her chest, she dumped her bag and ran into the lounge. All around her, the huge posters of her and Mayumi stared down, their faces glowing and in love. But Mayumi wasn't there. Nor were her Converse trainers, which she always left beside the sofa, or the stack of photography magazines piled on the coffee table.

CeCe let out a strangled cry and ran into the bedroom, flinging open the wardrobe. Mayumi's clothes had gone, the wooden hangers empty and clattering uselessly against each other. Every room told the same story: her toothbrush – gone; her camera equipment – vanished.

'No!' CeCe yelled. It was a heart-rending, agonizing sound.

She ran back to the hallway, pulling her phone out of her bag. Mayumi's was the last number dialled. She pressed it; it didn't even ring, just went straight to voicemail. She hung up and tried again. Same thing. The third time, CeCe didn't hang up.

'Mayumi?' she asked desperately. Her voice sounded shaky, positively unhinged. 'Mayumi, it's CeCe. Call me,' she pleaded, her voice thick with tears. 'As soon as you get this message. I need to speak to you. I need . . . Just fucking call me!' She slammed her finger down on the button, the tears rolling down her face as she began to sob uncontrollably. Her body sank down onto the floor, her legs too weak to hold her any longer.

Mayumi had gone. She'd left, and taken CeCe's heart and soul with her; all her hopes for the future. The apartment was completely clear of her presence, as though she'd never really been there at all. She *needed* Mayumi, CeCe thought desperately. She had to have her there in order to be able to design, to create. How could any designer function without their muse?

She clamped her hands down hard on top of her skull, pressing her palms into her temples. Her head felt as though it was going to explode. She couldn't think straight. Her breath was coming fast, and she was beginning to hyperventilate. She didn't care about anything except Mayumi – not Capucine, not her career, not anything.

She'd thought Mayumi loved her, but she didn't. She'd made a fool of her, used her. Jesus, her heart felt as if it had literally split in two, a physical pain slicing through her chest like a knife blade.

CeCe dragged herself to her feet and staggered towards the living room. Unnatural, guttural sounds were coming out of her; she was whimpering like a wounded animal. She felt primitive, unable to concentrate on anything but the pain. Tears were streaming down her face, her nose running freely. She wiped it on the back of her sleeve – a vintage Ossie Clark blouse that she'd thought looked cute teamed with a pair of high-waisted shorts. What did it matter if she ruined it? Nothing mattered any more.

She stood in the doorway to the lounge, swaying unsteadily. Her eyes focused on the huge poster of her and Mayumi. They were happy and smiling, looking directly into the camera.

'Bitch!' CeCe screamed, anger coursing through her body. She picked up a vase from the coffee table, filled with red roses that she'd bought for her, and flung it with all her strength. It hit the target, then fell to the floor and shattered, leaving the picture streaked with water, flowers scattered across the parquet floor amongst jagged shards of glass.

'Fucking bitch!' CeCe screeched again, her voice high-pitched like a banshee.

She stared at the poster for a moment, stained and torn, and felt a wave of determination sweep over her. If Mayumi wanted to be removed from her life, she would make sure it was complete.

With a loud cry, she launched herself at the picture, tearing it down from the wall and ripping it to shreds. She snatched at another photo of Mayumi, her dark eyes staring innocently at the camera lens, and tore it into a dozen pieces. Then she made her way round the apartment, working herself into a frenzy as she pulled down every image, obliterating any evidence that the two of them had ever been together. With every rip, she let out a loud cry, like a tennis player going for the winning shot. It felt good to exert the energy.

Finally CeCe stopped and stood back, panting and exhausted. The flat was covered in scraps of black-and-white paper, drifting down from the ceiling like some bizarre snowstorm. If CeCe looked hard enough, she could make out the individual features. Over there was one of Mayumi's eyes, staring at her accusingly.

Not far from that lay her nose; a little closer and she could make out the curve of a breast, a piece of a shoulder blade.

CeCe fell to her knees amongst the pile, picking up a handful of paper and letting it trickle through her fingers.

'What did I do?' she moaned helplessly, staring at the mess around her. Every single picture had been destroyed, she realized, with a piercing stab of regret. She scrabbled at the fragments, trying to put them back together, but they were all mixed up, impossible to repair. CeCe pawed helplessly at the pieces of Mayumi's face. She sifted through the pile and found a pair of lips, raising them to her own in a tender kiss before letting them flutter to the ground.

Then CeCe lay down on top of the pile, her body exhausted with effort and emotion, and sobbed as though her heart was broken.

Dionne's car sped down the Avenue Montaigne. It was the most fashionable street in Paris, home to stores such as Christian Dior, Chanel and Louis Vuitton. Dionne watched from behind dark glasses, remembering how she'd been for endless castings and fittings along here, how she'd modelled for most of the names on the Avenue. She let her hand slip to her bump, deep in thought as she cradled it. Well, there would be no more of that now.

The car pulled up at her destination, and Dionne checked over her outfit one last time. Black tailored trousers that she'd had custom made to fit her expanding proportions, a white tank top clinging proudly to her baby bump, with a smart black jacket and six-inch Louboutins, defying the fact that she was almost five months' pregnant. She'd had Frédéric from Premier Salon come over to her apartment to do her hair in a long, straight weave, and she was beautifully put together, her nails

French polished, her make-up immaculate. She was fighting for her career, and she was going to do it looking fabulous.

She stepped out of the car, pleased to note that there were no photographers in sight. Thank God for the French paparazzi laws – it would have been a nightmare if she was in the States or the UK. Then she strode boldly into the offices of Elite.

'I have a meeting with Lionel Vartan,' she informed the young girl on the front desk. She didn't bother to introduce herself – as far as she was concerned, everyone knew who she was.

She was right. '*Bien sûr*, Mademoiselle Summers,' the girl said, recognizing her immediately. 'If you'd like to follow me . . .'

Dionne was gratified; she didn't like to be kept waiting.

She was shown into a meeting room where four people sat behind a desk, waiting for her. There was Lionel Vartan, the head of the agency, Vice President Antoine Hardy, Sabine Blanc, her agent, and Jacqueline Cresson, her regular booker.

Dionne thrust out her chin defiantly. They were really pulling out the big guns for this. It wasn't a good sign. She had a fight on her hands and she knew it.

'Dionne.' Sabine spoke first. She rose from her seat and kissed Dionne on both cheeks. The others leaned across the table to shake hands formally, refusing to look her in the eye.

'How are you?' Sabine asked.

'Well, thank you,' she said tightly.

'And all is well with the baby?'

Instinctively, Dionne's hand went to her stomach. 'Yes, thank you.' She didn't want to get into pleasantries. They weren't there for that. Sure enough, Sabine resumed her seat and indicated that Dionne should do the same. She sat down carefully, trying to maintain her dignity as the bump unbalanced her.

'Dionne,' Lionel began, sitting forward importantly. He was silver haired and sharp-suited, an air of quiet authority about him. 'As you know, you've been with Elite for a long time now. We've always done everything we can to support you. You've consistently been one of our most successful models as well as one of the most . . .' He paused. '. . . Spirited. And controversial.'

Dionne remained silent. She glared at Lionel, her dark eyes like chips of ice.

'The issue of the photos,' Lionel began, a look of fake concern crossing his brow, 'it's not a subject we want to speak about, but unfortunately we have to. Have you seen them?'

'I was there when they were taken,' Dionne retorted frostily.

'So you're admitting they're you? They're not faked?'

Dionne hesitated, feeling caught out. 'I was young,' she stated bluntly. 'Sixteen, and at the beginning of my career. I didn't really know what I was doing, and he talked me into it—'

'Save the sob story for the Oprah interview,' Antoine cut in nastily. He was a small, weaselly man, with an overly Botoxed forehead and obvious hair plugs. Everyone knew about his predilection for young boys who were barely legal, and here he was, playing the outraged moral guardian with her. It made her sick.

At that moment, Dionne hated every single one of them behind that desk. All of them, smug and sitting in judgement of her, enjoying every minute of it. She'd had some furious bust-ups with them in the past. In fact, now she thought about it, she'd fought with every single person around the table at some point, believing she was bigger than them. Bigger than the agency itself, even. And they'd had to acquiesce to her demands, placate her when she was throwing a tantrum, feed her ego simply because she'd insisted upon it. Now the tables had turned, and they were revelling in it.

'What it comes down to is this . . .' Sabine put her fingertips together in a triangle shape, her hands moving up and down to emphasize every word. 'We no longer feel in a position to be able to represent you.'

Dionne opened her mouth to protest. She'd suspected this was coming, and all her fears had been proved right.

'Please, let me speak, Dionne,' Sabine interrupted, holding up her hand for silence as though they were in kindergarten and Dionne was misbehaving.

Whatever, bitch, thought Dionne furiously. *I'll get mine soon and you won't know what's hit you.*

'We've taken the liberty of preparing this statement,' Sabine said, sliding it across the desk to Dionne. 'It will be released to the press as soon as this meeting is over. You'll notice that it's neutrally worded and doesn't apportion blame. As we've worked together for so long now, I think we'd all prefer it not to get . . . acrimonious.'

'You can't fire me,' Dionne spat. *Screw not getting acrimonious.* 'What, is it because of the pictures? Or because I'm pregnant?' she challenged them.

'Dionne, this isn't just based on the rather unfortunate incident that's recently come to light. We've had a number of complaints about you from some of our biggest clients. They say that you are late, uncooperative and downright rude. There have been reports of verbal abuse and even sexual harassment. Word gets round, and we have our reputation to consider.'

'Bullshit,' Dionne burst out. 'You've been wanting to get rid of me for months and this is the perfect excuse. Since when has nudity ever harmed a career? Look at Marilyn Monroe, Madonna, Carla Bruni. Hell,

374

I've posed nude for half of the designers out there. Anyone who's anyone's had their tits out in *Vogue*.'

'With all due respect, Mademoiselle Summers,' – *Oh great, now they'd gone all formal* – 'Those types of photos are rather less graphic. If it was simply a case of a few topless shots, it wouldn't matter. These, however, are essentially pornographic. You can see less explicit poses in a top-shelf magazine.'

'They were taken *six* years ago,' Dionne said in frustration. 'I was basically still a kid. All you need to do is put out a supportive statement, and the whole thing will be forgotten in a few weeks.'

'Don't think we haven't considered that. But the problem in this industry is that reputation is everything, and once you've endured a scandal like this, it's very hard to go back. When clients come to us they have a product to sell, and they need to exude a particular image. It has to be beautiful, sexy, aspirational – not slutty streetwalker.'

'To put it bluntly, Mademoiselle Summers,' Antoine cut in with relish, 'you can't sell lipstick when everyone's seen your cunt.'

'Fuck you.' Dionne got to her feet. 'You can't get rid of me like this. I'm pregnant – there are laws about this kind of thing. It's a breach of my fucking human rights.'

'Yes, but there are also laws about turning up on time and doing your job properly,' Antoine said shortly, and his tone was cold. 'If you fail to do that, which you have, I think you'll find we are quite within our rights to terminate your contract. I'd be very careful what you say from now on. Our lawyers don't respond kindly to threats.'

'No? That's a shame. 'Cos I'm gonna sue this agency so hard that by the time I'm finished with you, you'll be lucky to be operating out of a backstreet in Pigalle.'

'Mademoiselle Summers, this isn't America. You can't sue at the drop of a hat, and our judges don't take kindly to time-wasting cases brought purely out of vanity. Ask your legal representatives to check your contract. I think you'll find that you . . . what's the phrase? Ah, yes. Don't have a leg to stand on.'

He stood up, indicating the meeting was over. But Dionne was already heading towards the door. She was so angry she was shaking, and she wasn't hanging around to be spoken to like this. She knew the stress wasn't good for the baby, but she couldn't help herself from getting into a fight.

She pulled open the door so her voice could be heard all the way down the corridor. 'Screw the goddamn lot of you,' she screeched. 'You'll regret the day you ever fucked with Dionne Summers, I promise you that. You will fucking regret it.'

Alyson didn't think she'd ever been so busy in her life. She was throwing herself into every challenge, working her butt off to make Kennedy's Dubai a success. At the end of every day she collapsed into bed exhausted, but she was happier than she'd ever been.

Her days were filled with meetings, dealing with architects, lawyers and contractors. She'd engaged a PR firm and an events company for opening night, although she was heavily involved in the arrangements herself. She'd come to realize that she was something of a control freak, eager to be in charge of everything and oversee it all. But this was Aidan's big night, and he was trusting her. She didn't want to mess it up.

Aidan himself had to fly back and forth between Europe and the Middle East, but Alyson loved it whenever he was around. It was nice to have someone there to talk things over with at the end of the day. They'd resumed their old tradition of sharing a bottle of red over dinner, and dined out all over Dubai.

'Research,' Alyson had joked.

'Sure. Put it on expenses,' Aidan grinned, looking impossibly handsome as his smile lit up his face.

It was during one of those dinners that Aidan dropped the bombshell.

'There's something I want to discuss with you,' he said. His voice was serious, his eyes unable to meet hers.

'Sure,' Alyson said easily, although her heart began to beat a little faster, an unexpected feeling of nerves sweeping over her. She could tell by his tone that this wasn't something minor – that he hadn't simply had a change of heart about the paint colour or the floor plan.

Aidan hesitated, playing uncomfortably with the stem of his wine glass. He gripped it tightly, twisting it between his thumb and forefinger, the pressure turning his fingertips white.

'Philippe Rochefort,' he said finally.

Alyson felt winded, as though someone had punched her in the stomach. She didn't want to think about him ever again, and Aidan was the last person she expected to bring up his name.

'Whatever he's done, I don't care—' she began fiercely, but Aidan cut her off.

'Hear me out,' he pleaded. 'The word within the industry is that his business is struggling. Not Rochefort Champagne – his own company, Rochefort Enterprises. Apparently he's overreached himself with these new properties in the States, and the recession has hit him hard.'

Alyson wondered why Aidan was telling her this.

She sat quietly as he spoke, trying not to interrupt until he'd finished.

'There's a few properties he owns – in Paris, and in the South of France – that would be perfect sites for Kennedy's. They're not officially on the market, but I've heard whispers he'd sell them and I could get them at a knockdown price. Of course, I doubt he'd sell them to *me*, so it would all have to be done quietly.' He looked at Alyson expectantly. 'What do you think?'

For a moment, Alyson couldn't speak. She was still in shock that Philippe's name had come up, even more so that Aidan wanted to do business with him.

If she was being honest, her initial instinct was no – there were too many memories, and she didn't want either of them anywhere near Philippe Rochefort again. But, on the other hand, it was Aidan's business and he had to do what was best for him – who was she to interfere, just because she had a personal dislike of the guy? There was no need for Aidan to have even told her – they weren't partners or anything; he was under no obligation. But he'd consulted her because he respected her opinion and didn't want to hurt her – something that Philippe would never have done.

Alyson understood now, in a way she hadn't before, that the two men had a grudge to settle. And if that's what it came down to, then Alyson knew who she wanted to win.

She looked Aidan straight in the eye, her lips curving upwards in a smile. When she spoke, her voice was steely. 'I think that sounds like an excellent plan.'

34

Dionne was standing on the street outside CeCe's apartment, feeling self-conscious. Her face was hidden behind enormous black sunglasses, but her tall, skinny frame and huge bump made her distinctive.

She pressed the buzzer.

'Hello?' said a man's voice. It was early afternoon and it sounded as if a party was in full swing in the background.

'Is CeCe there?' Dionne asked, confused.

'Sure, whatever, come up.' The door clicked and Dionne pushed it open, ascending the stairs slowly due to her expanding bump.

She wondered if she had the right apartment. She'd tried the last cell-phone number she had for CeCe, struck by a sudden, overwhelming need to speak to her old friend again, but the number didn't seem to be working. In desperation she'd rung Capucine and was put through to Jacques Perrot. He was pretty frosty when he found out who was calling – Dionne hadn't exactly endeared herself to CeCe's colleagues by trashing the label at every opportunity she got – but he knew their history and relented, giving her CeCe's number and home address.

'If you speak to her, try and persuade her to come in. Remind her she has a business to take care of.' He sounded pissed off and exasperated, not overly worried. Dionne got the impression that CeCe went AWOL on a regular basis.

She could hear music way before she even reached the third floor, the whole building pulsing to a throbbing base line. As she drew closer, people were bustling in the corridor, spilling down onto the staircase. Dionne didn't recognize any of them. She checked the address once more. Yes, this was definitely the right place.

Dionne walked up to the open door, her nostrils assailed by an overpowering smell of weed. She collared the first person she saw, a tall, lanky guy with glasses. He was wearing a velvet jacket and oversized spectacles, holding a cigarette in one hand and a glass of red wine in the other.

'Do you know where CeCe is?'

'Who?'

'Cécile,' Dionne repeated, leaning away from the curling stream of smoke. She'd battled hard to give up, and didn't intend to inhale this guy's secondhand toxins.

The guy shrugged amiably. 'No idea. Take a look inside.'

Dionne walked into the flat, feeling decidedly uncomfortable. She had a bad feeling about this.

The stench of weed was even stronger inside and there were people everywhere, dancing, smoking, making out. One girl was slumped in a corner, her eyes spaced out, while Dionne stepped carefully over a prostrate body. But there was no mistaking that this was CeCe's flat. There was a row of framed photos along the corridor, stills from the various Capucine shows. There were a couple of Alyson, of course, but Dionne was shocked to find a picture of herself, resplendent in white at the very first show in the Tuileries gardens. It was completely unexpected, and out of nowhere she felt a lump welling in her throat. Jeez, these pregnancy hormones really messed you up. She'd never been so emotional. Although, considering everything she'd been through in the last few weeks, that was hardly surprising.

The first room she came to was the kitchen. One guy was making a sandwich, another man was going through CeCe's cupboards – in search of what, Dionne didn't know – and a couple were pressed up against the counter, making out. It was like a goddamn commune, thought Dionne irritably.

'Has anyone seen CeCe?' she asked desperately. Sandwich guy shook his head. Everyone else ignored her.

'Hey, try the lounge,' he suggested, pointing with a stick of salami.

Dionne pushed through yet more people, the noise growing louder. The stereo system was thumping, some weird French electronic shit. She'd never been into French music.

'Get the fuck out of my way,' Dionne swore at a guy who stumbled into her path and nearly fell on her.

'Okay, lady, calm down.' The man held his hands up.

'Holy shit, would you look at how pregnant she is?' said someone else.

Dionne opened her mouth to reply, but at that moment she caught sight of CeCe. She was slumped against the far wall, curled into a ball beneath the window. Her frame was emaciated, her clothes hanging off her. Her skin looked grey, and there was old eye make-up smudged across her face. It was impossible to tell when she'd last brushed her hair.

'CeCe,' Dionne yelled, running towards her.

CeCe didn't respond.

'Leave her sleeping,' a guy said. 'She's pretty fucking weird when she's awake. She just keeps ranting and saying crazy shit.'

Dionne ignored him. She grabbed hold of CeCe's wrists, pulling her arms and shaking her whole body. Drowsily, CeCe opened her eyes, staring blankly at Dionne.

'*Va te faire foutre*,' she mumbled, before closing them again. *Fuck off*.

'Shit, CeCe,' Dionne swore. 'Come on.' She began shaking her again. Nobody around them paid any attention. 'CeCe, it's me. It's Dionne.'

CeCe's eyes opened. It looked like it was an effort. 'Dionne?' she mumbled uncertainly.

'Yes, it's me,' Dionne said eagerly, a wave of relief washing over her. 'CeCe, what the hell's going on? Who are all these people?'

CeCe tried to pull herself upright. Slowly, she looked around. 'I don't know . . .' she muttered. She fell back against the wall, her eyes beginning to close once more. 'Don't care . . .'

'Girl, what is *wrong* with you?'

'Just let me sleep.' CeCe sounded agitated.

Dionne was mad. She'd made the effort, coming all the way over here to make up with CeCe, and now she was in this state. Something was clearly very wrong, yet CeCe didn't appear to give a damn.

'No, I won't just let you sleep.' Dionne was shouting to be heard over the music. 'I'm getting rid of these people. This place is like a fucking crack den.'

'Whatever,' CeCe mumbled.

Dionne was furious now. She whirled around, eyes landing on the startled guy behind her. He was fiddling with the stereo, trying to change tracks.

'Get the hell out of here,' she yelled at him.

His eyes were dazed, his pupils enormous. He stared back, uncomprehendingly.

'Get out now. Move, you goddamn jerk!' Dionne screeched. She ran towards him, waving her arms, and he bolted away into the mass of people.

Dionne exhaled sharply. This was going to be impossible. With a burst of inspiration, she bent down to the stereo and pulled the plug out of the wall. The music stopped instantly, and the buzz of conversation died down.

'The party's over, get the fuck out of here right now,' Dionne yelled at the top of her lungs.

A skinny girl with braids in her hair, wearing a pink prom dress, looked her up and down. 'Just chill, bitch.'

'I won't fucking chill,' Dionne fumed. 'And don't call me bitch.'

'Isn't that Dionne Summers?' someone said.

'Yeah man, it is. Hey, I've seen her pussy!'

'Man, that was years ago. She got an *old* pussy now.'

Dionne saw red. 'Get out, all of you, or I'll call the police,' she ranted. 'Out! Go on, get out!'

She marched into CeCe's bedroom, flinging open the door. On the bed, a couple were making love, while another girl was rummaging through CeCe's closet, trying on her clothes.

'Party's over, fuck off,' Dionne told them sharply.

She was physically manhandling people now, pushing them towards the exit. There were protesting cries, and more lewd catcalls, but she blocked them out. Slowly people began to move, filtering into the corridor and down the stairs.

Dionne didn't stop until she was certain all the rooms were clear, flinging open windows as she went to try and get rid of the acrid stench. Then she slammed the front door, the noise reverberating around the now empty flat.

CeCe was sitting up in the same place Dionne had left her, tears rolling slowly down her cheeks. 'I'm sorry, Dionne. I'm so sorry.'

Dionne sat down on the floor beside her, wrapping her arms around her bony shoulders. CeCe clung to her, her body wracked with sobs. Dionne's cashmere scarf was stained with tears and eyeliner and God only knew what else, but she didn't care. She held CeCe until she began to grow quiet.

'Come on,' Dionne told her, helping her to stand up. 'I'll get us both some water.'

'Can I have brandy?'

'Baby, that's not good for you. How about a coffee or something?'

'I need a drink,' CeCe pleaded, becoming tearful once again. '*Please.*'

'I don't think you have anything left,' Dionne told her softly. 'Those bastards cleaned you out.'

'Check my room,' CeCe whispered. 'Under the bed.'

Dionne looked at her. Her body was shaking, and she didn't look healthy. Maybe alcohol *would* help, as a temporary measure. Sighing heavily, she headed to the bedroom, returning a few minutes later with an unopened bottle of Courvoisier.

'What do you keep one there for?'

'Emergencies,' CeCe told her seriously, already pulling off the plastic and unscrewing the cap. Dionne frowned as CeCe placed the bottle to her lips, swigging on it as eagerly as a baby calf suckling on its mother's milk.

'Hey, girl, take it easy.'

CeCe looked up at her with tear-stained eyes. 'I heard Elite fired you,' she said bluntly.

'Uh huh.' That wasn't the comment Dionne was expecting, but she was willing to run with it. 'Nowhere else will take me on – nowhere decent, anyway. I'm a liability, that's what they tell me. A risk. Turns out that a heavily pregnant diva with a pornographic past is pretty much unemployable, apparently. Look, CeCe . . .' She needed to get out what she'd come here to say. 'I'm so sorry about everything that happened between us. Really I am. It should never have happened – it just got out of hand, and I feel so bad about everything. Hey, I guess I always was a bitch, right?'

She raised an eyebrow ruefully, and CeCe smiled.

'You know if it had been up to me that job would have been yours? I'd have done anything for you, Dionne.'

'I know you would, honey. Come here.' She held out her arms, and the two of them embraced, CeCe's skinny body pressed against Dionne's bump. It was as though the years had rolled away, as though all their success had never happened and it was just the two of them again, curled up on the sofa after a night on the town, sharing secrets and dreams and ambitions.

'Congratulations on the baby.' CeCe sat up and pulled away, rubbing her hand over Dionne's swollen belly.

'Thanks.'

'Whose is it?'

'Ain't that the million dollar question . . .?' Dionne commented archly. 'But come on, CeCe. What the hell's going on with you, huh? Why are you living like this?' She waved an arm to indicate the carnage in the room.

There was a long silence. Finally, CeCe spoke. 'She left me.'

'Who?'

'Mayumi.' The name meant nothing to Dionne but she kept quiet, encouraging CeCe to talk. 'I loved her, Dionne. I was crazy about her. She was my inspiration, the only thing that kept me designing.'

'That's not true,' Dionne said gently. '*You're* the one who created all those amazing designs, not anyone else.'

'No,' CeCe insisted. 'I needed . . . I needed *her.*'

'What happened?' Dionne asked carefully. 'Did you have a fight or something?'

CeCe shook her head miserably. 'No, nothing like that. She walked out on me. I came home one day and she'd gone. Taken everything and left. She thought I wouldn't find her,' CeCe explained, her words slurring. 'I think she changed her number – I could never get through. I didn't even know where she lived. She was a student, you see, always told me her place was a mess and she didn't want me to see it.

'But I knew her timetable. I went to her university and waited until she'd finished her lessons. I saw her come out of the building. She looked perfect – exactly as I remembered her. But she was with a guy. They were holding hands and they didn't see me. I hung back, hiding in the crowd. And then they kissed.' Tears were rolling down CeCe's cheeks, and she took another long swig of brandy.

'You should have seen them, Dionne. It was like she didn't want to let him go, like it was a physical pain. Even when they withdrew, their fingertips were touching until the very last second. She was *never* like that with me,' CeCe wailed. 'I feel like she was playing with me, like she was never really serious at all. She left me for a *man.* It *always* happens,' CeCe burst out, glaring accusingly at Dionne. 'I fucking hate men.'

'Hey, I hear you, sister,' Dionne tried to joke, looking down at her belly.

CeCe stared at her. She looked utterly lost, her face streaked with make-up, the tears dripping from her cheeks. 'Hold me, Dionne. I miss her so much. I need her. I need someone . . .'

Dionne leaned across, taking CeCe's fragile body in her arms. It was clearly a long time since she'd eaten a square meal.

'I don't know what I'm going to do,' CeCe sobbed. 'My life is such a mess. I just wish there was some way out, some way to start again . . .'

'Hey, it'll be okay,' Dionne assured her, stroking her hair. It was lank and greasy, and badly needed washing. 'I know it doesn't seem like it now, but you'll get out the other side. You just have to hold on to that.'

'I just feel like . . . like there's nothing to live for.'

'You've had your heart broken, baby. I know it feels like hell now, but you'll get over it, I promise you.'

'It hurts so much.'

'I know it does, boo, but you'll find someone else. You're amazing, you know that? So talented and special.'

'Really?' CeCe looked up at her in disbelief.

'Uh huh,' Dionne smiled. She stroked CeCe's face, wiping the tears away with her thumb.

CeCe stared at her for a moment. Then she tilted her head upwards and moved towards her suddenly, her lips meeting Dionne's.

For a second Dionne didn't move, taken by surprise at the familiar feel of CeCe's kisses, her mouth soft and warm. But her breath smelt of stale alcohol, and the situation was all wrong. Shocked, Dionne pulled away. 'No, CeCe honey, I didn't mean . . .'

CeCe looked mortified, devastated by the rejection.

'You're all the same, aren't you?' she spat accusingly. 'I'm just some plaything to you straight girls. You used me, Dionne.'

'That's not fair—'

But CeCe cut her off. 'I broke my heart over you and you didn't give a damn. You used me to get what you wanted – that's all you ever do to people. You're a heartless bitch. I'm not surprised you're on your own now.'

Dionne stood up. There was no point in getting mad. She'd grown up a lot these past few weeks, and was learning not to fly off the handle at every little thing. CeCe was clearly wasted. She was hurt and lashing out, and Dionne knew it wasn't personal. She didn't even know if CeCe would remember what she'd said when she woke up tomorrow.

'Look, CeCe, I'd better go. Get some sleep, okay? I'll swing by tomorrow and check in on you. And lay off the brandy, yeah?'

'Just get out,' CeCe sobbed. 'I hate you, Dionne. You're a fucking bitch. Just get out.'

Without another word, Dionne got up and left the apartment.

After Dionne had left, CeCe sat on the sofa for a very long time, staring into nothingness. The silence that had long haunted her was oppressive – she'd managed to block it out with noise and people, becoming numb to life. But now it was back and she didn't know how to deal with it.

She stared round at her beautiful apartment, seeing it afresh for the first time. It was a wreck. Furniture was pushed over and broken, smashed glass littered the floor. One guy had clearly pissed in the pot plant – yellow urine sat on the wood around it – and a dozen cigarettes had been stubbed out in the soil. Some of her possessions were missing, presumably stolen, and someone had even graffitied her hallway, a spray-painted tag on the long white wall.

CeCe reached down beside her and picked up the bottle of brandy, taking a long, deep swallow. It helped. The alcohol dulled her sensations, blocking out real life. She took another swig. It almost hit the spot, but not quite. She could still feel. She didn't want to feel any more. If she did, all the misery came back to her: the mess of her business, the slow death of her career, the desertion of her lover.

Dionne said it would get better, but what was the point? CeCe didn't want to get better. She couldn't see that there would ever be anything good in her future again. She swallowed some more brandy, drinking for as long as she could until her body rejected it and she spat it back out. It ran down her chin, spilling over her clothes and the sofa. Dazedly, CeCe wiped her mouth.

Then she hauled herself off the sofa, the brandy bottle still tightly clutched in one hand, and headed for the bathroom.

Dominique Clemenceau sat stiffly in her apartment on her faux Louis XV armchair, her cream Persian cat seated on her lap.

At least that infernal music from the flat upstairs had stopped, she thought irritably. The situation had become interminable over the last couple of days. It had been the same ever since that eccentric designer had moved in. Dominique had never heard of her, but apparently she was very popular with the young people.

Her living habits, however, left something to be

desired. There were people coming and going at all hours of the day and night, undesirables hanging around on the staircase and the near constant smell of marijuana drifting round the building.

But, for now, the noise had stopped and the people had left. Dominique sat quietly, enjoying the rare sound of silence, until a peculiar noise caught her attention. It was as though she'd left a tap running somewhere, a constant *drip drip drip*. She stood up slowly, shooing the cat from her lap, and went to investigate.

She traced it to the bathroom and, as she opened the door, Dominique did something she rarely did. She blasphemed.

'*Mon Dieu!*' she exclaimed, as she saw the water dripping through the ceiling, landing in a puddle on her expensively tiled floor. Well, this really was the last straw. She'd put up with the partying and the drugs and the noise, but this was criminal damage! She was going upstairs right now to give that young lady a piece of her mind, Dominique vowed. She didn't care whether she was a famous designer or not – it still didn't give her the right to ruin other people's apartments.

Angrily, Dominique climbed the central staircase to the next landing and rapped sharply on the door. When there was no answer, she tried the handle and was surprised to find it opened.

'*Bonjour?*' she called out. '*Il y a quelqu'un?*'

There was no reply.

Hesitantly, she stepped further into the apartment, calling out again. The place was a pigsty – there was mess everywhere, graffiti on the walls, and all the windows had been left wide open, the curtains billowing out in the light breeze.

Dominique moved towards what she assumed was

the bathroom, conscious of the damage the water would be doing to her own apartment. Time was of the essence – she didn't want the ceiling to cave in.

Perhaps the stupid girl had gone out and left a tap on. Yes, she could definitely hear the sound of running water.

Dominique moved towards the bathroom and pushed open the door. What she saw made her eyes bulge, her shaky hands flying up to her mouth. Bile rose in her throat and she let out a bloodcurdling scream. Then she collapsed onto the floor, and everything fell silent.

35

Kennedy's Dubai was in utter chaos, and Alyson was right in the middle of it – literally. She stood in the centre of what was slowly beginning to take shape as a recognizable bar and restaurant, directing the whirlwind of activity all around her.

Aidan was flying in later today. It was almost a fortnight since he'd last been in the country, and Alyson wanted everything to be perfect for his arrival. Right now, that looked like a pretty tall order. There were still workmen everywhere she turned – carpenters, joiners, plumbers, all rushing to complete their allotted tasks. The electricians were installing the distinctive chandeliers overhead, while the walls were being given their final coat of paint. The finishing touches to the spectacular bar area were being fitted by the entrance, and even outside the beautiful wooden terrace was being sanded and varnished.

'Miss Wakefield? Where do you want this?'

Alyson turned round sharply, brushing away a strand of hair that had come loose from her messy ponytail and was snaking across her face. Her pale blonde hair was getting long; she was so busy she'd had no time to go to the hairdresser's, and her appearance was the last thing on her mind.

'Over there,' she directed, consulting her clipboard then pointing in the direction of the bar.

It was the Kennedy coat of arms, carved in Irish oak, and it had been shipped over all the way from Galway. Aidan had insisted on having one in every Kennedy's, a signature piece which would have pride of place above the well-stocked bar.

The man nodded, struggling to carry the enormous package shrouded in layers of polythene. Alyson watched in excitement as it was carefully unwrapped, thrilled to see that it had survived its journey halfway across the world intact. It was a beautiful piece, exquisitely carved and expertly finished, and it would look fantastic when it was finally erected.

Her BlackBerry began to ring, and Alyson snatched it up. It was one of her suppliers, letting her know the linen napkins would be late. 'Shit,' she swore. 'Well, can you give me an arrival time?'

She made a mental note to switch suppliers for the next order, and hung up.

In a matter of weeks, her role had extended way beyond its original, consultative brief, and she'd essentially become project manager of Kennedy's Dubai, overseeing everything while Aidan flew back and forth to Europe, attending to the rest of his business.

Alyson didn't mind. She'd become strangely fond of Dubai, with its insane weather and ever more extreme ways to beat nature. Not that she'd had much time to appreciate the shopping and sunbathing for which the extravagant Gulf state was famous. She'd been on a steep learning curve since the day she arrived, rapidly acquiring a wealth of knowledge on everything from banking in the emirate to its complex legal system.

When she'd taken the commission that night in Kennedy's London, riding high on a wave of enthusiasm and optimism, Alyson had only the barest idea of what it was like to conduct business in the Middle East. Sure, there'd been the odd photo shoot in Jordan, and a fashion show one time in Lebanon, but this was a whole different ball game.

Now she was dealing with accountants, foremen, interpreters, government agencies. She was learning about permits and licences, with a crash course in taxation and the strict alcohol laws. The emirate was keen to encourage overseas investment, offering favourable tax breaks as an incentive, but the flip side was a whole load of red tape and legalese.

And, of course, she had the added problem that some men out here weren't interested in dealing with a woman. Quite frankly, Alyson wasn't about to try and change their minds. If they wanted to lose out on business, that was their problem. She wasn't on a crusade. Instead, she concentrated on building a good reputation amongst the people she *was* working with, ensuring she was always courteous, professional and appropriately dressed, conscious that she was working in a Muslim state. Being young, blonde and female, she knew she had a lot to prove. She had to work twice as hard to be taken seriously.

But Alyson was up for the challenge. Naturally, it was stressful as hell, but she put her head down and got on with it – reading, learning, doing. It was a joy to finally be working for herself, to be able to channel her natural focus and dedication into her own company. Her work was no longer simply looking pretty and saying nothing, while everyone else around her got to have input and an opinion; now she was able to use her brain, stretching herself to solve problems and create solutions. It was everything Alyson had loved at Rochefort Champagne, but fifty times more challenging – and without the sleazy boss.

She was aware that Aidan was still pursuing his idea of acquiring some of Philippe's properties. Alyson hadn't asked him too much about it – she was still uneasy about mentioning Philippe's name, and she was aware that the negotiations were complex and confidential. Aidan hadn't wanted to reveal his identity, concluding – probably rightly – that Philippe wouldn't sell if he knew who the buyer was, so the whole deal was shrouded in secrecy.

In the meantime, all Alyson could do was work hard on Kennedy's Dubai and offer her support in that way. She'd promised Aidan she could do it, and she didn't want to let him down. Hell, she didn't want to let herself down. Kennedy's was her first client, the first commission Dante Consulting had taken on, and that was why she couldn't let her feelings for Aidan get in the way of her work. It would be completely unprofessional. And she *did* have feelings for him: she'd admitted that to herself now.

At night, when she closed her eyes, she could see his face; she longed to reach out and touch him, to trail her fingers over the soft skin of his cheeks, or run her hands through his hair and pull him close. Her dreams were full of him. She would wake up alone in her hotel room, her skin drenched in sweat, her heart racing – and it wasn't just the Gulf heat that was having that effect on her body. She wanted him, badly. It was more than just some silly crush – she was no longer the naïve young girl she'd been with Philippe. She'd known Aidan for a long time, and the realization had hit her suddenly, out of the blue: she was falling for him, and there was nothing she could do to stop it.

Oh, she would be crazy to act on it, she knew that well enough. There were a million reasons why it wouldn't be right, and Alyson could list every one. He was her client, they had to keep their relationship professional, they had a complicated history . . . But the more time she spent around him, the more she was inspired by him. His attitude fired her up, his enthusiasm motivating her to make a success of Dante Consulting. As long as she could channel all her passion into her business, hopefully that would be enough. Then she could throw herself into her career and repress all unprofessional thoughts and forget about Aidan.

Yeah right, she thought in despair. Who was she kidding?

But she had to try, so she attempted to smother her feelings and fill the gaping void inside by burying herself in her work. Luckily for her, there was never a shortage of that.

The clock was ticking to opening night, just over a week away now. A spectacular party had been planned, with fireworks, belly dancers, circus performers and all manner of extravagant entertainment. The guest list was high profile and exclusive – an eclectic mix of Arab sheikhs, Russian oligarchs, British footballers and their wives, as well as a handful of journalists and bloggers to help spread the word that Kennedy's was the place to be. Alyson had been working with a PR firm to get the word out there and help create a buzz in the press, both at home and abroad.

She was trying hard not to become the story herself. Naturally, the PR company were pushing Aidan as the face of the venture, and planning to do a lot of press with him personally, but when they found out that Alyson was somehow involved – Ally, the former supermodel who'd dropped off the radar – they were intrigued. What was the story there? Alyson explained briefly that they'd known each other way back when; had worked together in Paris before either of them had attained the dizzy heights they were at now.

The story was too good to resist. Alyson hadn't wanted to take part, but Dana, the pushy PR guru she'd hired, persuaded her it was a great angle. Alyson reluctantly agreed; if it helped make Kennedy's a success, who was she to argue? And so they'd invited journalists to Aidan's suite at the Madinat and done a series of interviews together.

A couple of reporters seemed more interested in their private lives.

'Your friendship goes back a long way, and you obviously have a great chemistry – has there ever been anything more than a working relationship between the two of you?' asked Anna Jones from *Dubai Living*, the British expat magazine.

Alyson froze, keeping her eyes fixed firmly on a spot on the floor, terrified that her feelings would be betrayed. Aidan smiled easily. He was great at dealing with the press: charismatic, warm and just a little flirtatious. The Irish charm surfaced easily, and he had an assured, laid-back air. It was what had made him so popular, as both a boss and a landlord, back at Chez Paddy.

'As you said, Alyson and I have a great working relationship, and we're good friends, but that's as far as it goes.'

'No mixing business with pleasure then?' Anna pressed, thinking she wouldn't mind a little pleasure-seeking with the eligible Aidan Kennedy.

'Exactly,' Aidan grinned at her.

Anna simpered and giggled, uncrossing then recrossing

her long legs in a flirtatious gesture. Unlike Alyson, who favoured concealing trouser suits, Anna was flouting convention in a short skirt.

Alyson smiled weakly to back him up, but the words were like a knife in her heart. Aidan couldn't have put it any more plainly – they were just friends, nothing more, and she'd been stupid to ever think they might be. She blamed it on Dubai itself; on getting swept up in the magic and unreality of the place, just as she'd feared when she'd first arrived. It didn't help that she spent night after night out here alone, and it was so long since she'd been with a man. Aidan probably had a different girl every night, she thought, killing herself at the thought. Women flocked to rich, handsome men like him – she'd seen it with Philippe.

'Miss Wakefield, the cutlery's arrived. Where should I put it? Miss Wakefield?'

With a start, Alyson realized one of the workmen was trying to speak to her.

'Oh . . . put it over there,' she gestured vaguely, feeling flustered.

'Daydreaming on the job?' said a voice behind her.

'Aidan!' Alyson whirled round. Damn, he looked so handsome in a light-grey suit, the collar of his shirt unbuttoned due to the heat. She was completely thrown, suddenly horribly embarrassed that he should see her with her hair a mess, no make-up, and a scruffy old suit that she'd put on to work in the dusty environment. She'd planned to go back to her room and change before he arrived. 'I didn't expect you until later.'

'I like to keep you on your toes,' Aidan grinned. 'Nah, I finished up a little earlier than I expected in London so I took the earlier flight. How's everything going?'

'We're getting there,' Alyson assured him, trying to sound calm and in control, and not as though the guy she wanted most in the world was standing just inches away from her, looking the hottest she'd ever seen him.

'It's changed so much since the last time I was here.' Aidan looked round admiringly. 'It's really taking shape.'

'I hoped we'd have everything in place by the time you arrived, but you've beaten me to it.' Alyson's voice revealed a trace of disappointment – she'd wanted everything to be perfect for him so he could see how hard she'd worked.

'That doesn't matter. It looks great,' Aidan assured her.

Alyson walked him round the space, filling him in on the changes that had taken place. Nothing to do with the fact that while she was talking shop she could try and ignore the way her heart was thumping wildly, the way her stomach was tying itself in knots. Even though he'd taken her completely unawares, she was thrilled he was here. Just being around him made her feel happier, giddy like a child. She wanted to grin ridiculously.

'Okay, time for a break, Miss Wakefield,' said Aidan, when he'd seen the whole property. 'I'm taking you out to lunch.'

Alyson hesitated. She was reluctant to leave, even for an hour or so, as they had a tight schedule to keep to. And it was more than that – she was scared to be alone with Aidan, unable to trust her feelings around him.

'They can spare you for an hour,' Aidan insisted. 'And I promise we'll only talk about work so you won't feel guilty being away.'

Alyson smiled. It was so easy to give in to him. 'Okay,' she agreed. 'Let's go.'

Ten minutes later, they were seated in a casual little restaurant in the souk, an Asian-fusion place and one of their favourites. It was mid-afternoon and the place was dead, the lunchtime rush having been and gone. Aidan was glad they were alone. He didn't want anything to distract him from Alyson.

The truth was that he'd taken the earlier flight because he was missing her so badly. He knew it was crazy, but he couldn't stop thinking about her. He hadn't been able to concentrate on his work while he'd been in Dublin, so he'd flown to London, hoping that being there might bring him some focus. It was worse than ever. Since Alyson had stayed with him, everything reminded Aidan of her. His apartment seemed empty without her there, and when he went into Kennedy's, all he could think about was the night they'd been there together. He could almost picture the way she'd sipped from her water glass, the way she'd taken a delicate bite of her asparagus or how her cheeks flushed when she'd had a glass of wine. He remembered what she'd worn, the close-fitting clothes showing off her body perfectly, the shape of her small breasts crushed beneath the fabric, flaring out gently to those slim hips.

He had it bad. There was no denying it. He'd been ringing her up on the most spurious of excuses, just to hear her voice.

'I don't know who she is, but it's love,' his friend Niall had teased him when they'd gone drinking one evening. Aidan had thought a night out with the guys might be the way to stop thinking about Alyson, but he'd just become drunk and morose.

'I don't know what you're talking about,' Aidan denied it hotly. But Niall was right. He'd fallen for her, big style.

But Alyson had never given him any indication that she might feel the same way. It was all about work with her: she was so focused on that. It was almost as though he didn't exist outside of Kennedy's, Aidan thought resentfully. But he was determined to tell her how he felt – maybe after the Dubai launch. That way, if it all went wrong and she told him to go to hell, they never had to see each other again. He would move on with his life once and for all.

'So, how's everything going?' he asked neutrally, sticking to safe topics.

'Crazy,' Alyson replied. She looked stressed, but she forced a smile. 'Don't get me wrong, it's fantastic, but everything's getting a little hectic.'

'I really appreciate what you've been doing. You've done a great job.'

'Thanks.' Alyson sipped at her mineral water.

'And what about after this?' Aidan asked, trying to sound casual. 'Do you have anything lined up?'

'No idea,' Alyson shook her head. 'I haven't even thought about it. I've been so busy I haven't had time to look for anything else or start pitching for contracts. I'm hoping if this goes well I might get some work out of it. Hopefully you'll give me a great reference,' she grinned.

'Absolutely,' Aidan smiled back, unable to stop himself from checking out her body. Man, she looked gorgeous, even though she was wearing just simple, loose cotton trousers and a demure white shirt. She always looked polished, classically chic. 'Seriously, if I can help you out in any way, just let me know.'

'You've already helped me enough,' she told him honestly. 'Just thinking back to the state I was in when that story came out . . . You were my knight in shining armour,' she teased. She was only half joking. There was no way she'd have picked herself up and created Dante Consulting without him.

'Hey, I can't resist a damsel in distress,' he smiled, then immediately felt like an idiot. He watched as Alyson shifted uncomfortably on her chair, instantly regretting what he'd said. He'd made himself look stupid and embarrassed her. 'So you really don't have any idea where you'll be next?' he said, trying to move the conversation on.

Alyson shrugged. 'I could be anywhere in the world,' she said, sounding a little sad. 'I guess that's the beauty of this job, right? I get to see new places, learn new things . . .'

Aidan nodded. 'But you'll miss me, right?' he couldn't resist asking.

'Of course.' Alyson hesitated for a moment. 'I'll really miss you, actually, Aidan.' Her voice seemed to crack; she couldn't meet his gaze.

Aidan felt as though his heart was being compressed; his gut was tight with nerves. 'Alyson,' he said. There was something in his tone; she looked up immediately, her blue eyes searching his.

'Yes?' she asked eagerly.

Aidan wanted to throw caution to the wind, to just tell her how he felt and to hell with the consequences. He was feeling reckless, as if nothing else mattered. 'I don't know if this is the right time,' he began quickly, the words rushing out before he lost his nerve. 'But here's something I have to tell you. Shit,' he swore er his breath, as Alyson's phone started to ring. looked back at him anxiously, her expression apologetic. 'I'm so sorry, Aidan, I'm going to have to take this. I'm waiting to hear back from the printers – they're querying the menu.'

'No problem,' Aidan said automatically. The phone call had killed the mood, but he was still resolved to tell her. He had to.

'My God, that's not possible!' Alyson burst out in shock.

Aidan looked up sharply. Her face had turned ashen, tears springing into her eyes. Shakily she hung up, putting her phone down on the table. Her whole body was trembling.

'What is it? What's wrong?' Aidan demanded.

Alyson's mouth opened, but no sound came out. 'CeCe,' she finally managed to say. 'My old housemate, Cécile. She's killed herself.'

36

It was the afternoon of CeCe's memorial.

Her funeral had been held a few days before, her body taken back to her home village of Clochiers. It had been a family-only affair. Her parents had never reconciled themselves to CeCe's choice of career, and the fashion world wasn't invited. As far as CeCe's parents saw it, it was the industry itself that had killed their daughter. The intense pressure, the constant stress, the merciless criticism – that's what had driven CeCe to it, in their eyes.

She'd been found in the bath, her wrists slit. Her blood-alcohol level had been off the scale, and there had been other substances in her system too. A neighbour had discovered her, an elderly woman who'd nearly had a heart attack herself when she discovered CeCe's lifeless body.

Dionne was still in shock, still unable to believe what had happened. They'd only just reconciled, and now CeCe had been taken away from her in the cruellest way possible. She'd known CeCe was in a bad way, but she'd never imagined . . . She should never have left, Dionne told herself repeatedly. Surely the signs had been there, if only she'd bothered to look . . .

But could she really have done anything? She'd asked herself that question a thousand times since she'd heard the news, going over it again and again. She knew she had to let it go – it would destroy her if she continued to think about it.

She stood up carefully from the chair in front of her dressing table, checking her appearance in the mirror. The day was warm, and she wore a simple black dress, empire line to accommodate her growing bump. She turned sideways, looking in the mirror to see how much she'd grown, smoothing the dress down over her stomach. Now that the initial trimester was over, she was almost enjoying being pregnant. Dionne Summers, the eternal party girl, was looking forward to being a mom! She loved the feeling of new life growing inside her, seeing her body develop and change. She'd expected the experience to freak her out, but she was revelling in it. Her skin was glowing, her eyes bright, and it was such a joy not to deprive herself of food but to eat healthily for the sake of the baby.

It was bizarre to think that CeCe would never know her child. That someone who had been such a big part of her life, who'd been her closest friend at one time, wouldn't be here for the next chapter. She guessed that was how the world worked, but it was pretty shitty sometimes.

Dionne checked her watch – lately, she'd gone back to wearing the Cartier Tank David had bought for her – and realized that time was getting on. She didn't want to be late. It was hard to change the habits of a lifetime, but she was slowly getting there.

Dionne took a deep breath as she picked up her oversized Gucci shades. There were going to be a lot

of people there today that she didn't want to see –
Alyson Wakefield for one. But she would rise above it
all. Yeah, she was definitely mellowing in her old age,
becoming more mature. Of course, it wasn't just Alyson.
There were all the people from the fashion world who'd
turned their back on her as soon as things went sour,
cutting off ties and refusing to take her calls. She would
be *persona non grata* at this memorial, practically a
leper.

But she didn't care what they said. She was doing
this for CeCe.

It seemed as though the whole of the fashion world
was crammed into l'eglise de la Madeleine in central
Paris. It was amazing how popular you became after
you were gone, Alyson reflected cynically, thinking
of the flood of tributes in the papers from people
who'd written CeCe off a long time ago. The fashion
press had hounded her during the final weeks of her
life, but now those who'd slated her were queuing
up to pay tribute, speculating on what heights she
could have achieved if her life hadn't ended so
tragically.

Alyson had had enough of the industry's bullshit
and two-facedness to last her a lifetime. It was only
her ties to CeCe that had brought her back here today.
After all, CeCe had been instrumental in the launch of
her career – without her, Alyson would never have
taken her initial steps in the modelling world, or had
her first big break with Capucine. Whatever Alyson's
feelings about the industry as a whole, she couldn't
deny how good CeCe had been to her.

There had been press outside the church when she
arrived, shouting her name and trying to take photos.
Alyson's heart had been pounding already, without

having to run the gauntlet of the media. She'd hurried inside and slipped into the nearest pew, trying to calm herself. She glanced around quickly, but couldn't see Dionne. She was probably going to turn up late to get attention, as if it was a bloody movie premiere or awards ceremony, Alyson thought, feeling uncharacteristically vicious.

This whole situation was unsettling her. It was so strange, returning to Paris. She hadn't been back since before her ill-fated trip to Japan months ago, and it felt as though everything had moved on without her. Her apartment had an air of abandonment, like the *Marie Celestc*, a fine layer of dust settling over everything. The food in her kitchen had rotted, the clothes in her wardrobe belonging to another life. Just as soon as she was finished with Kennedy's Dubai, she would make arrangements to sell the apartment. Paris was no longer her home. She didn't know where home was now – she'd spent so long with Aidan, first in London, then Dubai – but it was time to move on. She guessed she'd just go wherever the wind blew her, chase up more commissions for Dante Consulting and travel with work. She was thinking of investing in an office space in London, of making a more permanent base there. That way she wouldn't be too far from her mother, and hopefully they could continue to build bridges.

This trip was like the end of an era, as though she was closing the final chapter of a book that had lain open for far too long. There were so many people here today that she recognized, the familiar faces of stylists, make-up artists, photographers. And right at the front of the church was the team from Capucine, to whom she owed so much. They'd backed her from the beginning, accepting her inexperience and pushing for her appointment – the decision that had provoked so much bile and fury from Dionne.

Today was, first and foremost, about CeCe, obviously, but Alyson couldn't help but feel it was the perfect opportunity to say goodbye to her old life. The girl she'd been when she'd first moved to Paris was a distant memory; now it was time to move on and discover who Alyson Wakefield could become.

A sudden ripple ran around the church, conversations tapering off as heads swivelled towards the entrance. Alyson turned to see what was happening. It was Dionne. She swanned in wearing enormous black sunglasses and swept straight to the front of the church, walking past Alyson without even seeing her. Everyone was watching. It was a long time since Dionne had been seen out in public, and Alyson couldn't help but stare – man, she was huge! But she looked stunning, Alyson had to give her that. She was positively glowing, and her body had filled out beautifully. She'd always had curves, but now her breasts were enormous, her booty ridiculous.

Alyson stood up very straight, her face neutral, fighting to keep her composure at the sight of Dionne just a few metres away from her. This was the woman who'd tried to ruin her career – her life, even. But Alyson had moved on – she had a new business, a new sense of purpose. She almost felt sorry for Dionne. The story was that she'd been kicked out of her agency, that she didn't know the identity of her baby's father. And of course, there had been *those* pictures that had gone viral on the Net.

Dionne had always been overly ambitious, living her life at breakneck pace, and now it was catching up with her. In the past, Alyson had felt inferior around her, boring and unexciting. Well, now she was the one in control, and Dionne was losing it. The thought calmed Alyson, helped her not to feel intimidated. But she couldn't take her eyes off the distinctive figure at the front of the church, her gaze boring into Dionne's back.

There was a flurry of movement as the priest emerged from the sacristy and everyone stood up. Then the church fell silent, and he began to speak.

The ceremony was beautiful and touching. Alyson had expected it to be full of fake sincerity, with fashion types spouting platitudes from the lectern, but it was surprisingly moving. In spite of the criticism, CeCe had obviously had some firm admirers within the industry, and the tributes were heartfelt.

Alyson came out of the church, caught up in the crowds that were milling around in the sunshine outside. A lot of people stared discreetly, but no one approached her. She felt lost and out of place, wanting to make a quick getaway, but she couldn't see her car in the mass of black vehicles lined up on the Place de la Madeleine. Never mind, she would rather walk – clear her head and get some perspective.

As she made her way through the throng, a hand tapped her on the arm. It was Jacques Perrot, CeCe's second in command at Capucine, who'd now moved up to head designer. Alyson had got to know him well during her time working for the label, and he'd given a moving speech calling CeCe an inspiration, a true original. He seemed genuinely devastated that she'd gone.

'Are you coming?' he asked. 'To the reception?'

'I . . .' Alyson hesitated. She just wanted to get away.

'CeCe always spoke very highly of you,' Jacques said. His eyes were ringed with red, his face pale.

'I know she was thrilled with the work you did for us. When you retired, she said we'd lost a special talent.'

Alyson nodded, not trusting herself to speak. His words were sincere, and they'd touched a nerve.

'Will you come?' Jacques pressed.

Alyson nodded once more.

'Come with me, share my car,' Jacques offered, holding out his arm to escort her to the black Mercedes that was waiting.

The reception was being held just round the corner, at the Ritz. It was a short journey, and they spoke briefly.

'What's going to happen to Capucine?' Alyson asked, voicing the question that had been the subject of much press speculation.

Jacques sighed. 'I'm going to finish this collection and show it as planned. It's what CeCe would have wanted, and it just feels . . . *right.*'

Alyson nodded in agreement.

'After that, I don't know. Perhaps the label will be wound up. I've had offers from other places, but my heart's with Capucine. It all depends on the reaction I suppose . . .'

He trailed off, staring out of the window. Alyson didn't press him. It wasn't really the right setting for small talk.

They pulled up at the Ritz shortly afterwards, running the gauntlet of press before they were swept through to the sumptuous Salon Louis XV.

'I thought CeCe would like it here,' Jacques murmured to Alyson as they entered. 'Coco Chanel lived here, you know, and CeCe was always a huge admirer of hers. Oh, the clothes were a little sedate, a little mono-chrome for her. But the way she changed fashion – she was a revolutionary. Who knows what CeCe could have achieved if she'd had more time . . .'

He smiled sadly as the crowd closed in on him, everyone wanting to speak to him and offer their condolences. Alyson glanced around uncertainly, wishing she hadn't come at all, that she'd just gone straight back to her apartment after the service. There were few people that she recognized and even fewer she wanted to speak to. In desperation she fled to the rest room. She would kill a few minutes in there, make herself presentable, then do the rounds and leave after a suitable juncture.

The bathroom was incredible, more sumptuous than most people's houses, complete with pale-pink marble and an enormous vase of coordinating orchids and roses. She was repairing her eye make-up in the ornate mirror – it had been an emotional ceremony – when the toilet door behind her swung open. She watched in the reflection as a woman emerged, her face half hidden by a mane of glossy black hair.

Dionne.

For a moment, neither of them moved. Their eyes were locked on each other, bodies frozen.

Then Dionne stepped forward deliberately, standing right beside Alyson as she slowly washed her hands. Their bodies were almost touching, but still neither of them turned to look at the other, their only view coming from the mirrored reflection. Alyson's hand was shaking as she applied her lipstick. She clicked on the cap and put it back in her bag, smoothing down her hair and turning to go. She was about to walk out when she hesitated.

There was something about today – the emotion, the reflection it invoked. It had made Alyson realize that life was too short. She'd spent much of the memorial remembering the early days, when all three girls had shared a flat together. Dionne and CeCe had been so close, but they'd always been good to her, inviting her out no matter how many times she declined. Hell, Dionne had even helped Alyson prepare for her first – and only – date with Aidan. Seeing her now, so physically changed, her body blooming and gloriously pregnant, Alyson couldn't help but think of new life and new beginnings.

'Dionne.' Alyson's voice was clear and steady.

Slowly, Dionne turned to look at her. 'Alyson,' she said neutrally.

Alyson swallowed. 'Congratulations,' she began. 'About the baby.'

'Thank you.' Dionne's tone was cool.

'I hope . . .' Alyson broke off, unsure of what she was trying to say. 'I hope everything works out for you.'

Dionne didn't respond. Alyson felt foolish, quickly picking up her bag and walking to the door.

'Alyson.'

The sound of Dionne's voice stopped her.

'I think . . . I mean, I know CeCe would have been really happy you're here today.'

Alyson turned around, her face softening. 'Thanks, Dionne.'

'Yeah. She was always a huge fan of yours – probably saw your potential before anyone else. I just . . . I guess I was jealous,' she admitted.

Alyson nodded. She knew how much it had cost her to say that. 'Yeah, well. Past history,' she said, with a lightness she didn't feel. 'I'm happy with my life now. I hope you are too.'

Dionne didn't reply. 'I miss her, Alyson,' she whispered eventually. 'I treated her really badly, but I wanted to make it right. I went to see her, the day she . . . She was in a terrible state, but I left her. I never imagined she would . . .'

'She loved you,' Alyson told her, matter-of-factly. 'Anyone could see it.'

'Not at the end,' Dionne shook her head. 'She hated me. Everyone hated me.'

'You didn't make it easy for yourself,' Alyson said wryly. She had no intention of soft-soaping her.

'No,' Dionne agreed slowly. 'You're right. I just wish . . . I wish there was something I could do to make it better. I'd give anything to go back to how it used to be – when it was the three of us, living in that tiny apartment. I had a blast.'

'You can't go back, Dionne. Too much has happened.'

'I know. I just . . . forget it.' Dionne wiped away a tear with the back of her hand. She didn't think it was possible to cry any more than she had these past few weeks.

In spite of everything, Alyson couldn't help but feel an empathy with Dionne. So much had changed since Alyson's rapid rise to fame, and they'd both been through the mill.

'I hear you've been having a tough time of it,' she said sympathetically.

Dionne turned on her. 'Yeah? Been enjoying it, have you? Well, don't worry about me, Alyson, I'm doing just fine.'

'No, I didn't mean . . .' Alyson trailed off.

Then the anger vanished as quickly as it had arrived, and Dionne seemed to crumple before her eyes. Alyson had never seen this side to her – vulnerable, and afraid. 'I don't know what to do,' she confided. 'My career is over. I'm not like you – I don't have brains. This is all I've ever wanted to do, and now it's finished.'

'No, it isn't,' Alyson insisted. She knew how much modelling meant to Dionne, even though she would never understand it. 'Look at what you've achieved already,' she told Dionne, remembering the pep talk Aidan had given her. 'You can do anything you want.'

'Uh uh,' Dionne shook her head. 'I had my chance, and I blew it.'

'Why don't you model for Capucine?' The idea came out of Alyson's mouth before she'd even had time to think about it. 'I spoke to Jacques earlier, and they're still going ahead. They'll show at Fashion Week in September. Why not?'

Dionne looked at Alyson as if she was an idiot. 'Because all I've ever done is slate their company, and by Fashion Week I'll be eight months' pregnant?'

'Right, and you never did anything controversial before?'

A look of understanding flickered across Dionne's face. There was a glimmer of curiosity in her eyes, and Alyson knew she'd got her interested.

'But . . . would they even have me?'

Alyson shrugged. 'No harm in asking. Jacques is a good guy – you know that. And can you imagine the publicity for Capucine? His first show at the helm, and he's got the world's most notorious model on the catwalk.'

'The world's most notorious model,' Dionne repeated the phrase, liking the way it sounded. 'Yeah, maybe it could work,' she wondered, her tone betraying her growing excitement. 'And if everyone sees me turn it around, it could get me back in the game . . .'

'Maybe,' Alyson agreed. 'But don't do it for that. Just get out there, do it for CeCe and show the world that you don't give a damn what they think.'

'Why don't you join me?' Dionne said casually.

'Huh?'

'Think about it – the perfect tribute to CeCe. The first time both of us will have been seen on a runway together. It would be huge.'

'No thanks.' Alyson shook her head. 'Been there, done that. My modelling days are over. Besides, I don't think I'm the draw I once was. The fashion world forgets about you pretty quickly if you let it.'

'Aw, come on, Alyson,' Dionne insisted. 'It would be awesome – what better tribute to CeCe? The two of us on the runway, an event that will never be repeated. Like you said, who gives a damn what anyone else thinks? Just do it for CeCe.'

Alyson stared at Dionne for a long time. She wondered if she might be right.

37

Fireworks exploded, shimmering dots of white light exploding high above the Madinat Souk like shooting stars. Guests crowded onto the terrace to watch the display taking place on the opposite bank. It was a spectacular evening, an undoubted triumph, and as far as Aidan was concerned, it was all down to Alyson.

He badly wished that she could be there beside him, that they could face the world as a couple and revel in their achievement together. But he knew that attending her friend's memorial was important to her, and he respected her for that. She'd put so much work into Kennedy's Dubai that only something major could have convinced her to miss its opening night.

Aidan stared round at the scene, enjoying the heady thrill of success. It was a glamorous, fashionable affair, exactly what he'd envisioned, with some of the emirate's biggest players present, taking full advantage of his hospitality. Waiters mingled amongst the invited guests, offering canapé-sized portions of their most popular dishes – shot glasses filled with minted pea soup and topped with crème fraîche; perfect miniature Yorkshire puddings containing roast beef and horseradish mousse; quail eggs rolled in celery salt and cracked black pepper.

'Aidan Kennedy!'

Aidan heard a voice behind him, then a heavy hand clapped him on the back.

'Congratulations, my friend, you've done an amazing job.' It was Eddie van Niekerk, a South African multimillionaire who'd made his fortune with a chain of gyms and health clubs. He was in his fifties, tanned and healthy as befitted a gym owner, with pale-blond hair and freckled skin.

'Thanks,' Aidan smiled, happy to accept the compliment.

'I mean it. This place looks unreal.'

'Well, I had a lot of help,' he confessed.

'Ah, you're too modest, Aidan.'

'No, really.' Aidan shook his head. 'I worked with a company called Dante Consulting, and they really pulled this whole thing together.'

Eddie frowned. 'I don't think I've heard of them.'

'No?' Aidan feigned surprise. 'They're relatively new, but they specialize in international relocation. The MD, Alyson Wakefield, is fantastic.'

'Alyson Wakefield . . .' Eddie mulled over the name. 'Sounds familiar. Didn't she used to be an actress or something?'

'A model. And it was a long time ago,' Aidan said meaningfully. 'She's running her own business now, and it's very successful. Young, dynamic – totally on the ball.'

'Interesting.' Eddie nodded thoughtfully.

'Yeah. They specialize in companies expanding overseas, helping out with the red tape and offering local knowledge, that kind of thing.'

'You know, Aidan, I'm considering moving into the European market myself. Things are going well back home, and I think it's time to export some of that van Niekerk magic overseas,' he grinned. 'Do you think that's something they could advise me on?'

'I'm sure it would be.'

'Great. Listen, do you have her number? What was the company called again?'

'Dante Consulting.' Aidan scribbled it down on the back of his own business card. He was more than willing to spread the word for Alyson. He was so proud of everything she'd achieved and knew how desperately she wanted her business to succeed. More than anything, Aidan wanted her to be happy.

He was missing her like crazy, devastated that she couldn't be here to take the credit for tonight. Even worse was the fact that she'd gone before he'd had a chance to tell her how he felt. She'd caught a flight to Paris shortly after she'd got the phone call about CeCe, and there hadn't been a right time before she left. Understandably, she'd been too cut up about her friend.

But it was eating him up inside, not knowing how she felt. He hadn't been with a woman since Alyson came back into his life, and he was getting pretty frustrated in other areas too.

The next time he saw her, he would tell her at the first opportunity he got. Aidan was head over heels in love with Alyson, and he needed to know if she felt the same way.

Dionne lay back on the ultrasound table, her top pushed up below her breasts, her trousers pulled down to her pelvis as Dr Martine Chrétien, the obstetrician, smeared warm gel over her enormous stomach. She was at the American Hospital of Paris, about to have her final scan. The sensor was placed over her bump and within seconds the image appeared on the

418

screen – her baby, so clear and recognizable, like a new person already.

Dionne felt a lump in her throat that wouldn't shift, an overwhelming feeling of love surging through her. 'Hi, baby,' she whispered, giving a little wave.

She looked up at Alyson, standing beside her, mesmerized by the black-and-white image. Her eyes were shining wet, her expression incredulous. 'It's amazing,' she breathed, reaching out for Dionne's hand. Dionne took it, squeezing tightly. They smiled at each other, a shared moment between them.

The two women were gradually rebuilding their friendship, and Dionne had invited Alyson along today, thinking it might be the perfect gesture to help their reconciliation. It was her way of apologizing, of putting everything that had happened between them in the past. What better way to celebrate new beginnings than a new baby?

Dr Chrétien moved the scanner carefully over Dionne's stomach, producing a perfect image. It was so clear, so perfect. The heartbeat was strong. Dionne choked up when she heard it, the new life pumping away. *Her* baby.

The obstetrician turned to her with a smile. 'Everything is fine, Mademoiselle Summers. The baby's very healthy.'

Dionne sighed in relief, as Alyson smiled.

'The scan is extremely clear,' she continued. 'In fact, I can make out the sex, I'm ninety-nine per cent certain. Would you like to know?'

Dionne hesitated, her heart beginning to race a little faster. She stared at the screen, wondering if she could make it out, but she couldn't see clearly. She turned to Alyson. 'What do you think?'

Alyson shook her head. 'It's up to you. Your call.'

Dionne thought about it. She'd had the nursery

painted in tones of yellow and cream, but if she knew what she was having, she'd be able to completely redecorate. And she could start buying clothes in the appropriate colour – she'd seen all the adorable little boy and girl outfits in Baby Dior, but stuck to white and neutrals. Above all, she was curious. This baby whom she'd carried for eight months now, who had caused such a seismic shift in her life . . . she wanted to get to know it a little better.

'Yes,' she replied firmly.

'You're sure?'

She nodded quickly, before she could change her mind.

Dr Chrétien looked at her and smiled. 'Congratulations, Dionne. You're having a girl.'

The rest of the day felt a little flat after the morning's excitement. Dionne returned to her apartment, saying she needed to rest, so Alyson went back to her own flat, feeling tearful and emotional. It had been mind-blowing, such a rush seeing the images of Dionne's baby on the screen like that. Dionne was going to be a mother! Alyson could hardly wrap her head around the idea – crazy, irresponsible Dionne was going to take care of another person for the rest of her life.

But Dionne was changing, Alyson could see it. She'd calmed down, prioritized. The focus in her life had finally shifted, from being all about her to being all about her baby. A girl. Dionne was going to have a daughter.

Alyson felt herself well up once more, as she slammed the door to her apartment and stood there, drinking in the silence. She wondered if she'd ever have that. A child, a future, a reason to concentrate on something other than herself.

She flopped down on her sofa, her thoughts

automatically coming back to Aidan, where they always seemed to end up these days.

She'd been trying to contact him for hours, wanting to know how the launch had gone, but she couldn't get through. His phone was switched off. It was frustrating, but she guessed that was a good sign. Hopefully it meant it had been such an amazing night that he was still sleeping it off. She hoped there wasn't a more sinister reason behind it – that now the job was finished he was no longer interested in speaking to her. She wondered if she would see him again – did they even have a reason to keep in touch any more? She thought they were friends, but perhaps Aidan didn't see it like that. Perhaps he thought of their relationship as nothing more than a business transaction.

Alyson stared listlessly up at the ceiling. She didn't know what to do with herself, all alone in the apartment that didn't feel like hers any more. She supposed she should get round to calling a real-estate company to put it on the market. Or maybe she should get out her laptop and do some research for Dante Consulting. If the launch had gone well and Kennedy's Dubai was a success, then she needed to strike while the iron was hot, try and take on some more clients.

The buzzer to her apartment rang out, and Alyson groaned, dragging herself up from the couch.

'*Allo?*'

'Mademoiselle Wakefield?' It was the porter from the front desk. 'There is a gentleman here to see you. Shall I send him up?'

'Who is it?' Alyson asked in confusion. *A gentleman? Maybe Jacques from Capucine?*

'He says his name is Aidan Kennedy.'

Aidan! Alyson exhaled in shock.

'Yes, please, send him up,' she managed to stammer, before hanging up the phone.

Shit! She estimated she had just over a minute before he arrived at her door. Alyson raced to the nearest mirror, frantically trying to smooth down her hair and quickly slicking on some lipstick. She shoved the cluster of empty mugs from the coffee table into the dishwasher and stared blindly round the apartment. *What the hell was Aidan doing here?* Had there been a problem with the launch, or—

But there was no time to wonder any more as the next moment he was there, right outside her door. Alyson opened it to let him in, and thought she might faint with pleasure. He looked incredible in just jeans and a black T-shirt that picked out his thick, dark hair and the smattering of stubble that indicated he hadn't had time to shave before he arrived. His skin was lightly tanned from the hot Dubai sun, his eyes the brilliant blue of the Arabian Gulf.

'Hi,' she said shyly. Her heart was still thumping from the burst of adrenaline she'd got tidying the apartment, her skin lightly flushed from the exertion.

She felt ridiculous suddenly, as though she wanted to run and hide. What was wrong with her? It was Aidan! She'd spent the best part of three months with him, so why couldn't she act normally now?

'Hi,' he grinned, strolling lazily into the flat and looking around. 'Nice place.'

'What are you doing here?' Alyson burst out. 'Not that it's a bad thing, but I didn't expect . . . How was the launch? Was everything okay?' She couldn't seem to stop talking.

'I left straight after it ended. I haven't slept in what seems like a couple of days, so forgive my dishevelled appearance.'

Alyson didn't think she'd ever seen him looking so hot.

'In case you were wondering, the opening was amazing.'

'Really?' Alyson squealed in delight, realizing she'd been staring at him. He grinned at her, and she felt her stomach somersault, looping the loop like a fairground ride.

'It went perfectly. I couldn't have asked for anything better. And all thanks to you.'

Alyson blushed at the flattery.

'We make a great team, don't you think?'

'The best,' Alyson agreed. Her heart was hurting so badly she didn't think she could take it much longer. 'Would you like a drink?' she asked, groping for something to say. Her voice had somehow gone up an octave.

Aidan laughed. 'No thanks, I'm okay. I have something a little more urgent to talk to you about.'

'What?' Alyson asked in alarm.

'Alyson, I've tried to say this so many times, but I've been thwarted at every attempt,' he joked, his delicious Irish accent sounding sexier than ever. 'So, if I'm out of line, or you want to tell me to go to hell, then I promise you, I'll walk out of that door and never come back.'

Alyson's breath was coming fast as she wondered what he was about to say, if it was possible that—

'Alyson, I'm crazy about you. I always have been. I can't stop thinking about you. That's the reason I came here today. I just needed to tell you – I couldn't bear to wait any longer . . .'

Alyson could hardly believe what he was saying. It was everything she'd dreamed of, everything she'd fantasized about.

'Aidan,' she breathed, and before she knew what was happening, he'd taken her in his arms, kissing her so softly, so exquisitely. His lips touched hers, warm and delicious, but he took his time. He wanted to savour this moment.

Alyson felt weak, as though her legs wouldn't hold her up.

'Is this what you want?' he asked tenderly.

'Oh, Aidan,' she murmured, 'I've wanted you for so long. I never dreamt that you'd . . . I was so afraid.'

'Well you don't have to be afraid any longer,' he assured her. 'I'm here, for as long as you want me.'

'I'll always want you,' Alyson managed to say.

'Then I'll always be here.' He kissed her again and she smelt the delicious tang of his skin, the musky, manly scent of him. Alyson felt a sweet sensation of heat, low in her groin, but there was no need to rush – she knew that this time it would lead to fulfilment. Aidan wasn't going anywhere and neither was she. She wrapped her arms around him, wanting to lose herself in his arms, his lips, his body.

His kisses were soft, just the lightest trace of stubble brushing against her cheek. She wove her fingers through his hair, tracing the smooth skin on the back of his neck, able to do all the things that had haunted her dreams during the long, hot, sticky nights in Dubai.

Aidan's breath was warm against her neck, his hands brushing lightly against her body. She moaned as his palms slid over her breasts, letting out a groan of longing as she felt her nipples tighten beneath the thin fabric of her top. She wasn't wearing a bra, and the sensations were heightened, the rough texture of his thumbs circling the tiny, pale-pink buds.

'Aidan . . .' With shaking fingers she unbuttoned his shirt, finding the tanned, muscular chest below, a smooth covering of dark hair in the centre. He looked so young, so virile. Compared to Philippe, he was a veritable Adonis.

He pulled her close, and she could feel his hardness pressing against her. He was as eager as she was, both of them desperate to take their time but unable to do so. They'd wanted this for so long they had no sense of control, slaves to what their bodies were telling them.

Aidan slid the fabric of her top down below her breasts, catching his breath at the sight of her body, the delicate, pale skin creamy and flawless.

'You're perfect,' he breathed, as he bent down to her, his mouth closing round her nipple as he lightly sucked and licked.

Alyson gasped, her back arching as she pressed herself into his hands, longing for him to take her completely. Then her fingers slid down between his legs, feeling him through the thick fabric of his jeans. She let her hand move along his length, as Aidan groaned.

'Alyson,' he told her. 'I can't hold on much longer . . .'

She stared at him, her pupils dilated, the irises black. 'This way,' she murmured, as she took his hand and led him towards her room. They collapsed onto the bed, removing clothes in a frenzy, delighting in discovering each other's bodies for the first time.

As they lay naked together, Aidan poised above Alyson, about to enter her, he paused, looking her straight in the eye.

She lay beneath him, almost shaking with anticipation. Her lips were parted, her skin flushed.

'I love you, Alyson,' Aidan told her, his eyes tender and full of wonder, as though he couldn't believe that they were finally together.

Alyson's arms were wrapped around him, her hands stroking the smooth skin on his back.

'I love you, too, Aidan,' she told him. 'I love you, too.'

38

Dionne was in her element. She was swanning around backstage at the Capucine show, the centre of attention, and she adored it. Everyone wanted to speak to her,the press desperate to interview her about her scandalous past and her triumphant return. If there was one thing the media liked better than a fallen star, it was a resurrected one.

And Dionne played the game to perfection. She'd completely transformed from the diva she once was and now she charmed the reporters, being polite and gracious, taking the time to talk to whoever wanted to speak to her. More than one reporter who knew the Dionne of old commented privately what a difference it was, how she was almost unrecognizable from the stuck-up, difficult bitch they were used to dealing with.

Backstage it was chaos – there were people everywhere, designer-clad bodies packed tightly together, with blaggers downing all the free champagne they could lay their hands on, and fashionistas who hated each other kissing the air beside each other's cheeks. Because Capucine was trying to turn around its fortunes and get the media onside, reporters had been given unprecedented access to the whole show. Cameras and journalists were everywhere backstage, running around like kids in a candy store, and there was no privacy. Not even the model changing area was off limits, with girls having microphones thrust in their faces as their make-up was being applied, photographers snapping away as the models tried to get a little down-time.

The atmosphere crackled with electricity, and Dionne thrived on it, as vital to her as food and air. She didn't realize how much she'd missed it. And maybe, just maybe, this would be the beginning of bigger things; this one show would be the catalyst that relaunched her career. Yes, she was doing it for CeCe, but she was hopeful for herself too.

The music was pumping, and the energy was almost tangible. Dionne was blossoming, positively glowing. Her bump was enormous – she looked ready to burst – and her dresses had been specially made to accommodate it. Jacques had joked that he might design a diffusion line of maternity wear. Her opening dress was gorgeous – full-length and sweeping, with layer upon layer of plum chiffon, a sweetheart bodice and lace detail that covered her upper arms. The colour was rich, the fabric light and airy, so comfortable to wear in her expectant state.

For once, this was a show she might remember, Dionne thought, as she gratefully took a sip of orange juice. No alcohol, no drugs – it was kind of weird to do a show and not be high or drunk. But she was glad of it. She wanted to remember every second and she knew this was going to be special.

'Dionne – do you have time for a couple of questions?'

'Of course.' Dionne smiled radiantly at the reporter, moving in front of the camera.

'First of all, congratulations on your pregnancy.'

'Thank you.'

'Do you know if you're having a boy or a girl?'

Dionne smiled mysteriously. 'I really can't say,' she replied. She'd signed a big-money deal with a magazine for the first photo shoot – hey, she was a single mom and she had to make ends meet.

'This is your first ever show for Capucine. Are you looking forward to walking for the label?'

'Oh, totally,' Dionne gushed. 'I can't wait! I mean, I think everyone's finding it very strange today, to be here without CeCe, but this is the best tribute to her. Jacques Perrot is an amazing, talented designer, and he's done a fantastic job on this collection. Because of him, CeCe and her legacy live on.'

A runner passed by and tapped her lightly on the arm. 'Mademoiselle Summers? You're needed in make-up.'

'Thanks. I have to go,' she apologized to the reporters, breaking into an excited grin. 'Duty calls.'

Only a few streets away, Aidan and Alyson were seated nervously in the offices of Philippe's lawyers, on the rue de Castiglione. It was a prestigious area and the office reflected that. It reeked of old money – all leather armchairs, dark wood-panelling and bookcases lined with weighty-looking tomes. This was the final stage in Aidan's acquisition of Philippe's properties. His lawyers had checked over the contract already and all he needed to do was sign.

Alyson had gone with him for moral support, her hand resting on his arm as they waited for the *avocat* to finish preparing the documents.

Jean-Baptiste Le Clerc looked like a typical lawyer: grey, middle-aged, well dressed in a classic pinstriped suit. After what seemed like an age, he turned the papers around and pushed them across the antique mahogany desk to Aidan.

'Monsieur Rochefort signed earlier today,' he explained. 'All that's needed is your signature.'

'Thank you,' Aidan nodded, trying not to show his anxiety. His hands were shaking slightly as he picked up the Cartier pen, hovering above the paper just below where Philippe had signed.

Alyson stared at the page, at the familiar handwriting and that confident, scrolling signature that she knew so well. It was like a relic from another time.

She wondered if Philippe had looked into who he was selling to: she assumed not. If the rumours Aidan had heard were correct, Philippe had had more pressing issues on his mind recently, like trying to rescue Rochefort Enterprises from the brink of bankruptcy. He'd be so eager to offload his unwanted properties that she doubted he'd waste time checking who the buyer was. Besides, Alyson doubted he'd recognize Aidan's name. He'd probably never even appeared on Philippe's radar, the older man never imagining that the young manager from the tourist bar all those years ago was set to become his rival.

But for Aidan, this was personal, Alyson realized that now. It was about proving a point to himself, and to the rest of the world – but particularly to Philippe. He'd arrived, and no one was ever going to make him feel small and insignificant again.

Aidan leaned forward, scribbling his name three, four times, in all the places that the lawyer indicated. And then it was done.

'Congratulations, Mr Kennedy,' Monsieur Le Clerc smiled. 'The sites are now yours.'

'Thank you.' Aidan replied, looking visibly relieved. 'Now, if everything's concluded . . .'

'Of course,' Monsieur Le Clerc said pleasantly. 'You are free to leave.' He held out his hand. Aidan rose to his feet and shook it, then he and Alyson left the office.

Outside on the pavement, Aidan pulled Alyson to him, kissing her deeply as the brilliant sunshine beamed down on them. They were giggling with excitement, their faces radiant with happiness.

'So,' Aidan began, as they came up for air. 'How would Dante Consulting feel about working on another couple of Kennedy properties? I mean, it would involve working *very* closely with the owner for the next few months at least . . .'

'Oh, Aidan, that would be perfect,' Alyson cried, throwing her arms around him. They kissed once again; this time it was long and lingering. As they broke apart, something caught Alyson's attention. A car, a black Mercedes, pulling up outside the offices they'd just left. There was something horribly familiar about the whole scenario, Alyson realized instinctively, her skin beginning to prickle before her brain even worked out what it was. A chauffeur stepped out of the car, moving round to open the passenger side door as a man stepped out. Time seemed to stop. Alyson's breath caught in her throat.

It was Philippe Rochefort.

He looked older than Alyson remembered – his hair was thinner and increasingly grey around the temples. There were large bags under his eyes; his skin had an unhealthy pallor and his face was bloated, as though he'd been consoling himself with a little too much of his beloved whiskey and soda. His recent financial troubles had obviously taken their toll, his natural arrogance and vigour were now visibly dimmed. Alyson couldn't help but compare him with Aidan, and with how young, handsome and vital he looked. He was in the prime of life, at the top of his game. In contrast, Philippe looked haggard, a broken man.

He emerged from the car and straightened up, glancing warily around him. Then his gaze fell on Alyson, their eyes locking. She let out a little cry, stumbling in shock, and clung onto Aidan to steady herself. He put his arms around her, holding her upright, and Alyson sank into his embrace. His body was warm and solid, his strong arms making her feel safe.

Philippe took in the two of them, his gaze sliding from Alyson to Aidan. His eyes narrowed in dislike, hatred even, but there was something else there – it was defeat. A look of recognition, of understanding, flitted across Philippe's face, and in that moment he knew – knew that he'd been beaten by this younger, hungrier man.

Aidan smiled, savouring his moment of triumph. He squeezed Alyson's hand tighter, holding her close, and together they moved on.

'Where the fuck is Alyson?' Jacques Perrot yelled. He dragged his hands through his hair, his eyes bulging in fury behind his black-rimmed glasses. Backstage at the Capucine show, the crowd around him turned to stare.

'She's just called,' an assistant informed him urgently. 'She'll be here any second.'

'Thank Christ for that,' retorted Jacques Perrot.

Alyson was as good as her word, flying through the door minutes later.

'I'm so sorry,' she apologized breathlessly. 'This morning overran – it was something I couldn't get out of.'

'That's okay. You're here now,' Jacques told her, trying to stay calm but failing completely. It was a look Alyson remembered well from countless designers. Any show was a trip, a complete adrenaline rush. You were flying by the seat of your limited-edition pants, and there were a million and one things that could go wrong.

'We'll get you into hair and make-up in a moment. Would you mind doing some interviews right now? Everyone's dying to speak to you.'

'No, not at all,' Alyson lied. She hated the press with a vengeance, but she owed it to Jacques. Her stomach lurched as he led her over to the gaggle of reporters. Christ, she'd forgotten how terrifying this whole thing was, how badly she used to suffer from nerves. She tried to remind herself to breathe, in through the nose and out through the mouth.

This was absolutely the last time she was ever doing this, she promised herself. She knew the rush afterwards would be unbelievable, but she didn't care. There was no way in hell she was ever setting foot near a runway again. Not even as a guest. After tonight she was done with the fashion world – the Capucine show would be her swansong.

'Alyson, this is Jean-Paul and Sophie from Elle Online,' Jacques explained, introducing the cameraman and the extremely young, immaculately groomed reporter.

Alyson said hi briefly, then they were ready to go, the camera rolling almost instantly.

'Ally, this will be the first runway you've walked in almost a year. What was it about this show in particular that made you want to get involved?'

Alyson took a deep breath, trying to stay clear and concise, to give Sophie the answers she wanted. 'I'm a huge admirer of Jacques' work – his eye for detail is simply exquisite. And, of course, it's the perfect tribute to CeCe. She was one of my good friends, as you know, so it's just the perfect way to honour her memory.'

'Great.' Sophie flashed the camera a dazzling smile.

'And, Jacques, are you pleased to have Ally out there for you today?'

'*Absolument*, I couldn't be happier. She's always been something very special – it was a great loss to fashion when she retired, so the fact that she's been persuaded to come back for this show means a lot.'

Sophie turned to Alyson. 'So, does this herald a permanent return to the catwalk for you?'

Alyson smiled, shaking her head. 'No, this is just a one-off show that I'm doing for CeCe.'

'And what do you think she'd have made of today?'

The microphone was shoved roughly under Alyson's nose, uncomfortably close. She took a small step back. 'I think she'd be very proud. She originated these designs, and I think she'd be thrilled to know how much everyone here today has fallen in love with them.'

'Absolutely. Moving onto happier subjects – what is that enormous sparkler on your finger?'

Alyson felt her cheeks grow hot, holding her hand up to the camera at Sophie's bidding.

'Oh my God, is that an engagement ring?'

'Yes, it is,' Alyson admitted, her face growing even redder.

'So who's the lucky man?' Sophie demanded.

Alyson hesitated. 'I'd really rather not say. As I'm sure you know, I like to keep my private life private . . .'

'Thanks, guys,' Jacques smiled, much to Alyson's relief. 'We'll speak with you later.' He kissed Sophie on both cheeks and she wrapped up the interview as Jacques steered Alyson away from the cameras and towards the backstage area.

Dionne and Alyson stood in the wings, just yards away from the catwalk. Beyond that sat the great and good of the fashion world, everyone who was anyone packed into the incredible space – Rihanna, Olivia Palermo, Vanessa Paradis, and even Anna Wintour – had all turned out. Celebrities and editors dominated the front row, the hierarchy stretching all the way back, with a few lucky students and interns given standing room at the rear of the venue.

Dionne took a deep breath, smiling reassuringly at Alyson. They'd both walked several times already during the show, but now they were gearing up for the finale. Both of them wore white – the traditional wedding dress – but the two women couldn't have looked more different. Jacques had worked with their natural body shapes, celebrating the differences between them.

Alyson was ethereal, fragile as a thread of gossamer. Her waist was tiny, her wrists narrow, her whole frame slender like a bird's. The dress Jacques had created was straight up and down, like a sheath, held loosely in place by thin spaghetti straps. The neck sank in a deep V shape, a soft neckline skirting the edge of her small breasts, then falling straight to the floor. It was simple, elegant and beautiful.

By contrast, Dionne's was enormous, overblown – and gorgeous. The full skirt jutted out from the hips, layered and billowing, with enormous puff sleeves and a square neckline that displayed her overflowing breasts. It looked like something Marie Antoinette might have worn. The irony wasn't lost on either of them that she was wearing virginal white while eight and a half months' pregnant.

It was crazy to think that, almost three years ago to the day, both of them had been involved in Capucine's first ever show, just metres away from here, in the Tuileries gardens. And now Dionne was hoping that this would be her big comeback. Alyson had been great about it: she'd picked up enough PR tips while setting up Kennedy's Dubai and the pair of them had plotted how to get Dionne maximum exposure. They'd met again under the unhappiest of circumstances but, in spite of everything, a real friendship had blossomed.

Yeah, she'd definitely mellowed over the past few months, Dionne realized. She'd learned that life ran more smoothly when you weren't a bitch – that people responded positively, and life just become pleasanter. Before, where she'd instinctively lashed out at people, she'd learned to take things calmly and chill. Backstage, the hair and make-up people barely recognized her. They could hardly believe it was the same demanding diva that they used to work with. Okay, so she'd blown it with Elite, but Alyson had recommended Dionne to her old agency, IMG, and they'd scheduled a date to meet very soon. It was all looking promising. Besides, the scandal had done wonders for her profile – it was through the roof.

Dionne turned to Alyson. 'Ready to give them the money shot?'

Alyson nodded and held out her hand. Dionne took it, and together the pair of them stepped out onto the catwalk. The flashes were blinding, the music pounding, the snappers going crazy as they sashayed side by side down the runway, stepping together in perfect time. The audience cheered, rising to their feet in a standing ovation, as a picture of CeCe was beamed onto the backdrop behind them. It was a stunning black-and-white shot; she looked beautiful and serene, her gaze fixed on the camera.

Dionne broke into a huge smile, her white teeth dazzling as she blew kisses at the crowd. It was the cheeky, sassy side of Dionne that the audience loved. Alyson waved shyly, her diamond catching the flashlights and dazzling the onlookers. She'd refused to take it off for the show. Dionne followed Alyson's gaze and caught sight of Aidan on the front row – the guy she'd helped Alyson get ready for a date with all that time ago. He was on his feet, smiling broadly and looking so proud he might burst.

She stared deeper into the crowd, trying to see if David was there, but there were too many faces, the flashbulbs too bright to make out anyone clearly. She'd sent him an invite. She hadn't heard anything back, but she hoped he had come. They'd been seeing each other recently – meeting up occasionally, just as friends. Things were cooling with Esther, it seemed, and although Dionne knew she had a long way to go to rebuild his trust, she was hopeful they might have a future together. She had the overwhelming feeling that this baby was his.

But then, it almost didn't matter, Dionne realized. She was a strong woman, successful and ambitious, and she was going to look after this baby – her little girl. She would work and she would provide for her – with or without David. Her daughter was the most precious thing in the world to her, and no man was going to distract her from that.

They reached the end of the runway and the pair stopped, striking a pose. The applause grew louder, mingled with whoops and cheers, as the camera flashes popped incessantly, like firecrackers in the auditorium.

As Dionne looked out over the cheering crowd, she felt a surge of pure happiness pulsing through her. It was as though nothing else mattered – as long as she was up here, the world couldn't touch her. She stood tall, her head held high as she drank in the adoration.

This was what she had been destined for; what she had been born to do.

Dionne Summers was back where she belonged.

ACKNOWLEDGEMENTS

To my fantastic agent, Maddy Buston, for her superb guidance, incredible skill, and for giving me the opportunity to pursue the career that I've always dreamed of.

To my amazing editor, Kate Bradley, for editorial brilliance and unwavering positivity, and the equally wonderful Hana, for her never-ending stream of brilliant ideas. Thanks to Sarah, Elinor, and the whole team at HC for all their hard work behind the scenes.

Huge thanks to my fabulous friends who've been so supportive and forced everyone they know to buy copies of Idol – especially Amy, Cleo and Christina. Vicky, for all your input over the years and all of the boozes. The hilarious folk of Improvisers Anonymous – Kat, Jodyanne, Dave and Mike. Also Lesley, Beverley, Lucinda, Callan and Rudy Barrass. Caroline at Somer Design for my website. Ross's friends (and their mums!) who bought copies, and Sally, Brian and Alison, for taking Idol worldwide!

Thanks so much to everyone who bought a copy of Idol, the lovely readers who wrote to me to say how much they enjoyed it, and all the bloggers and tweeters who've been fantastic – your support is greatly appreciated!

To Ross, for coping with Carrie when deadlines are looming, and getting Caroline back afterwards (hope it's worth the wait!) Oh, and I promise I'll sign this one . . .

And to my Mum and Dad – my Mum, for not disowning me after she'd read *Idol*, and my Dad, for not reading past chapter two.